CLOSE
HER
EYES

BOOKS BY LISA REGAN

CLOSE HER EYES

LISA REGAN

bookouture

Published by Bookouture in 2023

An imprint of Storyfire Ltd.
Carmelite House
50 Victoria Embankment
London EC4Y 0DZ

www.bookouture.com

ISBN: 978-1-83790-234-7
eBook ISBN: 978-1-83790-233-0

In loving memory of Ann Bresnan

PROLOGUE

Her flesh burned away like tissue paper. The smell hit her first, even before the pain. Some part of her mind had already closed down, trying to protect her, but she knew it wouldn't be enough to shut out the agony that was coming. A thin coil of smoke rose from the apparatus he had used. He tossed it aside, metal clattering against concrete. He gave a low whistle as he regarded his handiwork. Then he licked his lips, looking more satisfied than she had ever seen a human being look. As the pain struck her, first with a searing punch, and then in hot, intolerable waves that made her entire body shiver, he looked even happier. A glance at her hip revealed that it was no bigger than an index card. Gritting her teeth, she wondered how something so small could hurt so much.

She had burned her hand once, getting it caught in a cloud of steam from a pot she'd been handling. It had been horrific. It seemed to go on for days, no matter what remedies she tried. But this... This was something else altogether. He paced back and forth before her as she writhed on the floor. She opened her mouth to beg him for something, anything. To untie her, to let her go, to splash it with cold water, at least.

As if reading her mind, he knelt next to her and tangled his hand in her hair. His breath smelled like stale beer. He whispered into her ear, "You're not going anywhere."

Now she wondered what else he was capable of, and whether or not she'd ever see the outside of this rancid room again. If she did, one thing was for sure: she was going to run, as far and as fast as she could, and never look back.

ONE

A small explosion boomed from the direction of Josie Quinn's backyard. From her place at the kitchen table, she heard an object thump against the outside of the house. Seconds later, there were shouts. The sooty smell of smoke filtered into the room. Josie's twin sister, Trinity Payne, leapt up from her seat and ran to the back door, flinging it open. Josie followed, snatching up the small fire extinguisher that she and her husband kept next to their microwave. Thick gray smoke rolled through the open door as Josie and Trinity pushed outside. Josie held the nozzle of the extinguisher like a weapon, waving it back and forth, searching for the source of the smoke.

On the edge of the small patio outside the kitchen door, flames rose from a mangled gas grill. Josie's husband, Noah Fraley, backed away from it, covering his face with his hands, while Trinity's boyfriend, Drake Nally, batted at the flames with his coat. On the grass, Josie and Noah's Boston terrier, Trout, barked furiously, jumping nervously from side to side, but thankfully staying out of range of the fire. The once-chrome lid to the grill now lay in a blackened heap near Noah's feet.

Their home's white siding bore a dark smudge the approximate length of the lid.

"Get out of my way," Josie said, nudging Drake aside. "Trin, get my dog, would you?"

Lightning fast, Trinity shot across the patio and scooped Trout into her arms. Drake and Noah joined her on the grass, well away from the grill.

Josie pulled the fire extinguisher's pin and aimed the nozzle at the flaming grill. Spraying from side to side, and keeping even pressure on the lever, she put the fire out in seconds. Once she was finished, she put the spent extinguisher onto the patio and strode over to Noah.

"I'm fine," he said as she cupped his cheeks with her hands and stared into his face. A clump of hair on the left side of his head was singed but he didn't look injured. His hazel eyes offered a silent apology. He reached up and clasped her wrists, pulling her hands from his face. "Really," he added. "I am."

Trinity hugged Trout's wriggly body to her chest and regarded Drake with a withering look.

He grinned at her, holding his charred coat in both hands. "I'm fine, too, by the way."

Trinity shook her head. "How many grown men does it take to grill a steak?"

Trout whined.

"We weren't even grilling yet," Noah said. "Drake was showing me how to work it."

Josie took Trout from Trinity and kissed the top of his furry head. "It's February."

Drake said, "You can grill all year round. Besides, it's like, forty degrees."

Trinity pointed at Drake's coat. "That's ruined. Throw it away. Also, you live in New York City. What business do you have teaching someone how to grill?" She looked at Josie. "And why do you and Noah even have a grill? You can hardly even handle the kitchen."

"Hey," Noah protested.

Josie shook her head. "She's not wrong."

Noah appeared to give it some thought and then declined to argue. The two of them were well known among family and friends for their legendary lack of culinary skills. Josie was a disaster when it came to cooking. She had burned more cookware than she had prepared food. From the standpoint of her waistline, marrying Noah hadn't been a very sound strategy. He was only passable in the kitchen. If not for the kindness of friends, who often had them over for meals or dropped things off, they'd subsist almost entirely on takeout. Recently, their friend's seven-year-old son, Harris, had challenged them to up their game in the kitchen. It wasn't going very well.

Noah said, "This was not our fault. I got this thing from a guy at work. He was getting rid of it. I figured it would be good to practice on."

Drake piped up, "I think there was a leak in the line. Maybe that's why he was getting rid of it."

Ever the journalist, Trinity launched into a list of statistics about grill fires and explosions. Drake continued to smile at her. He was still stupidly in love with her, Josie thought. No one could look at another person that way while they talked about properly operating a gas grill if they weren't stupid in love. Josie buried her face into Trout's fur and laughed.

When Trinity finished, Noah said, "Duly noted."

Josie said, "Do we not get enough danger on the job?"

Josie and Noah worked for the Denton City Police Department, she as a detective and he as a lieutenant. Denton was a small city in Central Pennsylvania, nestled in a valley surrounded by several mountains and bordering a branch of the Susquehanna River. Drake was an FBI agent from the New York City field office.

Noah sidled over to Josie and slid an arm around her waist. With his other hand, he stroked Trout's face and was rewarded with several anxious kisses. "We'll get it cleaned up."

Drake added, "And we'll go get takeout for dinner."

With one last glance at Noah, Josie followed Trinity back inside, carrying Trout along with her. Once seated at the kitchen table, she put him onto the floor. He immediately flopped down and laid across her feet. Either he was still having anxiety or he was sensing hers—or both. He had an uncanny ability to sense when she was distressed or sad, even when she wasn't fully cognizant of it herself. Josie looked down and watched his little chest rise and fall with each breath. It wasn't a mystery where her anxiety came from this time. Noah. Explosion. Those two things should never go together. With a small shudder, she tried to tear her mind away from what could have happened right in their backyard, instead keeping her attention on Trinity, who sat across the table, her laptop open.

"You were going to tell me what you were working on," Josie said. Her throat felt scratchy. She wasn't sure if it was the combo of smoke and fire-retardant chemicals or if it was the tickle of unease. How neither Noah nor Drake had been injured just now was a miracle. Without being too obvious, she worked through a breathing exercise that her therapist had taught her. Dr. Rosetti had more breathing exercises than Pennsylvania had trees, it seemed, and none of them worked for Josie. Not yet, anyway. Well, the one where she breathed in for a four-count, held it for a seven-count, and let it out for eight seconds helped a tiny bit, but Josie wasn't entirely sold.

Still, she sucked in a breath, mentally counting to four, and then held it for seven seconds.

Trinity raised a brow at her. "The men are fine."

Josie exhaled slowly, silently counting to eight. "I know."

She repeated the exercise, keeping her eyes on her sister. They were identical twins but as always, even in casual clothes and minimal makeup, Trinity seemed to have a sheen that Josie could never replicate. Her shoulder-length black hair was shinier and bouncier than Josie's locks. Her skin had a healthy glow, whereas Josie often looked pale and tired from too much work and too little sleep. Also, Trinity's face was unblemished whereas Josie had a scar that ran from her right ear, down her jawline, and under her chin. It was old and faded but still noticeable.

Trinity said, "Sometimes it's harder to focus on what actually happened than on what could have happened, huh?"

Josie nodded. Trout let out a stuttering sigh. She could feel his little body relaxing against her feet as she worked through another four-seven-eight breath.

In the middle of the table, Trinity's cell phone buzzed. A name flashed across the screen: Hallie Kent. Trinity looked at it longingly. "Go ahead," Josie told her.

Snatching up the phone, Trinity muttered a thank you and swiped answer as she left the room. Josie had gone through several rounds of her breathing exercises by the time Trinity returned. She felt marginally better.

"Sorry," Trinity said. "That's the source for this new case I've been working on."

Josie motioned to the chair Trinity had vacated earlier. "Sit. Tell me about it."

Trinity plopped back down. "Do you really want to hear about this?"

Josie nodded. "Of course. Between your show and my job, it's even harder to carve out this time together. Let's not waste it."

She almost added that they'd already lost so much time together in their lives. Although they were twin sisters, they'd only known about their true relationship for six years. Their parents, Christian and Shannon Payne, lived two hours away. When Trinity and Josie were three weeks old, Shannon had left them in the care of a nanny. A woman from the Paynes' cleaning service, Lila Jensen, had set their house on fire and abducted Josie. Everyone believed that Josie had perished in the fire, so no one looked for her. Lila brought Josie to Denton and used her as a way of getting back together with a former boyfriend, Eli Matson. She told Eli that Josie was his daughter. Back then, they didn't have DNA testing and Eli hadn't had any reason to believe Josie was not his daughter. He'd loved her fiercely and raised her as his own until his death when Josie was six years old. After that, Josie had been left in the care of Lila, who was evil and abusive. It was Lila who'd given Josie the scar. Eli's mother, Lisette, who Josie always believed was her grandmother, had fought to get custody of Josie, finally winning when Josie was fourteen, and bringing some peace and stability to Josie's life.

It wasn't until Josie and Trinity were nearly thirty years old that a murder case Josie had been assigned to solve unraveled the tangled skein of Lila's many lies and brought them together as sisters. Back then, Trinity had been a reporter for their local news station, WYEP. Now, she had her own show on national television called *Unsolved Crimes with Trinity Payne*.

Trinity said, "This woman—Hallie Kent—sent in a request to the show that we look at her foster sister's death. She first contacted us months ago—last summer—but she's been really persistent. The team that handles our submissions didn't even tell me about it at first because it didn't look like much."

"You said death," Josie said. "Not a murder?"

Trinity's eyes sparkled. "That's where it gets interesting. It was ruled an accident by the county medical examiner but Hallie and pretty much everyone in the town, including the police, have always believed it was murder. No one has been able to prove it."

Josie frowned. "That's not an unsolved case, Trin. What if it really was an accident? What will it do to her family if your investigation turns up the same result?"

"What if I don't get the same result? What if there is something everyone's missed and we have a chance to catch a killer?" Sensing Josie's discomfort, Trinity added, "Or our investigation puts the question to rest once and for all, and Hallie Kent gets the closure she's been looking for these past ten years. If it turns out to really be an accident, we don't run it as a show, that's all. I really want to help this woman if I can. Besides, she lives an hour away in Everett County."

Josie arched a brow. "That's the real reason you and Drake decided to drop by for a visit."

Trinity pouted. "That is not the reason, dear sister. We came to see you two. I can't help it if Everett County is close."

Josie laughed. "Sure. Okay."

Trinity pointed a perfectly manicured nail in Josie's direction. "Please. There have been plenty of times we've visited only to have you get called into work on some big, important case. You're always on call!"

Josie rolled her eyes. "I'm not always on call, Trin."

She was tonight, though, but she didn't say that out loud. Denton's investigative team consisted of Josie, Noah, Detective Gretchen Palmer, and Detective Finn Mettner. Noah and Gretchen were off. Mettner was working the evening and night shift, and Josie was on standby in case he caught more cases than he could handle. Josie was hoping he had a quiet night. She hoped they'd all have a quiet night with no more explosions.

The back door flew open, admitting Noah and Drake. The faint smell of fire still clung to them. "We were thinking," said Drake. "That we should all go out together."

Noah patted his singed hair. "I'd get a shower first, of course."

Josie looked over at her sister. Trinity smiled, "It is Friday night!"

Drake raised a brow. "What do you think about axe throwing? There's a place over on—"

Josie held up a hand to silence him. "Let me stop you right there. You two are not going axe throwing after you almost blew yourselves up."

"Dinner and a movie it is," said Noah.

They went to Josie's favorite restaurant. Josie was having the best time she'd had in months. Later, as she settled into her seat at the movie theater with a giant tub of popcorn between her and Noah, she felt her phone vibrate inside her coat pocket. Passing the popcorn off to Noah, she pulled her phone out and groaned when she saw Mettner's name flash across the screen.

"I knew you'd get a call!" Trinity said from her seat on the other side of Noah.

Josie looked over at her sister long enough to see Drake hand her a twenty-dollar bill. "Every time," he mumbled.

Noah laughed. "Agent Nally, the eternal optimist."

Josie swiped answer. "What've you got?"

Mettner said, "A body. Along Hempstead Trail, on the bank of Kettlewell Creek."

TWO

The woman lay in a heap among the rocks next to the creek. Beyond her crumpled form, the murky water of Kettlewell Creek rushed and churned. Its level was high for February, and the wind whipped off its surface, reaching all the way up to where Josie stood along the asphalt trail that ran parallel to the water, now separated from the bank by crime scene tape. Hempstead Trail was on the northeast fringe of the city. Formerly it had consisted of a group of old houses two blocks to the east of the creek. The massive flooding a few years back had washed many of those houses away. The rest had been condemned and knocked down. City Council had ruled that the land would not support any new construction, so now it was considered a green area with a walking trail that spanned roughly a mile. Along the creek bank, Josie saw several of her colleagues picking their way carefully among the rocks, mud, and other debris as they took photos, sketched out the scene, and placed evidence markers.

Before she arrived, Mettner had called in their Evidence Response Team, headed by Officer Hummel. The ERT had cordoned off the scene from the road all the way to the water and set up lights throughout, turning the night to day. Josie found Hummel's SUV, its hatch open, and retrieved a Tyvek suit, booties, gloves, and a skullcap. Her coat was too bulky to fit beneath the suit so she shed it, noting that the temperature had dropped precipitously since the grill explosion in her backyard. Ignoring the cold that enveloped her, she made her way back to the crime scene tape. A uniformed officer stood guard, clipboard in hand, making sure that only authorized personnel entered. He signed her in and then held the tape up so she could slip beneath it.

The ground sloped downward toward the water. It was mostly weeds, brush, and some trash: discarded soda bottles, beer cans, some cigarette butts, and a few food wrappers. The Tyvek booties slid a little in the mud as Josie made her way down to where a bed of rocks met the swirling creek water. A couple of the crime scene techs nodded at her. She nodded back and kept going to where Mettner stood near the body. The county medical examiner, Dr. Anya Feist, was on her knees, checking for any obvious signs of injury or trauma. The victim was young, probably late teens or early twenties, dressed in jeans, a puffy dark purple coat, hiking boots, and a gray knit cap with a pompom on it.

It was the pompom that twisted Josie's gut.

Long, dark hair unfurled from beneath the hat, mussed. Strands lay across her right cheek while the rest of her locks were in disarray. One of her arms lay across her stomach while the other was extended over her head, its elbow bent. A gray, knit glove covered her right hand. The letters S.E. were sewn in black near the wrist. Her other hand was bare. Her feet were spread about a foot apart, one leg straight, the other bent slightly. She looked like a doll, haphazardly discarded.

"She fell?" Josie asked.

Mettner looked up from the notes app on his phone. "Oh, hey. Thanks for coming. We're not sure."

Dr. Feist gave Josie a grim smile. "Detective Quinn, always a pleasure." With a gloved hand, she touched the woman's chin and then her throat. "I don't see any evidence of injury at all. Help me turn her, would you? I took the photos I need. Hummel already took pictures for the ERT. He said I could move her."

Josie got down on her knees beside Dr. Feist. While the doctor clutched the woman's shoulder, Josie slid one hand behind her hip and the other behind one of her knees. Although her body was the kind of cold that only the dead could produce, her limbs were slack. She hadn't gone into rigor mortis yet. Slowly, they pulled her toward them. Josie held the woman in place while Dr. Feist brushed through the hair at the back of her head, searching for injuries. With a sigh, she said, "I don't see anything here. Could be a closed head injury. Could also be natural causes."

As they eased her back into place, Mettner pointed upward toward the road. "Could she have broken her neck on the way down? If she fell?"

Dr. Feist studied the woman's face. "I suppose it's possible, but that's not a very steep incline. If she fell at the right angle, maybe. It's also possible that she went into cardiac arrest or had a heart attack and fell."

"She's pretty young for those things, don't you think?" asked Mettner.

"It's still possible," Josie said.

"We'll run toxicology, too," said Dr. Feist. "It could be an overdose of something. I do see a lot of that in young people these days. There could be injuries that aren't visible. As I always say, I'll know more when I get her on my table." She stood up, wiping at her dirty kneecaps. "I'll go up and let the EMTs know they can transport her."

"Who found her?" asked Josie, watching Dr. Feist move carefully back up to the road.

Mettner swiped at his phone. "A woman named Jeanne Wack. She lives about a ten-minute walk from here. Her son is five years old. Evidently, they walk up and down this road every afternoon before dinner—it was still light out when they found the body. Her son looked down toward the water and saw purple, told his mom a lady was sleeping near the river. Ms. Wack made him wait up top while she checked on the victim. There was no pulse so she called 911. She said she didn't recognize the deceased, and they did not see anyone else on foot nearby."

Josie looked down at the woman's face. Her eyes were open, brown irises fixed upward, unseeing. "Does she have any ID on her?" Josie asked.

Mettner nodded. He walked a few feet toward the water and pointed to an evidence marker that sat beside a brown purse. It was medium-sized with a long strap, and it rested on top of a flat rock, its zipper open. "We found this here. There was a wallet inside with a driver's license belonging to nineteen-year-old Sharon Eddy of Denton. She lives a few blocks away."

Josie squatted down and peered inside the purse. "She's got cash in here and a phone."

"Yep," said Mettner. "Not a robbery, then." He shifted uncomfortably from foot to foot, nearly losing his balance as his booties slid against a muddy rock. As he righted himself, a flush crept up his cheeks. He cleared his throat. "Nothing taken, no signs of injury, no external signs that she was sexually assaulted. I screwed this up, didn't I? By bringing in the whole team. She slipped and fell, didn't she?"

Josie moved closer and stared up at him. "What do you think?"

"I think if we find out later that this was a homicide and I had failed to secure the scene and have it processed, I'd be out of a job."

Josie shook her head. She pointed back down at Sharon

Eddy. "If we find out later that this was a homicide and you had failed to secure the scene and have it processed, someone she loves would get neither the closure nor the justice they deserve, Mett."

He looked away. Josie patted his shoulder. "Has anyone gone to her home? Made contact?"

"Not yet."

Josie panned the area, noting the position of the body, its distance from both the road and the riverbank, as well as its position relative to Sharon Eddy's purse.

"What is it?" Mettner said.

"Her purse is standing straight up, like she set it down perfectly," Josie said.

Mettner nodded. "The odds of it falling just like that are pretty slim."

Josie gestured toward the road, where they could see the back of the uniformed officer and the fluttering crime scene tape. Other officers clad in white Tyvek moved along the slope, searching the brush for anything that might be important and bagging items they'd marked earlier with evidence flags. "If she fell hard enough to give herself a fatal head injury or to break her neck, it seems to me she would have had to tumble down this slope."

"Sure," said Mettner. A beat passed. His tone grew more urgent. "Her clothes aren't dirty, though."

Josie nodded. She began moving from one evidence flag to another while Mettner followed. "What are you doing?" he asked.

"Looking for her other glove."

"It's not here," Mettner said. "I already asked Hummel. They didn't find it anywhere."

Two EMTs worked their way toward the victim, carrying a backboard and body bag. Josie paused to watch them transfer Sharon from her deathbed of river stones inside the bag. She was glad for the care they took, treating the body as though it was made of something precious. To someone, somewhere, probably only blocks away, Sharon was extremely dear. Josie was sure of it, based on the initials lovingly sewn onto her remaining glove.

Mettner added, "You think someone brought her here after she was already dead."

It wasn't a question.

Josie turned back toward the road and started making her way up the incline. "This is the perfect place to leave a body. No cameras. No residences. Remote."

Mettner trudged after her. "You think she was murdered?"

"Can't make that determination yet," Josie said.

"But you have a feeling."

She stopped walking and turned back to him. "Yes. Come on, we'll go to her residence and see if there's anyone there."

THREE

Sharon Eddy lived in a small, narrow rowhouse five blocks west of the Hempstead Trail. A thin elderly woman answered the door, looking Josie and Mettner up and down. Leaning heavily on a cane, she reached up and patted her curly white hair. "Who're you?" she asked. "I'm not ready for company."

Josie offered her police credentials. "I'm Detective Josie Quinn. This is Detective Finn Mettner. We're from the Denton Police Department."

The woman leaned forward. A pair of reading glasses appeared from the folds of her pink floral housecoat, attached to a chain around her neck. She settled them onto the bridge of her nose and studied the IDs they offered.

Mettner said, "We're sorry to bother you, ma'am."

She looked up at their faces. "It's after dinner."

Josie said, "We know. We were hoping to talk to you about Sharon Eddy. It's our understanding that this is her residence."

Fear flashed through her rheumy eyes. "Shar's my grand-daughter. Is she okay?"

A pang of sadness hit Josie like a slap. She did not want to tell this woman that her granddaughter was dead. While they weren't always responsible for death notifications, the task did fall on the detectives' shoulders now and then. It was one of the worst parts of the job. Softly, Josie said, "Mrs. Eddy? May we come in?"

Her lips smacked together. She removed her glasses, tucking them back inside her housecoat and coming up with a crumpled tissue which she used to dab at both eyes. "Rosalie," she told them. Hitching a shoulder, she turned and limped away from them, knuckles white over the handle of the cane. "Come in, then. Tell me what kind of trouble Shar got into."

Josie and Mettner followed her inside. The living room was narrow but long with threadbare gray carpeting. On a muted television mounted to a wall a prime-time drama played. Across from it, a long brown couch took up the entire length of the room. Diagonally across from that was a matching recliner sporting a cushion for lumbar support. Rosalie dropped into it and fussed with her cane, trying to fit it into the space between her chair and the end table. "Hope she didn't get into the drugs," she muttered. "Her momma was into the drugs something awful. Been in prison for a spell. On and off, that one. Never stays out long. I was hoping Shar would go the opposite way."

Josie waited until Rosalie was settled in her chair, birdlike hands folded neatly in her lap. Her slippered feet hung off the floor an inch, making her look smaller than she already did. Josie shored herself up for what was to come.

Mettner knelt next to the chair and rested a hand on its arm.

"Oh boy," said Rosalie. "Been a long time since a man got down on one knee." A smile wavered on her lips. She covered Mettner's hand with one of her own. Her voice dropped so low, it was difficult to make out the words. "It must be bad, then. Real bad."

Josie was not a big believer in delaying bad news. Working your way up to it didn't make it any easier to hear. "Mrs. Eddy, your granddaughter, Sharon, was found dead this evening. A mother and her son found her on the creek bank a few blocks from here."

Rosalie kept patting Mettner's hand until the movement became rhythmic. Her head bobbed up and down, as if she were still listening to words only she could hear. They gave her some time to absorb the news. When her body stilled, she found the crumpled tissue again and pressed it to one cheek, then the other, trying to staunch the tears flowing down her face. "What happened to my Shar?"

"We're not sure," Mettner said. "There were no visible signs of injury. We'll know more when we finish our investigation."

Josie said, "We're very sorry for your loss, Mrs. Eddy. Is there anyone we can call for you?"

Rosalie lifted her hand from Mettner's and pointed to a small table next to the front door. "Over there. My cell phone. Shar insisted I have one even though I can hardly use it. If you look on there, you'll find my brother's name and number. Albert. He lives a couple of hours away, but he'll come and help me take care of my Shar."

Mettner stood up and walked over, searching for the phone. Once he had the number, he stepped onto the porch to make the call.

Josie took his place, squatting down next to Rosalie's chair. "Mrs. Eddy, I know this is a terrible time, but I was wondering if you could answer some questions for me about Sharon. If you're not up to it, we'll come back later."

"Ask me now. I know how this goes. Lost my parents, my in-laws, two of my siblings and my husband. Once the shock wears off, I won't be much use to anyone."

Having lost her first husband and her own beloved grand-mother suddenly, Josie could relate. She took in a deep breath, trying to focus on the investigation. "Sharon lived here with you?"

"Yes," said Rosalie. "Just the two of us. It's been just the two of us for ages. Since she was about ten. Her momma just couldn't take care of her anymore, not like she should have. That one found trouble wherever she went. Like I said, she was in and out of prison for drugs. When Shar was ready to go to high school, I decided the two of us should make a clean break, so we moved here. She just graduated from Denton East a year ago."

"Where did you move from?" Josie asked.

"Bellewood."

Forty miles away, Bellewood was the Alcott County seat.

"How did Sharon do at Denton East?" Josie asked. "Did she make friends?"

"Sure, some friends. She's a good girl." The tissue clutched in her hands was now sopping with moisture. Josie found a box of tissues on one of the end tables and handed several more to Rosalie.

"Was Sharon in college?" asked Josie.

Rosalie shook her head. "Couldn't afford that. We thought maybe one day. She works at the animal hospital about fifteen minutes from here. She doesn't do anything fancy. She just answers phones and cleans exam rooms, that sort of thing. Whatever needs doing. She sure did love it."

Josie said, "Is that where she was headed this afternoon?"

"She left for her shift there this morning. Around six thirty. I wasn't expecting to see her till later tonight. Sometimes they do surgeries at the animal hospital. My Shar always stays late if there's a big surgery, to sit with the cat or dog. She says she feels bad for 'em that they're in pain and disoriented and can't be with their owners. They don't pay her to do that. She does it because in her own heart she can't stand the thought of those babies being alone. 'Fur babies,' that's what she calls them."

Josie felt the yoke of sadness tug at her body more forcefully. "Do you know if she made it to work today?"

"I assume she did, but if she didn't, they would have called her, not me. She's grown now. Handles her own responsibilities."

"Okay," said Josie. "We can find out when we leave here. Do you know how Sharon got to work today?"

"She walked, same as always. It's close enough to walk as long as it's not raining or snowing. She only takes the car to work when she absolutely has to—trying to save money."

Josie nodded. "Speaking of vehicles, before we got here, my colleague checked and saw that a Ford Focus is registered to you at this address. We saw it outside. Sharon didn't have her own car?"

"No. Couldn't afford it. She always used mine. Paid for gas and repairs herself. I don't use it much anymore, anyway. Don't get around so great anymore."

Josie asked, "Was Sharon seeing anyone that you know of? Dating anyone?"

Rosalie shook her head. "There was some boy she liked. Oh, I don't remember his name, but it doesn't much matter. I don't think either of them had much time for dating. I know she didn't. Not with the hours she worked."

"How about her friends?" Josie asked. "Do you know any of their names?"

Rosalie rattled off some names which Josie committed to memory. "They don't come here much. Shar meets them. All their numbers should be on her phone. Everything about her is on that phone. You'll probably get a lot more from that than from me. I love my granddaughter, but she had her own life. That's how I wanted it. I didn't want her to feel like she always had to stay here and take care of me, or something."

Josie smiled. "I understand. We found her phone, so we'll get a warrant for its contents and take a look. Do you know if Sharon was taking any kind of medication?"

"Don't think so," Rosalie said. "You can check in her room if you'd like. Top of the steps, first door on the left."

"Thank you," said Josie.

Mettner stepped back inside. He crossed the room and handed Rosalie her phone. "Albert is on his way."

Rosalie nodded. She looked back toward Josie. "You're going to ask me if Shar did drugs, aren't you? That must be next."

"Yes," said Josie.

"If she did, I never saw it. Couple of times, I smelled liquor on her but never saw her with anything else. Doesn't mean she wasn't, just that I didn't know."

"I understand," said Josie. "One last thing. Sharon was wearing a glove—knit, gray, with her initials."

"I made those," said Rosalie. "They're her favorite. She's had them since the sixth grade. Wears them every winter. A few times I had to darn them. I told her this year I wasn't sure if I could do it. My hands hurt so much now."

Mettner said, "You sewed her initials into them?"

Rosalie nodded. "Some girl in the seventh grade stole them and tried to say they were hers. After we got them back, I put her initials on each one. Never had a problem after that." She went silent. In the stillness, Josie sensed Rosalie's newly minted grief creeping in all around them like a toxic cloud of pain. She offered a hand and Rosalie took it. Her skin was clammy. She'd started trembling. It wasn't visible but Josie felt it in their fused hands, a low current working its way from her to Josie.

"Had she lost one of them recently?" asked Mettner.

Rosalie shook her head. "No, no. That would have been a crisis. Don't know why she loved those gloves so much." She looked past both of them at the front door. "You never know with these kids. You never know with anyone."

"Know what?" asked Josie.

"What people hold onto."

FOUR

The search of Sharon Eddy's room turned up a few bottles of liquor, some birth control pills, and a vape pen with no cartridges. If Sharon had been using any type of drugs, she hadn't kept them in her small bedroom. After years on the job, Josie generally found that parents or other caretakers of high school or college-aged kids knew very little about their kids' true activities, but in this case, it appeared Rosalie Eddy was basically correct about her granddaughter's activities—or lack thereof.

Back downstairs, Josie sat with Rosalie while Mettner knocked on the doors of her next-door neighbors. He returned with a woman in her forties who promised to sit with Rosalie until her brother arrived. Josie pressed a business card into Rosalie's hand and told her to call them if she had any questions.

Outside, they walked down the pavement to their vehicles. Streetlights cast small circles along the sidewalk. The temperature had dropped even more since they'd been inside Rosalie Eddy's home. Josie pulled her coat tighter around her shoulders, zipping it up all the way to her chin.

Mettner said, "That didn't give us much to work with."

Josie stopped at her SUV. "No, it sure didn't."

He took out his phone and scrolled through the notes he'd taken at the scene earlier. "That Hempstead Trail has no cameras nearby, so any type of video footage is out. I can run a check on LPRs in the area."

LPRs, or license plate readers, were a valuable tool that the police department used in many different cases. Denton PD had equipped three of their patrol vehicles with cameras that linked up to their mobile data terminals. As those cruisers moved throughout the city, the cameras scanned the license plates of all moving and parked vehicles and sent an alert to the officers if any vehicles that had warrants out on them had been stolen, or had suspended tags. If any of the LPR devices had been near the creek trail where Sharon Eddy's body was found that afternoon, it would have picked up which vehicles were nearby.

"Guess we should do a geo-fence, too," Mettner mumbled.

Josie smiled. "You don't say."

On their last big case, Mettner had given Josie quite a bit of ribbing over her use of geo-fence warrants and yet, a clue Josie found among the results of those warrants had led to a break in the case.

Mettner gave her a tight smile and tapped away at his notes.

A geo-fence was a location-based technology police used to draw a virtual boundary around a specific geographic area and then trace which smart devices, such as cell phones, were inside that perimeter during a certain time period. Geo-fence warrants had first been used by law enforcement in 2016. In other states privacy concerns had been raised, but as things presently stood in Pennsylvania, they were viable tools police could use in their investigation. A geo-fence would give them the phone numbers of any cell phones that were on and operating near the creek trail where Sharon Eddy's body was found in the hours before Jeanne Wack's son saw her purple coat.

Josie said, "LPRs, geo-fence, and we need a warrant for the contents of her phone as soon as possible. We also need to establish a timeline. She left for work at six thirty this morning. We need to find out if she got there or not."

Mettner looked at his phone. "It's after business hours. You think the animal hospital has someone on-site after hours?"

"I know the place," Josie said. "It's an emergency facility for animals, so yeah, they've got staff on around the clock. Let's head over there now and see if we can find out whether or not Sharon Eddy showed up for her shift this morning."

He pointed to his car which was parked a few spaces back from hers. "Want me to drive?"

Josie shook her head. Popping her trunk open, she found a flashlight. "No. I want to walk."

Mettner scratched the side of his face. "Boss, I'm pretty sure it's below freezing now."

She closed the trunk and flashed him a smile. "What's the matter, Mett? Can't take a little cold?"

Before he could answer, she set off. In her mind, she calculated the most direct route from Sharon Eddy's home to the animal hospital. By the time she turned onto the pitch-black Hempstead Trail, Mettner had caught up to her.

"Why are we walking?"

Josie snapped on the light and panned it back and forth across the trail as they walked. "Why do you think?"

"We're following in her footsteps."

Josie slowed down when they came to the area where Sharon had been found. The vehicles were all gone, but a slip of crime scene tape still fluttered where it had been tied to a tree. "You got it."

Mettner kept pace as she increased her walking speed, the

torch now moving back and forth across their path like a metronome. The only sounds were their feet crunching on the ground, the gurgle of Kettlewell Creek to their right, and an owl hooting in the distance. It wasn't hard to imagine they were the last two people on earth. Just before seven in the morning, it would still be somewhat dark since the sun didn't rise this time of year until a few minutes after seven. Although there was some traffic from residents who lived within a few blocks of Hempstead, it wasn't a well-used trail. It was entirely possible that Sharon Eddy had walked to work that morning without being seen by anyone.

Soon, the trail curved on to a residential street. "You check that side for cameras," Josie told Mettner. "I'll keep an eye out on this side."

Two of the houses they passed had cameras affixed to the sides of their front doors. Josie took one house while Mettner knocked on the door of the other. Ten minutes later, they met back in the street. "You get anything?" Mettner asked.

Josie shook her head. "Theirs is motion-activated and only goes off if someone comes onto their porch, so they didn't have anything. You?"

"Same thing," he sighed.

They trudged on. A block later, the back of the animal hospital became visible, a glowing neon sign announcing: "Juno's Pet Emergency Care." Three cars were parked near a set of doors. A sign affixed to those doors told them to go around to the front. Hot air whooshed around them as they stepped through a set of automatic double doors into a large lobby. A couple waited on a couch, faces pale and exhausted. The woman clutched a leash in her hand and stared across the room at a closed door. Josie's heart immediately went out to them. She and Noah had been lucky so far that Trout hadn't been in any accidents, or had any health issues that couldn't be cleared up with a course of antibiotics or some ointment. On the other side of the lobby sat another woman with a cat carrier in her lap.

They walked past all three people to the front desk where a man with a headset tapped furiously at his computer keyboard. His name badge read "Bryce." He fired off a barrage of questions into his mouthpiece as his fingers moved. He was so fast, Josie almost didn't register it when he told the person to please hold. Without looking at them, he shoved a clipboard across the desk. "We're not expecting anyone, so I know that you didn't call ahead. You really need to call ahead so we're ready for you. Fill this out and I'll get you in as soon as I can. I can't make any promises as to how fast you can be seen. We've got these two ahead of you plus several full rooms in the back."

When neither of them took the clipboard, Bryce looked up at them, probably realizing they had no pet. "Who do you have with you today?"

"Just us," Josie said. "We're not here for a pet emergency."

She handed him her police credentials. Mettner flashed his as well. Bryce's face paled as he took in their identification. He pressed a button on his keyboard and gave rapid instructions into his headset to his caller on what to do upon arriving at the ER. Then he clicked off and said to them, "What's going on?"

Mettner said, "We understand Sharon Eddy is employed here. We'd like to speak to someone about whether or not she showed up for her shift this morning."

"Sharon? She didn't. In fact, I was called in early to cover her shift."

Josie said, "She never showed up at all? No one saw her?"

Bryce pushed his mouthpiece away from his lips. "I was told she didn't show or call. The nurse on duty waited a half hour, called her cell phone, and got no answer." He waved at the waiting room. "I know it looks empty but trust me, this place is never slow. Not ever. This morning was a madhouse."

"How do you know that?" Mettner said. "About the nurse waiting for Sharon to come in and then calling her?"

"Because that nurse called me at home at exactly seven thirty-five and told me. Then she asked if I could hightail it over here to help out. When I got here at eight, it was packed from one end to the other."

Josie said, "Do you know if anyone tried to contact Sharon after that?"

For the first time since they'd shown up, concern broke through the stress of being overworked and busy. "Wait," said Bryce, holding up a hand. "Did something *happen* to Sharon?" He put great emphasis on the word "happen," as if it was some kind of code word for something unspeakable. Actually, in Josie's experience, it was exactly that. People always used it to refer to death. It sounded less harsh and final to say "something happened" than to say this person died.

She said, "We're afraid so. Sharon was found dead near Kettlewell Creek a few hours ago."

All the color drained from his face. Slowly, he pushed the mouthpiece back to his lips. One trembling hand reached for the phone receiver and pressed a button. Into the small microphone, he said, "Renee, I need to take a break. Can I send the calls over to you for ten minutes? Thanks." He clicked another button and then looked back up at them. In a raspy voice, he asked, "What happened to her?"

Mettner said, "We're not entirely sure yet. That's why we're here, trying to figure out when she was last seen."

His chest rose and fell with exaggerated motions.

Josie said, "Are you okay?"

"I'm fine, I'm fine. Sorry, nothing like this has ever happened here before and Sharon, well, she's just a kid." Bryce rolled his eyes. "I'm just a kid, too, I guess. I'm only a few years older than her but she's a *kid* kid, if you know what I mean?"

Mettner said, "I'm afraid we don't."

"She's really sweet and innocent. Life hasn't... messed with her yet."

Josie thought about what Rosalie had said about Sharon's mother. Life had messed with Sharon. It just hadn't ruined her kind nature. Josie knew what it was like to spend your early childhood with someone addicted to drugs. She was quite certain that Sharon's mother lacked the pure evil that Josie's own fake mother had possessed, but regardless, addiction was a challenge for any family and, for young children, it could often be confusing and even traumatizing.

"Was she murdered?" Bryce asked.

Josie glanced back at the three people in the waiting room. None were paying attention. The couple waiting for their dog bent their heads toward one another, having a private, tearful conversation. The other woman stared into her cat's cage, whispering reassurances. Turning back to the desk, Josie said, "We don't know any details yet. Can you tell us whether anyone had any contact with Sharon after the nurse made the initial call to her?"

"I know that the nurse called a couple more times and left messages. Sharon never called back. I think a couple of the techs wanted to call her grandmother, but I don't think anyone did. Like I said, it got crazy busy in here. Oh, no. Oh God. You don't think—if someone had called earlier—"

Mettner said, "We don't know what happened to her. It's impossible to say whether making contact with Mrs. Eddy would have had any effect on the outcome."

Bryce didn't look convinced. Josie said, "The nurse who called Sharon—is she here?"

He shook his head. "She left a few hours ago."

"Is there anyone here right now who was close to Sharon?" asked Mettner.

"Right now? I don't think so. Sharon worked day shift."

Josie took a business card from her pocket and handed it to

him. "There is a possibility that we'll need to speak with anyone on the day shift who knew or was friendly with Sharon. Either one of us or our colleagues will be back tomorrow during the day to speak with other members of your staff. In the meantime, if you or anyone else thinks of anything that might be helpful to figuring out what happened to Sharon, please call."

FIVE

They walked back to their vehicles in silence with Josie's flashlight leading the way. In spite of the light and Mettner's presence beside her, it felt as though the dark was chasing her somehow. She had the distinct and eerie feeling that Sharon Eddy's last moments had played out in this same silent void. The question was, had someone stalked and killed her, or was her death merely an unfortunate accident? They wouldn't know until the autopsy was complete.

Josie followed Mettner back to the Denton PD headquarters, pulling in beside him in the municipal parking lot at the back of the building. It was a huge, three-story, gray stone behemoth that sat in the center of town. Its ornate masonry, double casement arched windows, and bell tower made it look more like a castle than a police station. Formerly the town hall, it had been one of the first buildings to be listed on the city's historic register. Josie and Mettner entered on the ground floor and walked up two flights of steps to the second-floor great room. At this hour only a couple of uniformed officers used the common desks to fill out their shift paperwork. The permanent desks belonged to the investigative team: Josie, Mettner, Noah, and

Detective Gretchen Palmer. They had all been pushed together to make one large rectangle. To the side of them was the only other permanent desk, which belonged to Denton PD's press liaison and Mettner's girlfriend, Amber Watts. She was gone for the day. The Chief's office was just off the great room, but his door was closed. No light seeped from under it. Tomorrow, he'd be briefed on the Sharon Eddy case.

Josie helped Mettner with the reports and the warrants, spending a few hours at her desk before she left him to finish his shift so she could go home and get some sleep. Her house was silent when she arrived. Everyone had gone to bed, including Trout. From the bottom of the steps she could hear his snores, even behind their closed bedroom door. In the kitchen, Josie helped herself to a cold slice of day-old pizza, still too wired to sleep. She sat at the table and used her phone to pull up Sharon Eddy's social media profiles again. She'd looked through them at the stationhouse but hadn't found anything that raised red flags. Like so many people her age, Sharon had a lot set to public. Photos and videos of herself doing just about everything. A documentary of her life. The foods she ate, the clothes she wore, the shoes she bought, the animals she cared for at work. There were photos of her out with friends on the weekends, but it was mostly innocent—or she only posted the innocent parts because she was still technically too young to drink.

One photo taken the previous Mother's Day showed Sharon sitting side by side on a park bench with a woman whose face was almost identical to hers. This woman was older and thinner with red hair. There was nearly a foot of space between them. Their posture was identical—arms folded, legs crossed. Closed off. The two of them stared at the camera with weak smiles. The unenthusiastic caption read simply: *Mother's Day*. Josie wondered if Sharon had posted the photo of herself with her mother because she felt obligated. There were no other photos of the two of them on any of Sharon's social media plat-

forms. There were plenty of photos of Sharon with her grandmother, though. In every single one of them, Sharon hugged
Rosalie. They beamed at the camera. The captions read: *The
best*; *My ride or die*; *The amazing lady that made me who I am
today*; and *My favorite*.

Josie's heart ached to think of the grief Rosalie Eddy had in
front of her. She tossed her phone aside with a heavy sigh. It
slid across the table, bumping against Trinity's laptop and
dislodging a thick file folder she'd left on top of it. Josie lunged
across the table, fingers clamping the edge of the file before it
slid off the table and spilled its contents all over the floor. She
pulled it closer, reading the name Trinity had scrawled on its
tab: *Jana Melburn, Everett County, PA*. Most people did everything digitally these days, but Trinity still insisted on printing
out any and all materials she had gathered on the cases she
featured on her show. A photograph fluttered to the floor. A
young woman with curly flaxen-blonde hair and a heart-shaped
face wearing a cap and gown stood on a football field, flowers
clutched in her arms. Crowds of other graduates and their families milled behind her. She stood between a man and a woman,
visible only in profile as each of them planted a kiss on one of
her cheeks. A happy glow reddened her face. Was this Jana?
Were those her parents? They seemed young to have a high
school graduate. Trinity had said that Jana's foster sister was the
one who contacted the show. Were these Jana's foster parents?

It was tempting to open the file and review it. Josie's fingers
itched as she returned the photo to the file and then tucked the
edges of several pages flush with the folder. She carefully
placed it back on top of the computer. Trinity would gladly
share this with her—typically everything Trinity and her staff
uncovered or had access to was public record anyway—but Josie
didn't want to be presumptuous.

A creak on the stairs distracted her from the file. Seconds
later, Noah appeared in the kitchen doorway, bare-chested and

wearing a pair of sweatpants. Even after all the years they'd been together and all the times she'd seen him naked, her eyes were still drawn to his muscular chest and the thick, gnarled circle of scar tissue on his right shoulder. She'd shot him once. It was long before they were together, during a time when a vulnerable young girl's life hung in the balance and Josie wasn't sure who to trust. It turned out that Noah had been one of the good guys. He'd covered for her, helped her in that investigation and ultimately forgiven her. Still, she had not forgiven herself.

He walked over and planted a kiss on the top of her head. The smell of him and the warmth of his body made her dizzy. In a voice still thick with sleep, he asked, "Homicide?"

She stood up and faced him, smoothing his thick, dark locks down on his head. "We don't know yet," she said. She gave him a quick recap of the evening. As she spoke, his hazel eyes grew more alert. She could see him making calculations in his head.

He said, "She was somewhere between seven in the morning and when she died. If she wasn't in rigor yet, that means she died a couple of hours before her body was found."

"Right," said Josie. "Either someone took her, killed her, brought her back and dumped her body on the creek bank, or she went with someone, they dropped her back off at the creek bank and she fell to her death."

"From what you've told me about the scene—the purse standing straight up, the missing glove—she didn't fall."

"That's what I think, but we won't know until Dr. Feist does the autopsy."

Noah brushed her cheek with his fingers and tucked a strand of hair behind her ear. Josie wanted very much to lay aside her sadness over Sharon Eddy for a while by taking refuge in her husband's body. She leaned into him, resting her head under his chin. Her lips touched the hollow of his throat. He wrapped his arms around her. She whispered, "I'm on the morning shift tomorrow and you're not in until the afternoon."

"Yes," he breathed into her hair. His hands crept down her back, every touch setting her skin tingling.

"Which means we really won't be alone together until this time tomorrow night," Josie added.

His mouth found hers, kissing her slowly and deeply. When he was finished, he said into her ear, "Let's go upstairs and make the most of the time we've got right now."

A few hours later, they were showered, dressed, and downstairs, ready to join Trinity and Drake for breakfast. Afterward, Josie reported to work. Mettner had made no progress with the Sharon Eddy case. He hadn't gotten into Sharon's phone yet. It was password-protected so they needed to use the GrayKey to access its contents. Hummel had started the process, but it was still pulling information from the phone. The geo-fence results had come in. At six forty-three in the morning Sharon Eddy's phone put her at the end of the Hempstead Trail, about sixty feet before the residential street started. Then nothing. Either she or someone else had turned her phone off. The only smart device that had come close to Sharon Eddy's phone in the time frames they'd requested—early morning and within a three-hour range of when her body was found—was Jeanne Wack's cell phone. Wack had found Sharon and immediately called 911. The license plate readers hadn't hit on any vehicles that seemed to warrant further investigation. By late Saturday morning, Josie was urging Mettner to go home and get some sleep when Dr. Feist called her cell phone. Her voice sounded high and strange.

"Josie. Could you come to the morgue, please?"

Although Josie considered them more than just colleagues or acquaintances, Dr. Feist rarely called her anything but Detective or Detective Quinn. "Doc, what's going on?"

From across the desks, Mettner stared at her, his brow furrowed.

There was a beat of silence. Then, "I'm not in trouble, if that's what you're worried about. I just—please come to the morgue."

Josie was already on her feet. "We'll be there in ten."

"No," Dr. Feist blurted. She took in a shuddering breath. "I mean, when you say 'we,' you mean—"

"Mettner and me."

"No, please. Gretchen. Can you bring Gretchen instead?"

Gretchen wasn't due in until later that afternoon, but Josie was sure she could get her to meet them at the morgue. "Yes," Josie said. "I'll call her. We'll be there as soon as we can."

SIX

Denton's city morgue was located in the windowless basement of Denton Memorial Hospital near the end of a long hall of abandoned patient rooms that now held only dust and old equipment. The hall itself was a putrid color combination of yellowed floor tiles and grimy gray walls. As they approached the suite of rooms that served as Dr. Feist's domain, the smell of decomposition and death mixed with stringent chemicals enveloped them. Josie and Gretchen had become inured to it over the years.

"What are we walking into here?" Gretchen asked as they neared the autopsy room.

"Your guess is as good as mine," Josie mumbled.

In the center of the large exam room were two stainless-steel autopsy tables. On one of them rested Sharon Eddy's body, a sheet drawn up to her chin. Next to her, Dr. Feist paced, her movements short and jerky. One of her arms hugged her middle while the other fisted her skullcap, holding it beneath her chin. Her silver-blonde hair had come loose from its bun, swishing at her shoulders as she moved.

Gretchen said, "Doc?"

She stopped walking. "Thank you for coming."

Josie had rarely seen Anya Feist anything but calm and collected. There had been one case early on in Josie's tenure as a detective that had brought the entire town to its knees. The remains of nearly a hundred bodies had been recovered after Josie cracked it. They'd had outside help from the FBI, but still, Dr. Feist had been tasked with a great deal of work. It was the most tragic and horrific case Josie had ever seen, and in the months afterward, Anya had admitted to Josie just how badly the case had gotten to her. The stress had been so bad that she had lost weight, becoming gaunt and sickly. That was the worst Josie had ever seen her.

Until today.

Her eyes were red-rimmed from crying. Worry lines creased her face, which was pale to the point of being nearly translucent. A large blue vein in her right temple pulsed rapidly. Her lower lip trembled.

Josie said, "What's going on?"

Anya folded her arms across her chest and sucked in several deep breaths, her eyes looking everywhere but at them. "I finished the autopsy on Sharon Eddy."

"That's what's got you so rattled?" asked Gretchen. "Guess that means it wasn't accidental."

"It definitely wasn't."

Josie stepped forward and pressed the back of her hand to Anya's forehead. Her skin was cold and clammy. She said, "I'm fine."

Catching one of her wrists, Josie pressed two fingers on the inside of it. "Really? Because your heart is racing."

"Maybe we should go sit in your office," Gretchen said.

Anya batted Josie's hand away and looked back at Sharon Eddy. "No. No. We have to do this. I have to get through this. It took me hours just to work up the nerve to call you and—"

Josie said, "Okay, okay. We're here. We're not going

anywhere. Whatever's got you so freaked out, we'll work through it together."

"Talk to us," Gretchen said. "Just start at the beginning. Quinn brought me up to speed on the Eddy case. Tell us about the exam and autopsy."

"Yes, yes," said Anya. She turned back to the body. She began to recite her findings, settling easily into her role as medical examiner, the anxiety in her voice fading with each word. "Sharon Eddy. She's a well-nourished, well-developed nineteen-year-old female. No signs of any significant medical issues. No signs of sexual assault. We found what we believe are several different animal hairs on her coat. We've sent the samples off to the state lab."

Josie said, "She worked at an animal hospital. I'm not sure that's going to get us anywhere. Did you find any DNA on her body?"

"Nothing."

"How about injuries?" asked Gretchen.

"Although in the field we did not immediately find any evidence of injuries, once Ms. Eddy's body arrived here and her clothes were removed, I did note a bump on the back of her head which was well-hidden by her hair and the hat she wore. On autopsy it was discovered that she had a subdural hematoma."

"Is that what killed her?" asked Gretchen.

"While it certainly would have been enough to knock her unconscious, no. It didn't kill her. She was strangled."

Josie moved past Anya and stared at Sharon's throat. Even under the bright overhead lights, no marks were visible. "How do you know?"

Anya said, "There are some instances when the death happens so quickly that external bruising doesn't have time to occur. I did find a few spots of petechiae in her left eye, but the major finding that is consistent with death by strangulation is the focal hemorrhaging on her infrahyoid muscles."

Gretchen said, "Her strap muscles?"

Anya nodded. She must have noticed that Josie was searching her memory banks for strap muscles because she gave a soothing smile—looking more like herself than she had since they arrived—and pointed to Sharon's throat. "The infrahyoid muscles are the four pairs of muscles that sit in the front of your throat. More or less, they connect the jaw to the collarbone and support the structure of the neck. They look like straps—that's why we call them strap muscles. They start below the hyoid bone, which is below the jawline, and, like I said, they basically connect everything: hyoid, sternum, clavicle, larynx. You use them in swallowing, eating, talking... this is the very unscientific definition, by the way."

"Which we always appreciate," Gretchen said.

Josie said, "You said there was focal hemorrhaging on Sharon Eddy's strap muscles."

"Yes," Anya said. "Thumbprints, most likely. I've seen it before. The body looks fine on external exam with little or no bruising to the neck. Sometimes even the other hallmarks of deaths caused by strangulation are absent, like the petechiae in the eyes, the swollen tongue, bulging eyes, but when you perform the autopsy, a broken hyoid or bruised strap muscles will indicate that the victim was strangled. In Sharon's case, her hyoid is still intact but the injuries to her strap muscles are consistent with strangulation."

"Doc," Josie said. "We've had strangulation cases in the past. We had them last month in that big Collins case."

Anya's eyes filled with tears. "Yes," she murmured. "It's not that. That's not why I called. Listen, this is very difficult for me to talk about, and I understand that you will have to share it with your team. There's no way around that. I guess I just needed some time for it to sink in." She moved back to Sharon's side and carefully folded the sheet down until Sharon's torso and left hip were exposed. Josie noted a small tattoo on the inside of her left forearm, a butterfly. Her left hip was marked as well. Not a tattoo. Something else. "It's fresh," Anya said, voice husky. "Probably inflicted a few hours before she died."

Gretchen stepped forward. "Is that a brand?"

Segments of skin on Sharon's hip had been seared away, leaving red and purple blisters with charred edges, and making a distinct shape.

Anya nodded, lips pursed tightly. A tear slid down her face.

Before they could ask any more questions, she lifted her scrub top and then peeled her pants down just enough for them to see a matching brand on her left hip.

"Holy shit," Josie said.

Anya's was much more defined, even though the scar was older and her skin white and slightly raised, whereas Sharon Eddy's brand was still raw and bloodied. No bigger than the size of a coaster, it was a horseshoe shot through the middle with an arrow. The fletching on the arrow was represented by two lines on each side.

Anya said, "My ex-husband gave me this right before I left him over ten years ago."

SEVEN

Anya dissolved into tears. Gretchen stepped forward and gently pushed her hands aside, pulling her waistband back up and shirt back down. Then she took Anya into her arms, tucking the doctor's head against her shoulder and letting her cry. Josie covered Sharon Eddy back up, trying to order her thoughts. She'd known Anya Feist for eight years, and yet she hadn't even known that she had ever been married. The scar running down the side of Josie's face stung. She walked over to the two women and put a hand between Anya's shoulder blades, feeling the knobs of her vertebrae.

After a few moments, Anya's sobs subsided. She extricated herself from the two detectives and walked toward the back of the room where she found a couple of paper towels. Dabbing at her face, she said, "Thank you."

Gretchen said, "We've all got scars, Doc."

"And trauma," Josie said. "Just between the two of us, Gretchen and I have enough trauma to keep a whole army of therapists busy."

"For decades," Gretchen added.

Anya laughed. "I don't normally talk about it."

Josie pointed back and forth between herself and Gretchen. "Neither do we."

Some of the tension in Anya's shoulders loosened. "You're not angry? We've known each other for so long. Not just through work. Josie, you and I have lunch regularly."

Josie rubbed at where her scar ended beneath her chin. "No, not at you. I'm a little angry with myself for not making more of an effort to know more about you."

"Josie," said Anya. "I'm a closed book, just like you. Just like Gretchen. We do the job. We talk about the present. We try not to look back." She glanced at Sharon Eddy's face with a small shudder. "Until we have to."

Gretchen pulled her notebook out from her coat pocket and a pen from behind her ear. "When is the last time you saw your ex-husband?"

"About ten years ago," said Anya, twisting the damp paper towel in her hands.

Josie said, "No contact at all?"

"None. The first few years, after I moved here, I was a paranoid wreck. Always thinking I saw him on the street or following me in a car. But it was never him."

"You didn't press charges against him?" Gretchen said. "For the... branding?"

She squeezed the paper towel inside her fist. "Oh, I did. He pled down. His father intervened. Where we grew up, his dad had a lot of influence with everyone, including the county judges. In fact, my ex-father-in-law was on the town council for many years. As a result of his meddling, my ex-husband ended up on house arrest instead of prison. He was free in a matter of months. I kind of thought he learned his lesson after that but I couldn't be sure so I moved. Got this job. Started over. I've been happy here."

Her last statement was wistful, as if that happiness had now been tainted by the ugly intrusion of her past. She turned toward Sharon Eddy and stared down at the girl for several seconds, her expression tortured. Gently, she placed her empty palm over Sharon's eyes, closing them.

Gretchen said, "Can you tell us about the branding?"

Anya tucked the paper towel into her scrub pocket and pulled the sheet up over Sharon's head. Taking in a long breath, she turned back to them. "My ex-husband lived on a dairy farm. A family farm. Huge, very successful."

Josie said, "I know this was ten years ago, but I thought that farmers were moving away from hot branding to RFID tags."

Gretchen said, "What are RFID tags?"

"RFID stands for Radio Frequency Identification," said Josie.

Anya jammed her hands into her pockets. "They're plastic tags that farmers can affix to the ears of livestock to keep track of them. They usually have a number on them and are readable with handheld or stationary devices. Basically, it's like piercing the animal's ear rather than branding their skin. Freeze branding was in vogue for a while, and a lot of farms still use it as a more humane alternative to hot branding, but there was always a dispute over whether or not freeze branding really was more humane. RFID is far less barbaric than either of those, and yes, my ex-father-in-law moved to RFID tags as soon as they became available, before most farms in the country were using them."

Gretchen tapped her pen against her notepad. "Sounds like you were poised to inherit the farm."

"Vance was—that's my ex-husband's name. Vance Hadlee of Hadlee Farms."

The name was familiar. "Where is the farm?" Josie asked.

"Bly," Anya said. "It's about an hour from here. Like I said, it's a very small town. That's where I'm from. Vance and I were high school sweethearts. He was supposed to take over the farm. I was going to become a doctor. We actually broke up when I went away to college, but he kept showing up at my dorm. Even when I moved on to medical school, he was just always there. I'm not even sure I really loved him anymore. It just became comfortable. He wasn't abusive then."

Gretchen sighed. "They're never abusive in the beginning, at least not in obvious ways. It starts out with mind games, gaslighting, emotional coercion."

Anya nodded along with her words. One of her hands emerged from a pocket, holding the crumpled paper towel again. She used it to dab at a rogue tear that slid down her cheek. "Yes. Vance did all of those things. I didn't even want to get married or move back to Bly after medical school. I wanted to go to New York City and work in Emergency medicine. But he made me feel terrible for wanting that life. He implied that I thought I was too good for Bly, too good for this life he had planned out for us—without any input from me, mind you—and if I said I just want to explore this other avenue, it was, 'you don't love me.' There was no middle ground. No reasoning with him. Somehow, everything I said, no matter how reasonable it sounded, got twisted into me not loving him as much as he loved me or not prioritizing our relationship. I was never enough. Nothing was ever enough."

"Sounds like he was a master manipulator," Josie said.

Anya gave a dry laugh. "That, and the fact that I was just not prepared for it. I didn't see it. Not until it was too late. My parents died in a car accident when I was twelve. My uncle raised me. He was good to me—gave me a roof over my head, food in my belly, everything I needed—but it wasn't a close relationship. I was more like a boarder in his home. To say I was starved for love when Vance and I started going out together is an understatement. He was so sweet and fun in high school. Adventurous. He made me feel like anything was possible, and he had these eyes that looked like starbursts. I know that sounds ridiculous but it's a real thing. I found out when I went to med school. It's called central heterochromia."

Josie said, "Is that where each eye is a different color?"

Anya shook her head. Talking medicine, no matter how minor, seemed to put her on firmer emotional ground. "No, you're thinking of heterochromia iridium. Vance's eyes were the same but within each of his irises were several different colors. Brown closest to the pupil and then spikes of green and blue going outward. As a lonely high school girl, I was completely captivated by him. So yeah, later on, as an adult, I was not really aware of what was happening between us until I was in so deep that it felt impossible to get out."

"Did you go into Emergency medicine?" asked Gretchen.

Anya twisted the paper towel again. "I did, and as a compromise, I moved back to Bly and worked at a hospital an hour away near Philadelphia for a few days a week. Long shifts. But I was home there with him. Then he would schedule things for when he knew I'd be working and when I missed them, I was the bad guy. He felt like he never saw me at all. It didn't matter that I was doing what I loved or that I was the one making all the money. At that time, he hadn't even started running the farm. I didn't know it then, but he was having problems with his dad. Anyway, he wore me down over time with this idea that I didn't love him as much as I loved my job, and what kind of woman didn't love her husband more than her job?"

"You left the job near Philadelphia?" asked Josie.

Anya smiled weakly. "What do you think?"

Gretchen said, "But you kept practicing medicine."

She nodded. "There was a position open in the county for a pathologist. The current ME there, Garrick Wolfe, was willing to mentor someone with little to no experience. I had done a rotation in med school and enjoyed it. The pay was good. It was much closer to Bly than Philadelphia, and the hours were regular. Vance asked his father to talk with Garrick about hiring me. It almost seemed as though the decision had been made without my input at all."

Gretchen said, "Because it was."

"Yes. I know that now but at the time, Vance made it sound like good fortune, like it was meant to be. A sign that I should be home with him and not gallivanting off to the big city. 'Gallivanting.' That's what he called my work. I saved lives on those shifts but in his mind, I was just out having a good time with my doctor friends. It was a party as far as he was concerned."

"And he wasn't invited," Josie said.

"It was something he did not have control over," Gretchen pointed out.

Anya sighed. "Exactly. I didn't realize it then but he was slowly beginning to control every aspect of my life. It only got worse."

EIGHT

Anya let out a shuddering breath. She walked over to the stainless-steel counter lining the wall at the back of the room and deposited the balled-up paper towel into a waste bin beneath it. Leaning both hands against the countertop, she took several deep breaths. Josie and Gretchen said nothing, allowing her time to compose herself. After a long moment, she turned back to them. "My work was the one thing I had that was mine. It was the one place I felt truly free and like myself. Vance excised that independence right from my life."

"When did things become physical?" asked Josie.

"A few months after I started the ME job. We were fighting and he pushed me. I thought it was my fault because I made him so angry. I can't even remember what the stupid fight was about, and even having learned about domestic violence in school and having seen it in the ER, I didn't understand what was happening. It never even occurred to me that the push was bad. I just thought, 'we were arguing. It was the heat of the moment.' It didn't mean anything. The first time he pulled my hair or pinched me, I still didn't take it seriously. He was my husband. My high school sweetheart. We loved each other.

We'd built a life together. For all the fights, there were twice as many good times when he was caring and kind and tender. Then one day he twisted my wrist. I thought he was going to break it. My first thought was, how will I work?"

"That's when it hit you," Josie murmured.

Anya's hands were back in her pockets as if searching for something. They came up empty. "Weird, right? I never saw the escalation. Never. Until it was too late. There I was, completely enmeshed in this horrible situation. Getting out did not seem like an option at all. It wasn't even that I felt afraid to leave him at that point. It was that I had changed my entire life around for him—my career. His father had helped me get the position with the ME's office. His family had paid for our wedding. Our lives were so intertwined. Was I really going to blow it up over a sprained wrist?"

"It's very common, unfortunately," Gretchen said. "I'm sorry, Anya."

She got another paper towel from the dispenser and pressed it to her eyes, staunching the tears before they could come. "Me too. So yeah, it went from the sprained wrist to slaps to closed fists."

"Did he ever strangle you?" asked Josie.

"No. With Vance it was mostly pushing, pulling hair, punches. Like I said, the escalation seemed so slow and subtle that I barely registered that there was an escalation of sorts. I know that sounds unbelievable."

"No," Gretchen said quickly. "It doesn't sound unbelievable at all. Anya, that's how so many domestic abuse situations begin. It wasn't your fault."

Anya continued, "I didn't know what to do. I didn't want to involve the police. I still didn't really get it—that he was abusing me. It just seemed like a private matter. When he gave me my first black eye, I went to his father. Dermot was abrasive, gruff, and hard to read sometimes, but he had always been very fair.

He always put Vance in his place. In fact, the reason Vance hadn't yet taken over the farm was because he hadn't been going along with Dermot or following the plan for the farm. The truth is that Vance was lazy. He wanted the status of running the farm without doing any of the work. The reality was that he didn't even need the farm. He and his sister had a trust from their mother's family that paid out once they turned thirty. I didn't find that out until the divorce. It was never about the farm—it was about control. Dermot knew that. He'd never had a trust. He had to work to keep that farm going. Learn the business. Put in the time and labor. He and Vance were so different that way, but even when they were at odds, Vance listened to his father. For a while, things were better. Vance was furious with me for involving Dermot, but he didn't dare touch me."

Josie thought of her late first husband's father, Victor Quinn. He'd been horribly abusive to both Ray and his mother. As a child, Josie had seen it first-hand. Even when there was an uneasy peace in the household, Victor resented having to show restraint and it built up over time until he could no longer control it. "Your husband held onto that anger though, didn't he?"

Anya dabbed again at her eyes but this time the tears were too fast, spilling down her cheeks before she could stop them. "Yes. Again, I didn't see it coming. He was so angry with me, though—for humiliating him in front of his family by 'tattling' on him and for making our personal business known. He thought I chose his father over him. One night, we were staying over at the farm. He got into a fight with Dermot about when exactly he could take over. Dermot did not spare his feelings. He had a long list of reasons why Vance might never be ready to take over. Later that night, Vance got drunk. I went out to his workshop to collect him. Honestly, I was tired of it all. The ugliness. His bruised ego that never seemed to heal no matter how much any of us poured into it."

A sob rose in her throat. Josie watched her face go pink as she tried to swallow it back down.

Gretchen said, "Breathe, Anya. Nice and slow. It's just us here and we can stop any time you want."

"I don't want to stop," Anya said, wiping at her eyes again. "I want to get this over with. If I don't get it out now, I'm not sure if I can do it."

Josie touched her arm. "Okay. Then we'll stay until you've told us everything. Take your time."

Drawing in a deep breath, Anya straightened her spine and continued. "We argued. I told him the truth, finally, that I was unhappy, and I didn't want to be married anymore. There was a lot of ugliness that I'll spare you, including the fifteen hours he held me against my will. I'm not sure I want to relive it anyway. The end result was this." She patted her hip where the mark hid beneath her scrubs. Looking at Josie, she said, "Like I said, Dermot did away with branding long before I even met Vance, but what I didn't know was that as a child, Vance had developed a fascination with hot branding. He had been collecting different types of branding irons for years. He kept them in one of the old garages. He had tried most of them on the livestock even though it was not necessary, and Dermot forbade it."

"I can see why Dermot didn't want to give him the farm," said Gretchen.

"I didn't know until after. Vance came home to our little apartment each night and made his dad seem like the bad guy. He made Dermot sound so unreasonable, like this inflexible, crotchety old man who didn't take Vance seriously. It was all bullshit."

Josie said, "After that night, you left."

She nodded. Josie took the paper towel from her, now sopping wet, and threw it away. Anya hugged herself and rubbed at her upper arms. "I was lucky. Believe me, I almost lost my nerve about a dozen times. It wasn't easy. I felt tremendous guilt. He kept saying I ruined his life. It took years and a lot of distance for me to see the way things really were—how he manipulated and gaslit me to the point where he branded me like I was a piece of goddamn livestock, and I was the one who felt guilty."

Gretchen said, "It's more common than you know—the emotional coercion, gaslighting, and manipulation—not the branding."

Josie asked, "You pressed charges. He pled down and ended up on house arrest. You left town. What happened to him?"

Anya shrugged. "I don't know. I didn't look back, especially once the divorce was finalized. I was constantly on edge thinking he was going to come for me one day, but I didn't keep tabs on him. That was in my rearview."

"Fair enough," Josie said.

"It's been ten years," Gretchen said. "I understand why seeing the same brand on Sharon Eddy's body would upset you so much, but why would your ex-husband brand and then kill a girl in your jurisdiction? That's pretty brazen."

"And not smart," Josie said.

"True," said Anya. "Vance was smart, for all his flaws. But what else could this be except some sign from him?"

"And why now?" said Gretchen. "After all this time, why do it now?"

"I have no idea," said Anya. "I have no doubt he's still holding a grudge against me, but if he hasn't acted on it in almost a decade, I'm not sure what the catalyst is for him to start now."

Josie asked, "Who else knew about the branding incident?"

"The doctors and nurses at the local ER. The police. The prosecutor. My father-in-law and sister-in-law."

"No mother-in-law?" asked Gretchen.

Anya shook her head. "Mrs. Hadlee left when Vance was very young. Four or five, I think."

"Did anyone else know about the branding?" Josie pressed.

"Garrick. Like I said, he was my boss at the county medical examiner's office," said Anya. "I couldn't work for a while because of the pain." Her face flushed with the memory. One of her hands pressed against her hip. "You think that someone else did this? The brand—it wasn't a Hadlee family brand. Vance collected brands from all over the place. This was from his own —" she nearly choked on the words. "Personal collection."

"We have to consider every possibility," Josie said gently. "How many did he have in his personal collection?"

"Two dozen, maybe?" Anya said. "But that was ten years ago. God knows how many he's got now."

NINE

Two hours later, Josie and Gretchen had a warrant for any and all brands in the approximate shape of the marks found on Sharon Eddy's body to be served on Vance Hadlee at his farm in Bly, which was his last known address. Given the fact that Sharon Eddy had been missing for approximately twelve hours before her death, and Vance Hadlee lived only an hour away, it was entirely possible that he could have come to Denton, abducted her, taken her to a secondary location where he branded and likely killed her, and then returned to Hempstead Trail to leave her body. The secondary location was still a big question mark. Vance would have needed a fire and enough privacy to carry out the act without anyone seeing or hearing anything.

While Gretchen maneuvered her SUV onto the interstate, Josie spoke with dispatch. After hanging up, she said, "Dispatch will call the Bly Police Department and let them know that we're on our way and would like one of their officers to accompany us to execute the warrant. There's something else. I think." Josie hesitated. "I'm not sure if I should even mention it."

Gretchen gave her a quick glance. "What is it?"

"You know how I don't believe in coincidences, right?"

"That I do."

"Bly is in Everett County," Josie said.

"So?"

"Trinity's been visiting. She's actually looking into a case in Everett County right now for her show. The town could be Bly."

"Did she tell you what the case involved?"

"We didn't get very deep into it." The file folder atop Trinity's laptop flashed through Josie's mind. "I just know it was the Jana Melburn case."

"You think it could be related to the Sharon Eddy murder in Denton?"

"I'm not sure. It seems unlikely. Trin said that Melburn's older foster sister, Hallie Kent, contacted her producers about the case months ago. Kent had been trying to get her attention for a long time. On the other hand, without a deeper dive into that case, it's hard to say whether or not it's related to Sharon Eddy's murder—or to Anya."

"But we can't discount the connection. Trinity on a case in the same county where we're now pursuing a lead?" Gretchen said. "That's too coincidental. We'll have to ask Anya if she's familiar with it. You want to call Trinity now? Get a rundown?"

Josie tapped against the Mobile Data Terminal. "No. We'll be in Bly soon. I think we should prioritize finding out everything we can about Vance Hadlee and his farm."

Gretchen made a noise of agreement and focused on the road.

Josie switched back and forth between the MDT and her phone, running various searches and reading off her findings as she went. "The Hadlee farm is two hundred acres. Takes up a good bit of the southwest corner of Bly, according to these property records and map. It's been owned by Dermot Hadlee for nearly thirty-five years. It was originally owned by his wife's family. Her name was Susanna Blount. It was the Blount Family Farm for generations. As far back as these records go."

"When did it switch over to the Hadlee Family Farm?" asked Gretchen.

Josie read off the year. "Maybe that was the year they got married." Josie did some calculations in her head, based on Vance's age. "No, this would have been when Vance was about six or seven years old that it changed over."

"After Susanna left her family," Gretchen said.

"She abandoned a farm that had been in her family for generations, and her own children," Josie said. "Her life with Dermot must have been pretty bad. Maybe the proverbial apple didn't fall far from the tree."

"We may never know," said Gretchen. "But if Dermot still owns it, then he's stood by his decision not to hand it over to his son."

"Looks that way. Dad didn't give him the farm but he's still living there," Josie said. Turning back to the map, she added, "Gretchen, looking at all the structures on this farm again, I think we should call one of the guys to come help with the search warrant."

Gretchen said, "Do it."

Josie made some calls, first to Noah, then to Mettner. It was Mettner who insisted on coming in early for his shift so he could help them. "I caught the Eddy case," he told her. "Let me do it. Noah can stay and pick up any other calls that come in while we're in Bly."

Josie didn't argue. She called Noah back and he agreed with their plan. When Josie hung up, Gretchen asked, "Can you pull up a photo of this monster?"

Josie moved to a police database to pull up Vance's driver's license. As expected, he did not look like a monster at all. The worst ones never did. They looked just like everyone else, hiding their capacity for evil beneath a veneer of normal. Vance was no different with his square face, sharply cut jaw, long, straight nose. His central heterochromia wasn't visible in the photo. His eyes simply looked brown. His hair was also brown, now graying at the temples, slicked back from his face. The only hint that something unpleasant lurked beneath the surface was the corner of his mouth lifted in a smirk. Josie tapped a finger on the screen and Gretchen took a quick glance at it.

"What else can you find on him?"

Josie went back to searching. "Eighteen years ago, he was a star football player for Bly Hollow High School. Hmm. Looks like his dad, Dermot, coached the team back then."

"Dairy farm, town council, high school football coach," said Gretchen. "Dermot had his hands in everything."

Josie kept searching. "I don't see anything else here about Vance other than a bunch of articles about his high school football exploits."

"Criminal record? Beyond what Anya told us about?"

Josie ran a new search. "He's been clean since then."

"On paper," Gretchen muttered. "If his dad got him out of serious jail time with Anya—after what he did to her—God only knows what he's gotten him out of since. It's very rare for someone like that to just stop."

Josie clicked out of his record. A shiver ran up her arms. "Maybe he's gotten away with things for so long that he's become brazen enough to brand and kill young women in the city where his ex-wife is now the medical examiner."

"We'll just see about that."

TEN

The Bly Police Department was approximately ten miles from the Hadlee Family Farm. It was housed in a modern, gray glass-and-brick building on a few sprawling acres of land. It looked more like a recreation center than a police department, save for the handful of cruisers resting in the parking lot. Inside, a desk sergeant scrutinized their credentials and asked them to explain why they were there. Then, after they told him, he asked again. And again. Josie was growing impatient by the time a loud male voice boomed, "What the hell are you doing here? I told you everything you need to know. I know you reporters have to be persistent, but you have some nerve showing up here like this."

Josie looked up from the desk sergeant to see a man in his mid-fifties approaching from a hall behind the lobby desk. Dressed in a dark blue uniform, the nameplate above his left breast pocket read: *Grey.* He pointed a finger at Josie. She looked behind her but there was no one else in the lobby. Looking back at his red face, she quickly put together what was going on. Josie had pissed a lot of people off in her line of work, but only her sister could produce that shade of red on a police officer's face.

"I'm not who you think I am," she told him.

As he got closer, she got a whiff of cologne, not unpleasant. "I know exactly who you are," he said.

"I'm Detective Josie Quinn from the Denton PD. You're thinking of my sister, Trinity Payne."

He pulled up short, looking momentarily confused.

Gretchen said, "It's true. They're identical twins."

Still not convinced, Grey looked to the desk sergeant, who shrugged. "That's what her ID says."

Grey appraised her once more. Josie turned her head and used her index finger to trace the scar along the side of her face. "My sister doesn't have one of these. As you can see, not even copious amounts of makeup can completely cover it up."

Grey took a step back and ran a hand through his thick salt-and-pepper curls. "I'm sorry. I—"

Gretchen said, "Do you watch Trinity Payne's show?"

He looked away. "Sometimes. Listen, I'm sorry. I didn't know she had an identical twin."

Josie said, "Trinity mentioned she was looking into a case in this area."

His eyes narrowed. "You here about that case?"

"Jana Melburn?" Josie asked, noting the small tightening of skin around his eyes when she said the name. "No. We're here about Vance Hadlee."

The desk sergeant, looking bored now, said, "They've got to serve a warrant over at the Hadlee farm. They're looking for someone to go with them. The Chief was gonna send Belkin."

Grey held up a hand to silence him. "No. Belkin's busy. I'll do it." He moved closer and extended a hand, first to Josie and then to Gretchen. As they shook, he said, "Sergeant Cyrus Grey. I'm sorry for the confusion earlier. I can accompany you over to the Hadlee farm if you bring me up to speed on whatever it is you're working on. Walk with me."

They followed him into the suite of offices, Josie giving him the rundown. "Yesterday, in Denton, the body of a nineteen-year-old female was found on the riverbank. Her name was Sharon Eddy. She was a resident of Denton. There were no visible injuries to her person at the scene. However, on autopsy, our medical examiner found that she'd been strangled."

Gretchen said, "There was also a mark on her body that leads us to believe that Vance Hadlee may have been involved in her murder."

They passed a few offices, each with windows providing views inside. Some of them were occupied by officers in uniform and one was occupied by a woman dressed in civilian clothes. No one looked up as they passed. Stopping outside an empty office, Cyrus laughed. "Vance Hadlee? You're kidding, right?"

Josie said, "We know he has a history of violence."

Cyrus's face darkened. He looked up and down the hall, but no one was around. "This about his ex-wife?"

"What do you know about his ex-wife?" asked Gretchen.

He pushed the door open and beckoned them inside. "I know he did a number on her when all was said and done, and that she stuck around long enough to make sure he paid for it."

"Did he, though?" Josie asked. "Pay for it? He didn't even go to prison."

Cyrus plucked a set of keys from his desk. Then he met her eyes, his dark gaze penetrating. Josie stared back unblinking until he looked away first. "It's really uncanny," he muttered. "This twin thing. You and Trinity Payne."

Josie said, "We know that Vance Hadlee had a fascination with branding. We know that he had a collection of cattle brands and that he used one to mark his ex-wife. The same brand was burned into Sharon Eddy's skin yesterday before her death."

"In the same place on her body," said Gretchen.

"How do you know all that?"

"We spoke with his ex-wife," said Josie.

He gave her a tight smile. "How did you know to talk to her? That was a domestic case. The details—the photos, in particular —were never made public out of respect for her."

Gretchen said, "She's the Alcott County medical examiner. She performed Sharon Eddy's autopsy."

"Hmmph." Cyrus scratched his nose and led them into the hallway. "You know, the brand that Vance used on her was taken into evidence. He never did get it back. As per our policy here, it was destroyed five years after his conviction. He pled guilty, so there were no appeals that required us to keep it longer than that."

Josie said, "He collected brands, according to Dr. Feist. He could have gotten another."

"I suppose." Cyrus locked his office door. "Anya—Dr. Feist —is just up in Alcott County, huh? She didn't go very far."

"She shouldn't have had to leave at all," Josie pointed out.

Ignoring her, he said, "Vance has been clean ever since. His dad kept him on the straight and narrow."

"You can't know that for sure," said Gretchen.

He stopped near one of the cruisers outside and looked at them. "Sure I can. This town isn't that big. It's pretty rural. The folks in Bly tend to stay here and travel in the same circles they've always been in and that includes Vance Hadlee. He hardly ever leaves the farm. I'd know if he was up to something. No one's even seen him with another woman since his wife left."

Josie glared at him. "Does Dermot Hadlee pay you to cover for him?"

Shock slackened Cyrus's face, but he quickly covered it with a polite smile. "Dermot had his influence in certain matters around here. I won't say that he didn't. No one's ever come forward with proof, but there have been rumors. As far as I'm concerned, my obligation is to uphold the law. I stand by that. Now, do you want me to take you to the farm or do you want to insult my integrity a while longer?"

Gretchen looked at Josie and then at Cyrus. "We can insult your integrity on the farm just as easily as we can standing right here."

Josie saw the jolt go through him. She couldn't be sure if he was holding back anger or laughter but for a long moment, he said nothing, his lips pursed tightly. Josie took out her phone and checked the time. "Our colleague is meeting us at the farm, so yes, let's go there."

Gretchen smiled and pointed at their vehicle. "That's us. We'll follow you over."

Wordlessly, he got into his cruiser and fired up the engine, revving it hard. As they walked back to their own car, Josie made sure they didn't cross directly in front of his vehicle.

ELEVEN

Josie stared down the barrel of a twelve-gauge shotgun. In spite of the cold February air, a bead of sweat formed at the nape of her neck and rolled down her spine. At the other end of the gun was an older man, likely in his seventies. Thinning white hair swathed his scalp. One side of his face drooped slightly, wrinkles folding upon wrinkles. Watery blue eyes looked from Josie to Gretchen to Cyrus. The shotgun wobbled slightly in his hands. From her periphery, she noticed one of his legs shaking. Josie unsnapped the holster at her waist and curled her hand around the grip of her pistol.

Under her breath, Gretchen said, "What the hell is this?"

They had driven through the farm entrance, marked with a big wrought iron sign, and down the long dirt driveway until a large stone farmhouse came into view. They'd made it out of their vehicles and to the bottom of the steps that led to the wraparound porch when the front door slammed open and the man emerged, brandishing his weapon.

Cyrus said, "Dermot, put that down. It's Cy. Everything's fine."

Dermot stepped closer to the edge of the porch, swinging

the shotgun from side to side. Another sweat droplet snaked down Josie's spine. She heard the sound of Gretchen unsnapping her own holster.

Cyrus sighed. "Dermot, come on. It's me, Sergeant Grey. These two are with me."

Dermot's lips smacked together as he struggled to speak with one side of his mouth paralyzed. All that came out was a grunt. Behind him, the front door swung open. A woman emerged, dressed in a flannel shirt, jeans, and muddy boots. Long brown hair flowed down her back. She strode over to Dermot and easily lifted the shotgun from his hands. Expertly, she pushed the action release lever aside and broke open the shotgun, extracting the two unfired shells. Gun cleared, she pocketed the shells. Holding the shotgun at her side, barrel toward the floor, she pointed to a nearby rocking chair. "Dad, go sit down."

Dermot glared at her, anger flashing in his eyes.

She held her ground. "We talked about this, Dad. You can't just point a shotgun at people. Go sit down while I find out what's going on here."

He kept his fiery gaze on her face for a beat before hitching a leg and dragging it across the porch to the rocking chair. It creaked as he settled into it. He kept his eyes on the trio of police officers.

"I'm sorry," said the woman, waving them toward the steps. "What can I do for you, Cy?"

No explanation was given for Dermot Hadlee's behavior, but it was obvious that he'd had some kind of medical issue, likely a stroke, and that this was not the first time that he'd pulled a shotgun on guests. That Cyrus had chosen not to warn Josie or Gretchen was another matter altogether.

Cyrus introduced Josie and Gretchen. "They're here to speak with Vance and, uh, serve a search warrant."

The woman put the gun aside, leaning it up against one of

the wooden balusters, and walked down the steps toward them. "Lark Hadlee," she said. "Can I see some identification?"

Josie took her sweaty palm away from her pistol and produced her credentials. Gretchen did the same. Lark studied them, her expression impossible to read. "You want to talk to Vance about what?"

"A murder," said Josie.

If Lark was surprised, she didn't show it. She folded her arms across her chest and looked pointedly at Cyrus. He threw his hands in the air. "Nothing I can do about this, sweetheart. Not my circus. I'm here as a courtesy."

Dermot managed to say, "Get him."

Rolling her eyes, Lark spun on her heel and walked back up the steps. She threw the front door open and screamed for Vance.

While they waited, Josie and Gretchen exchanged a look. They hadn't found any evidence that Vance Hadlee had remarried, and given the family resemblance, it appeared that Lark was his sister. When Vance didn't appear, Lark went inside. Behind them, tires crunched against gravel. Seconds later, Mettner pulled up behind Josie and Gretchen's vehicle. He hopped out, drawing an angry glare from Dermot and a weary look from Cyrus.

From the porch, Josie heard Dermot hiss what sounded like "Whoosis?"

Cyrus said, "I imagine it's another detective from Denton." He looked at Josie and Gretchen. "That right?"

Mettner walked right up to Cyrus and extended a hand, introducing himself. Cyrus stared at his outstretched palm for a moment, as if it were covered in something disgusting. Mettner didn't move. Instead, he added, "I'm here to assist with the search warrant."

With a sigh, Cyrus shook Mettner's hand. Turning back to Dermot, he said, "I was right."

Inside the house, a door slammed. Lark's voice rang out, her words faint but audible. "I don't know. Just get the hell out here. Dad said."

A few more minutes passed in awkward silence, the only noise the creak of Dermot's rocking chair. Finally, Vance emerged from the front door, wearing a stained white T-shirt and jeans that he hadn't bothered to button up. His boots were unlaced, and half his hair stood on end. The same smirk they'd seen in his driver's license photo snaked across his face. He stopped on the porch, taking in the scene. Then he sauntered down the porch steps, keeping his gaze on Cyrus.

"Cy," he said. "My condolences. We were real sorry to hear about Piper."

Cyrus's posture stiffened. The flush of anger Josie had seen at the police station rose again in his cheeks. Before he could respond, Lark emerged onto the porch. "Sorry we weren't at the service," she called out. "Dad had the flu."

Cyrus swallowed and quickly changed the subject, introducing Josie and Gretchen—and now Mettner—to Vance. He explained why they had come, including everything they'd told him at the Bly Police Department.

Three horizontal lines creased Vance's forehead as his eyes moved from Cyrus to Josie, Gretchen, and Mettner. Up close, Josie saw what Anya had been talking about when she said his eyes were like starbursts. On less of a scumbag, they might even be attractive.

"Wait just a minute," he said. "You think I killed someone?" He shook his head, hard, his hair rearranging itself into a new picture of disarray. "And you think I—I branded this woman? Are you crazy?" Turning back to Cyrus, he said, "What's this about Anya? I haven't seen her in ten years. You know that, Cy. Everyone knows it. She left and never looked back."

Josie said, "The same type of brand that you used when you

assaulted your ex-wife was used on our victim before her death."

Gretchen launched right into questioning, trying to keep him off balance. "Do you know Sharon Eddy?"

Some fleeting emotion flitted across Vance's face. Josie couldn't decide if it was alarm or confusion but she was certain he recognized the name, though how he and Sharon Eddy might have been connected was a mystery. Josie and the team hadn't found anything at all linking the two, but they had yet to do a truly extensive investigation into Sharon Eddy's life. The corners of Vance's mouth tightened. He cast around, looking at everyone else for help. None was forthcoming. Dermot glared at his son, the healthy side of his mouth curled in a sneer. With a sigh, Vance answered, "I don't know anyone named Sharon Eddy."

Josie had come prepared with a driver's license photo of Sharon. She took out her phone and pulled it up, turning it toward him so he could see it. Lark walked down a few steps and peeked over his shoulder. Vance's expression was blank. The name had sparked some recognition but not her face. Unless he was a very good actor. "I don't know her. Never saw her."

"Where were you yesterday?" asked Mettner.

"I was here," Vance said.

"All day?" asked Josie.

"Yeah, all day. Lark, tell them."

She turned away and went back to the porch, now standing beside Dermot's chair. "He was here all day."

"How about your vehicles?" asked Gretchen. "Were all the farm vehicles accounted for all day yesterday?"

"Yes," said Lark and Vance in unison.

Gretchen took out the warrant and handed it to him. "We understand there are a number of structures on the premises."

They had looked up a satellite view of the farm on Google

Maps before writing their warrant. There was the house, two large cowsheds, a milking parlor, two silos, a barn, two large garages, and one smaller garage. Anya had told them that Vance's workshop was in one of the old garages.

Josie said, "We have a warrant to search the premises for hot branding implements."

Vance let out an incredulous laugh. "You're kidding me, right? Is this some kind of joke? What happened between me and Anya all those years ago was a private matter. You have no right—"

"You were convicted of assault," Josie pointed out. "You left a permanent scar on her. That was not a private matter, Mr. Hadlee. It was a crime, and no, this is not a joke. We're going to search the farm for branding implements. Please stay here with Sergeant Grey."

Vance looked to Cyrus for help, but Cyrus only shrugged. "The law is the law, Vance. You know that."

"This is bullshit," Vance said.

Cyrus said, "If it is, then you have nothing to worry about. Let them search."

Vance turned back to Josie, Gretchen, and Mettner. "Did Anya put you up to this? Why is she bringing this back up after all this time?"

Gretchen said, "All Dr. Feist did was perform the autopsy on Sharon Eddy, as per her job. She merely reported her findings to us. We're here of our own accord."

"We'd like to get started," Mettner added.

Lark stepped forward and beckoned them. "Come on, I'll show you around."

TWELVE

Lark led them inside the farmhouse, through a large living room where a fire smoldered inside a huge hearth, then through a dim dining room, and into a hallway. From there, they followed her up a set of wooden steps that were so old, they sagged in places. Upstairs, a threadbare carpet lined another hall. Elaborate floral designs meandered across the wallpaper from floor to ceiling. There were four doors in all, each of them white and closed. Nowhere in the house were there any photos, or even the bare minimum of home decor. The place could have been cozy with the right touch, but all it was under the auspices of the Hadlee family was utilitarian. It was a place to live, but it didn't feel like a home.

Lark pointed at the last door in the hallway. "This is my brother's room. I'm guessing you want to start here."

Josie said, "We'll need to have a look around the entire house, but this is as good a place to start as any." She nodded toward Mettner. "Detective Mettner can start at the other end of the hall, and we'll meet him in the middle. That sound okay to you?"

Lark nodded.

Mettner snapped on a pair of gloves and walked toward the other end of the hallway, disappearing behind one of the doors. Lark gestured toward Vance's bedroom door. "I'll wait right here and then I can take you around when you're done." She glanced back in the direction Mettner had gone and lowered her voice. "Peel the carpet up behind his nightstand. That's where he keeps things he doesn't want my dad to find. At least, that's where he used to keep them."

Josie snuck a glance at Gretchen, long enough to see from her expression that she was just as intrigued by this offering. Outside, Lark had towed the family line: Vance had been home the entire day yesterday. All the Hadlee vehicles were accounted for that day. But here, away from Dermot and Vance, there was a crack in the united front.

Josie said, "Lark, did you physically see your brother yesterday?"

Jamming her hands into her jeans pockets, Lark shrugged. "No. Usually I see him in the morning for the a.m. milking. We start around four or four thirty. Go till six or six thirty. As long as it takes. My dad can't help as much as he used to since the stroke. His right side doesn't work all that well, so it makes a huge difference if Vance helps. He's usually still up from the night before. Sometimes he helps me, sometimes he doesn't. On the days that he does, after we finish, I get on with the daily stuff while he goes back to bed. For the afternoon milking we usually have a couple of kids from the high school come out to help. We used to have people come and work for us but a few years back, my dad figured out he could get 'interns' from the local school so now that's what we do."

"Did you see Vance yesterday at all?" asked Gretchen.

"No. I didn't actually see him," Lark said. "But I wasn't here. I was out doing the work. If he went out, I didn't notice. Vance spends most of his time here, in his 'workshop,' or taking one of the ATVs out around the pastures checking for breaks in the fences that he then 'assigns' me to fix. Although, since Dad's stroke last year, he's been taking the bobcat out along the north edge of the property to dig. He got it into his head that he wants to put in a pond." She rolled her eyes. "'Cause that's what we need. Him digging for a pond instead of helping us run this farm."

Josie said, "That doesn't sound very fair."

Lark sighed. "Yeah, well, Vance never had any real interest in farming, only the income it provides and the status it gives him in town."

"What about your dad?" asked Gretchen. "What does he do during the day?"

"He can still drive, so sometimes he goes into town for supplies. The guys at the tractor supply load the truck up for him. I unload it for him when he gets back. If he's not on a supply run then he's in one of the big garages, working on the tractors. One of 'em's always broke. It's not so easy for him anymore with his limitations but he manages, and what he can't do, I do for him."

"Did you see Vance on Thursday?" asked Gretchen.

Lark nodded.

"You saw him Thursday," Josie said. "But not yesterday. When was the next time you saw Vance after Thursday? Physically?"

"Physically? Just now, outside."

"He wasn't at the a.m. milking today?" asked Gretchen.

"No. He missed it again. I can do it myself, no problem. It just takes longer."

"If you had not seen him since Thursday," Josie said, "how did you know he was here when we arrived?"

"I heard him come in around three in the morning. When he gets drunk—good and smashed, not the drunk where he's angry and mean but the drunk where he's just obliterated—he falls a lot. He fell in the hall here. I heard him cursing."

"You didn't come out of your room?" asked Gretchen.

Lark looked behind them again, as if she expected someone to be standing in the hall. Whether that someone was Mett or Vance, Josie couldn't tell. "I never come out when he's drunk if I can help it."

"Okay," Gretchen said. "You stay here while we search his room. Also, we're going to need the names and contact information of anyone who helped with the afternoon milking yesterday."

Lark said nothing. Reaching over, she pushed the door open.

Josie snapped on a pair of latex gloves, as did Gretchen, and they entered Vance's bedroom. The smell of sweat mingling with stale beer hit them immediately. A queen-sized bed took up most of the room, a blanket and sheet rumpled at its foot. A large wooden dresser spanned one wall. On top of it were two framed photos: one of a much younger Dermot, a woman who bore a striking resemblance to Lark, and two small children. The Hadlee family. They were sitting on a picnic blanket, huddled together. The ends of Dermot's mouth lifted in what Josie supposed could pass for a smile. His wife, Susanna, wore a smile that wasn't much more convincing than his, and yet she was still striking with high cheekbones, full lips, and long glossy locks split by a white forelock which stood out against her otherwise dark hair. The only thing out of place was what looked like a clunky hearing aid in her left ear. Vance sat in his mother's lap and grinned at the camera. Lark stood behind her parents, unsmiling. The photo had none of the crispness of modern-day pictures and had started yellowing around the edges.

The other frame held a photo of a smiling couple on their wedding day. Josie froze when she realized it wasn't Dermot Hadlee and his wife, but Vance and Anya. They stood in a rolling green pasture under a white arbor decorated with flowers and gauzy white fabric. Vance's smile was wide, his expression reflecting the happiness of wild abandon. Anya's was more subdued. Maybe she hadn't consciously known or understood it at the time, but some part of her deep down must have had doubts about the marriage for which she had repeatedly sacrificed her career ambitions.

Gretchen's voice made her startle. "Divorced ten years and still has the wedding photo on his dresser. No way has he moved on."

A chill rolled up Josie's back, nipping at the hair on the nape of her neck. "Not a chance," she whispered so that Lark wouldn't overhear. Vance's smirk flashed through her mind. He didn't miss Anya, she was sure of it. He was angry with her for what he thought she had done to him. Making a 'private matter' public. Humiliating him. Saddling him with a criminal conviction. That was the perspective of an abuser. What Anya had really done was stand up for herself, hold him accountable for his actions, and leave a dangerous and toxic situation.

Gretchen said, "It doesn't even look like Anya."

Although it was clearly a younger, curvier, fresh-faced Anya, Gretchen was right. It looked nothing like the woman they knew. Even her dress was an elaborate, over-embroidered affair that Josie couldn't imagine Anya choosing for herself. "It doesn't look like her because it's not her. Not anymore."

Feeling like a voyeur, Josie quickly turned away and helped Gretchen search the room. They found porn magazines, condoms, several hundred dollars in cash, what looked like cocaine, and several small baggies filled with pills. Unfortunately, it wasn't quite enough to make a case for Vance to be charged with possession or possession with intent to distribute drugs.

No branding implements.

The compartment under Vance's nightstand held only family photos from his and Lark's early childhood when their mother was still living with them on the farm. As Josie flipped through them, she saw Susanna Hadlee's smile change over the years. It was bright and joyful on the day of her wedding and shortly after the births of her children. Then, as the kids grew into toddlers, the muscles around her mouth seemed to get stiffer. Her smiles were mechanical, forced. The light in her eyes slowly extinguished, like a dying candle at the end of its wick. Then there were no more photos. Again feeling like a voyeur, Josie stuffed the pictures back into the compartment and covered it.

After searching the rest of the room and finding nothing, they returned to the hall where Lark waited. She gestured toward the room next to Vance's, which turned out to be hers. They searched it, finding nothing of concern other than a pocketknife beneath her pillow. They didn't ask her about it. Josie was pretty sure she knew why it was there. Once Mettner had concluded his own searches of his assigned bedrooms, all of them moved downstairs.

Methodically, Lark took them through the rest of the house. They found nothing. Outside, Dermot, Cyrus and Vance sat in chairs on the porch. Vance and Dermot glared. Cyrus maintained a blank expression but given the way he tapped his foot against the porch floorboards, like he was listening to a tune no one else could hear, he seemed to be enjoying the spectacle of the Hadlee farm being searched. Josie was relieved that the vehicles were at the side of the house, out of view of the men. The Hadlees had two pickup trucks—one black and one silver— a red SUV, and a white sedan. Lark pointed to the newest truck, silver gleaming in the sunlight. "That's the one Vance drives. Normally."

Gretchen approached it. "Normally?"

Lark pointed to the small white sedan. "Sometimes he drives that old piece of crap. When he doesn't want Dad to know where he's been. The truck's got GPS. That old car does not."

They started with Vance's truck. Inside was a lot of garbage, including several empty bottles of liquor. The other vehicles were cleaner and more well-kept. None had any branding implements inside or Sharon Eddy's missing glove. When they finished, Lark said, "I'll take you back to the other buildings. Might take you a while—they're pretty spread out."

She started walking away, deeper onto the property, and they followed. Ahead, the roofs of the cowsheds came into view, two small humps. Here at the back of the property, the smell of animals, feed, and manure mixed together to create a powerful stench. Gretchen coughed and wiped at her eyes. "Good lord," she muttered. "I'm not sure what's worse: a dead body or this."

Mettner laughed softly. "You get used to it."

"You do," said Josie. "But it's pretty unpleasant."

"Not something I'd want to get used to," Gretchen answered.

Mettner pointed at the cowsheds. "We should split up again. I can take those."

Josie nodded. "Good idea. We'll work on the smaller buildings. Meet up later."

He strode ahead of them. Lark banked right. As they walked, more buildings came into view. She pointed to the closest one. "Vance spends a lot of time inside the smaller garage. That's where... it happened, you know?"

Josie hurried to keep up with her, Gretchen still trailing a few steps behind. "What's that?"

Over her shoulder, Lark said, "The thing with Anya."

THIRTEEN

Lark crossed a wide patch of grass and turned onto a muddy path marked by parallel tire marks. "My dad calls it 'that business with Anya,'" she added.

Josie and Gretchen caught up, flanking Lark as more structures appeared. The first freestanding garage they came to was small and old. A bay door was held fast by a padlock affixed to the door handle about a foot from the ground. Lark fished around in the pockets of her jeans until she came up with a set of keys. As she bent to work the key in the lock, her flannel and the white T-shirt beneath rode up, exposing a strip of pale flesh above her waist. Near her left hip was a curved line of pink, raised flesh. It started below her waistband and disappeared beneath her shirt.

Josie used an elbow to nudge Gretchen in the ribs, but her eyes were already locked on the mark. The door groaned open. In the center of the bay was an old ratty orange couch that sagged on one side. A scuffed end table held an ashtray filled with cigarette butts. A half-filled bottle of vodka sat beside it. A small wood-burning stove took up one corner of the room. The walls were lined with shelves filled with various tools and equipment. One of the shelving units held brands. Dozens of them in all different sizes and shapes. Josie and Gretchen walked over and began searching through the shelves.

Lingering near the doorway, Lark said, "Dad took away his branding iron furnace after what happened with Anya."

Josie looked over her shoulder long enough to see that Lark's gaze was fixed on the wood-burning stove. Quietly, she added, "But he's got other ways."

Gretchen turned away from the shelves. "Sounds like you have personal knowledge."

Lark said nothing.

"He's hurt you," Gretchen pressed.

Josie's fingers paused over a brand in the shape of an H. "Lark, are you afraid of your brother?"

"Afraid of Vance?" Lark laughed. "No. I'm not afraid of him. I know exactly what he's capable of and it doesn't frighten me."

Gretchen said, "That brand on your back—he gave that to you, didn't he?"

Lark didn't respond.

Josie asked, "That wasn't scary?"

"Hurt isn't scary," Lark said. "It's just pain. My brother is a lazy piece of shit who gets off on making people feel small and vulnerable. He's a parasite. He can hurt me all he wants. Why would it scare me?"

"You never worry he might kill you?" Gretchen said.

"No."

"But you think he's capable of killing someone," Josie said.

Lark folded her arms across her chest again. "Of course he is, but he won't kill me. He needs me to run this farm. Dad won't live forever and without me, he'd run this place into the ground. After our father passes, I'll buy him out. Give him a deal he can't resist. I've got money my mom's people left us in a trust. He'd take my half in a heartbeat. Once this place is mine, I'll make sure he never sets foot on this farm again."

Gretchen asked, "You never thought about going to the police after he hurt you? Like Anya did?"

"So our dad can get him off just like with Anya? Bring him right back here? When you live with a tiger, you don't antagonize it."

Gretchen said, "If you've got money from your mother, why stay here? Is it enough to start over somewhere else?"

Lark's chin jutted forward. "Why should I leave? This is my farm more than it is his—more than it is my dad's at this point. I run this place. I love it. Why should I give it up because of them?"

"Fair point," Gretchen said.

Moving another set of brands in the shapes of various letters aside, Josie found a box of condoms tucked at the back of the shelf. "Does your brother entertain women here?"

"Yeah. Don't ask me which women because I don't know them. I just know he picks them up at some local bar. I sometimes see them leaving when I come out for the morning milking."

Josie made a mental note to visit the local bars and ask around about Vance Hadlee. "Deputy Grey said that no one has seen your brother with a woman since Anya left."

Lark laughed. "Cy loves to think he's got his finger on the pulse of everything that goes on in this town, but he doesn't. He's got no idea what goes on. He's hardly left the house in the last four or five years, other than for work."

"Why's that?" asked Gretchen.

"His daughter, Piper. She got shot in the head by her husband, years ago, and she's been a shell of a person ever since. The bullet didn't leave her with much. Cy's been taking care of her."

"She passed away recently," Josie said. "You told Cy you were sorry to have missed her service."

Lark nodded. "Yeah, it was real sad. Folks in town said her body finally gave out."

If what Lark said was true and Piper's husband had shot her, he could be charged with murder even if she died years later, as long as her death was related to the injuries sustained in the shooting.

"What happened to Piper's husband?" asked Josie.

"Went to prison for a while." She leaned back and craned her head from side to side as if checking to see if anyone was outside. Looking back at Josie and Gretchen, she shifted her weight from foot to foot. Licking her lips, she said, "He, uh, got out last year. It was, uh, after Dad's stroke. Anyway, he didn't come back to Bly, which is probably good. He wasn't liked much even before that."

"What's his name?" asked Gretchen.

"Mathias Tobin," Lark answered.

"Why didn't people like him before?" asked Josie.

They were far off-topic now, but Lark seemed like she wanted to talk, to get some things off her chest. They'd already learned more about Vance and his daily routine as well as his shaky alibi than they'd gotten when they first showed up. Josie couldn't imagine what it was like for Lark, living with Vance and Dermot all the time. Based on the photos in Vance's secret compartment, Lark was a couple of years older than him, which meant she was approaching her mid-forties, and yet she was single with no family of her own, still living on this farm. Surely she had friends and got away from the farm now and then, but day-to-day life must have felt isolating. It wasn't the worst thing to keep her engaged in conversation, even if it was about Cyrus's son-in-law.

Lark said, "Everyone here thinks he killed some girl ages ago. Police said it was an accident so he was never charged or questioned or anything, but once the rumors start, you can't stop them."

"Jana Melburn?" asked Josie.

Lark's brows shot up in surprise. "How do you know about it?"

Skirting the question, Josie smiled. "Seems like you can't talk to anyone around here without her name coming up."

Lark nodded. "Small town, small county. People got real hung up on that case. She was a receptionist at one of the local doctor's offices. We've only got two around here, so pretty much half the area knew her. I'd met her, since that was the office we've always used. Everyone agreed she was real sweet, and they were right. Pretty, well-liked young girl turns up dead? People couldn't stop talking. It was the mystery, I think. Was she killed or was it an accident? Gave folks something to talk about. Everyone had an opinion or a theory. I don't think anyone ever cared about Jana Melburn. Her death was just entertainment."

Before Josie could ask more questions, a cell phone rang. All three of them checked their pockets, but it was Lark who took out her phone and swiped answer. From her end of the conversation, it sounded as though Vance had grown tired of waiting for Josie, Gretchen and Mettner to finish their search. After a brief conversation, Lark hung up. Stationing herself at the garage entrance, she said, "Keep going, and take your time."

Josie and Gretchen finished searching every last nook of the garage. There were forty-two brands in all but none matching the kind that had been used on Sharon Eddy. Silently, Lark led them to another garage which they checked. Nothing was found. They met up with Mettner after that and the three of them searched the rest of the farm. Hours later, they were exhausted, hungry, stinking of cow dung, and empty-handed.

As they walked back to the house, Mettner drew up beside Josie and tapped her elbow. She took one look at his face and knew he wanted to discuss something but not in front of Lark. Josie coughed, drawing Gretchen's attention. They'd worked together for so long that it only took a waggle of her eyebrows and a brief nod in Mettner's direction for Josie to communicate that she and Mettner needed a moment alone. Gretchen focused her attention on Lark and began to ask questions about the farm. Josie and Mettner slowed until they were several paces behind Gretchen and Lark.

"What is it?" Josie said.

"There are guns all over this property," Mettner said. "Shotguns, rifles, even two handguns—one in Dermot Hadlee's bedroom and another out in one of the barns."

"I'm not surprised," she said. "Dermot Hadlee pointed a shotgun at us when we got here."

Mettner shook his head. "My point is they're all unsecured, and Vance Hadlee is not supposed to have access to firearms. Not after what he did to Dr. Feist."

"You're right," Josie agreed. "But you know for a fact that he, his father, and even his sister are just going to say that none of those guns belong to him."

Mettner made a noise of exasperation. "What are you saying? We shouldn't do anything?"

"I'm not saying that at all," Josie said. "We should absolutely do something. I'm just saying that it probably won't go anywhere."

As they rounded the front of the house, Josie noticed Vance leaning against the porch railing, a grin from ear to ear. Cyrus stood beside his cruiser, watching as they tromped over. "You three look whipped. Get what you came for?"

Mettner said, "What we found were a total of five firearms on the premises that are unsecured."

Cyrus said nothing. His expression didn't change.

Vance said, "So what?"

Mettner looked up at him. "I think you know that you are

prohibited from possessing firearms due to your aggravated assault conviction."

Vance's grin widened. "Good thing I'm not in possession of any firearms, then."

"But because the firearms on this property are not secured, you have access to them, which means you can be charged with persons not to possess a firearm."

From the rocking chair, Dermot hissed. "Bullshhhiiittt."

Lark didn't speak but covered the smirk on her lips with one hand. Vance looked from Mettner to Cyrus. "Cy, tell this piece of shit that I am not in possession of a firearm."

From her periphery, Josie saw Gretchen's hand go to her holster. Mettner kept his gaze on Vance, unblinking. Josie looked at Cyrus, who dropped his chin to his chest and closed his eyes. Slowly, he shook his head.

"Cy," Dermot rasped.

Vance slowly made his way down the steps, coming within a few feet of Mettner. He pointed a finger at Mettner's chest. "Let me give you a piece of advice, jackass. You don't come onto my farm and start lobbing accusations around. I don't know who the hell you think you are, but—"

Mettner cut him off, voice firm and clear. "Mr. Hadlee, I'm not in the habit of taking advice from felons who treat women like livestock. You have been found to be in possession of firearms. You will be charged accordingly."

He waved a hand toward Cyrus, who still stood near his cruiser, head low and bobbing back and forth. After a beat of silence, he opened his eyes and looked up at Vance. A heavy sigh issued from somewhere deep in his chest. "Get in the goddamn cruiser, Vance."

Dermot stumbled to his feet, the rocking chair clattering to the ground. Lark rushed to his side, clasping his weak arm in her hands. "Daddy, no."

A flush crept across Vance's face. Hands fisted at his sides, he took another step closer to Mettner.

"Dammit, Vance," Cyrus said. "Get over here. Don't make me cuff you, for chrissake."

Josie heard the sound of Gretchen's holster unsnapping. To his credit, Mettner stood straight and still. For every ounce of menace oozing from Vance Hadlee's body, Mettner showed twice as much confidence.

Cyrus opened the back door of the cruiser. "Vance."

After a few more seconds during which Josie could feel the tension like a thick cloud enveloping them all, Dermot said, "Go."

Vance glanced at his father. Then, head lowered, face redder than before, he strode over to Cyrus's car and got into the back.

Cyrus closed the door and looked back at Josie, Gretchen, and Mettner with a look of utter exhaustion and irritation. "Are there any other hornets' nests you three want to poke before you leave?"

Josie said, "We've got to visit your local bars. Vance frequents them."

Surprise flashed across his face, but he quickly covered it. "Guess you're wanting me to make some introductions."

"No," Gretchen said. "We're giving you the courtesy of telling you that we'll be continuing our investigation here in your jurisdiction."

Mettner said, "I'll come back to the station with you. Fill out any paperwork that needs to be done."

Cyrus didn't acknowledge Mettner. He opened the driver's side door and stood behind it, eyes squinting against the setting sun as he regarded them. "Well, you two ladies have fun on your pub crawl. I'd like to say it's been a pleasure, but it hasn't. Hope I don't see any of you around here again."

FOURTEEN

There were two bars in Bly and neither of their bartenders would admit to having Vance Hadlee as a patron. The locals, who were packed inside each bar for their Saturday-night outing, were even less excited to see two police officers from out of town than the Hadlee family had been, and refused to speak to them at all. If they wanted to know about Vance's nighttime activities and the women he entertained, they weren't going to find out from either bar. Exhausted and starving, they found Mettner waiting for them in the Bly PD parking lot and drove back to their own stationhouse in a caravan, only stopping once for takeout. After filing their reports and bringing both Noah and the Chief up to speed on everything they'd discovered that day, Josie's and Gretchen's shifts were over.

At home, Josie stood inside the foyer, car keys still in hand, and waited for Trout to come darting to her from another room. But he didn't. The only thing that reached her was the delicious scent of a roast, followed by voices from the kitchen. There was only one person who could make those sorts of smells come from Josie and Noah's kitchen, and that was their friend Misty DeRossi. Josie's stomach rumbled in response to the stimuli.

"I'm home," she called out.

Seconds later, the *click-click* of Trout's nails on the hardwood floor sounded. He came barreling out of the kitchen straight toward her with Misty's seven-year-old son, Harris Quinn, in tow. Josie knelt down, prepared to catch one or both of them so they didn't knock her over.

"JoJo!" Harris hollered, jumping into her open arms. She hugged him tightly and then released him to give Trout back scratches. Once he was sufficiently petted, Josie got up and the three of them went to the kitchen.

Misty stood by the stove, using a masher to pulverize potatoes in a large bowl that Josie hadn't even realized they owned. She was more at home in their kitchen than Josie and Noah. In fact, they welcomed her visits because it meant they'd get a good meal. Plus, they'd get to spend time with two of their favorite people. It hadn't always been that way. Years ago, after Josie and her first husband, Ray, separated, he'd started seeing Misty. Josie had been overcome with jealousy. She'd hated Misty, but after Ray died, Misty gave birth to Ray's son and Josie had fallen instantly in love with him. It had taken a marathon of baby steps for the two women to bridge the gap that Josie's resentment had built, but they'd done it. Now, Josie couldn't imagine her life without Misty or Harris.

"Oh hey," Trinity said. She and Drake were at the table, already stuffing their faces with an appetizer Misty had whipped up. Spinach puff pastries, by the look of them. Josie wondered if she'd added cream cheese this time. She leaned over and snagged a piece from Trinity's plate. Harris tugged at Josie's free hand. "JoJo, Mom has something really important to talk to you about."

Josie sat down and Harris climbed onto her lap. Imitating Josie, he reached across the table and tried to take puff pastry from Drake's plate. Lightning fast, Drake caught his small hand.

Misty said, "Harris, don't take food from other people's plates."

"But JoJo did it," Harris said.

With a devilish grin, Drake let go of Harris's hand and reached across to tickle under his arm. Josie barely kept him on her lap as he recoiled, giggling. When he calmed down, Drake handed him two puffs.

Josie looked back at Misty. "Is everything okay?"

While Harris was focused on his food, Misty rolled her eyes. "It's fine. Or it will be after you talk to him." She pointed the masher at Harris.

Josie looped an arm around his waist and squeezed. "What's going on?"

He shrugged. Around a mouthful of food, he said, "Ask Mom."

"No," Misty said. "You need to tell her."

With a sigh, Harris turned so he could look at Josie's face. "Mom says I have to talk to you about the Woodsman because I have so many nightmares now."

"The who?" said Trinity.

Harris picked up a puff and squeezed it between his thumb and forefinger. Cream cheese oozed from the ends of it. When he didn't answer, Josie said, "Harris, who is the Woodsman?"

Misty dropped the masher into the sink and walked over, lovingly tousling his blond hair. "It's okay, honey. Talk to Aunt JoJo. I promise you'll feel better."

He took a deep breath, held it for a couple of seconds, and released it. "The Woodsman is a man, and he lives in the woods and he takes little kids and never brings them back to their moms."

Drake said, "That sounds pretty scary."

Without looking up from his puff, Harris nodded.

Josie said, "Where did you hear about this?"

His feet swung back and forth. "School."

"Kids at school told you about this... this Woodsman?" Josie asked.

Another nod.

Trinity said, "In my experience, kids at school are notoriously unreliable sources."

Harris snuck a look at her. She smiled.

Misty said, "Apparently, they're all talking about this... man. I don't know where it started or why, but now he's having nightmares almost every night and no matter how many times I tell him that the Woodsman isn't real, he doesn't believe me."

"Because he is real, Mom!" Harris protested, meeting Misty's gaze.

Josie hugged him again. "Actually," she said. "He's not. You know how I know?"

"How?"

"Because I work for the police and if some man was lurking around in the woods taking children, we would know about it. Not a single parent in Denton has reported their child missing, and we've had no reports of any man in the woods trying to take children."

He looked at her and she could tell by his expression that he still had doubts. "The next time you talk to Uncle Noah, he'll tell you the same thing."

This seemed to help, although he didn't sound completely convinced when he said, "Okay."

Drake said, "You know, when I was your age, the kids at school used to say the same thing. There was a scary man in the woods, and he was after all of us, but it turned out they were wrong. There was never a man. Those were just rumors."

"Yeah," said Trinity. "We had very similar rumors at my school, too."

Harris looked from Drake to Trinity. "What's rumors?"

Josie held him while the adults gave him a crash course in rumors. Her thoughts drifted back to Lark Hadlee and what she'd said about the Jana Melburn case. *Once the rumors start, you can't stop them... Everyone had an opinion or a theory. I don't think anyone ever cared about Jana Melburn. Her death was just entertainment.*

Josie would have to talk to Trinity about the case when they were alone. For now, she would just try to enjoy the evening with her family—both biological and found. The truth was that she was glad for their company, especially with Noah still at work. She felt like the experience at the Hadlee farm had left some kind of foul residue on her psyche. The normalcy of having dinner and watching a movie with people she loved felt wonderful and yet, as the night wore on, thoughts of the case found their way into her mind. She couldn't stop thinking about Rosalie Eddy. Maybe it was because she reminded Josie so much of her own late grandmother. Maybe it was because she'd been so brave and yet so practical. The stoicism with which she had handled news of Sharon's death was reminiscent of how Lisette Matson had handled so many tragedies in her life. Like Lisette, Rosalie was a woman of steel.

Once in bed, Josie tossed and turned most of the night, eliciting groans from Trout, who slept at her feet. She was still awake when Noah slid into bed between three and four a.m. Wordlessly, he rolled toward her and gathered her in his arms. She felt the warmth of his bare chest against the thin back of her T-shirt. The feel and smell of him sent an instantaneous wave of relaxation through her body. Tension drained from her. He nuzzled her ear. "Why are you still awake?"

"Why do you think?"

"Mett told me about Sharon Eddy's grandmother—what she was like. He said she reminded him of Lisette."

When Josie said nothing, he added, "We'll get this guy, Josie. I promise."

"Did you get anywhere today? After Gretchen and I left?"

He kissed the hollow behind her ear. "Will you sleep if I tell you?"

Her fingers found his forearm and traced the muscles from wrist to elbow. "Maybe. If not, you can clear my head."

He chuckled, his breath in her hair. "I'm happy to clear your head at any time. We talked with Sharon Eddy's coworkers. No red flags. No ex-boyfriends to be concerned about. No stalkers. No inappropriate clients. No one seen hanging around in the weeks or days before her murder. She never complained to anyone about anything. No beefs with anyone that we could turn up. We got into her phone finally. Nothing much on there either. The GPS on the phone puts her at the edge of the Hempstead Trail at six forty-three in the morning. Then nothing."

"Someone turned it off," said Josie.

"Yeah. Someone smart enough to know that we'd be able to use it to follow Sharon's movements if it had been on. That's a dead end. We tracked down her friends. Talked with them. Same story as her coworkers—nothing concerning leading up to her death. There was a guy she had been seeing casually."

"Who?" Josie asked.

"James Michael Bishop, Jr. We ran a background check before we tracked him down. He was clean."

"Does he have an alibi?" asked Josie.

"Does he ever," Noah breathed, squeezing her more tightly. "Turns out he's an EMT with the city. Young, new. Guess who's been mentoring him?"

Josie felt the weird combination of discomfort, sadness, and affection that she always felt when Lisette Matson's long-lost blood-related grandson came up. "Sawyer Hayes."

"Yes," Noah said. "Bishop was on shift with Sawyer the day that Sharon went missing and was later killed. In fact, that morning he saved a little boy at a daycare in West Denton who was found unresponsive. It was pretty impressive, to hear Sawyer tell it."

"Bishop must be good. Sawyer isn't impressed by much." Josie sighed. "Sharon had good taste in men. Did you find any connection between Sharon and Vance Hadlee?"

"None."

Josie sighed. "That leaves us nowhere."

"Not necessarily. We're still on Vance Hadlee," Noah said. "By the way, we reached the high school kids who helped Lark Hadlee with the afternoon milking. They didn't see Vance at all on Friday. His alibi is non-existent. Just because we couldn't find the connection doesn't mean it's not there. At least he's off the street."

Josie thought of the way Dermot Hadlee had managed to control so much of the day's events, even with the physical limitations his stroke had left him. She had no delusions that Vance Hadlee would spend any significant time behind bars, if he was even charged at all.

Josie turned her body so she could face Noah. She ran a hand through his thick hair and kissed him. "I don't want to talk about this anymore," she whispered.

He didn't hesitate, answering her kiss with his own, lips hungry and insistent. As his hands found all the right places on her body, he said, "Then we won't."

FIFTEEN

Josie woke alone mid-morning on Sunday, annoyed when she saw how late she had slept. She wasn't due into work until the afternoon, but while her sister and Drake were visiting, she wanted to be present as much as possible. After a quick shower, she found Trinity peering out the kitchen window while Trout snoozed on the runner near the sink.

"What's going on?" Josie asked, joining her sister at the window.

"Grill lessons, take two," Trinity said as Noah and Drake emerged from the side of the house, wheeling a brand-new grill into the backyard.

"This is why he let me sleep," Josie mumbled. "I would never have agreed to this."

The two men paused near the back door, having some sort of discussion. After a minute, they each grabbed a side of the grill and hefted it off the concrete walkway and onto the grass. Once it was twenty feet from the house, they set it down. Noah knelt down and opened the tiny cabinet beneath it, studying its insides.

Trinity said, "Twenty bucks they destroy that thing in the next hour."

Josie groaned. "That is not a bet I want to take. I don't even want to know how much my husband paid for that. In February, no less. Who grills in the winter?"

"You'd be surprised. Early in my career I did a piece on Tips for Winter Grilling. Besides, maybe he's learning now so he can grill a lot in the summer."

Josie looked at her sister with a raised brow. "He will not use that thing all summer long. That's a bet I'll take."

Trinity smiled, catlike. "You're on."

Josie walked over to the coffeemaker, stepping over Trout. She fished two mugs from the overhead cabinet and poured them each a coffee. "I need to know about this case you're looking into. The one in Everett County."

Trinity assembled the creamer, sugar, and spoon at the kitchen table. "Really?" she said, eyes alight. "Why the sudden interest?"

Josie sat down and pushed a mug across the table toward Trinity. "The murder we caught yesterday has a connection to the town of Bly. That's all I can say."

Trinity dumped several ounces of half-and-half into her coffee. "It has to do with my case? The Jana Melburn case?"

"No. I don't know. Gretchen, Mett, and I had to pay a visit to the police department there, and one of the officers thought I was you."

"Dressed like that?" Trinity blurted out, pointing at Josie.

Looking down at her Denton PD polo shirt and black slacks, Josie said, "What's wrong with this? These are work clothes."

"Not important," Trinity said, stirring sugar into her coffee. "What did the officer say?"

"He was kind of upset," Josie said. "Said he'd told you everything you needed to know."

Trinity scoffed. "That's a crock. I made two right-to-know requests for the Jana Melburn case file and both times I was denied. Everything I need to know is in that file. Sure, I got some standard crap from an officer there, but it certainly wasn't much. My source, Hallie Kent, knows much more than he told me. She knew someone in records at the police department and managed to get copies of a lot of stuff, at least until that person retired, but it's not everything. Not enough. There could be things in there that could help me break this wide open, but I can't access them because I'm stuck going through these officers."

Josie leaned across the table and took the creamer, sugar, and spoon, preparing her own coffee exactly the same way as Trinity. "I'm not sure having someone in records making copies of police files and sneaking them to a civilian is legal."

"If you're a police officer worried about what's admissible in court," Trinity said. "That's not my problem. I have a source and she is reliable."

"Right," said Josie. As a journalist, Trinity wasn't held to the same standard of evidence as police. She wasn't building a case that would go to trial. She wasn't limited by police or evidentiary procedures. She would never be faced with an onslaught of motions to suppress evidence from defense attorneys. She wouldn't have to exclude things from her story because someone somewhere along the line hadn't followed procedure to the letter. It wasn't even necessary for her to disclose her source on air, as long as they were reliable, and she could verify the facts or documents provided by them. "Was the officer you spoke with Sergeant Cyrus Grey?"

"I'll tell you." Trinity disappeared upstairs and returned moments later with both her laptop and the file folder that Josie had nearly knocked over the day before. She flipped the folder open and started paging through a stack of her own personal notes. Josie recognized her handwriting. "Yes, Sergeant Grey was one of the people I spoke with at the Bly Police Department. He was not very forthcoming. He said Jana Melburn's death was an accident and I should 'let sleeping dogs lie' because it might be painful for her family to drag all this back up again after so many years."

Josie took a sip of her coffee, the taste of it heaven. "Didn't you say it was Jana's family who contacted you? Her foster sister, right? Hallie Kent."

"Yes. Jana Melburn didn't know her biological family," Trinity said. "She grew up in a foster home in Bly along with Hallie."

From the back of the file, she pulled up a printout of a satellite view map from Google. Pushing her own coffee aside, she unfolded it and smoothed it out on the table. Several pages had been taped together to create the full picture of Bly. Josie recognized the large gray building in the center of town that housed the police department as well as the Hadlee farm several miles away.

Trinity pointed to a collection of houses a few miles from the police station. One of them had been circled with a red marker. "This is where Jana grew up. A local couple fostered several children, including Jana and Hallie. When Hallie was about sixteen, the husband died of pancreatic cancer. At that time, the couple only had Hallie, Jana, and one other foster child, a boy named Mathias Tobin. The wife kept the three of them since Hallie and Mathias were teenagers— sixteen and seventeen—and close to aging out. Jana was seven years old and quite attached to her older foster siblings, and the woman didn't want to disrupt their lives unless it was absolutely necessary. She decided that she just wouldn't take in any more children. Didn't want to do it without her husband. About a year and a half after her husband died, she passed as well. Heart attack."

"What happened to Jana, Hallie, and Mathias?" asked Josie.

"All of them had to move out of the foster home. Hallie and

Mathias were adults by then. They both had jobs since they were old enough to get them, so they scraped up some money and rented a house. They got approval for Jana to stay with them until she aged out of the foster care system. They took care of her. Raised her like she was their child. I think I told you it was Hallie who contacted me."

Josie said, "She stayed in Bly all this time?"

Trinity nodded. "Hallie said she couldn't leave after Jana's death. It didn't feel right. Jana was like a daughter to her, and she couldn't leave the place where Jana had died without some kind of resolution. Hallie never believed that Jana's death was an accident, but she's never been able to prove otherwise. When my show launched last year, she immediately started contacting the team. She thought with my local connection to Central Pennsylvania, that I would want to look at the case. Unfortunately, I didn't see her messages until recently. Once I did, I agreed to look into it."

"How recently?" Josie asked. It still nagged at her that the very weekend that Sharon Eddy turned up murdered, her body bearing a clear sign from the killer that he was trying to get Dr. Feist's attention, Trinity was in town to look into a case from the county where Dr. Feist used to live and work. There had to be some catalyst, something that had set Sharon Eddy's murder into motion. Josie just couldn't figure out what it was—yet.

"Last year. Late summer, early fall," Trinity tapped the folder. "It's taken me some time to put all this together."

A loud bang sounded from the backyard. Trout's head snapped up. He looked around the kitchen and, seeing no immediate threat, went back to sleep. Trinity sprang up from her chair and peeked outside. "It's okay," she said. "Nothing's on fire. Yet."

Josie went back to studying the map. Two other locations had been circled and marked. The first was what looked like a gas station. Trinity's notation read: *last seen*. Then, what appeared to be a few miles from there was another mark, this one a wooded area sandwiched between a two-lane road and a lake. The note read: *body found.*

Plopping back into her chair, Trinity tapped a finger over the gas station. "Jana Melburn did not have her own vehicle. She hoofed it everywhere or got rides from people. She was attending community college at the time so all her money went toward tuition and books. Her foster brother, Mathias, had a pickup truck. Old, beat-up. No GPS. He often gave her a ride when she needed one—if he could. On this night, May 15, 2013, around nine p.m., Jana Melburn had left her home and walked to this gas station where she bought a Coke and a pack of cigarettes. While she was inside, Mathias pulled up and started pumping gas. He had come from work and was heading home from there. Jana went outside. They talked for about five minutes. Mathias pulled away. Jana walked off."

"She wasn't going back home?" asked Josie.

"Here is where it gets really interesting. Mathias told the police and Hallie that Jana said she was meeting someone, but she wouldn't say who. When he pressed her, she said something cryptic like she was trying to find out where they came from."

"What does that mean?" asked Josie.

"Mathias said he assumed she was talking about birth parents. Remember, he, Hallie and Jana were all foster kids. Anyway, he told the police that he found it suspicious that she'd be meeting someone to talk about her birth parents at nine o'clock at night and even more suspicious that she wouldn't give him any more information. He told her she should drop it and just come home with him since it was late and dark, but she refused. She was an adult, he said, and so he let her go. He says he did try to follow her in his truck but lost her when he got stuck at a traffic light and she turned onto a side street."

"So he just went home?"

Trinity shrugged. "He says he drove around looking for her

for a while—he wasn't sure how long, maybe an hour—and when he didn't find her, he gave up and went home. He tried calling her, but she didn't answer. It went right to voicemail. The police believe she turned her phone off after she left the gas station because they weren't able to ping it or use it to see where she had been the night she went missing. Then he thought maybe he had overreacted. He'd been acting as her father for ten years and now she was nineteen. He thought maybe it was time to give her some space. So he went home to bed. The next morning, he and Hallie realized that Jana hadn't come home. They called the doctor's office where Jana worked and found out Jana had not shown up for her shift that morning."

It sounded eerily similar to the Sharon Eddy case.

Trinity continued, "Both Hallie and Mathias tried calling Jana's phone, but still no answer. They contacted the police. Because Jana was nineteen, they wouldn't take a missing person's report until she'd been missing for twenty-four hours. Hallie and Mathias searched for her. They called everyone Jana knew but no one had seen or heard from her. They looked everywhere they could think to look but couldn't find her."

"Mathias, Jana, and Hallie all still lived together at this point?" asked Josie.

"Yes," said Trinity.

"Did Hallie see him that night when he came home?"

"Unfortunately, no. She was working at the textile manu-facturing company she was employed by at the time. Her shift ended around midnight. When she got home, both Mathias's and Jana's bedroom doors were closed. She assumed they were both sleeping."

"Which means Mathias had no alibi. Does Hallie believe Mathias's claims about what happened the last time he saw Jana alive?"

"Yes," Trinity said. "She says that Mathias wouldn't lie about something like that."

"Did Hallie have any idea who Jana was meeting with?"

"No. Hallie says Jana never said a word about trying to find her birth parents. She was shocked to hear it, actually. It had never come up among them before."

"Hallie was never suspicious of Mathias at all?"

"Hallie told me that for all intents and purposes, Mathias was Jana's father. Hallie says she and Mathias both took their roles as stand-in parents to Jana very seriously. Therefore, Mathias would never hurt Jana. Hallie says he would never hurt anyone."

"But everyone else in Bly thought he would and had."

Trinity nodded. "Mathias Tobin had an unfortunate history of accusations against him going back to high school."

SIXTEEN

The coffee sloshed in Josie's stomach. "What kind of accusations?"

"Three girls he went to high school with accused him of sexual assault. Charges were brought and then dismissed when the girls recanted."

Josie raised a brow. "Trin, don't you think this is a case of 'where there's smoke, there's fire?' If he was credibly accused of violent assaults, it's not a stretch to think he killed Jana Melburn."

"Yes, that was the problem," Trinity said earnestly. "That's why when people found out he was the last person to see Jana alive—besides the gas station clerk who watched the two of them talk—they immediately assumed he had killed her. He admitted to following her in his truck. It's not a stretch to think he killed her."

"But there was no evidence of homicide?"

Trinity flipped through a stack of pages inside the file folder and found a report, which she pushed across the table to Josie.

Autopsy Report. Name of Decedent: Jana Melburn.

While Josie skimmed the report, Trinity recounted the salient points. "She was found in a ravine on the side of the road, next to Latchwood Lake, about two miles from the gas station. No visible signs of injury. Nothing taken from her."

Josie felt a prickle along the back of her neck. Again, the circumstances were strangely similar to Sharon Eddy's case. She found the cause of death: blunt head trauma. Manner of death was accidental. Reading further, she found that although Jana hadn't sustained any bruising, lacerations, or abrasions anywhere on her body, she had sustained multiple severe fractures to both the back of her head and her eye sockets as well as a subdural hematoma and general bleeding around the brain. "Trin," Josie said. "Someone cracked her head like an egg."

Trinity's eyes glowed with a steely determination. "I know."

"But this was deemed an accidental death."

"You see now why I want to take this on."

Josie sighed. She found the name of the medical examiner who had prepared the autopsy report. Dr. Anya Feist. Her stomach dropped. She pointed to the name. "This is why you're here."

Trinity sighed. "I know Anya. I don't need you to make an introduction."

"But you're going to go after her. This report—if you believe that Jana Melburn was murdered, that means this autopsy report is wrong. It means Anya was wrong and justice wasn't served."

Trinity stared at her.

Josie said, "You wanted me to smooth things over."

"Not smooth them over. Mediate, maybe. If it came to that. Like I said, I know Anya. I respect her. Deeply. Especially after her work on the missing girls case. She was relatively new to Denton when that happened. The work she did was incredible."

And it had taken its toll. On all of them, but especially Anya, who'd performed dozens of exams and autopsies on the bodies of young women.

Trinity added, "But Anya's human, not perfect. She would have been young when Jana Melburn died. Well, not young, probably around thirty or so, but she wouldn't have had very much experience as a medical examiner. She could have gotten it wrong."

"And if she did?" Josie said. "Then what? You go on national television and crucify her?"

"No," Trinity said. "I ask her to tell me her side, to explain her reasoning. If it got to TV, I would give her a chance to present her side of things. Josie, I told you, I don't even know if there's enough here for a show. I'm just asking questions."

But Josie knew from the set of Trinity's jaw and the fire in her eyes that she was already committed to doing an episode of *Unsolved Crimes with Trinity Payne* on the Jana Melburn case. Maybe she had not consciously committed or devoted any show resources to it as of yet, but there was no way she was letting this go, one way or another.

"I don't like this," Josie said.

Trinity slid a hand across the table until her fingers touched Josie's. "You've never avoided the truth, even when it meant that people you cared about and respected had made huge mistakes. All I want is to try to set the record straight once and for all—homicide or accident?"

Josie sighed. "What else do you have?"

Trinity passed over a few more reports, starting with the initial missing person's report and the reports prepared after Jana's body had been found. As Josie read through them, a more complete picture began to form. According to Mathias Tobin, when he ran into her at the gas station, Jana Melburn indicated that she had planned on meeting someone to discuss her birth parents, but she would not say who or where they planned to meet. However, police found no evidence among any of her personal belongings that such a person existed, much less that a meeting had been planned. Nor were they able to glean the information from interviews with friends and coworkers. Even Jana's phone had yielded nothing. In spite of what appeared to be an exhaustive investigation, police hadn't uncovered a damn thing. Not a name, a text, an email, a letter or even a strange phone number. If Jana had truly been in touch with someone regarding her birth parents, Mathias was the first and only person to whom she mentioned it.

"Did anyone ever try to track down her birth family?" Josie asked. "To see if she'd been in touch with them or anyone connected to them?"

"Hallie did," Trinity said. "Turns out that Jana's mother died in childbirth. Her dad was already in prison, which is why Jana got put into foster care in the first place. Apparently neither of them had relatives willing to take her on. Her father was killed in prison when she was five. No one ever came looking for her. The only biological family Hallie could find were distant cousins who live elsewhere in the country— nowhere near Bly. None of them would admit to having tried contacting Jana."

Even if they had, Josie thought, there wasn't any evidence of it. Mathias's story sounded like a lie. Josie returned her attention to the reports. Two days after Jana was last seen, she was found at the base of a steep ravine beside Latchwood Lake, at the bottom of which were several large rocks. She had no injuries that might indicate a struggle, only massive head injuries.

"You can't prove this was a homicide," Josie said. She looked up in time to see Trinity's severely arched brow and added, "And I'm not saying that to somehow protect Anya. I'm saying it because it's true. You can't prove murder."

"The injuries prove it," Trinity argued. "Josie, you've been doing this a long time. Those are the kinds of injuries you only see when someone falls from a tall building or is hit by a car or —" Here her hands waved excitedly. "If someone is smashed in the head with a baseball bat or something!"

Josie said, "It's hard to make a judgment call without having seen the place she was found, but if the ravine was as steep as these reports suggest, she could have died from a fall."

Trinity riffled through the pages of the file again until she came up with a photograph. She slid it across the table. "This girl did not die from an accidental fall."

Jana Melburn smiled up at Josie. It was a school photo. Senior year would be Josie's guess. Just as in the graduation photo, her curly blonde hair tumbled to her shoulders. This photo was crisper and showed freckles across a pert nose. Brown eyes with flecks of gold.

"What do you know about Mathias Tobin?" Josie asked.

Trinity found another photo in the file and handed it over. This one was a candid shot of a young man standing in a small kitchen, monitoring a pot on a stove. The same man from the graduation photo, only much younger. He wore a pair of white football pants and a black T-shirt, the sleeves of which had been torn off, revealing muscular arms. His dark hair was long and slicked back. An embarrassed smile played on his lips as he turned his head to look at the camera. His nose was slightly crooked as if it had been broken and never reset properly. He didn't look a day over twenty.

Trinity said, "Nothing yet other than what I've told you. I'm supposed to meet with Hallie the day after tomorrow to go over the file and try to fill in the things I don't know yet."

She pushed another photo toward Josie. In this one, Jana, Mathias, and Hallie were on a beach. A teenage Jana sat atop Mathias's shoulders, her arms thrown out to the sides. Next to them, Hallie looked up at Jana, her head tossed back in laughter. Behind them, ocean waves rolled in.

Josie said, "I am pretty sure Mathias Tobin went to prison for a while after the Melburn case. For shooting his wife in the head."

"What?" Trinity gasped. "You're kidding, right?"

"I have a source, too. If what she told me is accurate, his wife's name was Piper. Check it out."

Trinity flipped open her laptop. "Oh, I will. I did an internet search on him and didn't come up with anything at all."

"Try accessing the Everett County criminal dockets then," Josie said. She shuffled through the documents Trinity had shared. "In terms of the Melburn case, I can't imagine what you don't know yet. This file looks pretty complete."

"I doubt that," Trinity said. "The Bly Police Department is hiding something. I can feel it."

On Josie's second pass through the witness statements, a name caught her eye. Carolina Eddy. The clerk at the gas station. The other last person to see Jana Melburn alive.

It couldn't be a coincidence.

Josie's phone rang. Anya Feist's name flashed across the screen.

Trinity sighed. "More work."

Josie pressed the phone to her ear. "Dr. Feist?"

There was no response, just dead air followed by some rustling. Then came the voices, as if from far away.

A man: "I just want to talk."

Dr. Feist: "There's nothing for us to talk about. Please leave my home."

A snicker. "You gonna call the cops? Like you did the other day when a body turned up in this city? Why would you bring me into some shit like that? Why? After all this time?"

"I was doing my job, Vance."

The name was a hot poker to Josie's gut. Clutching the phone in her hand, she ran out to the backyard. "Noah," she called. "Anya's in trouble."

SEVENTEEN

Josie's body slammed into the passenger's side door as Noah took a sharp turn onto a backstreet. Her phone bobbled in her hands, but she caught it before it fell onto the floor. Pressing it against her ear, she heard Anya and Vance's voices still. Noah punched a finger against the screen on the console, where the hands-free call feature displayed his conversation with Mettner. The call disconnected.

"He's on his way," Noah said. "With a backup unit."

Josie kept half her attention on him and the other half on Anya and Vance, although now it was mostly Vance lodging ten years' worth of built-up complaints about his ex-wife. "You did me real dirty," he was saying. "After everything I did for you..."

Looking at the buildings flashing past, Josie calculated it would take ten, possibly fifteen minutes for them to arrive. "My God, Noah, hurry," she said.

He hammered the heel of his palm against the horn, beeping at the two vehicles in front of them. They pulled to the side and let him pass, although one of the drivers gave them the finger. "She'll be okay," Noah said.

"We don't know that," Josie said. Her stomach was in her

throat. All the coffee she'd had that morning threatened to come back up.

Noah sped up, beeping any time a car got in front of them or a pedestrian hinted at moving into the street. "This guy is supposed to be in jail. What the hell happened?"

"Dermot Hadlee happened," Josie said. "He's got sway in Everett County."

"Well, he doesn't have shit in our city. Why didn't Anya call 911?"

On Josie's phone, Anya said, *"There is nothing for us to discuss, Vance. Please leave now."*

Josie said, "Because she would have to tell the 911 operator what was happening. That would take time and she'd have to do it in front of him. I already know the history—and the danger—so she figured either I'd pick up and hear them and race over there or it would go to my voicemail, and I'd have a recording of what could be her last moments."

Noah took another turn so sharply that the tires squealed. "We're not going to let that happen."

Vance was talking now. *"...think I'm leaving now? After all these years of you hiding from me? You're out of your mind. You're gonna pay for what you put me through, you stuck-up bitch."*

Acid burned the back of her throat. "Noah," she croaked.

Vance's voice stopped abruptly. Sirens sounded in stereo—coming from the receiver and outside the car—as Noah screeched onto Anya's block. Mettner's car and a patrol unit had pulled up in front of Anya's quaint little townhouse.

Josie thought she heard Vance's voice say, *"What the fu—"* before the sounds of men's voices drowned it out.

The car lurched as Noah stopped behind Mettner's vehicle. They jumped out together. Josie pocketed her phone and put a hand on her pistol grip. They'd put their vests on before they left the house. Racing up the front lawn, Josie took in the scene.

The front door was ajar. One uniformed officer circled to the back of the house while the other followed Mettner inside.

Vance's voice sounded from inside. "What the hell is this? You called the damn cops? You bitch!"

Josie was through the door last. The living room looked just as it had the few times Josie had been there: decorated in whites and yellows. A small couch and wingback chair. Coffee table. Television atop a small console. Fresh flowers and bright pastel abstract paintings. She had expected destruction, but everything was in its place. Vance stood in the center of the living room while Anya stayed behind the chair. Through the crush of bodies now filling the room, Josie met Anya's eyes. Fear gave way to guarded relief. Josie edged around the wall of officers facing Vance and took her hand off her pistol grip to reach out to Anya. Her clammy hand seized on Josie's, squeezing hard. Josie pulled Anya away, toward the kitchen but still within view of the living room.

Mettner said, "Sir, I'm going to have to ask you to come with me."

"Fuck you," Vance said, spitting at Mettner. It landed on his shirt, but he didn't move. Didn't even acknowledge it, which seemed to make Vance even angrier. "You got a personal problem with me, pig?"

Mettner said, "I'm just doing my job, sir, and right now, that's asking you to come with me."

The uniformed officer moved closer, and Vance backed away. "You're kidding me, right? I'm talking to my wife."

"Your ex-wife," Noah corrected. "You're not welcome in her home."

"The hell I'm not," Vance said.

Mettner said, "Mr. Hadlee, let's step outside and talk."

Vance panned the room, that cocky smirk curling his upper lip. "Four police officers to 'talk' to me for wanting to see my damn wife? Are you nuts? This is police brutality. You better believe I'm going to sue the shit out of your department. I'll have every single one of you in the unemployment line in a month. Don't believe me? Look how fast I got out of the trouble you tried to put on me yesterday."

Mettner said, "You're welcome to take up any claims you believe you have against us with an attorney at a later time. Right now, come with us."

When he didn't move, Mettner calmly spoke again, "Mr. Hadlee, we can do this the easy way, where you step outside and talk with us, or we can do this the hard way where we arrest you. Your choice."

Noah said, "Let's go."

Vance did not cooperate, instead taking a slow scan of the room. Josie's heartbeat ticked upward. Then she caught a glimpse of the agility that had made him a football star in high school. Moving so quickly that he was little more than a blur, he charged forward. All of them yelled at once, instructing him to stop, but it was too late. Vance was already flying toward Mettner. Before anyone could react, Vance slammed into him. The two of them fell to the floor. Noah and the uniformed officer descended on Vance, yanking him away from Mettner, but not before he landed a punch just beneath Mettner's left eye. Seconds later, Vance's face was mashed into Anya's carpet. The uniformed officer snapped on a pair of cuffs while Noah read him his rights.

Josie left Anya in the kitchen doorway and went to Mettner, offering him a hand. She helped him up while Noah and the uniformed officer carried a squirming, protesting Vance toward the door.

"This won't stand!" he hollered. "I'll sue! You'll all pay, including you, Anya. I was just trying to talk to you! Who calls the police when someone's trying to talk?"

A welt was already forming on Mettner's cheek. Josie said, "You okay?"

"Yeah." Touching his face, he muttered, "That son of a bitch."

Anya stepped forward, reaching for him. Holding the back of his head with one hand, she probed the abrasion with the fingers of her other hand.

"Ouch," he said.

From the doorway, Vance snarled, "You son of a bitch! Don't touch my wife!"

Josie noticed a shiver work its way through Anya's body as her eyes moved to the door, watching as Vance finally disappeared, his wriggling form sandwiched between Noah and the uniformed officer. She released Mettner. "I don't think anything is broken," she murmured. "But you should get an x-ray and ice it up."

"Thanks, Doc," Mettner said. "But I don't need an x-ray. Not my first scuffle. How about you? Are you okay?"

Josie saw her hands tremble before she jammed them into the pockets of her jeans. "Yes," she said. "Thank you for coming. All of you. I wanted to call 911 but I was afraid that would make him even more agitated."

"You did the right thing," Josie said.

"What happened?" Mettner asked, taking his phone out and bringing up his notes app.

Anya looked around the room. "I was about to leave for work. I got outside and he was on the porch. I panicked. I haven't seen him in nearly a decade. I've been safe here all this time. I stopped looking over my shoulder a long time ago. I mean, I had the protection from abuse order when I left Bly, but that's just a piece of paper. It wouldn't have stopped him from trying to hurt me. For years I expected to see him at every turn, but he was never there."

"PFAs are good for three years," Josie said. "Did you ask for another one after the initial PFA expired?"

Anya nodded. "Of course I did. But after six years without

so much as a peep from him, I figured he had moved on, or at least stopped obsessing over me."

Josie thought of the wedding photo on Vance's dresser. They had no way of knowing whether or not he had ever tried to locate Anya or if he'd ever had plans to make contact with her again, but it was clear that his obsession was still there.

Anya added, "Not me. He was never obsessed with me. He was only obsessed with possessing me and then later, he was obsessed with getting back at me for what he perceived as me having wronged him."

Mettner looked up from his notes. "He clearly believes that you had some ill effect on his life because you turned him in for what he did to you and then left him. These guys can never take responsibility."

Getting back on track, Josie said, "You went outside, he was on the porch. What happened after that?"

"I rushed back inside here, and he came right in after me before I could even react. It happened so fast. I think he pushed me, but I can't be sure. It was a blur. My heart was pounding so hard—"

"It's okay," Mettner said. "You can apply for a new protection from abuse order here in Denton. You asked him to leave, and he didn't. He can be charged with trespassing."

"Which only carries a ninety-day sentence in this case because it would be considered simple trespassing," Josie said. "Still worth it, but—"

"It's only going to piss him off more," Anya said. "It will make things worse."

"Then we charge him with assaulting a police officer," Mettner said. "I'll press charges. It'll keep him busy for a while, hopefully in jail as well, and we can try to get a handle on this Sharon Eddy case. I don't think his father is going to have the kind of pull here that he does in Everett County."

Josie said, "Anya, you should still press charges against him for the trespassing. Especially if you're going to ask the court for a new protection from abuse order."

Anya shuddered. "I know, I know."

Mettner said, "If you're not comfortable staying here at any point, you can come stay with me and Amber."

"Or with us," Josie offered. "I'm sure that Gretchen would also be happy to have you."

Anya reached over and squeezed Josie's shoulder. A tear slid down her face. "I know. I know you're all there for me. Thank you. I will give it some thought."

Turning to Mettner, Josie said, "You might need that x-ray after all. Document your injuries."

Mettner sighed. "Yeah, yeah."

As he walked out the door, Josie said, "Speaking of the Sharon Eddy case, I need to ask you some questions about a case from Bly that might be connected."

Anya's eyes widened in surprise. "Really? What case is that?"

"The Jana Melburn case," Josie said. "Does it sound familiar?"

Anya shook her head. "Vaguely. Was it a homicide? I had some homicides during my tenure there. They were all residents of the city. Bradysport. It's the biggest city in Everett County, where most of our cases were from. If I recall, every single one of them was a result of disputes over drug territory. There were two gangs in Bradysport back then and they had frequent skirmishes over which of them controlled the southeast side of the city. Gunshot wounds, every single case."

"No," Josie said. "This was something different."

"You might talk to my mentor, Garrick Wolfe. He was with the county ME's office far longer than me."

"I can speak with him," Josie said. "But you performed the autopsy."

"Oh," said Anya. "Well, Josie, I've done hundreds, if not

thousands, of autopsies in my career. I don't remember them all."

"I know," said Josie. "I was just wondering if Jana Melburn stood out to you. Having spent the day in Bly yesterday, I can tell you there aren't many people there who haven't heard about her case. You really don't remember?"

Anya shook her head again. "I'm sorry, but not off the top of my head. When was this?"

Josie thought about the date of Jana's murder. "It would have been right around the time you left."

A sad smile played on Anya's lips. "I was a wreck then. That entire time period is a blur. I did my job, but all I could think about was how to get out of Bly and away from Vance forever. Tell me about the case. Maybe it will help me remember."

"Nineteen-year-old found at the bottom of a ravine," Josie said. "Next to Latchwood Lake."

Anya flinched. "Sounds like Sharon Eddy."

"I know. But Jana Melburn had massive head injuries. You ruled it an accident. People in Bly believed that a local guy named Mathias Tobin did it."

"Wait." Anya took a moment, eyes squinting as she searched her brain for the memory. "I do have a vague recollection of this, but Josie, that was ten years ago. During a time when I was nursing a horrific injury inflicted on me by my husband who I was sure was going to kill me when I finally left him. I never admitted this to anyone, God help me, but at that time? The only thing on my mind was the fifteen hours and forty-three minutes that my husband held me and tortured me. Every day, it replayed in my mind over and over. I did go to work because I needed the money to get away from him—to try to be safe. I went through the motions. Garrick took up the slack for me when he could, but it's entirely possible that I missed something. I'm sorry."

Josie nodded. "I understand."

Her entire body started to shake. "Since then, I blocked a lot of stuff out from that entire time period. I had to, in order to survive."

Josie closed the distance between them and pulled Anya into a tight hug. She stiffened for a brief moment even as her frame shuddered. "It's okay, Doc. I understand."

Slowly, some of the tension drained from Anya. After a minute, she wrapped her arms around Josie and held on. The trembling went on for so long that Josie started to worry that she was going into shock. "I'm going to do everything I can to keep you safe," Josie said into her ear. "All of us will."

She felt Anya nod. Noah appeared in the doorway and seeing them, quietly turned and left them alone. Josie wasn't sure how much time passed but she stayed in place until Anya's body stilled, and she extricated herself from the hug. Taking a step back, she wiped tears from her cheeks. Looking everywhere but at Josie, she said, "If you think it's important, I'll try to remember what I can. Jana Melburn, you said?"

"Yes."

"I'll think about it. Can you get me the autopsy report? That would help."

"Yes," said Josie.

"You really think the two cases are connected?"

"Possibly. I've got to talk to Sharon's grandmother again."

"If you find a connection after you talk to her, please let me know."

EIGHTEEN

Josie left Anya in the capable hands of her colleagues and went in search of Rosalie Eddy. She wasn't home. When Josie called her cell phone, Rosalie said she was at a nearby funeral home. Josie asked her to call back when she got home, but Rosalie insisted she come directly to the funeral home. The parking lot was deserted save for the vehicle Josie knew to be registered to Rosalie. Inside, Josie's feet sank into the thick burgundy carpet. After speaking with the director, Josie was led to a large room in the funeral home cellar where mock-ups of different types of caskets lined the walls. Rosalie, wearing a floral print dress, leaned on her cane, studying a simple wooden chest. As Josie approached, she looked over with a wan smile.

"They're all so expensive. Even the so-called 'cheap' ones, and every time I have to do this, they cost even more."

"I know," Josie said.

Rosalie raised a brow. "You're awful young to know something like that."

"I buried my first husband eight years ago and my grandmother three years ago, Mrs. Eddy."

Rosalie nodded. "I'm sorry to hear that. I'm sorry to make

you come here, Detective, but I won't be able to concentrate if I know I've got to meet you later. I'll be wondering the whole time what kind of news you've got. Let's just get on with it, if you don't mind. You do have news, don't you?"

Josie said, "Yes."

Rosalie studied her for a long moment. "It's not good."

"I'm afraid not. I've also got a few more questions." Josie looked around the room. She'd helped her late husband Ray's mother choose a casket in a room just like this. Later, she had chosen one for her grandmother with the help of Lisette's grandson, Sawyer. She'd never known there were so many choices.

Rosalie turned and moved slowly toward the door. "That's fine. Come now, there's a nice soft bench out in the hall."

A moment later, they were seated side by side on the cushioned bench. Josie looked up and down the hall, but it was silent and still. Sound seemed to get sucked away instantly in this place. Even their voices didn't feel like they carried very far. If someone approached, they'd never hear it. Josie said, "Are you sure about this? We could go upstairs, or outside. I can take you any place you want."

Rosalie patted Josie's hand. "Just get it over with, would you?"

"Right." Josie took a deep breath. "Mrs. Eddy, Sharon was murdered."

Rosalie closed her eyes. Her upper body rocked back and forth a few times. "How?"

"She was strangled," Josie said. "She had a subdural hematoma on the back of her head. The only other injury was a burn to her hip, like a cattle brand."

Rosalie's eyes popped open. "A cattle brand?"

Josie nodded. "We've been looking into other cases that might have similarities. Which brings me to my questions. Sharon's mother, your daughter, what's her name?"

"Carolina. Like the states. Why? You don't think she had something to do with Shar's death, do you?"

"When is the last time you saw Carolina?" asked Josie.

"'Bout a year ago. When Shar graduated from high school. It took me months to track her down. Her cell phone is always out of service, or she didn't keep up with the payments. Or she's in jail. That's where she was when I finally found her. I told her about Shar's graduation. She said she'd be out by then and would definitely be there. Of course, she missed it. Showed up two days later, not even an apology. Same old Carolina. She looked well enough, but in jail she always put on weight. Her skin would clear up. Couldn't get the drugs in there the way she does out here. But I could tell she was taking something already. I wouldn't let her see Shar. I don't think Shar wanted to see her anyway after she missed the big day."

Josie asked, "Do you know how to get in touch with Carolina now?"

"I could give you her number but I'm not sure it still works. Detective, you didn't answer my question. Did Carolina have something to do with Shar's murder? My daughter's been addicted to drugs from when she was a teenager. I know she's done some terrible things to feed her addiction, but I've never known her to be violent."

"That's not why I'm asking about Carolina," Josie said. "I'm wondering if your family used to live in Bly."

"Why, yes," Rosalie said. "That's where we're from. Left about seven years ago."

"When I talked with you the other night, you said you'd moved from Bellewood."

"Yes, we moved from Bly to Bellewood. The three of us: me, Carolina and Shar. It took about a minute for Carolina to get into all kinds of trouble. I took Shar and moved here. It was a fresh start. A real one."

"What do you mean?" Josie asked. "Are you saying you moved from Bly to Bellewood for a fresh start?"

Rosalie leaned her cane against the edge of the bench and smoothed her dress over her lap. "We had to after that business with that poor girl who died."

"Jana Melburn?"

"Why, yes. You've done your research, haven't you?"

"Not as much research as you think," Josie said. "What can you tell me about the 'business' with Jana Melburn?"

"If you know about her then you know she was seen at a gas station a couple of days before she was found dead. My Carolina worked at that gas station. It had a little minimart inside. They sold snack food and soda and cigarettes. That sort of thing. Carolina saw that girl the night she went missing. Jana came in and purchased a can of soda and a pack of cigarettes. Then she went back outside and there was that boy—the football player who molested those cheerleaders—and Jana stopped to talk to him."

"Did Carolina hear what they said to one another?"

"No," Rosalie said. "That's just it. She didn't hear a thing. She said she never even thought about it till a couple of days later when the cops came to talk to her. Jana Melburn talked to that boy for a minute or two and then she left. On foot. The boy pumped his gas and then he left. But it seemed like no one in town wanted to believe it was as simple as that. She said she felt pressured to say that the two of them had had some kind of heated argument when that just didn't happen."

"Who was pressuring her?" asked Josie. "The police?"

Rosalie nodded. "It started with them. They didn't outright ask her to change her story, but they would come around to the house and keep asking her, 'are you sure that's what you saw?' and 'are you certain that there wasn't an argument?' or 'are you absolutely sure they didn't have a physical altercation?' We both had the feeling they wanted her to change her story. Like it might make it easier for them to put that girl's death on that boy."

"Do you think Mathias Tobin killed Jana Melburn?"

Rosalie sighed. "How could I think one way or the other? I don't know enough to form an opinion. All I know is what people in town said. The boy was the last one to see her before she was found dead. The police found her body at the bottom of a ravine. She hit her head. Who am I to say whether someone is a murderer based on that?"

Josie found this reasoning to be exceedingly fair and logical, but she knew others didn't employ it when publicly commenting on a crime.

Rosalie continued, "Anyway, Carolina stuck to the truth. After a while, especially when the police didn't charge the boy with murder, people got upset with her. She was the last one to see both of them. It seemed like people wanted her to lie so they could get the boy put away. One lady came into the gas station and told her, 'you know that boy raped three cheerleaders and you can't tell a little white lie to get him put away forever.' I tell you, I was appalled. *A little white lie?* We were talking about someone's life. That was just the start. Soon it seemed like the entire town had turned against her. When the rumors that maybe Carolina had killed Jana started, I knew we had to leave."

"People said Carolina killed her?" Josie said.

"Like I said, she was the last one to see them both. People would come in and say to her, 'how do we know you didn't follow her and push her into the ravine?' Never mind that Carolina didn't even know the girl!"

"Was there video of the encounter?" Josie asked. "Did the parking lot have cameras?"

Rosalie shook her head. "I don't know. Carolina never mentioned that. Anyway, we moved to Bellewood but like I said, Carolina got into trouble in a hot second. That's when I took Shar and the two of us started over here. I stood by my daughter when she was being harassed over what happened to Jana, and I helped her as best as I could. That was a separate issue from the drug use, which was affecting my granddaughter. I had to do what was best for Shar."

A tear slid down Rosalie's cheek. Josie reached over and took her hand. They didn't speak for a long time.

Finally, Rosalie said, "You're asking me about things I thought were long in the past. My Shar was only nine years old when Jana Melburn died. What's happening?"

Josie squeezed her hand. "That's what I'm trying to figure out, Mrs. Eddy. There's some kind of connection between that case and Sharon's murder. I'm just not entirely sure what it is yet."

NINETEEN

Back at the stationhouse, the entire team was in the great room, including their press liaison and Mettner's girlfriend, Amber Watts. She perched on the edge of her desk, tablet in hand, and listened while Josie briefed Chief Chitwood on the Sharon Eddy murder case. He stood beside the detectives' collective desks, arms crossed over his thin chest, listening intently. When Josie finished, he said, "You're telling me that someone took this nineteen-year-old girl, Sharon, and before killing her and dumping her body near the creek, branded her with the same kind of brand that our medical examiner's asshole husband used on her ten years ago in an entirely different county?"

"Yeah," Josie said.

"You're also telling me that there is some famous case from that same county that you've managed to connect to Sharon Eddy during the course of your investigation? What's the name? Mel something?"

"Jana Melburn," Josie said.

"It's not famous," Gretchen said, regarding the Chief from over her reading glasses. "I've googled it. It never even made the local papers there. Never got any press at all. The only piece of information on this girl is her obituary."

"Not true," Mettner said. "There's a small thread on NetSleuths about her case."

"How did you find that?" Gretchen said. "I spent hours scouring the web."

Noah said, "He didn't find it. Amber did."

"Hey!" Mettner protested.

Amber laughed. "These online forums are gaining popularity. I went down the rabbit hole a few times after watching one too many *Datelines*."

Mettner said, "I don't understand how her case wasn't ever covered in the news."

"Because it wasn't a case," Josie said. "It was ruled an accidental death. The rest is all rumors and conjecture from people who lived in the area."

Chief Chitwood said, "Not every death is covered by the press, especially out in the middle of nowhere. Everett is a small county. Any news coming out of Everett County is coming from the city, Bradysport, where they have a pretty big drug problem."

"It's true," Amber said. "We get a lot of deaths here—and our fair share of murders—the press doesn't cover all of them. I know it's hard to believe in an age where everything seems like it's online and under the microscope, but Gretchen is right. There's nothing of substance about Jana Melburn online. Even the thread I found on NetSleuths doesn't say much."

Mettner nodded. "It's mostly multiple attempts by a user called HKent claiming to be Jana's mother to start new threads urging people not to forget about the case and to consider it a homicide."

"Hallie Kent," Josie said. "Jana's foster sister."

Amber added, "On one of the discussion threads she

started, there is a friendly argument among three to five people as to whether or not it was an accident. It didn't go anywhere."

"The police are keeping a tight lid on the file," Josie said. "Trinity hasn't been able to get much out of them."

Chief Chitwood frowned. "Your sister is doing a show about the case?"

"Not necessarily," Josie said. "She's researching it to see if there's enough there to do an episode."

"Find out who she talked to—her source," the Chief said. "You need to talk to them, too. There's a reason the case is popping up on her radar and ours at the same time."

"I agree," Josie said. "She's going to meet with Hallie Kent on Tuesday. I'll go with her."

Mettner steered the conversation back to Sharon Eddy. "The connection between the Jana Melburn case and Sharon Eddy is that Sharon's mother was one of the last people to see Jana alive."

Chief Chitwood said, "Then we need to find her mother."

"Working on it already," said Noah, pointing at his computer screen. "Carolina Eddy was in county lockup in Bellewood last month for drug offenses. Released on her own recognizance. Don't know where she's staying. Her last known address is a shelter in Bradysport. I called there and they haven't seen her in a week."

"Keep working at it," the Chief told him. "Quinn, what do we know about this Mathias Tobin?"

"He doesn't have a horse in this race," said Gretchen. "The fact that Dr. Feist ruled Jana Melburn's death an accident kept him out of prison—for that case, anyway."

"But his name keeps coming up, Palmer," the Chief said. "He was the other person to see this Jana Melburn last, from what Quinn said."

"Which makes him worth talking to," Noah said. "He did

live with Jana at the time of her death. Grew up with her. He probably knew her better than most people."

Josie said, "I looked him up. Lark Hadlee was right. He was convicted of attempted murder five years ago."

"Lark Hadlee also said he was out of prison," Gretchen pointed out. "But attempted murder is an easy twenty-year sentence."

"I know," said Josie. "His conviction was vacated. He was released seven months ago—last July."

"Why was it vacated?" asked Mettner.

"I don't know. I can only see the dockets, nothing more. I'd have to talk with the prosecutor in Everett County, or his attorney."

Gretchen said, "That explains why Everett County hasn't put out a warrant for his arrest for his wife's murder now that she's passed from her injuries. If his conviction for attempted murder was vacated, they'd have a hell of a time proving murder."

"What about Mathias himself?" the Chief said. "Can't we just go straight to him?"

"Just like Carolina Eddy, we can't find him," Josie said. "He doesn't even have a cell phone. Last known address is a halfway house in Bradysport. I called there and they haven't seen him in months."

"For crying out loud," the Chief said. "This entire thing stinks to high heaven."

Josie said, "Like I said earlier, Trinity is talking to Hallie Kent Tuesday. She might know something."

"You all better start finding some people and some answers yesterday!" said the Chief, his voice almost a shout. "This killer came into our city and murdered a girl because she had some tangential and meaningless connection to the Jana Melburn case, and then he left her body branded in a way only our medical examiner would recognize. He left her here the way a damn cat leaves its kills on its owner's porch. I won't have it. Not in my city."

Mettner said, "The good news is that if it's Vance Hadlee, he's locked up for now."

"It won't last," said Gretchen. "If his dad had enough sway and money to get him a plea deal for what he did to Anya, and to get him out of being charged with person not in possession of a firearm, he'll likely be able to get Vance out on bail pretty soon."

"He won't have sway here in Alcott County," Noah said.

"No," Gretchen agreed. "He won't, but he's got money. He'll be able to hire a good defense attorney. Vance will be out on bail in a day or two, I'm sure."

Josie's cell phone buzzed, dancing across her desk. The name "Needle" flashed across the screen. As it always did whenever Larry Ezekiel Fox contacted her, Josie's stomach filled with dread.

Noah said, "Who is it?"

The phone continued to hop around on her desk. "Nee—" she began and stopped herself. She was the only person who called Zeke by the childhood nickname she'd given him. Noah knew about it but no one else did. "Zeke," she corrected.

Everyone stared. While they didn't know that she had always called him Needle, they did know something of the history between her and Zeke. After Josie had been kidnapped as an infant, the woman posing as her mother, Lila, had gotten heavily into drugs. Zeke had been her drug dealer. At a young age, Josie had begun to think of him as "Needle" because he always brought her mommy needles. Although he didn't do much to stop Lila from abusing Josie, he had stepped in the couple of times during which Lila was doing her worst. Josie had lived her entire life being angry with him for not doing more and yet, as the years wore on, she couldn't help but wonder how much worse things would have been if he hadn't helped at the critical times that he did.

The phone stopped buzzing, the screen fading to black.

She still harbored anger toward him though she tried hard to fight it. Last year, during a case, he'd actually saved her life, taking a bullet for her. Josie had done her best to look after him since then, but Zeke wasn't much for being looked after. She'd given him her number in case he needed anything. This was the first time he'd used it. A strange feeling tickled the back of her throat. Worry? Had she crossed some emotional barrier that now allowed her to worry about the man who represented the worst time of her life? Zeke was a lifelong criminal and above all else, a survivor. He couldn't possibly need help.

He probably wanted something from her.

Her fingers brushed the screen. Did she want to deal with this right now?

As she pushed the phone away, it buzzed again, startling her. His name appeared once more. She glanced over at Noah. "It's up to you whether to answer or not," he said. "We can send a marked unit to the East Bridge to check in with him."

With a sigh, Josie picked up the phone. Ignoring the stares of everyone else, she said, "He's not going to talk to a uniform." She swiped answer and pressed the phone to her ear. "Zeke? What's going on?"

"JoJo?" he said, his voice scratchy. "Thought you might want to come down here. I'm pretty sure I'm looking at a dead body."

TWENTY

Near Central Denton, the East Bridge crossed a wide branch of the Susquehanna River. Beneath it, a hotbed of drug activity thrived no matter how hard the police department tried to stop it. A small number of the city's homeless population also lived under the bridge, taking shelter beneath tents and other makeshift dwellings. Zeke had made a home for himself in a small shack about a half mile down the riverbank, in a small copse of trees, away from the majority of people who congregated at the bridge. When they arrived, Josie and Noah found him sitting outside of it in a camping chair that Josie had bought for him a couple of months earlier. It was olive drab green, just like the threadbare jacket he'd seemed to have been wearing all of Josie's life.

A nearly toothless smile spread across his face when he saw her. His white beard was longer than she'd ever seen it, the ends of it yellowed. "JoJo!"

Josie handed him a carton of cigarettes. He cradled the box like he was holding a newborn, looking down at it almost lovingly. "What's this for?"

"It's not for anything, Zeke," she said. "Just take it."

He stood and disappeared into the shack, secreting the carton away. From inside, they heard his voice. "I sure do appreciate that, little JoJo."

Noah called back, "What's this about a dead body?"

Wordlessly, Zeke emerged, walking past them toward the river. Josie and Noah followed until they left the trees behind. Under their feet, the terrain turned to frozen mud and rocks. Ahead, the river rushed and churned. Josie couldn't help but think of the Sharon Eddy scene next to Kettlewell Creek. She looked all around them but didn't see anything out of the ordinary. Zeke walked them to the edge of the water and pointed across the river, at the sky. The sun was sinking fast, daylight fading. Above the opposite bank, three turkey buzzards and a handful of crows circled, sailing on thermals. Josie dropped her gaze from their outstretched wings to the ground directly across from them. The other riverbank had always been too steep for any of the East Bridge residents to utilize. A road ran alongside the bank, but it was little used, especially in winter when cars were more likely to find icy patches and go toppling into the water.

Noah said, "What are we looking at?"

But Josie saw it. Something red broke up the otherwise brown and gray brush along the incline that led up from the river to the road. She pointed at it. "There."

"How do you know that's a body?" Noah asked Zeke. "Lots of people toss their trash over there."

Zeke raised a brow at Noah, giving him only a passing glance before addressing Josie. His hands disappeared into his jacket pockets and came out holding a cigarette and lighter. "Last night I was out here taking a piss. I saw a pair of headlights. That's not that unusual. People do drive down that road sometimes, but these ones stopped right in the middle of the road. Then they turned away and next thing I know, I see brake lights. Same place."

Josie said, "You're saying the car stopped and turned so its trunk was facing the river?"

He put the cigarette between his lips and talked around it. "Yep. Then a couple minutes later, I heard something. Like something heavy falling, crashing down the bank. Then another noise like the trunk closing. After that, the car went back the way it came."

Josie asked, "What time was this, Zeke?"

"I don't know. Last night."

"Can you narrow it down at all? Closer to dinner time? Midnight? This morning?"

Zeke lit his cigarette and took a long pull, exhaling a cloud of smoke as he answered. "I don't know. It was late. I know 'cause it was real quiet. Probably middle of the night."

Josie knew he didn't have a watch. The only access he had to a clock was his phone, and she wasn't even sure how he kept it charged out here. Still, she had to try again, "Think, Zeke. Can you narrow the time down at all? Within a couple of hours?"

"How the hell would I know, JoJo? I was holding my dick, not my phone."

Noah said, "Why didn't you call someone last night, or even this morning?"

Zeke didn't even look at him this time, keeping his eyes on Josie. He pinched the cigarette between a thumb and forefinger. "It's not in my nature to be in other people's business."

Josie suppressed an eye-roll. "You don't say."

"Aw, come on, JoJo. I thought we was on good terms."

As good as it was ever going to get, she thought. He was still on the other side of the law with a long history of petty crime to his credit. She said, "Why did you wait to call me?"

He took another drag. Ash tumbled down the front of his jacket, but he didn't bother to brush it off. "'Cause I wasn't sure if it was trash or a body. Your boyfriend's right. People dump a lot of trash over there. The city always comes and does a big clean-up in the spring and fall but then people come and dump more. Anyway, it's when I saw the birds that I knew it wasn't trash." He used the cigarette to point at the buzzards again. "I only ever see them when they're picking at a carcass. Usually deer. Sometimes smaller game. Never did see an animal wearing red, though."

Josie said, "Were you able to see what kind of car it was? Make, model, color? Anything?"

He shook his head. "Sorry, JoJo. It was too dark."

"Did you see the driver?"

Zeke took one last puff of his cigarette before flicking it into the river. "It was too far away."

Noah said, "Could you tell if there was more than one person in the car?"

"Nope."

Josie knew from prior experience with Zeke that he wouldn't tell her anything unless they specifically asked. "What *did* you see, Zeke?"

He reached into his pockets again until he found another cigarette. He put it in his mouth, unlit. "I told you. A car. Lights. Noise. That's it. Like I said, it was dark and all the way across the river. But the dome light inside the car came on when the driver's side door opened. That was the only door that opened."

Josie asked, "Did you get any kind of a look at the driver when they went to open the trunk? Tall, short, fat, thin, male, female?"

He shook his head, the cigarette bobbing in his mouth. "Too dark to tell. The driver was just a dark shape."

"What about the car?" she asked. "Dark? Light? Sedan? SUV?"

He lit the cigarette. Smoke shot out through his nose. "Light, I think. Sedan. It was low to the ground. Not an SUV."

Josie looked at the red peeking out from the brush, gauging the distance. In the dark, with no streetlights and no other vehicles to provide illumination, it would be impossible to tell much else from this vantage point.

"Thanks, Zeke," she said, relieved that the words didn't feel like razor blades over her tongue anymore.

"Anything for you, JoJo," he said. The leathery skin around his pale gray eyes crinkled as he smiled down at her. "Say, you think you could get me a sleeping bag?"

TWENTY-ONE

The woman in the red coat had been dumped like garbage. From the road, Josie could see the path her body had taken down the incline, tamping down the dried brush and dislodging discarded beer cans and other trash as it rolled to its final resting place. She had landed face down, her arms and legs splayed in unnatural positions. Curly blonde hair shone in the waning sunlight, dried thistle caught in it. She wore a black skirt that had caught on a bramble and now rode up on one side. A black ballet flat clung to one of her feet. Her other foot was bare. There were abrasions on her legs where crows and buzzards had attempted to feast. Josie and Noah had had to scare off several of the birds when they'd arrived. The odor of decomposition had been unmistakable from the moment they stepped out of their vehicle.

Now, members of the ERT moved carefully and slowly around the body. Their white crime scene garb stood out in stark contrast to the brown winter tones of the bank. Josie and Noah had called them out to the scene after shooing the birds and confirming that what Zeke had seen was, in fact, a body. Noah had gone back over to the other riverbank with a couple of patrol officers to canvass the East Bridgers. It was a long shot, but they had to find out if anyone else had seen or heard anything the night before. Josie alternated between sitting in her warm car and standing on the shoulder of the road, watching the ERT work. Mettner and Gretchen had gone home to get some rest.

Gravel crunched behind her. Then she heard Anya's voice. "Another one?"

Josie glanced over at her. Her puffy blue winter coat dwarfed her thin frame. Her silver-blonde locks swished across her shoulders. Circles of red smudged her cheeks and the tip of her nose.

"Another body," Josie said.

"We get a lot of bodies," Anya said. "But this one so close to Sharon Eddy? Dump site next to water? I don't have a good feeling about this."

Josie didn't have a great feeling either. They stood in silence while the ERT brought out lights to battle the onset of evening. Hummel's team erected a pop-up tent over the body and pointed bright halogen lights at it. Finally, Hummel gave them the signal that they were cleared to enter the crime scene. They suited up and Dr. Feist retrieved her supplies from her truck. Getting down the steep bank to where the body was located proved difficult in their booties. Josie nearly fell twice. Anya stumbled as well but only once. As they reached the body, she took out her camera and began taking photos. Josie waited as she documented every angle. Flies buzzed around every part of the body, flitting from limb to limb. Here, the stench of death was much worse. Up close, the dirt that smudged the woman's clothes and clung to her hair was more noticeable, as were the places on the backs of her legs where the crows and buzzards had begun their gruesome work. Another wound gaped open on the back of her left hand.

Anya zoomed in on each one of them. "Scavenger birds,"

she said. "You can tell by the triangular shape of the wounds. These were made postmortem. If they'd occurred before her death, when her blood was still circulating, I'd expect to see a lot more blood."

Bone was visible where the vultures had taken flesh from her hand. Her fingernails were long and expertly manicured a bright red. Josie looked around for her missing ballet flat but didn't see it.

"Hold this," said Anya, thrusting the camera at Josie.

She took it and watched as the doctor knelt next to the body. First, she bagged the woman's hands to preserve any evidence that might be under her nails. "She's in full rigor."

"Does that mean she's been dead about twelve hours?" Josie asked.

Without looking up, Anya began riffling through her coat pockets. "You know I can't give you an exact time just based on that. I have to take her internal temperature and do some calculations based on the ambient temperature. It's pretty cold, which could slow the process, but you may be looking at a window of twelve to fifteen hours. I'll have a more definitive answer once I complete the autopsy."

If the victim had been killed twelve to fifteen hours ago, it would have been in the early-morning hours of Sunday. Anytime between one thirty and four thirty on Sunday morning. This was consistent with what Zeke had told them in terms of the body being dumped in the middle of the night.

Anya pulled a cell phone from the victim's coat pocket. Josie called for Hummel, who took it into evidence.

"Help me turn her over," Anya instructed.

"You sure you want to turn her over?" Josie said. "In full rigor?"

"Yes," said Anya. "Come on."

Josie set the camera aside and squatted beside Anya,

prepared to handle the woman's lower body. One of Anya's gloved hands reached for the victim's shoulder and froze.

"What is it?" said Josie.

"If—" She broke off, fingers trembling.

Josie looked to Anya's face. "If what?"

"Josie, if she's got a brand, like Sharon Eddy, I don't think I should be the one doing the autopsy. If Vance had something to do with this—" She stopped, eyes still on the victim's blonde hair.

Josie said, "It's okay, Doc. Go on."

"If she was killed sometime late Saturday night or early Sunday morning and then dumped here, it's possible Vance could have done it. He didn't show up to my house until almost noon today. Sure, he's in jail now but he wasn't when this woman was killed or when she was left here."

She was right. Although Cyrus had arrested Vance Saturday afternoon, they knew he'd been released almost immediately. That Dermot had been able to get him out of town lockup on a weekend in a matter of hours spoke to how much influence the man still had in Bly. That meant that Vance would have been home the evening before. Josie also knew that Vance had driven a pickup truck to Anya's house on Sunday. It had been parked along the street when they took him into custody. But the Hadlees also had a white sedan. He could have used that to kidnap and kill this woman, gone home, and returned several hours later to Anya's house in one of the trucks.

Anya added, "If there is any connection to him at all, then I shouldn't be involved. Even if there is only a possibility that he did this."

"I get it," Josie said. "Who do you have in mind?"

"There's an ME in Lenore County I'd trust to do it. I'm sure he would love to do it, actually. They don't get as many cases as we do."

"Let's take a look," Josie said.

Together, Anya taking the upper part of the body and Josie the lower, they muscled her stiff limbs so that she was face up. The first thing Josie noticed was the way the blood had settled to the lowest part of her body, causing her skin to turn an ugly reddish purple. The second thing Josie noticed was that her eyes were wide open. They'd been blue in life but now were covered in a milky haze.

"Corneal opacity," said Anya. "Normally you can clearly see the cornea, right?"

"Yes," Josie said, stomach turning as she stared into the woman's eyes. She was grateful in that moment that the woman had landed face down because she knew from experience that the first thing that scavenger birds usually ate were the eyeballs.

"Because the cornea is transparent. In the back of your cornea is a layer of cells—they're in a honeycomb pattern—and they regulate hydration or how much water or fluid makes it into the cornea. When we die, those cells break down and more fluid gets into the cornea, causing it to become less and less transparent. Usually, we'll see this about two hours after death and it gets more and more opaque as time goes on."

Josie said, "Can you tell the time of death by how opaque her eyes are?"

Anya gave a half-shrug with one shoulder. Her fingers were now gently pulling at the woman's lower eyelids. "You can, but it's not the preferred method. Also, the best way to determine time of death using corneal opacity is by removing the eyeball."

Josie tried to suppress her flinch, but Anya wasn't looking at her. Anya continued, "I can measure the level of potassium in the vitreous humor—that's the gel-like stuff between the lens of the eye and retina—and that will give me a good time of death. But really, it's just as easy to do it the way I normally do and use body temperature while taking into account the ambient temperature of where the body was found. But for that, I've got to get her to the morgue. Or, as I said, my colleague can do it."

Anya checked the woman's hairline and her mouth, looking for visible injuries. All Josie could see was more dirt and debris from the dry brush.

"I've been at this a while," Josie said. "Most bodies we recover—that are still relatively intact—have their eyes closed."

Anya checked around the woman's ears. "Open eyes after death is a lot less common than closed eyes. Usually if they're open postmortem, it's due to some kind of central nervous system tumor, liver failure or other disease. Sometimes medication. In this case, like with Sharon Eddy, it's probably just a result of muscle spasms that took place as the body was shutting down. Look at this."

She held the woman's chin up with one hand and used the other to point at a ring of bruises around the woman's throat. They were nearly indistinguishable from the discoloration caused by the settling of her blood, but Josie could make out a pattern. Fingerprints.

Shit, Josie thought.

Anya said, "Camera."

Josie picked up the camera and handed it to her. While Anya took photos of the woman's throat, Josie's gaze was drawn to something small and black beside the body. On closer inspection, she realized it was a purse. After pointing it out to Anya, Josie called Hummel over. He took photos of it and then carefully extricated it from where it had lodged under the body. "The strap broke," he noted. "Must have happened on the way down and then the bag got trapped under her."

His gloved fingers tugged the zipper open and then searched inside until he came up with a driver's license. He held it out so Josie could see. In the photo, the woman's blue eyes were warm and clear, exuding intelligence. Blonde curls, void of dirt or debris, fell to her shoulders. "Keri Cryer," she read. "Age thirty-five. She lives in Central Denton."

Josie committed the address to memory while Hummel

returned Keri Cryer's license to her purse and then deposited the purse into an evidence bag. Anya finished up her photos of the strangulation marks. She set her camera down and took in a shuddering breath. "Okay, Keri, let's have a look at your hip."

It took some tugging, but Josie and Anya finally pried the waistband of Keri's skirt and her underwear away from her hips. When they saw blistered flesh on her left side, Anya gasped. Josie stared at the brand. This one had even less clarity than the one they'd found on Sharon Eddy. Only the top of the horseshoe and one half of the arrow were seared into her skin. Above and below them were additional burns. Josie said, "She didn't make it easy for him. She must have fought back."

Anya wiped away a tear and leaned in to have a closer look. "You're right. He wasn't able to fully brand her."

"Or he just gave up," Josie said.

"Good," said Anya. She surveyed the body once more. "Let's hope she fought hard enough to take some DNA from him that will help you put him away for life."

TWENTY-TWO

Keri Cryer had lived in an apartment that took up the first floor of a two-story brick building in Denton's central business district. It was only a few blocks from where many of the city's businesses lined the streets. The parking was bad, but the house was within walking distance to just about everything a person might need. Josie and Noah had gone back to the station after Cryer's body was processed and removed from the riverbank to write up reports, prepare warrants, and find out as much information about Cryer as possible. She had no motor vehicles currently registered in her name. She had rented the apartment in Denton approximately five months earlier. Before that, she'd lived in Bradysport.

It wasn't lost on Josie that Keri Cryer had lived in the largest city in Everett County before moving to Denton.

They'd gotten a warrant to search her apartment and called the landlord only to find out that she lived on the second floor of the building. It was dark by the time Josie and Noah arrived. She was waiting for them on the front porch, the exterior light casting a circle around her. Josie estimated her to be in her early sixties. She was thin, dressed casually in jeans and a cream-colored sweater, over which she wore a purple shawl. A hand thrust from one of its folds as they crested the porch steps. "Scarlett Claire March," she announced. She shook Noah's hand first. "This is my place. You're the police?" Then she grasped Josie's hand in hers, her brown eyes brightening. "Never mind, I recognize you from TV. Well, I had no idea I'd be meeting someone famous!"

Josie gave her a tight smile. She certainly didn't think of herself as famous. She had appeared on television in her capacity as a detective dozens of times, but it was the *Datelines* she'd done with Trinity after their past was discovered that always made people feel as though they were meeting a celebrity. There were times that Josie regretted having done them, mainly when her notoriety caused people to dislike her on sight. Thankfully, this didn't seem to be one of those times. Josie ran a hand through her hair. "Miss March, as my colleague told you on the phone, we're here to talk to you about your tenant, Keri Cryer. We've got a warrant to search her apartment. She is the only tenant here, correct?"

"The only person I rent to, yes," Scarlett confirmed. "Though she's had a boyfriend over an awful lot lately. She said he's just 'staying' here sometimes, but he's here an awful lot."

Josie asked, "When is the last time you saw him?"

Scarlett shrugged. "Oh, I don't know. Two, three days ago?"

"Does he have a key to the apartment?" asked Noah.

"Certainly not. He's not on the lease!"

"Great," said Noah. "We'll just need you to let us in."

From somewhere beneath the folds of the shawl, another hand appeared with a key ring. "I'm happy to let you in, but in the lease I've got with Keri, it says I have to give her twenty-four hours' notice before I enter. Then again, if you guys are here, it's probably an emergency."

"In a manner of speaking," Josie said. She was loath to let Scarlett know that Keri was dead before the medical examiner had had a chance to track down and notify Keri's next of kin. Then again, the last they'd spoken to Dr. Feist's colleague, he hadn't had any luck locating that next of kin. Nor had Josie, using the police databases at her disposal. They'd have the contacts from Keri's phone as soon as Hummel used the GrayKey to get into it, but that might take a while.

As if reading her mind, Noah said, "Miss March—"

"Call me Scarlett, honey."

He smiled. "Scarlett, do you happen to have an emergency contact for Keri on file?"

She frowned. "Oh no. Something's happened to that poor girl, hasn't it?"

Josie said, "We're not at liberty to give out many details at this point, but we really do need to speak with her next of kin."

The keys jangled as Scarlett pressed them to her heart. "Next of kin," she echoed breathlessly. "Oh poor, poor Keri. That poor girl. Well, honey, I'm sorry to tell you that she hasn't got any next of kin. None worth knowing about, anyway. I'll tell you what. It's real cold out here. Why don't we go inside? You two can have a look at anything you need to see while I go pull her rental application and see who she put as an emergency contact. Then we'll talk some more."

Seconds later, Scarlett had the front door open. She led them through the apartment, giving them a short tour, flipping on lights as she went. It was small but quaint. The house was one of the older homes in Denton and still had the original wood wainscoting as well as thick vintage toile wallpaper depicting birds flitting from tree to tree. The furniture that Keri had chosen was more modern, inexpensive and not even enough to fill the space. There was one small couch in the living room. The dining room was empty. The kitchen had a small table with two chairs. There was one bedroom with a queen-sized bed and dresser. Unpacked boxes sat in almost every room. Once they were satisfied that no one was in the apart-

ment—including Keri's boyfriend—they snapped on gloves and
began to search.

Josie started in the bathroom where she found two of everything: toothbrushes, bath towels, washcloths, shampoos, soaps,
and other toiletries, some of which were marketed to women
and the rest to men. Scarlett was right. It sure did look as though
the boyfriend lived with Keri. Unless he was looking for a new
place. Then again, based on the three negative pregnancy tests
in the trash can, maybe he wasn't. She found Noah in the
bedroom.

"One pair of men's sneakers and maybe two days' worth of
clothes," he said, holding up a pair of men's jeans.

Either he didn't own a lot of clothes or he truly was only
staying there temporarily. "We have to find out who he is," Josie
said.

They kept searching for anything that might help them
figure out who would have wanted to kill Keri Cryer. There
wasn't much. In the living room, Scarlett waited near the front
door, shawl pulled tightly around her even though they were
now indoors. Josie said, "Do you know the name of Keri's
boyfriend?"

She shook her head. "I'm sorry to say I don't. I'm sure she
told me but I forgot. Mikey? Matty? Mark? I did find her emergency contact, but I don't think this is right."

"Why do you say that?" asked Noah.

Scarlett opened the shawl. In one hand was a sheaf of
papers stapled together. She held it out to Noah. "Her emergency contact is her old boss, but honey, she got fired. That's
why she came here."

Noah took the application and paged through it before
handing it to Josie. Her old employer was an attorney whose
name Josie didn't recognize.

Noah asked, "Was Keri an attorney?"

"A paralegal," Scarlett answered.

Josie asked, "Did she tell you why she was fired?"

Scarlett leaned against the front door, pulling the shawl closed again. "I do know. She told me. She told me everything. She was desperate to get this apartment. The rent's cheap on account of there's really no parking to be had around here, and to tell you the truth, it gets real noisy in this part of town. Lots of shoppers and traffic. There's a little bandshell one block over where the city council invites musicians to give concerts all spring and summer. It's nonstop. Every tenant I had before ended up leaving because it was too busy and too noisy. I took a chance on Keri. She didn't have a pot to piss in, really, but she was honest."

"Why was she so desperate?" Josie asked.

"She'd been unemployed for a couple of months and had just gotten a new position here in Denton. She needed a place to live. Her savings were almost gone, so she couldn't afford to stay in a hotel until she found somewhere. She had enough for the security deposit and first month of rent, and she had employment lined up. I tell you, I felt so sorry for her, I ended up cooking for her the first month she was here!"

"That was kind of you," Noah said. "To cook for someone in dire straits even after she'd been fired from her job."

Scarlett huffed a breath, sending her brown and gray bangs up in the air momentarily. "Oh honey, she didn't get fired for a real reason, as far as I'm concerned."

"Is that right?" Josie asked, trying to keep her talking.

"That sweet girl got fired for falling in love. Now if that's a legitimate reason to fire someone, I don't know what this world is coming to. Don't worry, it wasn't with someone married or anything like that. Or her boss. It was a client. They fired her because it was a conflict of interest or some nonsense like that."

Noah said, "The boyfriend who's obviously been staying here—was it him?"

"I believe so," Scarlett said. "He wasn't here in the beginning. Just started coming around a few months ago. She never said much about him other than that they were in love. They were going to start a family once they got on their feet. Apparently, they both grew up in foster care. Not together, though. She never told me his story, only that he'd been a foster kid like her except he never knew his family. Keri always knew who her family was but wished she didn't. Her mother and father are both in prison for burning down a house with a whole family in it."

Josie felt a prickle at the back of her neck. It couldn't be a coincidence that Jana Melburn, Hallie Kent, and Mathias Tobin had all been foster kids, just like Keri Cryer. "She told you that?"

Scarlett nodded solemnly. "I told you, this poor girl told me everything. I liked her more for it. She was about eight years old when her folks got arrested. They're serving life sentences. She had a couple of relations on her dad's side, but no one wanted her. Isn't that sad? A sweet person like Keri."

Josie didn't say it, but Keri might have been lucky not to end up with family members of a murderer who had no interest in raising her.

Noah said, "They're her next of kin. Technically."

"Technically," Scarlett agreed. "But they're no kin to her. She hasn't seen them or spoken to them in years. For a long time, she grew up thinking they were innocent. She went into law 'cause she thought she might help them get out. Couldn't afford law school so she worked as a paralegal. But then she told me that she got the case files. She used that—oh what's that law? The one where you can get public records?"

"The Right to Know Law," Josie said.

"Yes! That's it. She got the trial transcripts. Read them. Knew in her heart she'd been wrong about them all that time. 'A foolish child's dream' is what she called it."

Noah said, "But she worked for an organization whose aim was to free wrongfully imprisoned people?"

"No. She wanted to but it didn't pay enough, and the attorneys did most of the work. Not much need for her. She worked for a criminal defense firm. Then she fell in love with a client. Got fired. Found a job with a different defense attorney here and moved."

"You weren't worried that the client she fell in love with was a criminal?" asked Noah. "Since she worked for a criminal defense firm?"

Scarlett said, "She said he'd never been in any trouble. It was all just a big misunderstanding."

"I'm pretty sure that's what all criminals say," Noah said. "Particularly the guilty ones."

Scarlett shrugged. "I figured, why would she tell me the truth about everything else and not that? Besides, if he'd done something really terrible, wouldn't he be in prison?"

He would, Josie thought. Unless he had recently been exonerated and set free.

Josie said, "It sounds like the two of you were very close."

Scarlett smiled, the skin at the corners of her eyes crinkling. "Oh, I'm just a little lonely living upstairs by myself, is all. I took care of Keri as much as I could when she first got here. Then she started her job. Lots and lots of long hours. I tried to leave her alone so she could get on with her life."

"Do you know where she was yesterday or the day before? The last time she was here? What time she left?" asked Noah.

"No. I'm up to my ears in repainting my kitchen. Didn't take any notice."

Josie asked, "Would Keri have told you if she was having trouble with anyone?"

"Like who?"

Noah said, "Her boyfriend? Maybe things weren't as great as she made them out to be?"

Scarlett shook her head. "Oh no. I hear a lot from upstairs. All those two ever did was laugh and do the... other thing. No fighting. Believe me, if she didn't seem so damn happy, I would have said my piece about him being here all the time."

Josie said, "How about anyone else? New friends? Coworkers? Did she ever say anything?"

"No, nothing. Not to me, anyway."

"What about anyone hanging around lately? Lurking, maybe even watching the house?" Noah said.

"I haven't noticed anyone, but I've got video footage upstairs I can show you. I never looked for anything like that but that doesn't mean it's not on there. I just have the cameras in case something goes missing or there's a break-in. You'll probably see the boyfriend on there, too."

TWENTY-THREE

Scarlett's video surveillance footage captured the front of the house as well as part of the street. It also went back two weeks. She made a copy for them so that they could take it back to the stationhouse. They went through it, watching Keri come and go from her apartment with regularity. Her boyfriend also came and went quite frequently, sometimes with her, sometimes without her. Either Keri had made him a secret key to her apartment, or she'd been in the habit of leaving the door unlocked for him. The moment Josie saw him, she was struck by how familiar he looked. He was older and leaner now. His hair was shorter, and he seemed to walk with a slight stoop, but his nose was still crooked. Josie was certain it was Mathias Tobin. She pulled up his latest driver's license photo which was dated four months earlier. He must have gotten it updated after his release.

"That's a match," Noah said, looking from the driver's license photo to a still he'd pulled of Keri's boyfriend's face. "We're going to need to talk with him."

"I'll call Scarlett," Josie said. "And ask her to call us immediately if he shows up there."

"We should get the ERT over to her apartment and collect DNA just to confirm. I'll call them."

Josie said, "I'm also going to draw up a warrant to impound the Hadlees' white sedan. Hummel can process it for any evidence of Keri Cryer."

They worked through the night until dawn broke on Monday morning. By the time Gretchen showed up to relieve them, Josie's eyes were burning. The Chief arrived seconds later. Josie and Noah briefed them on the developments so far, and that they were waiting for Dr. Feist's colleague to finish the autopsy on Keri Cryer.

"Let me get this straight," said the Chief. "We've got a second victim with the same brand as Dr. Feist's husband inflicted on her ten years ago, and this second victim also has a connection to the accident case in Bly."

"Yes," said Josie. "This is a much stronger connection, though. A much more obvious connection."

"Because all of Bly thinks that our second victim's new boyfriend killed that girl? What's her name again? Jana Melburn?"

"That's it," said Noah.

"This boyfriend," the Chief said. "How's he look for these murders?"

Josie said, "Well, we've got him on video coming and going from Keri Cryer's house for the past two weeks. He was not there during the time that Sharon Eddy was missing and then murdered—"

"But we don't know where he was because we haven't been able to locate him in order to talk with him," Noah interjected.

"In terms of Keri Cryer," Josie said. "He left before her on Thursday morning and he hasn't been back since."

"That gives him time to kill both Sharon Eddy and Keri Cryer," Gretchen said, "Chief, you want to put out a BOLO on this guy?"

"I want you to talk to him," the Chief said. "That's for damn sure. Try to keep the press off this, but let's put out an alert. If any units see him, they should bring him in for questioning. You said he's got no car, right?"

Noah shrugged. "Nothing registered to either him or Keri Cryer."

The Chief frowned. "Hard to transport a body with no car. We know Keri Cryer was moved in a sedan."

Noah said, "Just because there's nothing registered to him or Keri doesn't mean he doesn't have access to a vehicle somehow."

"Which is why we need to talk to him," said Josie.

"Phone?" Gretchen said. "He's got to have a phone. How was he keeping in touch with Keri?"

"We haven't found anything in the databases under his name," Josie said. "But Hummel is working on getting everything he can from Keri Cryer's phone. I'm sure there will be something on there."

"What else do we know about this woman?" asked the Chief. "You find anything in her apartment?"

Josie said, "We found a lot of negative pregnancy tests, so her landlord wasn't lying when she said that Cryer and Tobin were trying to start a family. We found a laptop, which Hummel is processing. We also found some documents from her old firm, Downey, Downey & O'Neill. Termination letter, that sort of thing. We called them to see if they had any contact information for Mathias Tobin, but they wouldn't give us anything. I asked about Keri Cryer but they said they don't discuss HR matters."

"How about Keri Cryer's new firm?" asked Gretchen. "Get in touch with them?"

Noah said, "I spoke with her supervising attorney there. He said she was a good worker. Smart. Never had an issue with her. He did relate that two of her coworkers said they were meeting her for drinks on Saturday night at a bar a few blocks from her house, but she never showed."

Josie said, "We knew from the landlord's surveillance footage that she left her apartment on foot Saturday evening around nine p.m. We checked traffic cams and surveillance from nearby businesses. It took a bit as there are a few different routes from her house to the bar on foot, but we found her. We were able to follow her to about four blocks away from the bar. At that point, all we could pull was video of her lower body, basically, from a shop that is almost a full block away. Can't see shit. Just her stepping off the curb and walking up to a car—white sedan from what we can tell, too far away to see the plate—and talking to the person. Then she gets in. The car leaves."

Noah said, "We're hoping that once Hummel gets into her phone, GPS will show where she went."

"Doubtful," said the Chief. "If this is anything like the Sharon Eddy murder, then the killer convinced her to turn her phone off when she got into the car."

"But how?" asked Noah.

"Don't know," the Chief said. "Maybe you can ask this killer when you find him!"

Gretchen asked, "Did you get anything else from the traffic cams?"

Josie said, "We've got the car on some other cameras that local businesses provided. Nothing close enough or clear enough to see the plate or who was driving."

"LPRs?" asked Gretchen.

"Still working on that," said Noah. "But nothing so far. The cameras only follow them a few blocks, and once they're out of the business district, we've got nothing."

Gretchen said, "We'll send more units out this morning to collect footage."

The Chief said, "We also need to find out where Vance Hadlee was in the time period between Keri Cryer getting into that car and her body being dumped near the river. Let's not forget, this happened before he showed up at Anya's and punched Mett."

Noah said, "We'll see what we can find out although with him in jail here now, we'll have to go through his attorney."

The Chief folded his arms across his chest. "Let's go back to Mathias Tobin. Seems like violence follows him wherever he goes but nothing sticks."

"He wouldn't have known about the brand, though, would he?" asked Gretchen. "When we spoke with Anya, his name never came up."

"Ask her again," said the Chief.

Josie said, "We can, but Chief, these murders have connections to the Jana Melburn case. Mathias Tobin walked away from that with little more than accusations from the people in his town. Why would he now, ten years later, after having been set free for a completely different crime, draw so much attention to the Melburn case? All that does is bring unwelcome scrutiny back onto him. Again."

Noah said, "Josie's right. It makes no sense for him to be involved in this. He just got out of prison."

"But everywhere you look, his name comes up," said the Chief. "We need to find out why."

TWENTY-FOUR

Josie purred with pleasure as Noah kneaded her feet. She was stretched across her couch with her feet in his lap while Trout snored contentedly, pressed against her side. After sleeping most of the day, Josie and Noah had gotten up, showered, and taken Trout for a long walk. They weren't due to work until the next day so they were taking advantage of the downtime, although Keri Cryer and Sharon Eddy were never far from Josie's mind. She had texted Gretchen and then Mettner, who had come on shift to get updates, but so far there were few. They'd managed to get the Hadlees' white sedan impounded. Hummel was at work processing it. It was an older model and its GPS system had been disabled. There was no way to track where it had been for the last forty-eight hours. Lark and Dermot insisted that Vance had been on the farm with them even though, when pressed by Gretchen, Lark admitted she had not physically seen him since he returned from being locked up by Cyrus sometime Saturday evening. Neither had noticed whether the sedan had been missing or not for any length of time.

There had been no sightings of Mathias Tobin. Where had

he gone? He'd practically been living with Keri Cryer, and now that she was dead, he had not been back to her apartment. It still seemed like he had the most to lose by the new scrutiny that Sharon Eddy and Keri Cryer's murders had brought to the Jana Melburn case—not to mention that there was still no proof that he knew about Anya's brand—and yet, something about his disappearing act wasn't sitting right with Josie. She couldn't stop thinking about the fact that the women in his life—Jana, Piper, and now Keri—all turned up dead.

Josie wished she could talk with Trinity about the entire thing, but she'd just have to settle for accompanying her sister to Bly the next day to speak with Hallie Kent. Hallie had grown up with both Jana and Mathias. She'd been an excellent source of information for Trinity. Josie knew that Gretchen had contacted Hallie to see if she'd heard from Mathias but she had not. Still, if the team hadn't found him by tomorrow, Josie could dig a little deeper when she spoke with Hallie. Josie hoped she could shed light on a lot of things.

From the kitchen came the sounds of cooking—silverware clinking, pots clanging, something sizzling. Trinity and Drake had decided they would cook dinner. Neither Josie nor Noah had argued. The smells wafting from down the hall made Josie's stomach growl.

"This is what we should do from now on," she said. "Just have a constant influx of guests who know how to cook. We'll never cause a fire in the kitchen again."

Noah laughed. "We'd also get no alone time."

"Hmm," Josie said. "If we're choosing between alone time and food, I'd rather starve."

Before he could respond, the doorbell rang. Trout jumped up, ran to the door and began barking furiously. With a groan, Josie extricated herself from the couch and went to answer. Anya Feist stood on the front stoop, wrapped in a coat and knit hat, looking pale and distressed.

"Come in," Josie said.

Trout, recognizing her smell, immediately dissolved into a blur of butt-wagging and whimpers, jumping to lick at her gloved hands. Anya took a moment to squat down and greet him. Trinity appeared in the doorway to the kitchen, hands covered with potholders. When she saw Anya, her eyes widened. Josie shot her a look of warning. Although Josie had gotten a copy of Jana Melburn's autopsy report from Trinity earlier that day, and dropped it off at the morgue so that Anya could review it whenever she was ready, Josie hadn't told Anya about the possible television show focused on the Melburn case. She was relieved when Trinity disappeared back into the kitchen.

Standing, Anya looked around Josie's foyer. She sniffed the air. "This is a bad time. I'll come back."

"No," said Noah, walking in from the living room. "Stay. Trinity and Drake are here. We're just having dinner. I'm sure there's plenty. We'd love for you to join us."

Anya gave him a weak smile. "I'm not that hungry." She looked at Josie, as if seeking rescue.

Glancing at Trout, Josie said, "I was just about to take the dog for a walk. Why don't you join me?"

Looking relieved, Anya nodded. She waited while Josie bundled up and put on Trout's harness. It was dark outside, night falling early in the winter, but the streetlights gave off plenty of light. Once they were a half block away, Anya said, "I talked with my colleague in Lenore County. The autopsy on Keri Cryer is just what you'd expect. I'm sure you and Noah will be briefed the next time you're at work. Cause of death was manual strangulation. Manner, homicide. Time of death between midnight and two a.m. on Sunday. She had abrasions on her arms. Defensive bruising, most likely. There was a skull fracture as well that he thinks took place just before her death.

No sign of a patterned injury, so we don't know what she was struck with. It didn't break the skin."

"The killer is subduing them by hitting them over the head," Josie said.

"Looks that way. Keri Cryer had recently had sexual intercourse."

"The last time she saw her boyfriend was Thursday morning," Josie said. "Could it have been from someone else?"

"I can't say for sure, but it could definitely have been from the boyfriend. She could have had intercourse three to five days prior to her death, and it would still show up on exam. That's how long sperm can live inside a female body after sex. There was no evidence that intercourse was not consensual. My colleague took a sample and sent it off for DNA analysis. DNA was also removed from her coat. That's been sent out as well."

"Speaking of her boyfriend," Josie said, "we believe it was Mathias Tobin."

"Oh my God." Anya stopped in her tracks. She looked up at the darkened sky, taking deep breaths until she was composed. Trout pulled against his leash, not realizing they'd paused.

After a moment, Josie said, "Anya?"

She lowered her gaze but didn't meet Josie's eyes. Slowly, she started walking again. "That's why Gretchen asked me if I remembered Mathias Tobin and if he knew about the brand Vance gave me. We didn't get a chance to talk for long. I was busy with an accidental drowning case. I actually came to your place tonight to discuss the Jana Melburn case, which I'll get to in a minute. As far as Keri Cryer is concerned, it's quite possible that the two DNA samples we found on her body came from different people. That's why we send them out to be analyzed. Or maybe they didn't. God, this is just insane. I thought all of this was ancient history. I'm having a really hard time with all of this coming back up. Seeing Vance yesterday was like—" She floundered for words.

Josie rubbed her shoulder. "I'm sorry you're going through this."

Anya swiped at a tear that had leaked onto her face. "And everyone here has been so wonderful. If I had had all of you when I was young... if I'd had such a good support system then... I don't know. Maybe things would have been different. Maybe they'd be the same. Listen, I'm sorry I didn't come in for dinner. As great as everyone on the team has been to me, I'm just not up to... people tonight."

"I get it," Josie said. "It's probably for the best. Full disclosure? My sister is researching the Jana Melburn case with a view toward potentially doing an episode on it."

Anya groaned. "Oh no."

"I've asked her not to approach you for now. She has no idea what's going on with you and Vance, or here in Denton with the Sharon Eddy murder—and now Keri Cryer—but she agreed not to talk with you about it yet. I'm just not sure how much longer I can hold her off. You know how she is when she digs her heels in on something."

Anya laughed drily. "Yes. Of course I do. She's legendary. But I suppose I have it coming."

TWENTY-FIVE

They stopped as Trout paused to sniff the base of a telephone pole vigorously. Josie asked, "What do you mean?"

"I reviewed Jana Melburn's autopsy report. It brought a lot of things back."

Trout relieved himself on the pole and then went back in for another sniff. Josie waited for Anya to continue.

"That case was extremely difficult. From what I remember, the police had absolutely no evidence to suggest that Jana Melburn had been murdered. I went to the scene with them. It was very plausible that she fell, tumbled down the embankment, and hit her head."

Josie said, "The injuries to her head were catastrophic."

Anya held up a hand as they continued on their walk. "I know that, and I know it's hard to believe that a person could sustain such severe injuries in a simple fall."

"Her eye sockets were shattered. The back of her head—"

"I know," Anya interrupted. "But listen to me, in the absence of evidence of homicide, as a pathologist, you're obligated to rule the manner of death as accidental or undetermined. Josie, sometimes these freak injuries just happen. Believe me, I struggled with this case. You're right. Those kinds of injuries are not typically caused by a fall like that but they can be—the odds are extremely low but it *can* happen."

It was the same argument that Josie had used on Trinity the day before.

"You should know," Anya went on, "that even in light of that, I still wanted to rule the manner of death homicide. Just like you—and your sister—I couldn't get past just how catastrophic the injuries were."

They stopped again so that Trout could investigate a patch of grass. "Why didn't you?" Josie asked.

"My initial draft of the report ruled it a homicide," Anya said. "But I was pressured into changing it, and I'm sad to say that I caved. Like I said, it was a very difficult time for me. Please understand that I am not using my own personal crisis or the situation with Vance as an excuse, only an explanation."

"Who pressured you?" Josie asked.

"My boss. My mentor, Garrick."

Josie's arm jerked as Trout continued on down the street. She followed but kept looking over at Anya, whose gaze was locked on her feet. She tried to think of who benefited from the case not being classified as a homicide. Mathias Tobin. Assuming he was the person the police had had in mind as a suspect all along.

"When you discussed the case with the police," Josie said, "what did they think? Did they have a suspect in mind?"

"At the time? If they did, they didn't discuss that with me, but it wasn't within my purview to discuss suspects, only my findings. I do know that they were leaning toward homicide, just as I was, because of the injuries, but they had no evidence other than the injuries. They made that very plain. I think they were just as frustrated and baffled as I was, but what could we do?"

Josie said, "From what I understand, Mathias believed Jana

was going to meet someone the night she died. The police didn't discuss that with you? That she might have met someone and he killed her?"

"I had heard that, yes, but they couldn't find anyone or any evidence that there had been anyone she was meeting with. I'm telling you, there was nothing to go on."

"They didn't suggest that you list the manner of death as undetermined? As opposed to accidental?" Josie asked.

"If they did, I don't remember it."

"But you remember Garrick pressuring you to list it as accidental."

Anya nodded.

"I assume you know that Mathias Tobin became the main suspect in the case. Both the police and the citizens of Bly believed he had murdered her."

"I had no idea," said Anya. "I left shortly after Jana's death. I never spoke to anyone from Everett County or Bly again after that. Not until today when Vance showed up on my porch. I had no idea that this—this lore had grown up around Jana Melburn's death."

"Did you know Mathias Tobin?" asked Josie.

"I had to look him up in the yearbook. Took me a couple of hours to dig that out, but yes, once I saw his face, I remembered him. He was a year behind me and Vance in high school. Vance and I ran in the same circles with him. All the football players and their girlfriends hung around together."

"Did you know him well?"

She shook her head. "Not well, no. Not at all, really. I knew of him. I don't remember any direct contact with him, but I do remember that he was accused of sexual assault by three of the cheerleaders. I definitely wouldn't have had contact with him after that."

"What about the cheerleaders?" asked Josie. "Did you ever speak with any of them?"

"No. But they were a year behind me, too. They had their own clique and although I was Vance's girlfriend, I was not welcome in it. They thought I was stuck-up and snobby. Honestly, looking back, I'm not even sure how Vance and I ended up together or how I managed my way through high school. Without him, I would have been a loner, an outcast, even. I was far more into studying than football, and those of us who were focused primarily on academics were not treated well at that school."

"Do you know what happened in terms of those accusations?"

Trout stopped again, this time sniffing a holly bush on the edge of a neighbor's property. Anya rolled her eyes. "This I remember because it was so appalling. Mathias was charged and given an ankle bracelet, but he was still allowed to go to school and play football even though many people protested."

"Football more important than the safety of girls?" Josie said. "Unfortunately, in a lot of places, that is the reality."

"Yeah, well, it's an ugly one."

"I agree."

"Eventually, those girls recanted and the charges were dropped. I didn't like them—like I said, they didn't treat me well —but I was upset. I was afraid that somehow they'd been bullied into recanting or that they saw how the charges were already being handled with Mathias being prioritized over them and decided going through with a trial wasn't worth it."

"Did you ever talk with any of them?" Josie asked.

"No. Maybe I should have but who was I to talk? I ended up in an abusive relationship and didn't get out until my husband branded me for life."

"Did you ever talk to Vance about Mathias?"

"Yes. I expressed my disgust for what had happened a few times, but he said there was nothing to worry about because there was no way in hell Mathias had done what the girls said he did. Believe me, we had heated arguments over that. I didn't go to the games for the rest of the year. He wasn't happy."

"Were they friends?" Josie asked.

"No, I don't think so. I never saw them together except at football practice or games. I think it was just a matter of Vance defending his teammate. Plus, with Dermot coaching, Vance treated the team like family. You defend your family. Stand by them. He never said it out loud to me, but I think he thought that those girls made the whole thing up. The accusations were a stain on the whole team—that's how Vance saw it. God, I was such an idiot. Looking back, I can't believe I had feelings for him."

"You were a different person then," Josie said. "A kid. Let's fast-forward to the time that you prepared your autopsy report on Jana Melburn. The police had not discussed any suspects with you, and you had no inkling that Mathias Tobin or anyone else was or might be held to blame for her death?"

"No."

"Then why change the ruling from homicide to accidental? You could have made it undetermined."

Anya sighed. "Garrick. He knew the police had no leads, same as I did. He was concerned that if we ruled Jana's death a homicide—which would never be solved—it would cause a lot of fear and upheaval in the community. People would think there was a killer on the loose. If I ruled it undetermined, in some ways that might be worse than calling it a homicide. People would still be freaked out, thinking there was a killer on the loose. He thought the best thing for all concerned was to call it an accident."

"You can't rule someone's death an accident just because you think it's what's best for the community," Josie said.

Anya pressed a hand to her heart. "I know that and Josie, I swear to you, if there had been even a shred of evidence that pointed to homicide besides the extent of Jana's head injuries and my own instincts, I would never have gone along with it. But there wasn't. There was nothing. Also—" She broke off.

After a couple of beats of silence, Josie said, "What is it?"

"I don't even want to say."

"Tell me," Josie said.

"Garrick knew Dermot, my ex-father-in-law. They grew up together. They were friends. Vance was like a nephew to him. Garrick promised me that he would talk with Vance and do everything he could to keep him from coming after me once I left."

Josie's heart fluttered. "In exchange for listing Jana Melburn's death as accidental on the autopsy report?"

Anya grimaced. "Not exactly. He never said, 'Hey, make the manner of death accidental in your report and I'll keep Vance away from you for good.' It wasn't like that, but it did come up during our talks about the report. It was... implied."

Josie thought of the Anya she had seen in the wedding photo on Vance Hadlee's dresser. A woman much younger and almost unrecognizable from the woman who stood before her today. A woman with no family support of her own, manipulated into a life she didn't really want, abused, beaten, worn down. A woman who, once she found the courage to tell her husband she wanted to leave, had been violently assaulted and branded like cattle. A woman living in fear every moment of her life in a community where her husband's family had more power than the justice system.

If Josie had been in that position, would she have considered her mentor's implied offer to keep her abusive husband away from her in exchange for ruling a death accidental? Especially given the fact that there wasn't a shred of evidence to suggest that it was *not* an accident?

Josie knew a thing or two about making compromises and messy decisions from a place of fear. "I understand," she said.

Anya let out a breath. "Thank you. I'm not proud of it—that

I took this into account when I made my decision—but Josie, the only reason I was comfortable ruling Jana's manner of death an accident was because, as Garrick pointed out to me, if the police came up with evidence later that Jana had been murdered, we could always change it. But from what you've told me, they never did."

"You're right," Josie said. "As far as I know, but it didn't stop the public from speculating or casting Mathias Tobin as the villain."

"Because he was the last to see her alive?"

Josie nodded. "From what I've learned so far, he actually followed her that night until he lost her on a side street. He lived with her, too. They were foster siblings. In fact, he and his other foster sister, Hallie Kent, raised Jana from the age of nine. He was like a father to her. I think that gave people the belief that he may have had reason to kill her—that prior relationship —and the fact that he had previous allegations against him for a violent crime probably contributed."

"Well, if he did kill her, he did a hell of a job of leaving no trace of himself whatsoever. You said he was Keri Cryer's boyfriend? That is a direct connection to the Jana Melburn case —for which I performed the autopsy. Is he a suspect?"

Josie said, "He's a person of interest. We need to speak with him."

"Did you talk to Sharon Eddy's grandmother?"

"I did," Josie said. "Her daughter—Sharon's mother—was the clerk at the gas station where Jana and Mathias were last seen speaking on the night she went missing."

"My God. Sharon Eddy couldn't have been more than ten years old when Jana Melburn died."

"She was nine," Josie said.

"Why would someone do that? Why kill the child of the woman who saw Mathias and Jana together for the last time? This makes no sense. Keri Cryer's murder doesn't make sense either. Why kill the girlfriend of Jana Melburn's older foster brother? What does it accomplish?"

Trout stopped once more, this time scenting the air, trying to discern something neither of them could smell. "Anya," Josie said. "The killer is trying to get your attention. The connections to the Melburn case? You did the autopsy. The branding? That was a direct message to you. I'm really not sure about the correlation between the Melburn case and your branding, but what this killer has accomplished is to send a message to you."

Tears spilled down Anya's cheeks. "God. These poor women. They're both dead because of me. I can't— Who would do such a thing? Why go to all this trouble? If this killer has a problem with me, he should just come for me!"

"He's angry," Josie said. "And very sick in the head. Vance is the obvious suspect, especially given the brand and the fact that he's still harboring a lot of anger toward you, but Anya, is there anyone else from your past who might be angry with you?"

"Enough to kill two innocent women? No."

"How about just angry?" Josie said.

Anya bit her bottom lip.

"What is it?" asked Josie.

She looked away. "God, I just can't believe this stuff is coming up now. After all these years. That was the worst time of my life. I was an emotional disaster. I did things I'm not proud of—things I would never do now or ever again."

"Name someone who claims they've never done something they're ashamed of and I'll show you a liar," Josie said. "Just tell me."

"I had an affair. Well, not really an affair. I had been separated from Vance for months, waiting for the court to settle things—the assault on the criminal side and my divorce on the civil side. The person I was with, well, he was single. His wife had died the year before and his daughter was in college, although a month or two into our affair, she moved back in with him. She was still so distraught over her mother's death that she had to withdraw from school. But being together wasn't a good look for either of us. It was very complicated. At any rate, it wasn't serious, and I didn't think it would last. Because I didn't think it would last, I broke it off. Except I didn't tell him I was breaking it off. I just left. Without a word, and never looked back."

A sinking feeling settled into Josie's stomach. "Who was it?"

"Cy. Cyrus Grey."

TWENTY-SIX

Josie's mind was still reeling the next morning as she and Trinity drove to Bly. She kept coming back to Anya's revelations. First, there was Garrick pressuring her to make her ruling on Jana Melburn's autopsy report an accident for what he said was the good of the community. But what did he think would happen within his community? Why had he been so desperate for Jana's death to be ruled accidental that he had made a thinly veiled offer to Anya: do this and I'll make your abusive ex-husband go away for good? There had to be something more to Garrick's motivation than what Anya told her. Noah was going to track Garrick down while the rest of the team was still digging into Keri Cryer's life and trying to locate Mathias Tobin.

Then there was the revelation about Cyrus Grey.

Anya had gone on to make all kinds of justifications for the brief tryst. Cyrus had been kind to her. He'd made her feel safe, less alone. He had given her, in her lowest moments, the things she had craved for years, the things that she had gone without while she was with Vance. Being with him had been a brief respite from her harsh reality. It hadn't been love, but even if it had, carrying on a relationship with a police officer who was actively involved in the case against your husband was a huge problem. In the end, Cyrus had still represented a period in Anya's life that she wanted to close the door on forever.

Josie wondered how Cyrus Grey saw things.

"Are you going to do this silent trance thing the entire drive?" Trinity complained.

Glancing over, Josie managed a smile. "Sorry. I'm thinking about a case. A couple of cases."

"Oh, you're up to a couple now?"

Josie didn't need to look at her sister to know that one of her eyebrows was severely arched. "Yes."

"They're connected to my case? Both of them?" Excitement brought a breathless quality to her words.

"Yes," Josie admitted. "But you know I can't talk about them."

"We're going to interview Hallie Kent together."

"As a professional courtesy to me and as a favor from one sister to another, I'm asking you to leave this alone right now."

"But it sounds like this might be so much bigger—" She broke off. Then, "Promise me an exclusive."

"Exclusive what?"

"If this turns out to be a huge case, you only talk to me."

"Trin, I hate talking to any press. Besides, whatever this is, I think all the parties concerned deserve their privacy."

There were a few seconds of silence, filled only by the whir of the heater. "If I do an episode on Jana Melburn—"

"We both know you've already decided to do one," Josie said.

"Yes, I have, but it has to be approved by the producers and my network first. So if I do one and it's so deeply connected to whatever you're working on that the three cases can't be separated from one another, then you—as the police contact in Denton working your cases—give me an exclusive."

"I'm not promising anything," Josie insisted. "Let's be honest here. You don't need me for an exclusive. You'll get whatever you want whether I'm involved or not."

Trinity gave a little huff. "I'm choosing to take that as a compliment." She reached over and turned the radio up. "We'll just listen to music until we get there."

Hallie Kent lived in a small white house along one of Bly's main thoroughfares. Before Trinity could ring her doorbell, the door swung open, and Hallie welcomed them inside. A white couch and tub chair faced a dormant fireplace. Above the mantel was a television. The local news from WYEP played, its volume lowered to a barely audible buzz. So far, Denton PD had managed to keep both Sharon Eddy and Keri Cryer off the news. Hallie gestured toward the couch. Trinity and Josie sat side by side. On the end table was a framed photo similar to the graduation photo that Josie had seen in Trinity's file. In full cap and gown, Jana Melburn stood between a beaming Hallie and Mathias. In this picture, Hallie and Mathias each had an arm around Jana's shoulders. The three of them smiled at the camera, a tight and happy family unit. Next to it was another photo of them. Jana was younger, perhaps eleven or twelve. Again, she stood between Hallie and Mathias, who hugged her protectively. Hair and clothes soaked through, the three of them grinned proudly at the camera. Behind them was a sign for the log flume at Knoebel's Amusement Park in Elysburg. Josie recognized it from when she and Noah took Harris there last summer.

Hallie dragged the chair across the hardwood floor, turning its back to the fireplace and TV so that she could face them. As she did so, a gray cat darted across the foot of the fireplace. A small bell on its collar jingled. It stopped at the threshold to what appeared to be the kitchen and peered at Josie with striking green eyes.

Following Josie's gaze, Hallie said, "Oh, that's Flynn. She doesn't really like people."

"She's beautiful," said Josie.

The cat lifted a paw and licked it several times, all the while keeping her eye on Josie.

"Thanks," Hallie said. "She's a Russian Blue. I like her because she doesn't shed much. She really doesn't like company, though. I can't believe she's still in the room. She must like you."

As if to dispel her owner of that notion, Flynn scuttled off, disappearing into the kitchen. The bell jangled again.

"I guess I was wrong." Hallie laughed nervously. She ran her fingers through her short dark hair twice before clasping her hands in her lap. Her knuckles whitened. Breathlessly, she said, "Thank you so much for coming. I really appreciate it. You have no idea what this means to me."

Trinity smiled, turning on the charm that had won her millions of fans during her career on television. "It's my pleasure, Hallie. I'm just sorry it took so long for this meeting to happen. I hope you don't mind, but I've brought—"

Interrupting, Hallie said, "I know who she is—your sister. Josie Quinn. I recognize her from TV. I watched your *Dateline* episodes. I'm excited to meet you, too."

Josie forced a smile. "Hallie, I'm here about two current cases that I'm working in my own jurisdiction which I believe might have a connection to what happened to Jana."

"Someone from your department called me yesterday," she said.

"Yes," Josie said. "That would have been Detective Gretchen Palmer. I've got a few more questions. I can't tell you many details, but I'd like your permission to listen to your conversation with Trinity and perhaps ask some of my own questions."

Hallie smiled. "Absolutely. Where should we start?"

Trinity took her file folder out of her messenger bag and held it on her lap. "First, I want to thank you for sending the file you compiled. There's so much here. It's rare that we start out with so many documents."

Hallie smiled. "My friend Bella helped me. Bella Crooke. Like I told you, she worked in records at the police department." Her smile faltered. "I forgot to ask you the last time we talked— you don't have to reveal that she was the one who got me all these reports and things, do you?"

"No," said Trinity. "I don't."

"You don't need to talk to her, do you? 'Cause she was already nervous about helping me. Although since she's retired, it probably doesn't matter."

"No need to talk with her," Trinity reassured. She patted the folder. "All I need is what you've already provided. However, I do feel that there are a lot of things from the file that your friend wasn't able to get. I'm trying to obtain them but for now, maybe you can help. Jana did live with you at the time of her death, right?"

"Yes, Jana and Mathias, we all lived together as a family." She waved a hand around the room. "Not here. I had to leave that place a few years ago. Landlord sold the building."

"To your knowledge," Trinity asked, "did the police look into Jana at all? Check her phone? Talk to her friends? Coworkers? Anyone she went to school with?"

"Oh," said Hallie. "You mean did they actually investigate the circumstances of her death, or did they just call it an accident and move on?"

Trinity smiled. "Precisely."

"They looked pretty closely at her life, from what I remember, especially after Mathias told them that she had said she was meeting someone the night she died. That was a big deal. They thought if they could find that person, they'd find her killer. I did, too. I still don't know how they never found anyone. They had her phone. I know they looked at that. I could never get it back. Never got any of it back. They came to our place and searched her room. They took some things. She was studying biology at school. She wanted to go into medicine, study genetics. That's why she took the job at that doctor's office as a receptionist. Anyway, they took her textbooks, some papers she had written, her laptop. My understanding is that they never found anything. Like I said, my friend Bella had access to the file. She reviewed it and told me she didn't see that they'd found any leads. I mean, if they had, we wouldn't be talking right now, would we?"

Josie tried to recall what reports Trinity had shown her. "How about friends and coworkers? Do you know if the police interviewed any of those people?"

Hallie gave a slow nod. "Bella said there were some reports of interviews, yes."

"But none discussed the identity of the person Mathias said Jana was meeting that night?" Josie said.

"No. Not that I'm aware of."

Trinity said, "What about you, Hallie? Do you have any thoughts as to who it could have been?"

Hallie's eyes landed on the photos next to Josie. Lines creased her forehead. "I don't know. It's bothered me so much all this time. Jana told me everything. I mean, I was her mother! Well, sort of. Mostly. She would come home and tell me every little detail about her day. I knew everything."

Josie didn't point out that—particularly in her experience as a police officer—teenagers did not, in fact, tell their parents or even their mothers everything. Although parents almost always assumed they did.

"Then why wouldn't she have told you she was meeting someone that night?" asked Trinity gently.

Hallie swiped a knuckle beneath one of her eyes, catching a tear before it could roll down her cheek. Her voice was husky. "The only thing I can think of is that she was looking for her birth parents and she thought that if she told me, it would hurt my feelings. Maybe she didn't want me to be insulted. After all, she barely remembered our foster parents from before. We really were her parents, Mathias and I. Maybe she didn't want us to think she was ungrateful by trying to find them. I won't lie. I would have felt sad and maybe scared for her in terms of what she might find out, but I wish she had told me. I could have helped her. I did find everyone I could after she died—distant relatives. They didn't care about her. Had never been in touch. That was a dead end."

Josie said, "This is probably a long shot, but have you ever spoken with the gas station clerk that night? Maybe she talked with Jana while she was making her purchases?"

Hallie rolled her eyes. "You mean Carolina Eddy, drug addict and pathological liar?"

"You did talk with her?" asked Josie.

Beside her, Trinity was writing Carolina's name down and began searching the file folder for mention of her.

Hallie laced her fingers together and began twisting them in her lap. "Of course I did, the very next night when Mathias and I were looking for Jana. We went back to the gas station to find out if Jana had maybe come back or if Carolina had heard or seen anything. She said she didn't know anything, but she's got a reputation in town for lying. Who knows what she really saw or heard? She kept working there for a long time after Jana died. From time to time, I'd go in there and chat her up, try to see if she'd change up her story. Tell me the truth."

Trinity found the report and drew a star beside Carolina's

name. "You think this Carolina Eddy was lying about what she saw or heard the night Jana went missing?"

Hallie shrugged. "I don't know! That's the whole point. I could never believe her."

"Did her story ever change?" asked Josie.

Hallie shook her head, shoulders slumping. "No. It never did."

"Okay," said Josie, changing the subject. "Was Jana seeing anyone when she died?"

"No. She was completely into her studies. Like I said, she told me everything. She wasn't dating anyone."

Trinity said, "Hallie, I know you believe that Jana was murdered. Who do you think killed her?"

Hallie was silent for several seconds. Somewhere, far off in another room, a bell tinkled and then something made a thud. Ignoring it, Hallie said, "I don't know. I think it had to be this mystery person she had gone to meet, don't you? That seems like the most obvious explanation. I mean, I suppose it could have been random, or maybe someone she knew, but if it was someone she knew, wouldn't they have come under suspicion by now?"

Josie recognized the frown on Trinity's face. She wanted to point out the obvious—Mathias had come under suspicion precisely because he knew her and also because the mystery person that he claimed Jana told him about never materialized— but there was no way to say it without sounding insensitive. Instead, Trinity moved on. "I know that you want to find out what happened to Jana, and having reviewed the materials you provided for me, I agree with you that she was murdered. Now, there is nothing in this file to prove that except that her head injuries were so severe that I find it difficult to believe she sustained them in a fall."

"Yes!" Hallie exclaimed. Her body sagged with relief, fingers going still.

"Because I believe that Jana was murdered," Trinity said. "I'm prepared to do an episode of our show on her case."

"Oh, thank God," said Hallie. Her eyes were glassy with unshed tears. "I've waited so long and fought so hard to try to make things right. Every year it seems like more and more people forget about Jana. They stop caring. It's like—it's like she never mattered. Like our little family never mattered at all." Unlacing her fingers, she pressed a hand to her chest as the tears gleaming in her eyes fell down her cheeks. "It matters to me."

Trinity reached across and squeezed one of Hallie's hands. "I know, Hallie. I know it does. That's why I'm here. That said, you have to understand that there are no guarantees that an episode will help her case at all. Sometimes we uncover new information which leads to a case being solved, or we get a tip as a result of the show that then leads to the case being resolved. But most of the time, nothing happens. We do the episode and in spite of tips, we're left with exactly what we started with— and in Jana's case, it's not much."

"I understand," Hallie sniffled. "I'm willing to take the chance. I'm okay if nothing comes from it. I just want Jana to have a fighting chance."

Trinity smiled again. "Wonderful. Now, let's talk about Mathias. I know you believe that he didn't hurt Jana. But Hallie, I think there is a possibility that Mathias was responsible for Jana's death. I need to know that you're mentally prepared to face that if that is where all this leads."

Stricken, Hallie's face paled. She wiped her tears away. With her hands back in her lap, her fingers intertwined and twisted again. "Mathias did not hurt her. He would never hurt anyone."

Trinity said, "You told me yourself that he was accused of rape while he was in high school. Not once but three times."

"Yes, because you would have found out anyway and I

thought you should hear it from me, but he didn't hurt those girls. I'm telling you, he's never hurt anyone."

Josie wondered if Keri Cryer had known about the history of accusations against Mathias. Surely something like that would have come up during his trial for shooting Piper. Had Keri always believed in his innocence, like Hallie did? Josie said, "My understanding is that those girls simply recanted their statements. He wasn't proven innocent."

Hallie shook her head vigorously. "This damn town and its rumors. Every time something happens here, it's like that stupid child's game, Whisper Down the Lane, except that the person who starts doesn't have any facts at all."

Josie leaned forward, her elbows on her knees. "Tell us the facts, then, Hallie."

TWENTY-SEVEN

Hallie's knuckles blanched as she continued to fidget with them. For a moment, Josie worried that she might snap one of her fingers. From the direction of the kitchen came another noise like something had been knocked over, followed by the jingle of Flynn's tiny bell. Hallie didn't take any notice. Her eyes were locked on the photographs beside Josie.

"Take your time," Trinity added soothingly. "We're here to listen." She took out a legal pad and pen. "If you don't mind, I'd like to take notes."

Snapped back to the present, Hallie gave her a wan smile and nodded. "The rape allegations. Right. The assaults took place at parties, after games. There's a place around here, out in the woods, where kids go to party. Everyone knows about it. Even the adults know about it, but they don't bother to stop it. Like the football coach! He knew about it but he never said a word about the players going there. Anyway, one of the girls was assaulted there. It was dark and she'd gotten drunk and wandered away from the group. A few days after it happened, she told her parents, who had her go to the police. After that, someone who was at the party said they saw Mathias coming from the direction of where the girl had been assaulted. She told the police it was Mathias. Once it got out that she had gone to the police, two other girls came forward and said they'd been assaulted the year before under similar circumstances. They also said it was Mathias."

"What made them change their stories?" asked Josie.

"The case was going to trial. Mathias got a defense attorney from the public defender's office. Once he got discovery, he saw how flimsy the evidence was—there wasn't even DNA. They all initially reported that it was too dark, and they were too intoxicated to see well and then later they changed their statements to say that Mathias had done it. Anyway, the attorney was pretty certain that he'd be able to cast doubt on their testimony at trial."

"But it never got that far," Trinity said. "Did it?"

"No. The defense attorney was able to prove that in the two cases from the year before, Mathias was at work at the time those assaults occurred. They had time cards from his employer. He wasn't even on the team yet!"

"What about the other girl?" asked Josie. "The one who reported a few days after her assault?"

"During the preparation for the trial, she decided not to move forward. She said she could not say for sure that Mathias was the person who hurt her."

"But he was there that night," Trinity pressed. "Just like he was with Jana the night she was killed."

Hallie made a noise of exasperation. She stood and left the room. From somewhere in the house, Flynn's tiny bell rang again. Moments later, Hallie returned with a large photo album, its cover blue and cracked. She handed it to Trinity. "I know that no one prints photos anymore, but Jana liked having a physical photo album."

Josie looked on as Trinity paged through the album. Some photos were of young children with an older couple. As the kids got older, she recognized both Mathias and Hallie. Then another child appeared—about four years old, chubby and blonde. As she got older, it became clear that they were watching Jana grow up. At some point the couple disappeared, and the majority of the photos showed an adolescent Jana with teenagers Hallie and Mathias. The background changed as well, from a rustic-looking home to a cramped apartment. There were duplicate photos of the ones Trinity had in her file and the two that were framed on Hallie's end table. There were a few photos of just Hallie and Jana, but the majority of the album was filled with pictures of Mathias and Jana. Him reading to her; playing video games with her; helping her with homework; making crafts with her; giving and receiving a home manicure—with Mathias smiling widely as he showed off his blood-red nails. It was typical, Josie thought. The mom was rarely in any photos because she was always behind the camera.

Hallie stood over them as Trinity slowly flipped the pages. "I know what you're going to say: Mathias was accused of sexual assault, accused of Jana's murder, and then accused of shooting his own wife. But I'm telling you that he would never hurt anyone. He is gentle and decent. I've known him since we were children. You can see that. You can see how much he cared about Jana. When our foster mother died, he didn't have to take us in. He was out already. He certainly didn't have the resources to help me raise Jana, but he did it anyway. We were happy. We were a family. I don't just want to convince the police that Jana was murdered, and find her real killer, I want to clear Mathias's name."

Trinity closed the photo album and handed it back to Hallie, who hugged it to her chest as she returned to her chair. Flynn's bell, sounding more loudly now, announced her arrival. She dashed from the kitchen doorway to beneath Hallie's chair, peeking out at Josie and Trinity from between her legs.

"Hallie," Trinity said carefully. "When we were corresponding by email and when we spoke on the phone, you talked about Mathias, but you never told me that he went to prison for shooting his wife in the head."

Hallie's eyes went wide. Her fingertips dug into the cracked vinyl cover of the photo album. "He didn't do it. He did not do that. He was exonerated." With each statement, her voice rose an octave.

In a mild tone, Josie said, "What do you know about his wife's shooting?"

"We weren't able to find much information," Trinity added. "The press coverage of things in this area is practically non-existent."

Hallie's fingers relaxed. She stood and put the album onto the fireplace mantel under the television before resuming her seat. "I know. Bradysport gets all the headlines. No one cares what happens out here in the county."

"Start at the beginning," Trinity urged. "How did Mathias and his wife meet?"

"They were both working at the tractor supply place. He had been there a long time, and I guess she quit college or whatever so she started working there, too. They worked together for a long time before they started dating. They kept it a secret as long as they could."

"Why keep it a secret?" asked Trinity.

Josie remembered what Anya had said about her affair with Cyrus. His daughter had just dropped out of college at that time. Anya hadn't specified what year she'd been in but the oldest she could possibly be, assuming she started college at eighteen, was twenty-two, which meant that Mathias was significantly older than her. "They had an age gap, didn't they? He was a lot older than her."

Trinity shot her a look but didn't ask how she knew this.

Hallie shifted in her seat, crossing and uncrossing her legs.

"The gap was ten years, yeah. But I don't think that's why they kept it secret."

"Really?" Trinity said. "Ten years is a big gap."

"Maybe," Hallie said. "But they were adults when they met. I guess some people might find it weird, but really, that wasn't the reason they kept it secret. The real reason was that Piper's dad is a cop." Pausing, a blush crept up her face. She looked at Josie. "No offense."

Josie smiled. "None taken."

Hallie was right. Lots of people in relationships had age gaps. It wasn't uncommon. By Josie's estimation, there had been at least ten years between Anya and Cyrus when they'd had their affair, although Anya was already in her thirties by then. Still, Josie was certain the reason Mathias and Piper had kept their relationship under wraps had less to do with Cyrus being a cop and more to do with the accusations and rumors that followed Mathias everywhere. "Were they dating when Jana died?"

"No. They met after that. I think a year after she died, maybe? I know that they eloped two years after she died because it was right around the anniversary of her death. I was really upset with him at the time."

"Because he eloped?" Trinity asked.

From between Hallie's feet, Flynn pawed at the laces of her sneakers. Hallie reached down to shoo her away, but Flynn was undeterred. "No. I never cared about how he got married. That was his business. I just didn't understand how he could do it so close to the date of Jana's death. It felt wrong. On the first anniversary of her death, he and I had made a point to spend the day together. We had lunch at Jana's favorite restaurant and then we visited her grave and brought flowers. It helped us get through the day because we did it together, just like we spent almost ten years of our lives raising her like our own child. I just assumed that's how we would spend the anniversary of her death every year. I was blindsided when I found out he'd chosen to elope that day instead. He told me it didn't mean anything, that he hadn't chosen that date on purpose—they'd just decided to go for it. I could never understand how the date of her death meant so little to him, but what do I know?"

"Did Piper's dad find out that they'd eloped?" asked Josie.

Flynn kept clawing at the laces of Hallie's left sneaker until they were completely loose. Again, Hallie tried to stop her but was ignored. "Oh, yeah. Once they were married, they didn't bother to keep it a secret anymore. Piper's dad went ballistic. Then, to make matters worse, all her friends stopped talking to her."

"Why?" asked Trinity.

"Those stupid rumors. He was a rapist. A killer. He'd been getting away with it for years. That's what people said. Everyone in town thought the worst of him. None of it was true but that didn't matter. He even got let go from the tractor supply place shortly after they married because all those rumors kicked back up again. His boss thought he was too distracting. He had a hard time finding work after that. He'd get hired at a place, work there a few weeks, and when someone figured out his connection to Jana, he'd get fired again and be back out trying to find something. In fact, he was out looking for work one day and when he came home, Piper was on the kitchen floor, bleeding everywhere. He called 911 and the cops arrested him."

"What about the gun?" Josie asked. "Was it recovered?"

Flynn went to work on Hallie's other sneaker. Hallie didn't even try to stop her this time. "It was there. It was hers. She always had a gun. Her dad had taught her to shoot and bought her a pistol for self-defense. The police said it was a domestic dispute and that Mathias had shot her. Of course his prints were on it because it was their gun. It's not like he'd never touched it. Not that they looked very hard, or at all, but the police never found any other suspects."

Trinity said, "He didn't have an alibi?"

Hallie twisted her fingers together again. A flush crept up her face. Flynn continued to bat at her loose shoelaces. "Yes. He did. He was at the Hadlee Family Farm that afternoon, looking for work. He thought with Dermot having been his football coach and all, maybe he'd give him a job on the farm. Dermot said he'd think it over and yet when the police went to him to verify Mathias's alibi, Dermot told them that he hadn't seen him in years."

Trinity raised a brow. "This guy Dermot—his old coach—he lied?"

"Yes. I don't know why. We've never known why."

Having met Dermot, Josie was sure he had had his reasons. "Maybe Dermot lied for the same reason that the boss at the tractor supply fired Mathias. He didn't want the farm's reputation to be tarnished," Josie said.

Even as she said it, discomfort tickled the back of her neck. It was one thing to not give a person a job because you didn't want them associated with your business. It was entirely another thing to lie about something inconsequential and send someone to prison for a serious crime they hadn't committed. "Was Dermot Hadlee still on the town council back then?"

"Yes," said Hallie. She kicked off both sneakers and gently pushed them to the side so that Flynn could have full control over them. Immediately, the cat started wrestling with Hallie's left sneaker, her little bell tinkling.

Trinity looked over at Josie and then jotted down some notes.

Josie thought about how Carolina Eddy had been bullied into leaving town. How the citizens had wanted her to tell a white lie to send Mathias to prison because they believed he'd already gotten away with rape. Had Dermot been of the same mind after Piper Tobin's shooting? Had he considered Mathias a stain on the town and just wanted to get rid of him?

Trinity asked, "Mathias hired Downey, Downey & O'Neill to defend him. From what I've been able to glean in my internet research, they're a very experienced defense firm. It seems like they would have looked pretty hard for other suspects."

Hallie watched as Flynn dragged her sneaker toward the kitchen. "They would have, and they did when he finally hired them. When Mathias was first arrested, he had another public defender. Neither of us had money for a good lawyer. Downey, Downey & O'Neill came into the picture after he'd been in prison for a few years."

"Did you visit him in prison?" Trinity asked.

"Every weekend," said Hallie. "He was up near Erie so it was about a six-hour drive each way, but there was no way I was letting him rot in there alone. I told him I'd do everything I could to prove his innocence."

Josie asked, "You were the one who hired Downey, Downey & O'Neill?"

"Oh no. I still didn't have the money for that. I'd been trying to find a good firm that would take his appeal pro bono, but no one wanted to touch it. Then one day I went to visit him at the prison, and he told me that he'd gotten someone. I asked him how and he said not to worry about it. I was so happy, I didn't. I just wanted him to come home, and he seemed pretty confident about this firm."

Josie said, "Did you ever meet anyone from the firm?"

"Yes. Throughout the process I did meet his attorney."

"How about any of the paralegals?" Josie pressed. "Did you ever meet someone named Keri Cryer?"

She could feel Trinity's eyes burning a hole in the side of her face, but she ignored it.

Hallie gave a faltering smile. "I think. I don't know. There was a woman on the staff there that Mathias thought was really pretty and nice. He talked about her a lot. That might have been her name."

Before Josie could ask more questions, Trinity said, "But Mathias wasn't set free on appeal, he was exonerated, thanks to exculpatory evidence. I couldn't get any of the trial or hearing transcripts or the file from the DA—assuming they'd even give it to me—before we met." She turned and looked pointedly at Josie. "Maybe you have some of the files?"

Josie said, "No, I don't have any of the files. My department could not get anything from the law firm."

Satisfied, Trinity turned back to Hallie. "Without information from either the prosecutor or Mathias's attorney, I'm at a loss. Just like with Jana's case, neither Piper's shooting nor Mathias's exoneration were covered in the press. Do you know what the exculpatory evidence was?"

"A witness," Hallie answered. "He came forward and said that he'd seen Mathias at the time that Piper was murdered. Evidently, he hadn't come forward earlier because the police had never talked with him, but it was enough to free Mathias."

Josie said, "Where is Mathias now?"

Hallie frowned. "I don't know. Your colleague—Detective Palmer, you said? She called me yesterday to ask if I knew where he was or how to get in touch with him. I honestly don't know. I haven't seen him in months. When he got out, he stayed at a halfway house in Bradysport. I couldn't believe it. All those years of me driving out to Erie to visit him. All those years of us living together as a family before that, and he would not come home to me." She waved a hand around the room. "I mean, this is his home as much as it is mine. Believe me, I wanted him to come stay with me, but he said that he couldn't. The last time I spoke with him, which was about a month or two after he got out, he said he couldn't see me again until he had cleared his name."

"Why not?" Trinity asked.

"It wasn't safe. That's what he told me. He said when he cleared his name once and for all, we could be a family again. Then he disappeared. His phone number was disconnected soon after that. He never went back to the halfway house. I've been looking all over for him. I have no idea where he is or if he's even alive. I hope he is." Tears formed in her eyes. She swallowed. Flynn abandoned the sneaker near the kitchen doorway and sauntered back to Hallie, rubbing her body against Hallie's shins. "He's all I've got left."

Josie said, "Hallie, my team recently discovered that he's been staying in Denton."

Confusion creased her forehead. "Denton? We don't know anyone in Denton."

"Keri Cryer," Josie said. "She was a paralegal with Downey, Downey & O'Neill. Evidently she had worked on his case. They've been dating. He was staying with her. He was last seen there Thursday."

Flynn leapt up into Hallie's lap, nudging her hands to be petted. "Last seen? If he was there, can't you just ask her where he went? I really need to talk to him. I need to see him. I need to tell him about Trinity and the show."

"We can't ask Keri," Josie said. "Because she was murdered."

Hallie's hands lifted to cover her mouth. In her lap, Flynn froze, staring up at her. Voice muffled behind her hands, she said, "Oh my God. What happened?"

"I'm not at liberty to say," Josie replied.

Through gritted teeth, in a voice low enough for only Josie to hear, Trinity said, "I can't believe you kept this from me."

Josie said, "Hallie, is there any place that Mathias would go if he was in trouble?"

Slowly she shook her head. Lowering her hands to stroke Flynn's back, she said, "Here. He would come here. But I haven't seen him."

"All right," Josie said. "What I need you to do is to contact me immediately if Mathias comes here or contacts you somehow. Can you do that?"

Hallie leaned forward to take the business card that Josie offered her. "Of course," she said. Then, looking at Trinity, she added, "Will you still do an episode of your show on Jana's case? It's really important to me. I need your help to clear Mathias's name so he can come home once and for all."

Trinity's smile was sympathetic. "Yes. I'm still interested in doing the show. Just remember, Hallie, I can't make promises, but I'll do my best to present a clear and compelling episode about Jana's case that will hopefully generate some leads."

Josie said, "Hallie, who was the witness that came forward in Piper's case?"

"It was Dermot's son, Vance Hadlee."

TWENTY-EIGHT

Josie pulled away from Hallie's home, acid burning in her stomach. In the passenger's seat, Trinity scribbled like mad on her legal pad. A brief glance told Josie she was jotting down more questions. Endless questions. She'd interrogated Hallie about Vance Hadlee but all she'd managed to find out was what they already knew: his family owned a farm nearby and that he and Mathias had played football together at Bly Hollow High School with Dermot as their coach. If there had been talk of what Vance had done to Anya or anything at all about his marriage, it hadn't reached Hallie or she hadn't deemed it important enough to discuss.

While Trinity finished the interview, Josie texted the team. She wasn't sure what any of it meant but it seemed important—and strange—that Vance Hadlee had come forward to exonerate Mathias Tobin in his wife's shooting. Had Vance told the truth? Had Mathias really been at the farm to ask Dermot for a job the day that Piper was killed? Had Vance seen him? If he had, why not come forward immediately? Even as the question entered her mind, Josie knew the answer: Dermot wouldn't allow it.

Dermot controlled everything, and for whatever reason, he didn't want Mathias to be exonerated. Josie worked through the timing in her mind. Vance had only come forward months ago. Lark had told them that Dermot had had his stroke last year. Mathias had been freed seven months earlier—also last year. Was it possible that Vance felt emboldened to go against his father's wishes after the stroke and set Mathias free? Josie wondered if Lark knew anything about this or could shed light on it. Finding out would require getting her alone—no easy feat.

Regardless, Mathias had gone free.

Was it a coincidence that the recent murders in Denton started after Mathias was released from prison? No, it didn't make sense. To Josie's knowledge, Mathias would have had no way of knowing about Anya's brand.

Josie stopped at a red light, drawn out of her thoughts by the silence in the vehicle. She glanced over at Trinity. "Are you going to be speaking to me?"

Without looking up, she said, "I'm not going to lie. It upsets me that you've got information that I don't that could be relevant to what I'm working on. However, I do understand that you've got a job to do, the same as me. I've been in this business long enough to know that law enforcement can't tell journalists everything. I respect that. I can't promise not to look into this Keri Cryer thing in connection with Mathias, but in terms of my episode on Jana Melburn? It's got nothing to do with it. Whatever he did or didn't do after Jana's death isn't going to help me figure out what really happened to her—whether it was an accident or not. I want to keep the focus on Jana for now."

"Thank you," said Josie. The light changed and she began driving once more.

Trinity tapped her pen against her window. "That's the gas station where Mathias and Jana had their last conversation."

Josie made a noise of acknowledgment and glanced over. A familiar black pickup truck sat next to one of the pumps. Josie slowed and craned her neck to try to get a glimpse of the owner at the pump. Dermot Hadlee. They locked eyes for a brief moment. He glowered, head turning slowly as she drove past. If there was any doubt as to whether he recognized her from the search of his farm, his menacing expression put it to rest. Josie looked over to see if Trinity had noticed him, but her head was bent to her pad again.

Josie sped away from the gas station. She tried to put Dermot out of her mind, focusing instead on Vance Hadlee coming forward as a witness to exonerate Mathias. Even if she was right and Vance had only come forward after Dermot had been weakened by a stroke, why? He did not strike Josie as the altruistic type. Also, although Vance and Mathias had been on the same football team for a year, no one they'd spoken with yet had ever suggested that the two were friends. Hallie had not indicated that they were ever close. According to Anya, they hadn't been. So why would Vance come forward after Mathias had spent years in prison and swear that Mathias had been with him when Piper was shot?

Trinity looked up briefly and pointed her pen. "Turn left here. The place where they found Jana is about a mile from here."

On autopilot, Josie made the turn. Had Vance really seen Mathias at the farm at the time that Piper was shot? Or had he lied to get Mathias out of prison? And if he had lied, why?

"Make a right here," Trinity said, waving her pen at the windshield again. "This is the road."

There was simply no way that Vance had helped Mathias get out of prison out of the goodness of his heart. Either Vance had gotten something out of it, or he owed Mathias for something. They couldn't find Mathias to ask him about it. Keri Cryer might have known something—maybe Mathias had confided in her—but now she was dead.

"Slow down," Trinity said. "It's coming up in a half mile.

Hallie said there used to be a marker. A cross. The township keeps taking it down, but she puts it back up every time."

Josie tried to shake off her questions so she could concentrate on the road ahead. It was narrow, only one lane in each direction. To Josie's left was a rock face where the township had cut into the side of a mountain to make the road. On the other side, trees flashed past. In February their branches were barren, allowing glimpses of Lake Latchwood at the bottom of a steep drop-off. Josie wondered if Jana had attempted to walk this road in the dark on her way to meet the mystery person Mathias claimed existed, or if her killer had simply dumped her here after the fact. It seemed a treacherous road in broad daylight.

"Up there," Trinity said. "I think I see it."

Ahead Josie spotted a pink plastic cross affixed to a tree on the shoulder of the road. Her foot pumped the brakes as she searched for a place to pull over. The roar of an engine drew her attention.

"What is that?" Trinity asked.

In the rearview mirror, a big black pickup truck barreled toward them, going at least twice the speed limit. "Shit," said Josie.

There was a small spot to pull over, but it was on the opposite side of the road, against the cliff face. The roar got louder. Josie swerved into the oncoming lane and the truck followed.

Trinity's voice was high-pitched. "What are you doing?"

"Hold on," said Josie, jerking her SUV back into their lane. Again, the truck followed.

Trinity turned her upper body, craning to see behind them. "My God," she said. "He's going to cause an accident."

"I think that's the point," Josie muttered. She jerked the steering wheel back and forth again, but the truck stayed tight on her tail.

"What a psycho!" Trinity said. Her phone was in her hands. "I'm calling 911. This guy is going to kill someone."

I think that's the point. Josie thought. The truck bumped the rear of the SUV, giving them a jolt. Trinity let out a yelp. Josie felt the tug of the truck, pulling her vehicle back even as she sped up. The front of the truck had caught on the back of her SUV. As she pressed her foot harder onto the gas pedal, metal screeched. Something gave and the SUV surged ahead. It afforded her a few precious seconds to get ahead of the truck. Her lead didn't last long. Peering into her side mirror, she watched in horror as the truck got closer and closer, bearing down on them until she could make out the face of a man behind the wheel.

Dermot Hadlee.

His eyes glowed with rage. One corner of his mouth was slack while the other curled in a sneer.

Into her phone, Trinity said, "We're driving in a blue Ford Escape on Latchwood Cove Road. There's someone behind us. He's chasing us—"

The truck slammed into the back of them once more, sending their upper bodies whipping forward. Trinity's phone flew out of her hands.

Josie said, "Hang on."

Again, she pressed her foot against the gas pedal as far as it would go. The SUV felt like its rear was dragging somehow but still it lurched forward, surging ahead of the truck once more. This time, as soon as she had a car's length between them, she jerked the wheel to the right and slammed on the brakes, bringing them to an abrupt stop. Trinity screamed, bracing both hands against the dashboard.

"Are you crazy?"

The truck flew past them. Josie noted the license plate as it, too, screeched to a stop. Then she pumped the gas again, yanking at the steering wheel as she did, trying to turn the SUV around the way they'd come. Trinity's head was between her legs as she searched the floor for her phone. The truck's reverse lights came on. Josie kept it in her periphery as the front of the SUV kissed the guardrail along the side of the road. It was too narrow for her to turn around in one continuous movement. She'd have to do a three-point turn. Throwing the shifter into reverse, she started to back up as quickly as she could. She heard something clatter onto the roadway. The rear tires hit the object hard and then rolled over it, bucking them almost out of their seats. The back of Trinity's head smacked against the underside of the dash. The strap of Josie's seatbelt cut into her collarbone.

Sickness rolled through her stomach as she realized her rear bumper had fallen off. She'd just backed over it. It was stuck under the SUV.

"Shit," she said.

They were sitting ducks, their vehicle sideways across the two lanes of traffic. Josie shifted into drive and tried to accelerate but the tires only squealed, stuck on the bumper. As she tried to maneuver around it in the tight space between the rock face on one side and the guardrail on the other, she noticed that the truck was surging toward them in reverse, getting closer with each second. Then it stopped. For a fleeting moment, Josie paused her efforts, hoping they were safe, but then it started moving again, turning until it was parallel to them and then again so that the front of it faced them. There were no impediments to its three-point turn. Dermot's pale face was a smudge behind the windshield as the truck picked up speed, now a missile pointed right at them. Trinity's head popped up. Her phone was in her hands, but her eyes peered out her window at the approaching truck. "Josie!" she screamed.

Josie jammed her foot against the gas pedal so hard that it ached. The SUV bucked a few times before it finally heaved over the top of the bumper. But it was too late. As she tried to guide the steering wheel into the final part of the turn—toward escape—the truck punched into the rear passenger's side of her vehicle.

Then it kept coming.

Josie tried to control the direction of the SUV while the truck pushed into it, but it was like trying to wrestle a giant. The wheel slipped out of her grip. The vehicle spun. She tried to accelerate away from the truck, but it simply changed direction, sending them flying toward the guardrail faster. She tried to brake but it was no use.

"Josie!" Trinity screamed again.

The front bumper burst through the guardrail, making a shrieking sound. The hood of the SUV tipped downward. Josie felt the loss of control. Weightlessness. Then the whole world spun feet over head. Glass shattered. Her sister cried out. The seatbelt cut across her torso like a knife. Something hard made contact with her head. Before the windshield cracked in a thousand places, Josie saw a kaleidoscope tumble before her eyes. Water, rocks, trees, sky, trees, rocks, water. Her arms flailed to find something stable but there was nothing.

The final impact jarred her entire body and left her hanging upside down.

Time slowed. There was a rushing sound in her ears. Reaching up, she braced both her hands against the ceiling of the SUV, immediately feeling an ache in one of her shoulders. Next to her, Trinity hung limply.

"Trin," Josie said. It came out much quieter than she had intended. It was hard to talk while hanging upside down with a seatbelt cutting across your upper body. It was hard to breathe.

"Trin!" Stronger this time.

First, there was a whimper that sent a surge of relief through her, adrenaline numbing the pain that felt like it had infiltrated every cell in Josie's body. Trinity's hair swung, then her arms. One braced against the ceiling just as Josie had done. The other reached up and disappeared into her lap.

"Trinity," Josie said. "Are you okay?"

Panic edged into her voice. "I'm stuck. My foot is stuck. I can't move it."

"It's okay," Josie said. "It's okay. I think I can get out. I'll help you."

Josie took one hand off the ceiling so she could search for the seatbelt release. It took several seconds. Each one felt like an hour. Trinity's breath was labored. Whether from panic or some sort of injury, Josie couldn't tell. "Calm down," she told her sister. "I'm almost out."

The release button clicked beneath her fingers. The seatbelt snapped back. Josie's body fell, crumpling in a confused heap of limbs. Her head pressed awkwardly against where the ceiling met the windshield. She maneuvered herself so that she was at least, mercifully, no longer upside down. Dizziness took over as the blood that had rushed to her head drained into her lower body. Searching overhead, her fingers fumbled for the door handle, finding it and tugging at it. It took a few pushes and kicks to get the door open.

Trinity's voice dropped to a whisper. "Josie. Josie! Someone's coming. He's coming."

Josie was half out of the car, the lake water lapping at her feet. She stopped and listened. It was hard to hear over the pounding of her own heart, but there was definitely something or someone moving toward them on the bank.

Trinity's voice was high and squeaky. "Boots, Josie. I see boots."

"Hang on."

She stumbled out of the car, falling forward into the freezing lake. Water sloshed up and down her front, splashing into her face. Luckily it wasn't deep where she'd landed so she was able to brace herself against some rocks under the water. Quickly, she staggered to her feet and whipped around. One hand reached for her pistol, relieved when her fingers found its grip. She unsnapped the holster and drew it, moving around the vehicle to where Trinity was suspended. A sitting duck. A curtain of red fell over her vision. Hot fluid spilled from her scalp down her face. Her eyes burned. Blinking didn't help. As she rounded the front tires of the SUV, she saw, through the bloody haze, a large figure leaning down, extending a hand through Trinity's window.

Josie pointed her pistol at it. "Stop!" she commanded. "Get the hell away from my sister. Now."

The figure straightened and turned toward her, both hands held aloft, palms empty and facing her. "Just relax," he said. "I'm not going to hurt you."

Josie blinked again but more hot red moisture poured into her eyes.

The man said, "You're bleeding. A lot. Put that down and let me help you. That's why I'm here."

He came closer until she could finally make out his face. Cyrus Grey.

"Don't come any closer," she told him, trying to hold the pistol steady.

"I have to come closer, Detective. I'm afraid if you lose any more blood, you'll pass out."

She was chagrined to find out that he was right. Her entire body felt weak and unsteady, although it was more likely from the shock of being in a car wreck than blood loss. She couldn't give in just yet. "How did you know we were here?" Josie demanded.

He sighed in exactly the same way he'd sighed when Mettner had insisted on pressing charges against Vance Hadlee for possessing firearms. "One of you made a 911 call. I've got more officers en route plus a couple of ambulances. I was the closest. That's why I'm here now."

Trying to fight her overwhelming dizziness and fatigue, Josie hesitated until she heard Trinity cry out for help. When she heard a siren on the road above, she lowered her pistol and collapsed, sliding down into the bed of stones.

TWENTY-NINE

The emergency department of the small community hospital looked like every other emergency department Josie had ever been in: a waiting room that smelled like vomit and chemicals with cracked vinyl chairs and half-filled vending machines; curtained-off treatment areas; nurses striding from place to place with purpose; and patients in various states of agony, one of whom groaned loudly and continuously no matter what the medical staff offered. Behind a faded pink curtain, Josie lay on a gurney beneath five hospital blankets, holding gauze over the slice in her forehead. She had no idea how much time had passed. Her phone was lost. A nurse had come in and gotten her out of her freezing wet clothes, helping her change into hospital gowns—one opening in the front with the second one over the top of it opening in the back—and covering her up with as many blankets as she could find. After that, she asked Josie a number of questions while cleaning her face with saline and gauze pads. Many, many gauze pads. A doctor had come after, probing at the wound and flushing it out until it burned. Eyes watering, Josie resisted the urge to shove him away. He promised to return in order to give her stitches.

Her heart thudded in her chest. She hated hospitals. In her experience, nothing good had ever happened in a hospital. But this—laying beneath the glare of fluorescent lights, waiting for a doctor to put stitches into her face—brought her back to when she was six years old. The woman who had taken her from her real family and posed as her mother had tried to slice Josie's face off. Needle, or as she tried to remember to call him, Zeke, had walked in as the knife blade reached Josie's chin. In a rare moment of concern, he'd insisted Lila take Josie to the emergency room. Lila had, of course, lied about how the injury had happened, scaring Josie into keeping the secret. It had taken twenty-seven stitches to close the physical wound.

The emotional wound still festered.

Josie tried to do her four-seven-eight breathing exercise, but her body wouldn't calm down long enough to keep the breath in her lungs for a whole seven seconds. She tried to shift focus, tuning into the din outside her treatment area, her ears listening for Trinity's voice. She knew Trinity wasn't seriously injured because she hadn't stopped talking the entire ambulance ride, but she didn't know where the staff had taken her once they arrived. Her heartbeat sped up when she couldn't find Trinity's voice right away. Then came the ding of an elevator, the whoosh of doors, and finally, "...yes, yes. I called everyone. No. I haven't seen her yet. I'll find her after I hang up. I'm fine. Just a sprain, thank God. Right. I'll see you soon. Drake? Gotta go."

Some shouting erupted between a patient and a nurse, drowning Trinity out momentarily. Then Josie heard her voice once more. "Hey! Hey. Sergeant Grey."

Josie kicked off the blankets and threw her legs over the edge of the gurney. She counted to three before standing. Thankfully, the dizziness she'd felt earlier had passed. The achiness in her neck, shoulders, elbows, and knees had not. The nurse had put a scratchy gray pair of non-skid socks onto her feet to keep her from sliding on the tile when she walked.

Holding a piece of gauze to her head, she slowly made her way to the hall and turned left, following the sound of her sister's voice.

"Sergeant Grey," Trinity called again. "We need to talk."

At the end of the row of curtains, Josie turned right. Cold air whooshed up past the hospital-issue socks and over her bare legs. The hospital gowns didn't offer much in the way of warmth. Several feet away, Trinity sat in a wheelchair next to the nurses' station. Her right foot was elevated on the footrest. Cyrus Grey's back was to Josie. His head bent to gaze at Trinity. From the set of her jaw, she managed to look intimidating even seated with her hair in disarray and drops of Josie's blood splattered across her shirt.

"Miss Payne," said Cyrus. "How's the foot?"

Trinity glared at him. "Don't waste my time. You heard what my sister told you on the way over here. A man named Dermot Hadlee ran us off the road. He is the owner of Hadlee Family Farm, which is in your jurisdiction. Is he in custody?"

There was a beat of silence. Josie shuffled closer.

Trinity waved her phone in the air. "It's been hours. This man is clearly a danger. Why hasn't he been arrested?"

Cyrus gave what Josie had now come to think of as his signature heavy sigh. "Miss Payne, Dermot Hadlee had a stroke last year. He's not in very good shape. I highly doubt that he's the person who did this."

Josie drew up beside him. "I saw his face. I can identify him. If that's not enough, Dermot Hadlee has a black Ford F-150 registered to him." She rattled off the license plate number she had seen just before the crash. "On Saturday when my team executed a search warrant on his property, it was there. If you go to the farm now, you'll find that it has significant front-end damage."

Cyrus met her eyes. "What makes you think Dermot

Hadlee is capable of driving a truck, much less running you off the road?"

"Lark told us that he can still drive." When Cyrus didn't respond, she added, "He's capable of loading and pointing a shotgun at me."

Still, Cyrus said nothing.

"I know what I saw," Josie said. "Dermot Hadlee tried to kill us today."

Cyrus held her gaze for several seconds. Then he said, "Fine. Let's say he did. You're asking me to arrest a seventy-year-old stroke victim who has more clout in this town than God. What do you think is going to happen? Honestly?"

"I don't give a rat's ass how much clout he has," Josie responded.

Cyrus opened his mouth to speak but Trinity cut him off. "You know, Sergeant Grey, I've come to Bly to do an episode of my show on the Jana Melburn case centering around the question of whether it was an accident or murder, but maybe the real story is the corruption of your department and all the other local authorities: prosecutors, judges, town council. Maybe that's what the episode should be about. Is that what you want? Because I will have a camera crew here so fast, it will make your head spin, and I will crawl so far up your ass, the entire country will know what the inside of your colon looks like. If that doesn't incentivize you to do your job, then I'll place a call to my contact in the FBI's anti-corruption unit and ask them to look into this 'clout' you mentioned."

As Cyrus's face paled, Josie tried to hide her smile.

"Let's just take a minute, here," he said. "I'm not suggesting we do nothing."

"Really?" said Trinity. "Because that's what it sounds like."

He straightened up a little, drawing his shoulders back. "I always do my job, regardless of outside influences, and I will do it today. However, I don't mind saying that I find it hard to believe that Dermot Hadlee ran you off the road."

"Well, he did," said Josie.

Cyrus reached into one of his pockets and took his phone out. "Fine. I'll call the station and have him picked up. I will need a statement from both of you later, though."

Trinity said, "You'll have it, just as soon as we're released."

While Cyrus stepped away to make the call, Trinity turned her gaze to Josie. The fire in her eyes receded, replaced with concern. She opened her mouth to speak but a male voice from behind Josie called, "Miss Quinn? Josie Quinn?"

Josie turned to see the doctor from earlier. His smile did nothing to dispel the anxiety turning her stomach acids to molten lava. He said, "Time for those sutures."

Trinity touched her hand. "Want me to come with you?"

Josie swallowed. She was a grown woman. She wasn't six anymore. Hospitals weren't scary, and Lila was dead. "No. I'll be fine. Just, uh, find my husband, would you?"

Her feet felt heavy as she returned to her curtained-off area. The doctor was in his forties, pleasant and kind, just like the doctor had been when Josie was a kid. That doctor had known that something wasn't right but without young Josie admitting to what Lila had done, there was little he could do. She'd taken her stitches and gone back to Lila's house of horrors.

As he positioned all of his materials on the tray table, Josie tried to force the memory out of her mind. She'd been in the emergency room many times for various reasons since that incident. Why was this bothering her so much? Why were the memories bubbling so quickly to the surface? Why was she rattled?

The doctor snapped on gloves and produced a large needle. "I'm going to inject your scalp with this numbing medication. It's going to burn when I do it and it will probably feel funny for a long time, but I promise it's a whole lot better than giving you stitches without it."

Her therapist was always telling her that she'd never truly dealt with many of the things Lila had done to her. Josie didn't understand what Dr. Rosetti meant. Hadn't dealt with them? She'd lived them. She'd thought about them more times than she cared to admit over the decades that had passed. Wasn't that dealing with them?

As the needle pinched her skin and sent a searing sensation across her forehead, she was transported back in time. She was small, so small, and the medical staff had left her alone in the room with Lila.

Josie's chin was gripped tightly in her mother's hand, fingers squeezing against the bone and pulling at the skin around her wound. Her eyes watered with the pain. "Mo-mommy," she gasped.

Her mother's blue eyes were almost black with fury. When she spoke in an angry whisper, spittle sprayed across Josie's nose. "You don't say one fucking word, you got that?"

A gasp escaped her lips. The doctor pulled back, frowning. "Are you okay?"

She couldn't push any words out, so she nodded. He gave her a skeptical smile but then started to prepare to stitch. "You will feel a pulling sensation," he told her.

Suddenly she knew why she was having such a strong reaction to the situation, why her traumatic memories were flooding back so quickly and easily. Although she'd been in the ER dozens of times for dozens of reasons since Lila tried to slice her face off, she'd never experienced anything so close to what had happened that day—stitches in her face. But here she was, a grown woman, a police officer, capable, competent, strong—she had a gun for God's sake—and the memory had stolen all the air from her lungs. *Unprocessed trauma.* In her mind, she could hear the words coming from Dr. Rosetti's lips.

The doctor slipped the surgical thread through a needle. "I'm going to use the finest thread that we've got since this is along your scalp line. It will look ugly for a while, but I don't think this will scar. Get some vitamin E oil and once these come out, that will help you avoid scarring."

Her heartbeat felt out of rhythm. Unprocessed trauma or not, she was here and she needed stitches. There was no getting out of this. She thought about waiting for Noah. If he was there, she could do it. Or she could stop this and ask Trinity to join them. Before she could decide, she heard a very loud and familiar voice booming from somewhere outside the curtain.

"To hell with your procedures. One of my detectives was almost killed today. I know she's here and I want to see her immediately. Not in an hour or fifteen minutes or even five seconds. Now. Right now. Stop wasting my time and find her! Detective Josie Quinn."

The doctor grimaced. "Someone you know?"

Josie tried to smile but the motion made her whole head feel weird now that her hairline was pumped full of numbing medication. "My Chief."

As if on cue, the curtain was wrenched back. The Chief's face was as red as Josie had ever seen it. Behind him, a nurse looked on helplessly. She met the doctor's eyes and threw her hands in the air. The doctor said, "It's fine."

The Chief strode over to the bed. "Your sister told me it's just a flesh wound."

The doctor said, "Some sutures will take care of it."

Ignoring him, the Chief said, "Noah and Mett caught a missing kid. Lost in the woods near his house. They've got Luke and the dog out there searching for him. I told him to leave them and get his ass down here yesterday."

"Thank you," Josie said.

The Chief pulled a chair over beside the bed and plopped into it. He nodded for the doctor to carry on. Josie's heart fluttered wildly in her chest as the doctor fished the thread through her skin. Again, it was like she was being slammed back in time. All she could hear was Lila's angry voice, low and dripping with menace.

"I told you to shut up. Not one word. What I say is what happened, you got that? If you tell one person—just one person— what happened, you're going into the closet. Forever. And Daddy and Gram won't be able to save you. You understand that?"

Fear set her entire body into a quiver, and she felt a hot wetness spread down her legs and through her nightdress. She whispered, "I promise."

"Quinn!" The Chief's shout broke through the memory.

She couldn't turn her head to look at him with the doctor working on her forehead, but she tried to focus on him and not on what was happening in her own head. "Sorry," she muttered.

"I wanted you to hear it from me," he said. "The judge in Alcott County set Vance Hadlee's bail high—as high as was reasonable for the charges and circumstances—but his dad posted bond early this morning. He's out."

"Anya," Josie said, still trying to ignore the strange pulling sensation of the sutures being sewn into her skin.

"Gretchen went right to her house. Packed her up. She'll stay with them until things settle, but Quinn, we need to figure out what the hell is going on—hey, Quinn. You okay? You look like you're going to be sick."

Josie choked out, "It's the stitches."

The doctor said, "I can give you more lidocaine if you're feeling pain, but I loaded you up."

"No, it's not that."

She felt the Chief's eyes on her. Slowly, she lifted her hand and pointed to the scar along the right side of her face. By now, everyone on the team knew the origin of the scar.

The Chief's voice changed, abrasiveness muted. He said,

"Hey, Quinn, did I ever tell you about the time Kelsey fell on the playground and hit her lip on the edge of the slide?"

Kelsey had been the Chief's little sister. The Chief's father had also been a police officer, though a corrupt, dirty one. He'd made a habit of having inappropriate relationships with much younger informants that resulted in pregnancies. When Kelsey came along, the Chief was already twenty-five. Their father had no interest in raising her, so the Chief had done it.

"No," Josie said. "You didn't."

"Yeah, yeah. Took out a nice chunk of her lip. Doc had to reshape it and all. Only twelve stitches though. She was eight at the time. Scared shitless. Asked me to sing this song she liked. I always sang it to her. I have no idea why she liked it but she did. So I sang it right there in the hospital while the doc put in those stitches. She didn't even know he was doing it!"

Josie felt a new wave of anxiety. The Chief was not the warm and fuzzy type. Yes, Josie had seen a more tender side of him, but she couldn't imagine him singing... anything, really. She knew how difficult it was for him to express emotions—they were two peas in a pod in that sense—and she wasn't sure she could bear him making himself vulnerable before her. She was already teetering on an emotional precipice.

"Please don't," she said.

But he took a deep breath anyway, preparing to sing. She expected some kind of lullaby or a children's song. Something cute, sweet, melodic. Instead, he started belting out the worst, most tone-deaf version of AC/DC's "Back In Black" that Josie had ever heard. It was so bad and so jarring, that the doctor startled. Josie was grateful for the lidocaine when she felt the harsh jerk of the needle. The doctor paused, watching the Chief with a mixture of shock and horror. When it became clear that he wasn't going to stop, he resumed, finishing the sutures in record time.

The Chief stopped after the doctor hurried out of the room.

Satisfied, he leaned back in his chair and folded his hands over his stomach. The curtain pulled back again. Noah stood before them, one brow raised. He looked from Josie to the Chief and back before rushing to her side. He clasped her hand in his and her entire body started to relax. "Are you okay?" he asked. "It sounded like someone was torturing a cat."

THIRTY

Josie, Noah, and Chief Chitwood all crammed into Cyrus Grey's office. There were two chairs in front of his desk. Josie sat in one. Noah stood next to her, his palm warm on her shoulder. The Chief paced the small space behind them. Lucky for her, Noah had arrived at the hospital bearing a change of clothes and shoes. The numbing medication was starting to wear off, leaving a deep throb that seemed to encase her entire forehead. She'd chanced a glance at the wound in the hospital bathroom and was relieved to see that the cut was so close to her hairline that even if it did scar, it would likely not be noticeable. Now that she was out of the hospital and safe beside Noah, her adrenaline had started to recede. In its wake, every bump and bruise from the crash vied for her attention. Exhaustion weighed heavy on her limbs. Trinity had already given her statement and left after Drake came to pick her up. Josie had watched them go with a mixture of relief and envy knowing that lots of rest was in her sister's future. Trinity would be relaxing on Josie's couch before Josie could.

She reached up and squeezed Noah's hand. "Did you find the missing child?"

"I didn't, but our new rock star K-9, Blue, did. The kid had gotten pretty far so it took him about a half hour, but he went right to him."

"Happy ending," the Chief said. "That new K-9 unit has come in damn handy, if I do say so myself."

It was true. The team had balked at first because the new "K-9 unit" consisted of Josie's ex-fiancé, Luke, and his bloodhound, Blue. Their history was rocky. Initially it had been awkward, but after Luke and Blue helped crack a high-profile case the month before—and saved Josie's life—there were no more complaints. When the city council had denied the Chief's request for a dedicated K-9 unit, he turned to a nonprofit devoted to providing search and rescue dogs to police departments that otherwise could not afford to have full-time K-9 units.

"If only we could use him to find Carolina Eddy," Josie muttered. "Or better yet, Mathias Tobin."

"What did Hallie Kent have to say about Mathias Tobin?" asked the Chief. "I got your text, but give me the long version."

She filled them in on the conversation that she and Trinity had had with Hallie Kent.

Noah said, "Why would Vance Hadlee exonerate this guy?"

"I know. It's weird, right?" Josie said. She told him her theory that Dermot had forbidden Vance to give Mathias an alibi for reasons they did not know.

"We can sit around all night and try to figure out why Dermot Hadlee does anything," said the Chief. "But we really need to maintain focus on our murder victims. We should be thinking about all of this with them in mind. The connection between Vance Hadlee and Keri Cryer is that Keri worked for the law firm that took Vance's statement, which ultimately freed Mathias Tobin. But what's the connection between Vance Hadlee and Sharon Eddy? Aside from the brand?"

Josie sighed. "I don't know. Everything seems to be six

degrees of separation from Jana Melburn, though. Sharon Eddy's mother was one of the last people to see her alive. Dr. Feist did Jana's autopsy. She wanted to rule it a homicide or at least undetermined but her boss, Garrick Wolfe, pressured her into ruling it accidental."

"Why?" asked the Chief. "What was in it for him?"

Josie recapped the conversation she'd had with Anya about the autopsy and Garrick's implied offer to keep Vance from stalking her if she did what he asked.

"I strongly doubt this Garrick guy was worried about the community," said the Chief. "He's friends with Vance's dad. We're back to Vance, who doesn't have an airtight alibi for the day that Sharon Eddy was killed, and probably doesn't for when Keri Cryer was killed, either."

Noah added, "And if Hummel finds any traces of Keri Cryer in the white sedan we impounded from the Hadlee farm, Vance will be in even more trouble."

"But killing Sharon Eddy and Keri Cryer only served to draw attention to the Jana Melburn case. Why would Vance do that?" asked Josie. "He had no connection to her at all. Even if there was a connection that we're not aware of—hell, even if he killed Jana Melburn—why would he want to draw attention to it? The Keri Cryer murder has more to do with Mathias Tobin than with Jana Melburn."

"Then we look at Tobin," said the Chief.

"Right," said Josie. "But Vance is the reason that Mathias Tobin is a free man. Why would Vance kill his girlfriend?"

"We're missing something," said the Chief. "Or someone."

"Are we overlooking Garrick Wolfe?" Noah suggested. "I tracked him down but we haven't spoken with him yet."

Josie said, "Him pressuring Anya to rule Jana's death accidental only benefited Mathias in the long run. He wanted that case brushed under the carpet, so why would he want a microscope on it ten years later? Also, he helped Anya. Why would he be killing people to send her a message now?"

"We don't know," said Noah. "We have no idea what Garrick Wolfe knows. You said it yourself—he wanted the case brushed under the carpet. Why?"

"Find out," the Chief agreed. "Just like every other damn person whose name comes up in Sharon Eddy's murder investigation, he's got a connection to the Jana Melburn case."

"But he's got no connection to Keri Cryer," Josie said. "And no connection to Mathias Tobin that I can see—unless we just haven't found it yet. He did know about Anya's branding."

"But the brand has nothing to do with Jana Melburn," Noah pointed out. "Why is the killer even using it? What is he trying to say? These are two very different cases: Anya's domestic violence case and Jana's death, and yet everything comes back to Melburn except for the brand. Even Keri Cryer comes back to her in a way. Keri was in love with Mathias who was the last person to see Jana alive, not to mention her brother and father figure. The brand is the outlier. Maybe it's meant as a distraction to keep us from putting all of this together."

"No," said the Chief. "The brand is just another degree of separation from Jana Melburn. The brand was inflicted on the doc by Vance Hadlee, who exonerated the guy who was widely believed to be Jana Melburn's killer."

"Exonerated for another crime, though," said Noah. "Unrelated to Jana Melburn. From what this Hallie Kent has told Trinity and Josie, he's still the prime suspect in Jana's death."

Josie said, "But Mathias practically raised her." She thought about the photo album Hallie had shared. If the pictures were truly representative of the relationship between Mathias and Jana, then she could see why it was impossible for Hallie to believe that he'd harm her. He'd been fresh out of high school when he took on raising her. Taking on that responsibility was a labor of love and from all appearances, Mathias Tobin had loved Jana intensely. He'd been devoted to her. Doting.

Noah said, "You don't think Mathias Tobin killed Jana."

"I don't know," she said. "I just don't know. There's still no proof that Jana Melburn's death was anything more than a freak accident."

The Chief sighed. "We're gonna need one of those cork-boards with the yarn pretty soon. For the love of all that's holy, are you telling me we've got to solve the Bly Police Department's accident case in order to figure out who killed Sharon Eddy and Keri Cryer?"

Cyrus Grey appeared in the doorway, a sheaf of papers in one hand and Josie's phone in the other.

"Maybe not," said Josie. "The Sharon Eddy and Keri Cryer murders were a direct message to Anya. We just need to figure out who had the greatest motivation for sending that message."

Cyrus walked in and moved behind his desk, offering them a grim smile. He slid Josie's phone across the table to her. "One of my guys found this at the accident scene. Not much of a charge on it, but it's intact."

Josie mumbled a thanks and put it in her pocket.

Cyrus waved the pages in Josie's direction. "I've got your statement for you to sign. Dermot Hadlee was taken into custody two hours ago. I'm sure that his attorney is already hard at work on getting the charges dismissed."

He pushed the pages across the desk toward Josie, together with a pen. Ignoring it, she met his eyes. "Deputy Grey, where were you on Friday between six a.m. and nine p.m.?"

Noah said, "And nine p.m. Saturday until five a.m. on Sunday morning?"

THIRTY-ONE

A stillness settled over the room. Cyrus stood frozen, one hand on the back of his chair and one resting on his desk. Josie held his gaze and waited. In the silence she heard the clack of a keyboard from somewhere down the hall; the murmur of voices; a phone ringing; and footsteps passing by the door. Her forehead throbbed in time with her heartbeat.

Cyrus said, "Excuse me?"

"Friday," Josie repeated. "Where were you? Between six a.m. and nine p.m.? Saturday night nine p.m. into Sunday morning around five?"

"Are you—" He looked at Noah, the Chief, then back at Josie. "Are you asking me for alibis?"

Noah said, "We have a murder victim named Sharon Eddy."

"I'm aware of that," Cyrus said.

"She was the daughter of Carolina Eddy," Josie said.

His expression remained blank.

The Chief said, "Carolina Eddy was the clerk at the minimarket the night Jana Melburn was last seen alive."

Realization struck. Cyrus shook his head. "Jana Melburn.

Jesus. We're back on that. Are you helping out Trinity Payne, or what?"

"We're trying to solve a murder," Josie said. "Actually, we're trying to solve two murders now."

Noah said, "Our latest murder victim was Keri Cryer."

Cyrus said, "I've never heard of her."

"She worked for Downey, Downey & O'Neill in Bradysport. She was a paralegal for Mathias Tobin's defense team. Part of the team that ultimately got him exonerated in the attempted murder—now murder—of your daughter."

"Don't." Cyrus's face paled. His voice held a note of warning.

Josie continued, "We just found out that both of these victims have a connection to the Jana Melburn case."

Cyrus clenched his jaw before responding. "Those are pretty loose connections. Sounds to me like you're grasping at straws. Vance Hadlee didn't work out for you, so now you're just trying to pin these murders on anyone you run into down here? I'm just next in line till you eliminate every person in Bly? Do you even hear yourself? I am an officer of the law."

"Yes," Josie said. "But you're also a father who just lost his daughter."

He swallowed twice before speaking, voice husky. "I told you. Don't talk about my daughter."

Josie stood up and advanced toward his desk even though her head felt as heavy as a bowling ball. She put both palms on the desktop and leaned toward him. "I mean no disrespect to Piper." At the mention of her name, his hands twitched. Josie forged ahead. "What happened to her was horrible and tragic, but as an officer of the law, you have to see what I see. Were you on the staff when Mathias Tobin was accused by three cheerleaders of sexual assault?"

Cyrus bristled. "Just. I had just started in this department."

Josie continued, "You were definitely on the staff when Jana

Melburn died. You knew that Mathias was the last person to see her alive—Carolina Eddy notwithstanding—and you knew that the two of them lived together, that there was a prior relationship there. You knew that the majority of the people here in Bly believed that he killed her. It's not out of the question to think that maybe he went free because Anya Feist did not rule Jana's death a homicide. Then he married your much younger daughter."

A vein in Cyrus's temple pulsed. The twitching in his hands became so noticeable that he folded his arms across his chest, burying his fingers in his armpits.

Josie continued, "Your daughter married a man who had multiple allegations of violence made against him—both in and out of the confines of the justice system—and what happens next? He shoots her in the head."

She waited to see if he would protest, say that this could not be true given the fact that Mathias had been exonerated. He said nothing.

"You have spent years caring for your daughter because of the catastrophic injuries Mathias gave her, and then he walks free. Not only that, but he immediately moves on to another woman. He and Piper never got a divorce, did they?"

His silence was all the answer she needed.

"He never even came to see Piper once he was released, did he? Just moved on with Keri Cryer like his wife meant nothing to him. Then Piper dies. Now your daughter is gone, and her murderer is walking free—exactly the way he's walked free for the last fifteen years. I can't imagine what that must be like."

In a voice taut with barely concealed rage, Cyrus said, "If I was going to kill someone, I would kill that son of a bitch. Not innocent women. But I didn't. I don't even know where he is—not that I'm looking for him. There is nothing I can do about any of that now."

Noah drew up beside Josie. "Do you think that Mathias shot your daughter?"

Cyrus glared at him but gave no answer.

Josie pushed off the desk, fighting a wave of dizziness, and drew her spine up straight. "You don't believe Vance Hadlee? That Mathias was with him at the time of Piper's shooting? That Mathias had come to the farm to talk about a job?"

"You've met Vance Hadlee," Cyrus said. "Would you believe anything that came out of his mouth? The truth is, I don't know what to think anymore. Mathias lived with Piper. He found her. His prints were on the gun. There was no other evidence to suggest that anyone else had been there. Trust me, I looked. But you're right. There were allegations and rumors for years before what happened to Piper. After all these years, I figure that if it looks like a duck and quacks like a duck, it's a damn duck."

"Fair enough," said Josie. "Why would Vance Hadlee lie?"

"Because he's a piece of garbage. You really haven't figured that out yet?"

From behind her, the Chief said, "You never tried to find out? Never talked to him about why he suddenly came forward to exonerate Mathias?"

Cyrus gave one of his signature sighs. "Of course I did. I went at him so hard, I got reprimanded by my Chief. I was told to leave him alone. Leave all the Hadlees alone or I'd be out on the street looking for a new job. My, uh, Piper was still alive then. She still needed around-the-clock care, which meant that I had to keep this job."

Josie said, "What did Vance say when you asked him about it?"

"He came forward because Mathias was at the farm that afternoon. Claimed he hadn't said anything before because Dermot told him to stay out of it."

"Stay out of making sure an innocent man doesn't go to prison?" blurted the Chief.

Cyrus shrugged. "Vance said Dermot didn't want them to get involved in a murder case. Didn't want the farm name dragged into it. Dermot had dealt with the fallout from the rape allegations when he was coaching football. He told Vance to mind his business and he did. That is all I could get out of him."

Josie said, "Vance came forward after Dermot's stroke, then?"

"Yes, and like I told you before, I don't know what to believe anymore. Maybe Vance grew a conscience in the last few years and so when he saw an opportunity to do the right thing and get Mathias out, he went for it. Or maybe he's the same piece of shit he's always been and he just lied."

Noah asked, "Was Vance friends with Mathias? Or with Piper?"

"No. Not that I know of. The boys had been on the football team together in high school, but Piper never said anything to me about them being friends. I tried to turn something up once Mathias got off but I couldn't find a damn thing."

The Chief said, "Do you have a theory about why Vance Hadlee would lie to exonerate someone he wasn't even friends with?"

Cyrus gave a short laugh. "Knowing Vance? There was something in it for him. I don't know what, and now that my daughter's gone, I don't care."

"Really?" Josie said. "If a guy had helped my daughter's killer go free, I would care. I'd care enough to want to kill him. Or maybe frame him for murder."

THIRTY-TWO

Cyrus let out a long breath. "Man, you sound just like your sister, throwing out all these crazy theories. Again, I'm asking you, do you hear yourself? I'm a police officer. The law is the law. It's not my job to go around doing all kinds of vigilante shit. I don't know what you're trying to do right now, but if you think I killed Sharon Eddy or Keri Cryer, you're nuts."

Noah asked, "You really don't care why Vance gave that statement in Piper's shooting, or that he might have lied?"

"I did. For a while. Like I told you, I damn near got myself fired over it. Now? What difference does it make? What's done is done. Doesn't much matter how it happened. At the end of the day, my daughter is dead, and Mathias Tobin is free."

"That's it?" said Josie.

Cyrus shook his head. He lifted a hand and shoved it through his thick hair. In that moment, he looked haggard. "I'm tired," he muttered. "You have any idea what it's like taking care of someone who needs twenty-four-hour care, all while working a full-time job? Sure I had home health nurses, but that don't take away the stress of watching your child go through something like that. I just lost her a few weeks ago. I'm exhausted, and you all are not helping."

"I'm sorry for what you've gone through," Noah said, "and for your loss. I'm sorry we have to be here asking these questions, but you've got to understand that we've got a job to do. Mathias was your son-in-law. Did you—"

Cyrus held up a hand to silence him. "I don't want to get into this. I tried to accept him. I did my best, but it's like you said. He was older and he'd had allegations against him even if none of them stuck."

"Each time he walked away with no charges," Noah said. "That didn't drive you crazy?"

"Of course it did," Cyrus said. "It still does. But I told you. I'm tired. I'm not sure I've got any fight left in me. What's the point now? Piper's gone."

Josie's scalp tingled. She resisted the urge to touch her stitches, instead maintaining her focus on Cyrus. "Do you ever think that maybe if Dr. Feist had ruled Jana Melburn's death a homicide, things would have turned out differently?"

"Sometimes," he admitted. "Even though we didn't have much evidence, if she'd just ruled the manner of death a homicide, we would have at least had the green light to keep investigating, maybe ask the public for tips. We did what we could in terms of looking for the mystery person Mathias claims she was going to meet, but then Anya ruled it an accident. It was an open and closed case. She fell, she died. We couldn't keep devoting resources to it. But a homicide? Even a cold one would warrant some manpower, some digging."

Josie said, "Dr. Feist failed you."

"I wouldn't go that far."

Noah said, "Jana's injuries were severe. You didn't think that the homicide determination was appropriate based on those alone?"

"Personally? Yeah, of course I did. My gut told me she was

murdered but we couldn't prove it. Besides that, I'm not a medical examiner."

"No, you're not," Josie agreed. "But you said yourself that Anya's determination of the manner of death could have made a big difference. Maybe, given more time and resources, you could have found evidence that Mathias killed Jana. Maybe he would have been put away before he ever met Piper. Maybe you were bitter and angry with Anya."

"I don't deal in maybes," Cyrus said. "Only what's in front of me."

"You don't blame Anya at all for Mathias Tobin going free ten years ago?" Noah asked.

"I think a lot of people are to blame for that, myself included. I told you, there was no proof that he did it."

"But you personally must have a lot more anger toward Anya than other people might," Josie said. "You had a sexual relationship with her."

He held both hands up, palms facing Josie. "Hey, come on now. That's ancient history. I know you've got murders to solve, but you can just leave our private relationship out of it. That's got nothing to do with anything."

"You sure about that?" Josie said. "Were you in love with her?"

"I'm not going to answer that."

"Let's say you were in love with her," Josie said. "Then one day, she disappeared. No goodbye. No call or text or even a note. She was just gone. That had to hurt."

He swallowed again. "Anya did what she had to do. That's what I always figured. I never had any hard feelings about how things ended."

The Chief edged his way in between Josie and Noah, shooting an incredulous look at Cyrus. "Really?"

Cyrus's gaze swept downward, lingering on his desk. "I knew it wasn't serious."

Josie said, "But even if it wasn't, that was a shitty way for her to end things, and here you are ten years later burying your daughter with the knowledge that this woman you'd been in a relationship with, who didn't care enough about you or respect you enough to at least tell you she was leaving, potentially could have stopped Mathias Tobin, or at the very least, set into motion a series of events that could have put him away before he married Piper."

Cyrus didn't look up from his desk.

Noah said, "You two had an intimate relationship and you were also involved in her case against her husband. You were familiar with the brand. You saw first-hand what Vance did to her, and I'm guessing you also witnessed the psychological damage—the terror—he left her with. You would know how seeing that brand on another woman would affect her."

"I'm not even going to dignify that with a response."

Josie said, "Did Anya ever talk to you about why she ruled the death an accident?"

"Yeah, we talked about it."

"Did she tell you that her boss, Garrick Wolfe, wanted her to list the manner of death as accidental?"

"She ran all her cases by him."

Noah said, "Did she mention to you that Garrick had implied that if she ruled Jana's death an accident, he might be able to keep Vance from bothering her again?"

Cyrus didn't respond.

Josie said, "If you thought that Anya made a selfish decision when she decided to list the manner of Jana Melburn's death as accidental in exchange for her own safety and in doing so, inadvertently set Mathias Tobin on the path to your daughter, wouldn't you want to get back at her?"

Cyrus tapped against the pages on his desk. "I'd like you to sign this statement now so you all can get the hell out of my office."

Noah pressed on, "Where were you on Friday between six thirty a.m. and nine p.m.?"

Josie said, "And on Saturday from nine p.m. until five a.m. Sunday morning?"

"I was home. On Friday, I had the day off. I spent it packing up some of my daughter's things. On Saturday night, I was doing some housework and then I went to bed. Alone. I don't have an alibi for either of your murders. Happy? As to this absurd suggestion you are making that I went out and killed a couple of young women to somehow get back at Anya for her work on the Melburn case, you know as well as I do that if evidence surfaced at any time to prove that Mathias killed Jana, the manner of death could be changed. Sure, we couldn't go out looking for that evidence because of the accidental ruling, but that didn't have to be the end of it. There was just never enough there. If you don't believe me, I'll show you the damn file—as long as you promise not to share what we've got with Trinity Payne."

Josie said, "My sister already has most, if not all, of what's in that file."

Cyrus raised a brow. "That's not possible."

Noah laughed.

Josie said, "You've met her. You think it's not possible for her to get what she wants?"

"How?"

"A source," Josie said.

He stepped back and walked a small circle behind his desk chair. "A source, huh?" he mumbled. "Let me guess. Hallie Kent."

Now it was Josie's turn to stay silent. Although Josie had interviewed Hallie as part of her investigation into the Sharon Eddy murder, the exchange of reports, documents, and information had been between Hallie and Trinity. It was up to Trinity to decide whether or not to disclose the identity of a source.

Cyrus huffed. "You don't have to confirm it. I already know it was her. Did she tell you how she got the stuff? The truth?" He looked at each one of them but when they gave no response, he went on. "Yeah, okay. Why would she? Hallie used to work here. In the records department. She got fired for illegally copying material from that file. One of the other clerks in the department, Bella Crooke, caught her doing it and turned her in. Bella was about to retire. She was training Hallie to take over her position and that's when she caught her."

Josie bit back the desire to tell him that he was right—although Hallie's story about Bella Crooke's role had been much different. Instead, she asked, "Does Bella still work here?"

"She retired last year. If you want to talk to her, I'll call her. I'm sure she'd be happy to come in and verify what actually happened and the fact that Hallie is a damn liar. I guess Hallie wouldn't have been able to win the trust of Trinity Payne if she admitted to that. I knew Jana was her foster sister. Well, she always referred to Jana as her daughter. I knew she had an interest in the case. I understood her desire to know what was in the file—I probably would have done the same in her position, but I never thought she'd turn that stuff over to the press, especially after getting fired for taking it."

"Well, it's out there now," Josie said. "I've seen the reports. It's a lot. Maybe everything."

The vein in his temple started to throb again. "Goddamn Hallie Kent."

Noah said, "I get firing someone for making copies of case files, but why don't you want Trinity Payne to have the contents of the file? It seems like everyone knows everything there is to know already."

The Chief said, "He doesn't want the press to get the file because it will show the complete incompetence of this police department."

"No, not us," said Cyrus. "Anya."

"What are you saying?" asked Josie.

"I'm saying that if the contents of that file are made public—especially in something like the format of Trinity Payne's show—Anya will get crucified. It won't matter that there was never enough evidence to rule it a homicide. The public made up their minds a long time ago—in the complete absence of evidence of foul play, mind you—that Jana Melburn was murdered. The entire town has always believed that, and because Mathias Tobin saw her last, he must have done it. The public doesn't understand that you need more than conjecture to prove a homicide case. They'll look at what's in that file—what they don't yet know is in that file—and they'll blame Anya."

"Because of the autopsy?" Josie asked.

"Not just that."

The Chief stepped forward and pointed a finger at Cyrus's chest. "You need to show us what's in that file. Now."

THIRTY-THREE

Twenty minutes later, the four of them were in a conference room, crowded around a laptop that Cyrus had brought from his office. Josie sat in a chair beside him while Noah and the Chief looked over their shoulders. With a few clicks, he found a thumbnail of what looked to be video footage.

Cyrus pointed to the small square. "This is video of the last time Jana was seen alive. It's from the gas station."

"According to her mother," Josie said, "Carolina Eddy never mentioned this."

"She never had access to it. The owner of the station kept his security footage off-site. This way no one could ever come in, rob the place, and destroy the video. They could destroy the cameras but nothing that had already been captured. That's what he said, but I think what was really going on was that he'd be able to tell if his employees were ripping him off or not because they couldn't destroy footage."

Noah said, "You're saying Carolina Eddy didn't know about this video?"

"She knew they had cameras there, but she didn't have access to any footage. We never showed this to her. She never asked. We were never sure exactly what she witnessed since from behind the counter inside, she would only have been able to see a portion of the lot. We pressed her on it because what she told us and what's on this footage don't match up, but she stuck to her story."

The Chief said, "Play it."

Cyrus clicked on the thumbnail and the square enlarged to fill up the entire screen. The angle was from overhead, showing the gas pumps and a small part of the front door of the mini-mart. It was in color and surprisingly crisp. The date and time-stamp were in white on the bottom left of the footage. An older model, beat-up white pickup truck pulled up to one of the gas pumps. Mathias Tobin emerged, dressed in dirty jeans and a worn brown hoodie that bore as many stains as it did small holes. Mud crusted along the bottom of his heavy boots, which were unlaced. As he went to the pump and used a credit card to pay for gas, they could only see the back of his head. He slotted the nozzle into the truck's gas tank and leaned back against the pump, waiting as the tank filled. When it finished, he returned the nozzle, slapped the gas cap on the truck closed and waited for a receipt. It was then that Jana emerged from the mini-market.

She was dressed in tight black pants and a white jacket. Her curly blonde hair bounced over her shoulders as she approached the truck. In one hand she held a can of Coke, in the other, a pack of cigarettes. She stuffed the smokes into her jacket pocket as she pounded on the truck's hood. A grin spread across her face as Mathias startled.

He matched her smile when he turned and saw that it was her. Stuffing his receipt into his pocket, he walked toward her. Now they were both at the front of the truck, facing one another. They were only visible in profile. It was difficult to even see their mouths moving but Josie could tell by their body language and the way they each occasionally used their hands, gesturing in various directions, that they were having some sort of conversation. In the bottom corner of the screen, the seconds ticked past. Going on three minutes. Trinity had said they spoke for about five minutes before parting, but she'd gotten that information from Hallie Kent, who had evidently never seen this video.

"Hallie Kent didn't know about this video?" asked Josie.

"I don't know," Cyrus said. "I'm sure she had access to it. Maybe she didn't have time to find it before she got caught. Or maybe she saw it and decided not to slip it to Trinity Payne because it's so damaging to Mathias."

Noah said, "There is nothing concerning in this video. Nothing damaging to Mathias Tobin. Certainly, nothing that Dr. Feist should be worried about."

Cyrus held up a hand. "Just wait."

Another minute ticked past, then another. Just over five minutes had passed when something in Mathias's posture changed. He seemed to grow larger, looming over Jana. From the sliver of his face that Josie could see, his skin was flushed. His mouth moved more rapidly. Jana took a step back but didn't cower. She set the Coke can onto the hood of the truck and pointed in the direction of the road.

Mathias shook his head. He lifted a hand and stabbed an index finger in the air, aimed at her. If Josie had to guess, she would say he was probably shouting now. Still, it was impossible to tell what he might have been saying.

Jana put a hand on her hip and thrust her chin up at him in a universal display of "fuck you." She waited until he finished his tirade and then she uttered two words. Josie couldn't make them out. Maybe they were "fuck you."

She spun on her heel and started to walk off. Mathias stomped after her, seizing her upper arm and spinning her toward him. She tried to pull away. Words were exchanged. As they fought, their bodies moved, giving a better view of their faces at the moments in the video they were pointed toward the camera. It was still an odd angle, looking down on them from above, but it was possible a skilled lip reader could glean some of what they'd said to one another.

The struggle lasted about a minute. Mathias pulled at her, trying to drag her toward the truck, gesturing wildly with his free hand. Jana dug her heels into the gasoline and oil-stained concrete, protesting, her fingers trying to peel his hand from her arm. When that didn't work, she kicked his shin. His grip loosened and she tore her arm away, stepping out of his reach. He called out to her, but she shook her head, said something else, and then turned and ran. For a few seconds, he watched her. Then he snatched up the Coke can from the hood of his truck, got in, and sped off in the same direction Jana had gone.

A total of twelve minutes and thirty-nine seconds had elapsed.

Cyrus clicked out of the footage, returning it to a thumbnail in a bed of black screen. "As you can see, they argued. Heatedly. He put his hands on her and then he followed her. He always said he went after her to check that she was okay, but it sure doesn't look like it in this video."

The Chief said, "That's not enough to convict him of a murder."

"I know that," said Cyrus, turning in his chair so he could make eye contact with the Chief. "You all know that. The general public doesn't. The general public only knows that he was the last person to see her. We never released the details of what he told us. People figured it out when we went out searching for the mystery person Jana was supposed to meet. If this video got out, it would look very bad for Mathias Tobin— worse than it already did. People would look at this and convict him in their minds. Hell, around here, they did that without ever having seen this! Then they'll have a look at the autopsy report, authored by Anya. They'll say, how could she have seen this video and still ruled Jana's death an accident?"

Noah said, "Did she see this video?"

"We showed it to her but we agreed with her assessment that Jana getting into an argument and a physical confrontation with her foster brother two miles from where her body was found didn't prove she was murdered." He pounded a fist onto the table. "We could never get from here to there, don't you get that? But again, the public won't care about that. The public doesn't care about the burden of proof. They see what they want to see, and in this case, they'll see a medical examiner who didn't do her job, and that's simply not true. What the hell's gonna happen when your sister does an episode on Jana's case?"

Josie pointed to the computer screen. "Have you ever had this video studied by a lip-reading expert?"

Cyrus laughed. "You're kidding, right? I don't know how your department operates but in Bly, we don't hire forensic experts for closed cases. We don't usually hire them at all. You know how expensive it would be to get a lip-reading expert to review this tape? For what?"

He was right. Forensic experts were extremely pricey. Yet, if Trinity got her hands on this tape, the first thing she'd do would be to find one to review it. Then again, her network had practically unlimited funding. Josie met Noah's eyes. He knew what she was asking without her ever having to speak. Before Josie, he'd dated a woman who was deaf. He'd learned some sign language, but he'd also learned to read lips quite well. It had come in handy in prior cases.

He nodded at her.

She stood and gave him her seat. To Cyrus, he said, "I'm not an expert, but I'm pretty good at reading lips. Mind if I give it a try?"

Cyrus sighed. "We all tried that already. Half a dozen officers tried to read their lips. Didn't get anywhere."

"Just let me try," Noah said.

"Fine. Do what you want. I don't know how this helps your murder cases or protects Anya, but sure, give it a go."

Josie said, "Have you got a notepad? Pen? So we can write this down?"

He shot her a dirty look but then heaved himself out of the chair. He left the room and returned minutes later with a yellow legal pad and pen. He handed it to Josie and motioned for her to take his seat next to Noah. She held the pen in one hand, ready to transcribe what Noah said, even though leaning over the pad made her head swim. The numbing medication was almost completely worn off now. The stitches burned and the tender skin they held together pulsated.

Noah pulled the laptop toward him and played the video once more. He couldn't get anything from the first several minutes during which Mathias and Jana were mostly in profile. But once the physical altercation started, he was able to decipher some of what they were saying.

Leaning in toward the screen, he rewound, played, rewound, and played several more times, talking as he went. "He says to her, 'Don't go... sounds ridiculous—no, suspicious... you don't know... doing."

The Chief tried to fill in what they were missing. "Don't go to meet this person? This sounds suspicious. You don't know what you're doing?"

"I'm not completely sure," said Noah. "He pivots a little at that point. I can't see his face clearly enough. But here, he comes back around into the frame a bit more and says, 'Who? Tell me... can't let you go unless you tell me.'"

Cyrus leaned in, head between Josie and Noah, and peered at the screen while Noah replayed it. "You've got to be kidding me. You're getting all this just from watching this video?"

Noah said, "Watch his mouth."

As he replayed the segment for a final time, he mouthed the

words in time with Mathias. When Josie watched it with Noah overlaying the words, it was unmistakable.

Cyrus must have agreed because he said, "I'll be damned."

"What about her?" asked Josie.

Noah let the video play on. "She says, 'You can't tell me what to do.' Then something else. Then he says, 'But I can tell you what you should do. You're gonna get...' I think he says in trouble. She says, 'Get off me. Let go.'"

On screen, the two struggled, their bodies turning this way and that. Noah paused the footage. Rewound. Played again. "He says, 'Please don't do this. Don't go... sounds like a scam.' Then she says, 'You're wrong. I know what I'm doing. What if I told you...' Shit. She gets turned around in the struggle."

"There," Josie said. "Her face turns back. Can you figure it out?"

He played it several times. "She says, 'Don't you want to know the truth...' The rest gets cut off when she tries to pull away from him again."

The Chief said, "The truth about what?"

Cyrus shook his head. "The truth about her birth parents. That's what Mathias said in his statement. She was trying to track them down."

Something nagged at Josie. "But why would Mathias want to know the truth about her birth parents? Why wouldn't she say *she* wanted to know the truth?"

Cyrus said, "Maybe the lieutenant here is reading it wrong."

"It's possible," Noah admitted with a sigh. "We're not exactly getting the full conversation here. Only snippets."

"It's more than Bly PD had until about twenty minutes ago," The Chief said. "Fraley, see if you can decipher any of the rest of it."

They all quieted while Noah went back to work. Toward the end of the confrontation, as the struggle became more physical, their faces were only in a position for Noah to read their lips for short bursts. He only caught snatches of what was said. "Mathias says, 'You're wrong' and then I lose him but when he turns again, I just get him saying the word 'insane.' Jana says something I can't see that ends in 'it could be yours,' and Mathias says, 'you're crazy... don't know who is filling your head...' and then he turns away. Right here, his face comes back into the frame. He says, 'Whatever you are trying to do, please stop.' She says, 'Don't you want to know?' and he says—wait, I can't tell what he's saying right there but when he turns his head back, here, he says, 'promise you it won't end well. Stop being a meddling brat and come home with me.'"

At that point in the footage, Jana kicked him and ran off. Their faces turned away from the screen. Noah said, "That's it."

Cyrus said, "You sure about this?"

Noah shrugged. "I'm as sure as I can possibly be."

Josie said, "What does she mean when she says, 'it could be yours'?"

Cyrus stared at the screen where Mathias was frozen in time, watching Jana run away. "Hell if I know. She wasn't pregnant. I mean, that's what women say when they tell you they're carrying your baby, right? 'It's yours?' I suppose 'it could be yours' works just as well."

The Chief said, "I thought of that but then he says—" He leaned over Josie's shoulder and read from the notepad. "'Don't know who is filling your head' and then he calls her a meddling brat. That doesn't sound like they're talking about pregnancy."

Another sigh from Cyrus. "Well, I don't know what to make of any of this. If your read is accurate, Tobin wasn't entirely truthful. He and I never talked about it. We tried not to talk to one another at all, to tell you the truth. I didn't take his statement, but I've read it. He said she was going to meet with someone who could help her find her birth parents. This conversation could be about that, but it sounds like there's more to it. Whatever that is, only the two of them knew the truth. She's dead and I'm assuming he's missing. Otherwise you would have talked to him after Keri Cryer's murder. You said they were sleeping together."

"Yes," said Josie. "He was staying with her. He hasn't been back to her place. We don't know where to find him."

"Well, I can't help you there. We didn't exactly keep in touch. You were right about what you said earlier. He didn't try to see Piper after he got out. Just ran off. I didn't know he was with some other woman. I just figured he couldn't face us. Then when he didn't come to his own wife's funeral—" He broke off.

Josie turned in her chair and stared at him. "You think he would have felt welcome at Piper's funeral?" She didn't add the last part: *with you there?*

"If he didn't kill her, then yeah, he should have felt justified in being there. He should have felt justified in coming to see her as soon as he was out. He should have wanted to see her."

There it was, Josie thought. Cyrus hadn't complained about Mathias Tobin. He barely uttered a word about the man. Maybe he'd never believed that Mathias shot Piper. Maybe when he was exonerated, that had sat just fine with Cyrus. But not coming to see her once he was free and then not coming to her funeral was an admission of guilt in Cyrus's eyes.

Cyrus added, "Maybe they were on the outs already when she was shot. When they found Piper, her wedding ring was missing. I always thought maybe she took it off. Maybe they were breaking up and argued and she tossed it. Maybe that's why he didn't come back or try to see her. She was never well enough for me to ask her after the shooting. Still, he owed her the respect of coming to her funeral. At the very least."

"Did you ever ask him about that?" asked Noah. "If they planned to divorce? If he knew what she did with her ring?"

Cyrus shook his head. "Couldn't. Wasn't allowed to talk to him. Me being a police officer and her father. His attorney, my boss? They never let me talk to him. Once he went away, it didn't much matter."

A quiet knock on the conference room door interrupted them. Cyrus said, "Come in."

The door swung open. Anya stood there, eyes searching the room until they landed on Cyrus. Her face started to crumple and then she caught herself, pushed down the wave of emotion taking her over. Swallowing, she tried on a smile. It looked more like she was in pain.

She said, "Hello, Cy."

THIRTY-FOUR

Josie watched a few emotions flash across Cyrus Grey's face before he got control of himself. Shock, anger, longing, and then fear. They all waited for him to respond but nothing came. From behind Anya, Mettner appeared in the doorframe. "She wanted to come," he told the room. "But I didn't want her to be in Bly alone."

Anya and Cyrus were still staring at one another like no one else existed. When the seconds stretched on into awkwardness, Josie stood up and cleared her throat. Taking her cue, Mettner said, "There is actually something I need to talk to you about. Maybe out here in the hallway?"

If either Anya or Cyrus noticed Josie, Noah and the Chief leave the room, they gave no indication. Without tearing her eyes from Cyrus, Anya sidestepped to let them all pass through the door. Once in the hall, Josie left the door ajar. They may have been old flames, but Josie didn't trust anyone in Bly. She heard the low murmur of their voices as her team gathered in a tight circle in the hall.

The Chief said, "Do you really have something to tell us or

were you just trying to save us from... whatever that was in there?"

Mettner took out his phone and pulled up his notes app. "Hummel processed the Hadlees' white sedan. Unfortunately, he didn't get much."

Noah said, "No DNA? A hair, even?"

Mettner shook his head. "Nothing. However, Hummel asked Luke to bring Blue over, since he's certified in cadaver and he did alert on the trunk."

"Human remains?" asked the Chief.

"Yes," said Mettner. "Blue is trained to know the difference between human remains and animal decomposition. Luke said if he alerted then it is from a human."

Noah said, "But you just said that they found nothing in the trunk."

"The dog can still alert if there were remains in there at some point."

Josie said, "Which means there was a dead body in the trunk of that car at some point."

Mettner said, "Yes, but that's all we can say. I'm not sure it's enough if we can't put Vance in Denton on Saturday night into Sunday, or link Keri to his car in any way."

"It's circumstantial," Noah said. "But we might be able to work with it."

"No," said Josie. "We need more than that. We have to keep looking. What else do you have for us, Mett?"

He looked back at his notes. "Hummel also got everything from Keri Cryer's phone. Here's what we know. The GPS on her phone had her going from her apartment to about three blocks from where she was picked up. That was it. It was turned off at that point."

"Told you," said the Chief. "The killer made her turn it off. How about Mathias Tobin? Did you get a phone number for him?"

"Burner phone," said Mettner. "Gretchen is trying to track it, but I don't think it will go anywhere. There are some text messages between them, mostly concerning when he will be at her place, except for Friday and Saturday where he messaged her repeatedly asking her to please contact him as soon as possible. He called her at least three dozen times. In fact, it looks like they called each other most of the time. Obviously, we have no idea what the content of those calls was."

"What about the text messages?" asked Noah.

"Here is where it gets interesting," said Mettner, holding up an index finger. He looked past them to the conference room door. Quietly, Anya slid out into the hall, Cyrus in tow. Both their faces were flushed.

Anya said, "This is one of the reasons I wanted to come."

Mettner said, "There were a series of messages between Mathias Tobin and Keri Cryer that concern Garrick Wolfe."

"What?" Cyrus said.

Mettner swiped his phone and then turned it toward them. "It's easier if you just read it. These are the last messages between them before Keri Cryer went missing." He pointed to the screen. "The blue messages are from Mathias."

They all leaned in for a better look. Josie felt Cyrus's breath on the back of her neck.

Mathias: *I know you're angry with me but please try to understand.*

Keri: *I understand that you say you want a family with me but you're not willing to put your past to rest once and for all.*

Mathias: *This isn't about putting my past to rest. We don't need this in order to start a family.*

Keri: *You deserve for everyone to know the truth. You deserve that. You shouldn't be kept hidden like some dirty secret. You think you can move on from this but you can't. You don't see it, but I do. Have you even talked to Garrick?*

Mathias: *No, but I will. I promise.*

Keri: *I don't know why you won't just go to him. He paid your legal fees for years. Obviously, he is willing to help you.*

Mathias: *It's so much more complicated than that.*

Keri: *No. It's really not. You can choose yourself and a future with me but to do that, you have to also choose the truth and I don't think you really want to do that.*

Mathias: *I don't need to know the truth for us to have a future together.*

Keri: *Yes, you do. You absolutely do. I can't believe you don't see it or maybe you just don't care. I'm sorry M but I'm exhausted from it. I gave up everything for you and it doesn't seem like you're willing to do the same. I love you but I don't want to see you until you figure out what you really want.*

Josie said, "This exchange took place in the twenty-four hours after Mathias Tobin was last seen leaving her apartment but before she got into that car at the bus stop."

"Right," said Mettner.

The Chief looked at Anya. "How do Garrick Wolfe and Mathias Tobin know one another?"

Anya shook her head. "They don't. Or at least, ten years ago, they didn't."

"What can you tell us about Garrick?" asked Noah.

"He's a brilliant pathologist. He was a brilliant internist before that, but he has a drinking problem. A big one. He never said, but I heard around the office when I started working for him that he'd had to give up his practice and switch to pathology because of his drinking. 'He's better with dead people than living ones,' people used to joke in the halls. I never put much stock in it. He was good to me. Kind and caring. He always had my back. Always. His wife was the same way. It was them that I stayed with when I left Vance. After the branding."

Cyrus said, "Marie died a couple of years after you left. Brain tumor."

"Oh my God," Anya gasped. "I didn't—Garrick never—"

"Did he know?" Cyrus blurted. "Where you went? Did you tell him?"

She gave a small nod. The hurt that flashed across Cyrus's face was fleeting but unmistakable. Anya whispered, "I'm sorry, Cy."

Josie said, "Did Garrick and his wife have children?"

"No," Anya said. "Marie didn't want them. She said—" She paused, pain crinkling the skin around her eyes. "She said that Garrick would have had to choose between alcohol and a child and he always chose alcohol. She didn't want to have children if he was going to keep drinking."

"After she died, Mathias Tobin went to prison and then Garrick started paying his legal fees so that he could eventually be freed, whether on appeal or by exculpatory evidence," the Chief said.

"Garrick had enough influence with the Hadlee family to keep Vance away from you for ten years," said Josie. "Is it possible he talked Vance into making the statement that freed Mathias?"

Before Anya could comment, shouting erupted from the direction of the lobby. Josie looked up to see Vance Hadlee charging toward them. A female deputy chased after him, one hand on her holster. "Mr. Hadlee!" she shouted. "Mr. Hadlee, stop!"

But Vance's fury was laser-focused on Anya.

"You uppity bitch," he snarled as he closed in on her.

Anya visibly shrank, as if she were trying to make herself smaller, as if she were made of nothing but air. Her eyes bulged.

"You're just hanging out here with all your cop buddies, laughing at me?" Vance shouted. "While my dad is in jail? Because of you?"

Cyrus stepped in front of Anya. "Vance," he said. "Stop right there."

He was a few feet away from Cyrus when he froze. His chest heaved, fists clenched at his sides. A crimson flush stained his cheeks. Spittle ran down one side of his mouth. The female deputy caught up and put a hand on his shoulder, but he batted it away.

Cyrus said, "Vance, you need to calm down."

Mettner took a step forward. "What is he doing here?"

"He came to get his father out of custody," said the female deputy. "Dermot's out on bond. They're processing him out now. I'm sorry. We were leaving one of the visitation areas and he saw you here and..."

Mettner looked at Vance. "Well, Dr. Feist is also here, and she's got a protection from abuse order in effect against you which you're in violation of right now."

"You son of a bitch," Vance sneered. He looked from Mettner back to where Anya's face was just barely visible over Cyrus's shoulder. "You're fucking her, aren't you?"

Cyrus said, "Vance, you need to leave right now."

"You're banging my wife, you bastard. Who the hell do you think—"

Anya's voice quavered. "I'm not your wife, Vance. Please leave."

Josie moved sideways so that she was shoulder to shoulder with Anya.

Cyrus said, "Vance, if you don't leave now, we'll have to arrest you. I really don't want to arrest you twice in one week, and I definitely don't want two Hadlees in here at the same time."

Vance stabbed a finger in Mettner's direction. "I didn't sit on my ass for ten years so some pig could end up screwing my wife."

The female deputy grasped his shoulder more firmly this time. He tried to shrug her off, but she was ready for it. Cyrus stepped forward. "Vance, shut your mouth and get out of my station before I throw you in the same damn cell your father is vacating."

Josie wrapped an arm around Anya's shoulders, feeling her body tremble.

Vance registered the change in Cyrus's tone. The tension in his body slackened slightly. He turned his attention to Cyrus, who was now pivoting him away and pushing him toward the entrance. "Cy, these assholes are gunning for my family. Ever since they showed up at the farm, it's been nonstop bullshit. Now this piece of shit is flaunting the fact that he's doing my wife. Rubbing it right in my face—"

As they slammed through a set of double doors into the lobby, his tirade was cut off.

Anya went limp against Josie. Mettner turned to her. "I'm sorry, Doc."

She gave him a weak smile. "It's not you, Mett. Vance Hadlee has always been able to manufacture scandal from nothing, and he can make anything ugly."

THIRTY-FIVE

Cyrus returned to the hallway fifteen minutes later, looking pale and shaken. Josie couldn't tell if it was still Anya's presence having that effect on him or if Vance Hadlee had actually managed to put a crack in his ever calm facade. He looked at Anya but addressed all of them. "It's getting late. After dinner time. You all want to head over to Garrick Wolfe's place and talk to him, or you want to wait till the morning?"

Josie said, "We've had two women killed in our city in a matter of days. I don't want to waste any more time."

The Chief said, "Quinn, why don't you let Fraley take you home. Mettner and I can handle this."

She shook her head, which felt as unwieldy as a sack of potatoes. "No. I'd like to see this through. I didn't almost get killed by Dermot Hadlee today to back down."

Anya slid out of Josie's grasp and turned to face her. She cupped Josie's cheeks gently and tilted her head so she could see the wound from the car accident. "Resting after being injured is not backing down, Josie."

Mettner laughed. "Don't even bother, Doc. When she makes up her mind, there's no convincing her otherwise."

Josie extricated herself from Anya's grasp and managed a smile. "He's right about that. Really, I'm fine. Let's go."

"I'd like to go with you," Anya said.

No one protested.

Cyrus said, "I'm assuming you all don't need me to tag along and make introductions, then."

Josie said, "I think we'll manage."

To Anya, Cyrus said, "Take the south side up the mountain. The road on the north side is closed. The last storm that rolled through caused a landslide about three quarters of the way to the house. It's still not cleaned up."

"Thanks," said Anya.

Noah touched Josie's hand. "I'm on board with your plan, but Josie, when is the last time you ate?"

Anya added, "At least eat in lieu of rest."

"Fine," said Josie. "We'll grab a bite and then head to Garrick Wolfe's place."

"Then I'm going back to Denton," the Chief said. "You'll keep me posted. I've got Gretchen at work trying to locate Mathias Tobin and Carolina Eddy."

As Cyrus's instructions suggested, Garrick Wolfe lived on the top of a mountain at the end of a road that felt never-ending. At least, the south side road seemed that way. Josie wondered if the north side road, when it was open, was faster. Noah had found her some ibuprofen before they got on the road, dulling the pain in her scalp. Mettner drove with Anya in the passenger's seat while Josie and Noah sat in the back. No one spoke except for Anya, who gave occasional directions. They'd been on the same twisting, one-lane mountain road for what felt like an eternity before she told Mettner to make a left. Only a simple black mailbox marked the driveway. Luckily for Josie's pounding head, it was paved. It curved in two places before a large log home came into view. Parked in front of it was a four-door sedan. Light-colored. As they parked beside it and got out, Josie pointed in its direction. "If Garrick doesn't have an alibi for the night Keri Cryer's body was dumped, we should get a warrant for the car."

"You think Garrick is behind all this?" asked Anya.

Josie said, "I think we shouldn't rule anything out."

Small artificial exterior lanterns illuminated the front door. Light blazed from several of the first-floor windows.

Noah said, "Has he always lived here?"

"As long as I've known him," Anya answered. "It wasn't ideal in bad weather, but the rest of the time he and Marie were happy here."

She strode toward the front door. Josie was a few steps behind her. Close enough to see Anya raise a fist to knock on the door and hesitate.

"It's open," she said.

Before anyone could respond, Anya pushed the door open.

Josie said, "Wait."

Anya screamed. One of Josie's hands unsnapped her holster while the other reached for Anya's coat. Josie caught a piece of fabric, but it slid right through her fingers. Anya rushed forward and fell to her knees. It was then that Josie saw what had driven Anya inside. A white-haired man, probably in his seventies, lay on his back in an ever-widening pool of blood.

"Garrick!" Anya cried.

Josie's pistol was in her hands. She panned the room as behind her, Noah and Mettner fell into room-clearing formation. Her mind took in the details of the room like snapshots. Two recliners, one with a crumpled afghan on its seat. Standing lamp. Small round coffee table. Mug knocked on its side. Liquid staining the wood. The smell of whiskey. A bottle of Crown Royal but no cap. A hardback book on the round area rug beneath the table. A library edition with cellophane over its cover. Hardwood floors. Fireplace, smoldering. A darkened doorway to the left. Garrick, half-on and half-off the area rug.

No weapon, but plenty of blood.

Anya tore at Garrick's shirt, a light blue button-down now stained with blood.

Noah, the last one in, yelled, "Clear."

Anya probed at Garrick's chest and torso. The man's face was deathly pale and contorted with pain. One of his arms flailed up toward Anya but she brushed it aside. Leaning in closer to his chest, Anya muttered, "My God. Josie, help me. I need help."

Josie turned to Mettner and Noah. "I'll stay here. Clear the rest of the house."

It wasn't how they normally did things. Procedure dictated that they secure the premises before rendering aid, even if someone was dying, but Anya wasn't leaving Garrick's side. If nothing else, someone had to stay and protect her. Noah and Mettner came to the same conclusion within seconds.

Noah said, "Call 911."

Josie nodded and watched them head deeper into the house. She looked at the front door, standing ajar, then down at Anya and Garrick Wolfe. Anya took off her coat and used one of its sleeves to wipe away the blood covering his chest. Josie took out her phone and dialed 911, her gaze swinging back and forth from the front door to Garrick and Anya. As she rattled off details to the dispatcher, with Anya's help, she saw Anya clearing the blood around an inch-long wound on Garrick's right side. Blood bubbled out of it. The sound it made sent an instant wave of nausea through Josie's body. His torso labored as if a fifty-pound weight were on top of it.

Josie hung up. Anya pressed one hand over the wound. Again, one of Garrick's hands flailed upward. His blue eyes searched around the room, wild and afraid. His lips moved, forming words, but no sounds came. Anya said, "He's got a sucking chest wound. I need to seal this. What do you have? Do you guys have a kit in the car?"

Josie couldn't stop staring at his face. He was trying to tell them something. Somewhere else in the house, shouts of "Clear!" continued.

"Josie," Anya said in a loud, firm voice. "I need to seal this. Do you have a kit in the car? With a chest seal?"

Keeping her pistol at the ready, Josie ran outside to the car. She and Noah always kept a first aid kit in their personal vehicle. If you'd been on the job long enough, it was something you did. Her assumption was that Mettner also kept one. There was nothing in the glove compartment. Lifting the hatch at the back of his SUV, she found a mess of hunting equipment. She started yanking it out and tossing it into the driveway, searching for a first aid kit when she heard Anya's voice call out, high and forceful.

"Josie. I need help now!"

Josie abandoned the SUV and ran back into the house. Anya's upper body was angled awkwardly across Garrick's chest, her right elbow holding pressure on the wound while her hands worked to rip the cellophane off the library book. When she saw Josie, she said, "Put pressure on this wound while I figure something out."

Josie dropped down, Garrick's blood immediately soaking through the knees of her jeans. Anya took her elbow away and Josie placed a palm over the wound. Anya tore a square of cellophane off the book cover. Tossing the hardback aside, she looked around the room. "I need tape, dammit."

From another direction inside the house, Josie heard Noah call out, "Clear!"

Anya leapt up and ran over to the lamp. She disappeared behind the recliner. A second later, Josie heard rustling and tearing. The light in the room flickered as the lamp teetered.

Josie chanced a glance down at Garrick's face, alarmed at how rapidly he was losing what little color he had left. "Anya!"

Anya returned, dropping to her knees. Clutched in her hand were strips of black. "What is that?" asked Josie.

"Electrical tape. It was around the cord to the lamp." Anya set it aside and picked up the cellophane, pulling it taut. "We have to wait till he exhales, and then I'm going to put this over the wound. I need you to hold it in place while I tape it."

Josie's heart stuttered. When she felt Garrick's chest fall again, she lifted her hand and Anya placed the cellophane over the wound. Josie held it firm while Anya taped it on three sides. Garrick raised his hand again, hitting Josie's shoulder. His lips pressed together and then opened, trying to say something.

Anya smoothed his thinning white hair away from his forehead, leaving a streak of red. "It's okay, Garrick. The ambulance is almost here."

"Muh—" he gasped.

Josie couldn't shake the feeling that he was trying to tell them something. She leaned down, putting her face directly over his. "Don't try to talk," she told him. "Mouth it." Silently, she mouthed: *like this.*

Recognition flickered in his eyes. It took a few tries before Josie figured out what he was saying. At least, she thought she did.

Anya said, "I have no idea what he's trying to say."

"He's saying, 'my son.'"

Anya sat back on her heels, shaking her head. "He doesn't have a—" Abruptly, she went silent. Josie looked up at her, but she wasn't focused on either of them anymore. Her gaze was frozen to the doorway where Mathias Tobin now stood.

THIRTY-SIX

Josie jumped to her feet, pistol pointed at Mathias. "Don't move," she said. "Put your hands up."

For a fleeting second, he looked away from her and to Garrick. His face crumpled in pure anguish. Then he turned and ran. Josie yelled, "Get Mett and Noah." Then she ran after him. For the first time since they'd arrived, she felt the slap of cold air and the stillness all around. The further she got from the house, the darker it became. Pausing momentarily, she took her phone out and pulled up the flashlight app, simultaneously trying to scan the area around her. Once she had it on, she turned the beam outward, holding the phone beneath her pistol so that the light and the barrel of her gun were pointed in the same direction. She strained to hear anything in the silence.

Then came the sound of rustling. A twig snapped.

Josie turned in the direction from which it had come and ran toward a wooded area near the side of the house. "Mathias!" she called out. "Mathias Tobin! My name is Josie Quinn. I'm a detective with the Denton Police Department. I just want to talk."

She tried to move more quietly, listening intently for any

sound. Each time she heard it, she turned her body in that direction and picked her way through trees and over rocks and brush. Every movement she made sounded impossibly loud. Even her breathing seemed cacophonous. Soon she had to stop altogether and listen, then begin again. A few times, she pressed the flashlight beam to her side so that it wouldn't be visible. She tried to keep her body still until she heard him move again. He tried to match her movements, but she outwaited him every time.

"Mathias! Please stop running. I just want to talk!"

Footsteps rushed away from her. She followed. The trees gave way to a clearing. She panned the area with the flashlight, but the phone's beam was weakening. She was going to lose the charge soon. "Mathias! Talk to me. I'm investigating the death of Keri Cryer. If you cared about her, you'll help me."

She froze in the middle of the clearing, turning in a slow circle, the beam dwindling as the moments passed. Then Mathias materialized from the darkness, inches from the barrel of the gun, squarely in the middle of the light. Josie suppressed a gasp, tightening her fingers around the pistol's grip. "Put your hands where I can see them," she said.

His shoulders made a small movement. In her periphery she saw his two hands, pale and empty. "I'm not going to hurt you," he said.

She studied his face. All she saw was devastation. His cheeks were sunken. He hadn't looked quite this gaunt on the video Scarlett March had provided. The place where the bridge of his nose hooked was more pronounced in person. This close, she could see what she hadn't been able to see in the pictures of him, even in his driver's license photo. The eyelashes of his left eye were white-blond, whereas those of his right eye were dark. Staring so closely into his pupils, she saw that his irises were blue but in his left eye, there was a slight discoloration, as if a sliver of the pupil had turned brown. She wondered if someone had hit him. The whites of his eyes were bloodshot, his eyelids puffy.

He'd been crying.

"Keri's really dead?"

"I'm sorry," Josie said.

She watched him swallow down his emotion, the features of his face rippling as he tried to compose himself. "She hasn't returned my calls or texts. I knew she was mad at me—we had a fight—but it's not like her to make me worry. Someone killed her, didn't they?"

Instead of answering his question, Josie said, "I've got handcuffs in my pocket. Since you ran away from a crime scene and did not respond to my commands, I'd like to put them on you for the walk back to the residence."

Fear flitted across his face. He took a step back. "Please," he said. "Don't do that. I can't—I can't go back to prison."

Calmly, Josie said, "No one said anything about prison, Mathias. I just want to go back to my stationhouse in Denton and talk to you."

"I didn't hurt Keri," he blurted out. "I swear to you. I would never hurt her. Ever. I love her. Loved her." A tear slid down his cheek and he used a hand to wipe it away.

"Hands up," Josie reminded him.

He followed her instructions. It was automatic, she realized. A result of his foray into the criminal justice system. He said, "I told you, I'm not going to hurt you. I wouldn't hurt anyone. Not Keri, not Garrick. Not anyone."

"Then why are you running?" Josie asked.

"I can't—I can't tell you, and I can't risk going back inside until I get all this figured out."

"All of what figured out?"

He took another step backward, but Josie followed. The light was growing dimmer. Her forehead pulsed in time with her heartbeat. Some muted part of her mind realized she had no idea where she was or how to get back to the house. She had no idea if there were even other residences up on this mountain.

"Mathias," Josie tried again. "If you did nothing wrong then you have nothing to worry about."

He looked down, a noise coming from his throat that was half laugh and half sob. "You're naïve if you believe that."

In that moment, he looked utterly defeated. His body seemed to shrink down. Tears streamed down his cheeks now in earnest and he made no move to staunch them. His hands, aloft in the air, began to tremble. Josie tried to give him the benefit of the doubt. What if Hallie was right? What if he really wouldn't hurt another person—ever? He'd grown up in foster care and in an eighteen-month period lost the only parents he'd ever known, all while fighting rape allegations. By the time those were resolved, at the tender age of eighteen, he'd taken his younger foster sister and raised her—something he didn't have to do. It was a weighty responsibility that most eighteen-year-olds would run from. Then one night, he'd had an argument with Jana in the parking lot of a gas station. He'd clearly thought she was in danger—insane—for doing whatever it was she'd been planning. He'd asked her to stop. Two days later she was dead, and ten years later, he was still under a cloud of suspicion for her death. Back then, he'd managed to move on, marrying Piper Grey, and starting a life. Then one day, he came home to find her with a bullet in her head. He went to prison. When Garrick Wolfe stepped in and hired a firm to have him exonerated, he was finally free. Again, he found someone to love. They were trying to start a family. Now she was dead, too.

"Mathias," Josie said softly. "Who's doing this to you?"

He looked up, searching for her eyes. Josie lowered the flashlight a fraction so that he could see her. His entire face changed, agony giving way to soaring hope. He looked like someone had seen him for the first time in his life.

He swallowed. "It's complicated."

Josie said, "I can handle complicated. Give me a chance."

She could see in his eyes that he was wavering. Then she saw the decision and she knew what it was, recognized the response from her own past trauma. No matter how kind or helpful or sincere someone seemed, the best course of action was always to trust no one.

"Mathias," she pleaded. Her phone's flashlight began to fade rapidly.

They stayed frozen in place as it died completely. For a brief moment, her phone flashed to the starting screen, her cell carrier's logo dancing across it, and then everything went dark.

Nearby, an owl cried.

In a voice so small, Josie could barely make out the words, Mathias said, "Dermot Hadlee."

A jolt went through her. "I'm putting my gun away, Mathias." She slid it into her holster and snapped it in place. "Talk to me. Right here. Right now."

"I'm sorry," he said, and then she heard the crunch of his steps moving away from her.

Her arms shot out, as if to catch him, and she stumbled forward. She tried again to follow the sound, feet scrabbling over rocks as she moved out of the clearing. When his breath became audible, she knew he was close. His voice came again. "Don't get any closer."

Again, she reached out. Her feet hurried forward.

Then she stepped into nothingness.

There was a split second of horrifying realization as her body dropped through the air. She'd stepped off some precipice. A cliff or a wall. Her arms flailed for something to hold onto and then her entire body was wrenched briefly upward before it dangled, suspended over a black chasm. The seams where her sleeves attached to her coat cut into her armpits. Hands grappled with the fabric at her shoulders.

"Reach up," Mathias huffed. "Grab my hands."

She tried to reach both hands at once but immediately began to slide out of the coat. A scream tore from her throat. She waited for free fall to come but it didn't. Her heartbeat stopped. In her head she counted. One. Two. It kicked back to life, thundering in her chest.

"Easy," Mathias said, breathing heavily. "One hand. Just one. I've got you."

Josie used her right hand, snaking it up—slowly, slowly—until she felt his hands.

He said, "Take one of my hands. Just one. I'll hold onto your coat with the other. One at a time, okay?"

"Yes," she gasped.

In spite of the cold night air, sweat started to pour down her face. Her newly sewn scalp burned like someone had thrown alcohol on it. They worked together in small movements, tiny increments, until Mathias had both her hands. Then he pulled. She kicked lightly until her feet found purchase along the cliff face. She pushed up as he pulled her over and onto solid ground. Her lungs wheezed. Every muscle in her body shook. She squeezed her eyes tight against tears, glad that it was too dark for him to see them. She said, "Thank you."

She felt a warm palm on her shoulder. Then he said, "Stay here till first light. Don't try to go back before that."

"Wait, what? Mathias, no!"

His voice came from several feet away as he retreated. "I'm sorry."

THIRTY-SEVEN

A search team found her just before dawn, curled on her side, shivering and drifting in and out of sleep. The next hours went by in a blur. Noah. Mettner. Anya. An ambulance. The hospital again. Cyrus. She was exhausted. So delirious with fatigue that she kept wondering if she'd imagined the entire thing with Mathias. Except that her cell phone was at the bottom of a forty-foot ravine.

"He saved my life," she told all of them when they asked what the hell had happened.

They were standing around her bed in the emergency department. Noah and Mettner were covered in dirt, five o'clock shadows darkening their jaws. Anya looked like she'd been on a slip and slide lubricated with blood. Only Cyrus looked pristine in his clean, freshly pressed uniform. But looking in his eyes, Josie saw that he wasn't much better rested than any of them. Lines creased his forehead as he looked at her doubtfully. "Mathias Tobin saved your life?"

Josie touched her forehead. A nurse had been in to clean the wound, her nimble fingers probing the sutures before she declared that Josie would be just fine with a little antibiotic ointment. Now the greasy salve clung to her fingertips. "Cyrus, how well do you know your former son-in-law?"

He didn't answer.

"Cy?" Anya said.

He wouldn't look at her. "It was embarrassing. My daughter marrying a guy who'd been under suspicion for both sexual assault and murder."

"That make you any better than the community?" asked Noah. "Convicting him in your own mind without ever giving him a chance?"

"It wasn't like that," Cyrus said. "I tried to know him, okay? He was closed off."

Josie thought of the way Mathias had responded to her commands from muscle memory. "Because you're a police officer. He was probably wary of you after what happened in high school and then with Jana."

Mettner cleared his throat. "Boss," he said to Josie. "Garrick Wolfe is still in surgery. He might not make it. We can't question him. Did Tobin say anything?"

"He said he didn't hurt anyone. He said that he hadn't hurt Keri or Garrick. I asked him—I asked him who was doing this to him—"

"Doing what?" Cyrus asked.

"Trying to ruin his life for the last twenty years. He said Dermot Hadlee."

Cyrus said, "Why would Dermot Hadlee try to ruin Mathias's life?"

"I don't know," Josie said. "I'm just telling you what he said. He was afraid. I could see it in his eyes."

"We're talking about a seventy-year-old stroke victim," Cyrus said. "There is no way Dermot Hadlee could have been at Garrick Wolfe's home last night and stabbed him."

Mettner said, "He left the station before we did."

"But we didn't see anyone leaving the property," Noah

pointed out. "Garrick had just been stabbed. There were no other vehicles. The house was clear. It had to be Mathias."

Images of Mathias flashed through Josie's mind. Him standing in the doorway, looking stricken. Him trapped in the circle of light from her phone, looking defeated. "Mathias didn't have any blood on his person. If he'd stabbed Garrick, there would have been something."

"Then he changed his clothes," said Mettner.

"No," Josie sighed, eyes heavy and gritty. She was having a hard time keeping them open. "I'm sure it wasn't Mathias."

Anya's voice drew everyone's attention. "If there was someone else, they could have come up the north road. Parked near the downed trees and walked the rest of the way. Slipped in, stabbed Garrick, and gotten out before we arrived."

Josie swung her gaze toward Cyrus. He said, "She's right."

"You've got a team processing the house, right?" asked Mettner.

"Of course," Cyrus said. "We borrowed a team from the state police. They're up there now. If there's any DNA, any evidence that points us in the direction of someone, they'll find it."

"If Mathias had changed out of bloody clothes and stashed them somewhere, they'll find that, too," said Mettner.

"Who would know the layout?" asked Noah. "Know how to get up there to the house in the dark and back?"

Anya said, "Vance."

"Why would Vance try to kill Garrick?" Mettner asked.

No one answered.

Noah said, "I thought that Garrick was good friends with the Hadlees."

Anya nodded. "He is, always has been. He and Dermot have been friends since they were little boys. Dermot's not easy to get along with but I never witnessed any bad blood between them."

"There's no beef between them," said Cyrus. "Back when Garrick was practicing medicine, he delivered Dermot's kids."

Josie could barely push out any more words. They'd given her some painkillers when she arrived. Something slightly stronger than regular Tylenol. Now she could feel it take hold of her body. "Kids," she said.

"What's that?" Noah said, squeezing one of her hands.

"Garrick," Josie said, "is Mathias Tobin's biological father. Mathias... door... Garrick said, 'my son.'"

Her eyes slid shut. She heard Cyrus say, "Is she okay? She's not making sense."

Josie felt Anya's warm palm against her cheek. "She's exhausted. She's also right. Garrick is Mathias Tobin's biological father."

Mettner said, "I don't understand. What's that got to do with the Hadlees?"

"Nothing," said Noah.

Mettner added, "Also, Vance was the witness who exonerated Mathias. If the Hadlees were hell-bent on ruining Mathias's life, why wouldn't they let him rot in prison?"

Cyrus said, "Anya, how in the hell would you know that Mathias is Garrick's son? Because Garrick said, 'my son' when you were patching him up at his house? He'd been stabbed four times."

This was news to Josie, but Anya had prioritized sealing the sucking chest wound and by the time that was finished, Josie was chasing Mathias through the woods.

Anya said, "Before they took him into surgery, Garrick told me."

Cyrus's voice was angry. "You're just telling me now that you were able to speak with him? The damn medical staff wouldn't let us near him!"

Anya made a noise of frustration. "A lot has happened in the last twenty-four hours, Cy. Give me a break."

Cyrus eased his tone. "Garrick told you Mathias Tobin is his son? Did he happen to mention who stabbed him?"

"He doesn't know who it was," Anya answered. "He said the person was dressed in black from head to toe with a bala-clava covering their face. It happened so fast he couldn't iden-tify anything about them."

Noah sighed. "Of course."

Mettner said, "What else did Garrick tell you?"

"He said he'd had an affair. Mathias ended up in foster care. I don't know why his mother couldn't raise him. We didn't have a chance to talk about that, but—" The sound of paper rustling reached Josie's ears. Before she faded out, she heard Anya once more. "He wrote his last will and testament on the back of this nursing note in case he doesn't make it. He left everything he owns to his son, Mathias Tobin."

THIRTY-EIGHT

Josie felt Noah's fingers trail down her cheek. Emerging from sleep, she was first aware of how warm and comfortable she finally felt. Her feet touched Trout's silky body. The scent of Noah's aftershave stirred something in her. She opened her eyes to his face, backlit by the daylight streaming into the bedroom windows. A smile sent a pinching sensation through her forehead. She reached up to touch the stitches. They felt tight and hard, sore.

Noah said, "They look better than they feel, I'm sure."

"They hurt," Josie said. "How long have I been asleep?"

"Twelve hours," he said.

"What day is it?"

"Thursday."

Slowly the memory came back to her. The confrontation with Mathias. Nearly falling off a cliff. The team finding her at dawn on Wednesday. The community hospital in Bly. The return home. Sleeping, eating, and finally, more sleeping.

She started to sit up, eliciting a groan from Trout. Her entire skull pounded like someone was playing a staccato beat against it. The rest of her body felt like a toothache. "I'm going to need some ibuprofen," she told Noah. "And an update."

He disappeared into the bathroom and returned with two pills. Josie sat all the way up and took them dry. Noah said, "Take your time. Anya's here. We'll be in the kitchen when you're up to it."

A half hour later, Josie was beginning to feel human— though still sore all over—as she joined Noah and Anya in the kitchen. Trout followed her anxiously, staying near her feet. Noah handed her a cup of coffee already made just the way she liked it. "Trinity and Drake went out to brunch," he said.

Josie sat down across from Anya. "Did you run into them before they left? Did Trinity bother you?"

Anya smiled. One of her thin hands curled around a coffee mug. "I can handle Trinity. I'm worried about you. I thought I'd stop by and see how you were feeling."

"Like I got run off the road into a ditch and then later that night, almost fell off a cliff. I'm fine, Doc." She took a sip of her coffee, a feeling of pleasure flooding her body. She glanced back at Noah, who stood with his hip leaned against the kitchen counter. "Did you tell Trinity that Dermot's already out on bail?"

He poured himself a cup of coffee. "I sure did. She's on the warpath now. She's prepared to dig up anything she can to destroy him. I'm talking scorched earth."

Josie laughed. "Trinity going scorched earth? I almost feel sorry for the guy. Almost."

Noah said, "There must be something there though for her to dig up. Otherwise, why would he have come after the two of you?"

Josie said, "We could ask him, but I'm sure his lawyer won't want that."

Anya said, "How did he even know you were in town?"

"We drove past the gas station where Jana Melburn was last seen. He was pumping gas. He saw me."

Anya stared into her mug, head shaking sadly. "I don't understand. Dermot was always reserved. Stoic. He was strict with the kids—he was never warm or fuzzy—but he was never violent. Not that I saw. I wonder if the stroke has impaired his judgment. He has never been a hothead. He was always very calculating. Careful. Him trying to hurt or kill you and Trinity? It's very out of character for him. I'd expect it from Vance, but not Dermot."

"They're both hiding something," said Josie, taking another sip of her coffee. "But they're not going to tell us what it is, so we have to work whatever leads we've got."

Noah said, "Gretchen got a warrant for the light-colored sedan owned by Garrick Wolfe even though the Hadlees' sedan appears to have had human remains in the trunk at some point. Hummel's still processing Garrick's car but he was able to download the GPS history. Garrick Wolfe is a no-go. He's been in Bly for weeks. The only places he goes are the grocery store, the cemetery, and the liquor store. Sometimes a local bar."

Josie downed the rest of her coffee, already feeling more clear-headed. "Garrick is off the suspect list but did he make it through surgery? Is there any way we can talk with him? He might know things that will help our investigation."

Anya sighed. "I called the hospital. The surgery didn't go well. He had extensive internal damage. His bowel was punctured in two places. His body did not tolerate the repairs very well. The surgeon is worried about peritonitis—that's an infection. It seems he is still bleeding internally somewhere in his abdomen and may need another surgery. He's in critical condition. The doctors have him intubated. They're not sure if he's going to pull through."

Josie said, "I'm sorry, Anya."

Anya's eyes shone with unshed tears. "I'm the one who's sorry. Garrick was truly good to me. So was his wife, Marie. They took me in, protected me. Garrick even protected me after I moved away, but I left them behind just like I left Cyrus. I mean, I said goodbye to them but once I left, I never looked back. It seemed like the only option at the time, the only way I could survive emotionally, to cut off that life like it was a gangrenous limb, but now I wonder if I made a mistake. I'm going to drive to the hospital today and be with him. It's the least I can do. He's got no one else."

Josie said, "He's got Mathias. Any word on him?"

Noah shook his head. "Nothing. He's good at hiding, that's for sure. Last I checked, the state police were still processing Garrick's house—although that was hours ago. Anyway, at that time, Cyrus said that they'd found some personal items that looked as though they belonged to a man in one of Garrick's spare bedrooms, including the burner phone that Mathias had been using to call Keri Cryer. It's got a ride-share app on it. That's how he was getting around. That's how he got to Garrick's without his own vehicle."

"Mathias was staying with Garrick," Josie said. "Makes sense. He wasn't with Keri all the time, and he didn't keep much in the way of clothes there. Hallie Kent said that Mathias went from prison to the halfway house in Bradysport and then she lost track of him. There was a two- to three-month gap before he started showing up at Keri Cryer's apartment. He was probably with Garrick. No one would have thought to look for him there. He must have spent some time there since he was familiar enough with the terrain around the house to navigate it in the dark. Did they find anything else at Garrick's house?"

Noah frowned. "Like Sharon Eddy's glove and Keri Cryer's shoe?"

"I have to know," said Josie. She couldn't get the encounter with Mathias out of her head. Her gut told her he was innocent even though absolutely nothing they'd found so far had proven it.

"No."

Relief washed over her. At her feet, Trout sighed and nuzzled his head against her ankle.

"The only odd thing they found was a bone fragment. The coroner said it's very old, though."

Josie recoiled. "They found a bone fragment inside his house?"

Anya said, "Human?"

"Human, yes," Noah said. "The Everett County medical examiner is pretty sure it is a skull plate. They'll send it for testing but they're not sure they'll get DNA from it."

"Where was it?" Josie asked.

"In a metal box in Garrick's garage. Cyrus said the lab will try to pull prints from it. There were a few other items inside the box. A piece of clothing, also old and badly degraded. What they think might be a necklace of some kind, and also perhaps a hearing aid, but they're not sure. Everything was caked in dirt and badly deteriorated. Like I said, we'll know more once it's all been through the lab."

Josie looked at Anya. "That sounds like a box of serial killer trophies."

"No," Anya said. "Garrick would never... I don't know why he would have those things, but he would not hurt anyone."

Before Josie could ask more questions, a cell phone trilled. Each of them checked their pockets. Noah took his out and swiped answer. After listening for a moment, he said, "Got it. Yep. I'll ask her."

He hung up. "That was Mett. Gretchen's off. He located Carolina Eddy at a shelter in Bradysport. We've also got an armed robbery in East Denton. One person injured."

"You mind taking the armed robbery?" she asked. "I'd like to go with Mett to talk to Carolina Eddy."

He leaned in and kissed her. "Only if you promise not to go off any cliffs."

She smiled, breathing him in. "Just trying to keep up with you, husband."

THIRTY-NINE

Josie and Mettner followed Anya to the hospital in Bradysport where Garrick Wolfe had been transferred the night before for surgery and where he was currently in the ICU. They waited for her to exit her car, cross the parking lot, and enter the building before pulling away and heading toward the homeless shelter nearby. Over the course of the investigation, using the phone number Rosalie Eddy had provided, Gretchen had routinely pinged Carolina Eddy's phone. Rosalie was right. It had been out of service. But they kept pinging it in the hope that she'd get it turned back on—and she had. In fact, Carolina had called Rosalie the evening before, which Rosalie reported to the Denton PD immediately after hanging up with her daughter. Carolina wouldn't tell Rosalie where she was staying but with the phone turned back on, Gretchen was able to pinpoint its location: a homeless shelter that Rosalie confirmed Carolina had frequented in the past.

Josie just hoped she was still there.

Mettner drove the car through the streets of Bradysport, weaving through residential areas with modest homes until he came to a block of streets that contained several businesses.

They were nearly at the shelter when Josie saw Carolina going into a laundromat, a small mesh sack of clothes over her shoulder. "Stop," Josie told Mettner. "I think that's her."

He parked nearby. "You sure?"

She looked much more emaciated than the photo that Josie had seen on Sharon Eddy's social media and the last driver's license photo they'd found for her in the TLO database, but Josie was certain. "That red hair stands out," she said. "Come on, let's have a closer look." As they walked up to the laundromat, Josie peered inside the windows. The inside was narrow and long with another entrance in the rear. Besides Carolina, Josie saw only one other patron, a man. His head bobbed to music coming from a pair of blue earbuds as he stuffed his wet clothes into a dryer. Behind him, midway between the front and back entrances, Carolina took off her coat, tossed it onto a nearby chair, and then dumped the contents of her mesh bag onto a table and began riffling through clothes.

Josie said, "Go around the back."

"What?"

Josie pointed to the rear door. "She's a runner. Trust me. Go around the back. Wait by the door."

He stared at Carolina as she searched through the pockets of a pair of jeans. "How do you know she's a runner?"

"Mett," Josie said. "I just know."

"Meet you in there then," he muttered.

Josie waited until his shadow appeared in the center of the rear door. Carolina was still oblivious, shaking the empty bag for any leftover contents. The other patron now sat on a bench, scrolling through his phone. His head still moved to music coming through his earbuds. Josie went inside. As she got closer to Carolina, she saw that she was searching her clothes' pockets for change. A small pile sat on the table next to her things. Not enough to do a load of wash. As Josie came within five feet of her, her head whipped up. In person, Josie was struck by the near-perfect facsimile of Sharon Eddy's face. In a universe where Carolina wasn't firmly in the grip of drug addiction, they might have even passed for sisters. Except for the red hair, of course, and the faint yellow tint of her skin. Even the sclera of her eyes was yellow.

Josie said, "Carolina Eddy."

Carolina went still, watching Josie like she was a wild animal that might attack. She took Josie in from head to toe. Denton PD polo shirt under a slim black coat that did little to conceal the gun at her hip. Brown slacks, boots. Josie could practically see the word form as if in a thought bubble over her head: cop.

She ran.

By the time she reached the back door, Mettner had stepped inside, a wall preventing her from getting out. "Stop," he told her. "We just want to talk."

Carolina turned back toward Josie. There was a spring in her knees as her weight shifted to the balls of her feet. Ready to run.

Josie said, "We're not here to arrest you or give you any trouble of any kind. We just want to talk."

Carolina's head swiveled back to Mettner. Josie could see her calculating whether or not she could make it around him to the outside, but his frame took up the entire door. He softened his tone. "Miss Eddy, we're actually here because we have some bad news."

Carolina rocked back on her heels. "Bad news? Is it my mom?"

Josie said, "No, it's your daughter, Sharon. She was killed on Friday. Your mother gave us your number. We've been trying to locate you. I'm so sorry."

They weren't there to give a death notification. They already knew that Rosalie had told her about Sharon, but Mettner's approach worked. Immediately, Carolina's posture went slack. She shook her head. "I talked to my mom last night. She told me." Her head bobbed toward the table of clothes. "I was trying to do some washing so I have something clean to wear to the funeral."

Josie reached into her pockets and came up with a handful of dollar bills. She held them out. "You need ones, don't you?"

She stared at the money. "I don't have change."

Josie shrugged. "Don't worry about it."

Carolina took the money as if Josie might bite her, moving in fast, snatching it, and then stepping away even more quickly. As she went over to a vending machine that dispensed single-load portions of laundry detergent, Josie and Mettner followed. They made sure to keep her between them in case the uneasy truce broke. A quick glance toward the front of the store told Josie that the other patron hadn't even looked up from his phone.

Mettner produced his credentials, introducing himself and then Josie. Carolina didn't bother to look at either of their IDs. She inserted a few dollars into the machine and started punching buttons. "If you're still here, I guess you've got questions."

"We do," said Mettner.

Carolina took the small box of powdered detergent over to the table and started gathering up her clothes. "I wasn't in Denton when Sharon was killed. I haven't seen her in a long time. She doesn't want to see me, and I don't blame her. I never blamed her. I guess my mom told you what a screw-up I am."

Mettner said, "Your mother told us you've struggled with drug addiction for a long time."

Carolina gathered the clothes into her arms. With a sigh, she said, "You don't have to church it up. I know what she thinks of me."

Josie said, "We're not here to talk about Sharon's murder, Carolina."

She walked to the nearest washer, but a sign taped to it read: *Out of Order*. "Then why are you here?"

Mettner said, "We're here to talk about Jana Melburn."

Her response was instant. "Who?"

"Ten years ago, you were working at a gas station in Bly," Josie said.

Her shoulders stiffened. As she walked to the next washer, her gait was more careful. "Oh, that," she said. "I, uh, don't remember much about that. Like you said, ten years. I was pretty messed up back then—taking a lot of stuff—and I've been even more messed up since then, so I don't think I can help you."

As she started to stuff her clothes into the washer, one of her socks fell and landed on the floor. She bent to pick it up. For the first time, Josie noticed just how ill-fitting her T-shirt and jeans were, both too small even for her frail body. The hem of the T-shirt rose up to her rib cage, which was painfully visible. There, on the left side of her back, near her kidney area, was a small brand. It was old, the ridged skin a pale pink. Not as old as Anya's looked, but still from a long time ago. The shape was a heart with a squiggly line going straight through it.

Josie swallowed. She looked over at Mettner to see if he'd noticed it. He gave her a small nod.

"Okay," Josie said. "Then let's talk about Vance Hadlee."

Carolina came up with the sock. Her eyes bulged. "I don't want to talk about him."

"But you know him," Josie said. "Pretty well, wouldn't you say?"

"I don't know what you mean."

Josie thought of the drugs and cash in Vance's room. "Vance has an addiction problem, too, doesn't he?"

Carolina turned and backed away from them until her body touched the washer. "I don't know."

"How did you like spending time with him on the farm? We heard he likes to entertain ladies in his workshop," Josie said.

Mettner added, "I can't say all the ladies enjoy it, though."

Carolina clutched the sock to her chest, looking back and forth between them. "You think he hurt me. That's why you're here? He didn't."

Josie motioned toward her left side. "So that brand he gave you—it was consensual?"

"I said—I said it was okay. He's weird. A little kinky, okay? We were high as hell. I didn't care."

Mettner said, "How long were the two of you in a relationship?"

Carolina looked down at the dirty sock, as if it might have the answers. "We weren't in a relationship like that. It wasn't ever serious. We just—we could be ourselves around each other. That was all."

"What do you mean?" asked Josie.

"He never cared about me using, okay? It never bothered him. Not once. He'd come find me when he was bored or upset or he needed something. He usually complained about his dad being an asshole. Sometimes, if he was really going through it, he'd get all emotional and cry about his mom dying."

Mettner said, "I thought his mom left when he was a kid?"

Carolina shrugged. "I don't know. Maybe she did. Maybe I'm remembering wrong. Listen, man, we'd get fucked up together, mess around a little, he'd talk or cry or whatever. I'd listen. That's all. We weren't ever going to get married or anything. Trust me, he is never going to get over his wife."

"When is the last time you saw him?" asked Mettner.

"I don't know. Five or six months ago. I've been away, you know?"

"Were you seeing him ten years ago?" Josie asked.

"Ten years ago? I've been seeing him since high school—" She broke off, realizing her mistake. "I, uh, listen, I don't really want to talk anymore, okay? I just want to get this done." She held up the sock as if offering it to them and then she turned and threw it into the washer.

Josie said, "Let's talk about Jana Melburn then. You were the last person to see her."

"No, no, I wasn't," Carolina said over her shoulder as she pressed a series of buttons to start the washer. "That guy was the last person to see her."

Mettner said, "But you lied to the police about what happened."

She turned back toward them, her fingers now tugging at a strand of her hair. "No, I didn't. I—"

Josie said, "We saw the video, Carolina. What you told the police and what was on the video were very different things."

She curled the hair around her index finger. "So?"

"So," Mettner said. "What we can't figure out is why you would lie. You didn't even know Jana Melburn, did you? Or the other guy?"

"No, I didn't know them."

"Then why bother to lie about what happened between them?" Mettner pressed.

She twirled the hair around her finger, loosened it and twirled it again.

Josie said, "Did you hear what they were arguing about?"

Carolina didn't answer right away. Josie and Mettner waited. It was a technique that Josie found extremely useful in both interviews and interrogations. Saying nothing. Most people had to fill the silence eventually. Except that Carolina didn't.

Josie tried again. "The only reason I can think of why you would lie about something like that is because you were protecting someone. It can't be Mathias Tobin. You say you didn't know him. Jana was dead. Was it your mother? Sharon? Did you hear something that put you in danger?"

Still, she said nothing. She pulled so hard at her hair that several strands broke off and floated to the floor. Jaundiced eyes blinked slowly at them. Josie wondered if she was trying to will them away, will this conversation over.

"Carolina," said Josie. "When is the last time you went to the doctor?"

Immediately, her free hand went to her face, touching the skin beneath each cheek, one side after the other. She gave a nervous laugh. "It's that obvious, huh? I thought maybe it wasn't to other people. Red hair doesn't go well with this look, does it? I thought about dyeing it dark like my mom or Sharon. They both got the dark hair. My grandmother had red like me. They say it skips a generation."

Her voice had become skittish, almost breathless. Josie had the feeling she would just keep talking if they didn't stop her. "Jaundice is usually a sign of liver failure. Is that what the doctor told you?"

Carolina nodded. "At the ER, last time I OD'd. Too many drugs for too long. I was hoping to get through Sharon's funeral without my mom seeing me like this, though." She touched her forehead.

"Did they talk about treatment?" asked Mettner.

Carolina laughed. "Treatment? For someone like me? Even if I had insurance or could afford it, I'd have to stop using to get better, and I'm not going to do that. I'd like to think I would stop but that's a lie. Nah. I'm going out like this. This is it. Could be a couple more years or could be a matter of months. All I know is I'm going to try to be obliterated right to the very end. Starting after Sharon's funeral."

Mettner said, "Fair enough. But if that's what you're going to do, don't you think Jana Melburn's family finally deserves to know the truth about the night she died? I know you had a difficult time being a mom and that your relationship with Sharon was strained, but wouldn't you want to know what really happened to her?"

Josie counted off the beats of silence in her head. When she got to seven, Carolina muttered, "Yeah. I guess. I know my mom would. My mom deserves that after raising her so well."

"Then tell us," Josie said. "Tell us what you heard the night you saw Jana Melburn arguing with her brother."

Carolina used the back of her wrist to swipe at a tear that rolled down her cheek. Sniffling, she said, "Am I gonna have to give a statement or something?"

Mettner said, "Probably, yeah. Depends on what we find out and what it means to the case. After we talk here, we can drive over to the Bly Police Department and get it all down on paper."

"Bly?"

Josie said, "Jana's case is in their jurisdiction. We don't make those rules. Whatever you tell us, you'd have to repeat to them and make a written statement. They would be the ones to act on what you tell them, if necessary."

Mettner added, "We have a guy over there that we trust. You can talk to him, and just him."

"Who?"

Josie said, "Cyrus Grey."

Carolina gave a slow nod. "His daughter died. Yeah, I know who he is. I guess he's okay. Then again, I guess it doesn't much matter if what I'm about to tell you gets me killed. I'm going to die anyway."

FORTY

They sat on a bench with Carolina between them. She talked low and fast, keeping her eyes on the washer's timer across the room from them as it counted down from forty-two minutes to zero.

"I didn't hear much of what they said," she explained. "I looked out the window, saw they were arguing. I went to the door so I could hear better. I didn't want to open it and draw attention to myself 'cause then they would stop. But I heard some stuff. He wanted her to come home with him, but she was going out to meet with someone. She said it was important. She'd been working on getting 'the information' for weeks. The guy, Mathias, said it was a scam or something like that, blah blah blah, but basically he didn't want her meeting with this guy."

Mettner said, "Did either of them say the name of the guy?"

"No. Not that I heard. He tried to get the name out of her but it didn't seem like she was going to tell him. They had a fight. Like, a physical fight, sort of. He was trying to stop her from going."

They waited for her to say more but she kept silent. Over her head, Mettner caught Josie's gaze. She could see the question in his eyes. That was it? That was Carolina's big revelation? Then why had she said that what she was about to tell them might get her killed? Josie looked at Carolina's hands, tangled in her red locks, twisting until more and more dried, damaged strands of hair fell away. One of her heels drummed against the tile. She turned and looked at Josie. "Either of you got a smoke? I could use a smoke."

"I'm sorry, we don't," said Josie. She was reminded of Needle—Zeke—and the way he held information close, only giving it up if she asked precisely the right questions. It was infuriating and yet it was one of the things that made him so savvy and able to survive on the street year after year—and stay out of trouble with the police for the most part.

"Carolina," said Josie. "Do *you* know the guy Jana Melburn was going to meet that night?"

"Well, yeah," Carolina said. "It was Vance Hadlee."

Josie was surprised and yet, at the same time, not surprised at all. Everything seemed to come back to the Hadlees. The bodies of Sharon Eddy and Keri Cryer had the literal marks of Vance Hadlee on them.

Over Carolina's head, Mettner stared at Josie as if she'd just performed a miracle. He said, "How do you know?"

As if it was the most obvious thing in the world, Carolina said, "'Cause he told me."

"Vance was helping Jana find her birth parents?" Mettner asked.

Carolina wrinkled her nose. "What? I don't know nothing about that. I just know they were together that night."

"Were they seeing one another?" asked Josie.

Carolina shook her head. "No, it wasn't like that. I mean, yeah, Vance would have liked to... what'd he say? 'Defile' her. He wanted her real bad, but she wasn't into him. I'm pretty sure that wouldn't have stopped him, but then she was dead so it didn't matter."

Mettner said, "He talked about Jana?"

"When I asked him about her, yeah. Just so happened, he was out back of the gas station that night after my shift. He looked a mess. Like, he was really strung out, but he said he hadn't even taken anything yet. He wanted to get high. We took a walk. There's an area not far from there that's pretty much hidden from everything. Well, I think someone built a house there a few years ago but back then it was just a lot with a bunch of trees on it. If he was coming to meet me after my shift, that's where we went."

"You did this often?" asked Josie.

"Yeah. Few times a month. Sometimes more. When his wife was ignoring him, he said, which she did a lot. He was always complaining about her. I'm pretty sure by that time she'd already left him. The divorce was turning him into a monster. He really didn't deal well with it. He complained nonstop about how she kept telling all these lies about him to everyone and getting him into legal trouble. I was trying to get him off the subject, so I asked him where he'd been all night. He said he was with someone. I said, someone like a woman? He said a girl, way too young for him, and it went all wrong. He said he might be in big trouble. He never said her name. I didn't find out till a few days later when the whole damn town was flipping out over her body being found."

"How do you know he was talking about Jana Melburn?" Mettner asked.

Carolina reached up and massaged her throat. "'Cause of what happened next. We were getting real high and I started ribbing him about the girl. Asking, well, how young was she? Is that why you're gonna be in big trouble? I said you think you're in deep shit with your old man right now 'cause of what happened with your wife, wait till he finds out you're a cradle-robbing perv! Well, he just burst right into tears. He said that wasn't the problem. I said, what in the hell did you do? Did you run her over with your truck or something? I was half joking, but he completely lost his shit. Went batshit crazy."

"In what way?" asked Josie.

"He tried to kill me. Slammed me against a tree and started strangling me. Said I could never tell anyone about her. That she knew him or that they'd met. He said I could never tell anyone what I heard. He said blink twice if I understand, so I did. After I caught my breath, I was mad at him. I said, all these years we've been doing this—the drugs and the sleeping together—and I've never told a single soul. No one could even tell we knew one another. Whatever he did was none of my business. That's when he kind of told me."

"Told you what?" asked Mettner.

Her fingers lingered over her throat. "That he'd met this girl along the road a few blocks away where no one would see her get into his truck. He'd met her somewhere. She wanted to talk to him. He never did say about what. I don't think he cared. I think he was just trying to get in her pants. He took her to the farm. They had an argument and he hit her."

"With what?" asked Josie.

She shrugged. "I don't know. He didn't say, or I didn't remember. He just said he hit her again and again. She went unconscious. He thought she was fine at first 'cause there was no blood or bruising or anything. Then he tried to wake her up, but she was dead. So he took her and left her by the lake. There was only one girl who turned up dead next to the lake right after that, so I know it was Jana Melburn. Anyway, Vance was super paranoid for weeks and weeks after that. Like totally freaking out. Kept going on about what if he left DNA on her somehow? What if they figured it out? Then the cops ruled her death an accident and it all went away."

Mettner said, "Did Vance ever talk to you about Mathias Tobin?"

Carolina shook her head. "No. Well, that's not true. One

time, yeah. Last time I saw him. He was wrecked 'cause he had just given some statement. He said it was to help get a guy out of prison. The guy who shot his wife in the head. The cop's daughter."

"Piper Tobin, Sergeant Grey's daughter," said Mettner.

"Yeah. He said he gave a statement to some attorneys that that guy was with him when she was killed so that he could get out of prison."

"Why was he 'wrecked'?" asked Josie.

"He said he was going against his dad. I told him not to worry. His dad had had a stroke a month or so before that. He wasn't exactly in shape to give Vance hell."

Josie asked, "Was Vance worried that his dad might somehow punish him for giving that statement?"

"I don't know. He always had big hang-ups about his dad. After the stroke, Vance was even more of a mess than usual. Kept saying he thought he knew who his dad was, but after the stroke he found out things that changed his mind."

"Things like what?" asked Mettner.

"I don't know. Don't think he told me."

A barrage of feelings flooded Josie's consciousness with each new revelation. Sadness that bright, sweet young biology student Jana Melburn who, at nineteen, was working at a doctor's office to put herself through college, had had her life snuffed out. Vance had thrown her away like she meant nothing. But she'd meant a great deal to Mathias Tobin and Hallie Kent, who had loved her and raised her.

Anger that Vance Hadlee had killed her as if it were his right to do so if his anger flared hot enough. He swaggered around Bly like he owned the place, like he was above the law, like he had every right to hurt women: Anya, Lark, Jana, even Carolina, in spite of her admission that the relationship between them was consensual. Then there was confusion.

What information had Jana been seeking from Vance

Hadlee? It couldn't be about her birth parents. Hallie had tracked down her biological family. There was no connection between them and Vance. Josie searched her memory banks for anything that could possibly have brought Jana and Vance together. It only took a few seconds. The doctor's office where she worked. Lark Hadlee had told Josie and Gretchen that the Hadlees were patients there. Josie had no doubt that Vance had noticed Jana right off. But why had Jana wanted to meet with him?

What things had Vance found out after Dermot's stroke that had made him so agitated? One of the first things—maybe the only thing—that Vance had done after Dermot's stroke was to free Mathias. But why? What did Dermot have against Mathias? If Mathias hadn't shot Piper Tobin, then who had?

"Carolina," Josie said. "Did Vance ever say anything to you about the murder of the cop's daughter? Did he know who killed her?"

She shook her head. "He didn't say much except that her husband wasn't the one who did it."

Mettner said, "Do you think Vance did it?"

"How should I know?"

"Because it seems like Vance told you everything," Josie pointed out. "Did he ever talk about who killed the cop's daughter?"

"No. He didn't much care about her, just that this other guy wasn't in prison."

They had a lot of pieces to the complex puzzle that had formed in the town of Bly over the years and later spilled over into Denton, and yet the picture was incomplete. What were they still missing?

Mettner said, "Carolina, Vance Hadlee tried to kill you. He admitted to you that he had killed a young woman and dumped her body like it was trash. Why would you keep a secret like that?"

What he didn't say was that it wasn't only morally wrong but legally, it made her an accessory to murder. Josie didn't mention this either. Any charges that might be brought against her would be squarely in the hands of the district attorney of Everett County. All Josie and Mettner could do was deliver her to Cyrus so he could take her statement and then perhaps accompany him when he went to arrest Vance. Hopefully, with the national press scrutiny that Trinity could bring to bear, neither Vance nor his father would be able to get him out of jail, even temporarily.

Carolina eyed the washer, which still had sixteen minutes to go. Slumping against the wall behind her, she said, "You're making a pretty bold assumption that I'm a good person. Since you talked to my mother, you ought to know better." When neither of them responded to that statement, she continued. "The truth? I loved him. I've always loved him. Still do, maybe. Or maybe not, now that I've finally told his secret."

She must have felt Josie stiffen next to her because she looked over and met Josie's eye. "I know what you're thinking. How could I love someone like him? Cheated on his wife, did drugs, killed a girl. It's because he never judged me. Not one time. He knew exactly who and what I was, and he was fine with it. No judgment. I never even got that kind of treatment from my own family."

FORTY-ONE

Josie stood next to Mettner in the corner of the hospital cafeteria, a paper cup of coffee in hand, and listened as Cyrus gave Anya the news about Vance. As agreed, Carolina Eddy had given her written statement to Cyrus at the Bly Police Department, after requesting several accommodations. Some were easy: coffee, a meal, cigarettes. Others were more complicated, and required Cyrus to set up some fast and furious meetings with his superiors as well as the county DA. Carolina was convinced that once she signed her statement, her life would be in danger.

Josie, still nursing the wound on her forehead, couldn't argue.

The county set her up in a hotel for the next few days, at least until Vance could be taken into custody and they were sure that he wouldn't be released on bail. After Carolina was firmly ensconced in her hotel room, Cyrus started the arrest warrant. Even though the Jana Melburn case wasn't theirs, Josie and Mettner decided to stay to see things through, especially with Anya in Bradysport. Cyrus had wanted to deliver the news to her personally. With Garrick still on a ventilator and unresponsive, they'd all gathered in the cafeteria.

Josie watched Anya's face go through a carousel of expressions as she listened to Cyrus. Shock. Sadness. Anger. Deep hurt. Guilt. Shame.

"I had no idea," she said. "I mean, I often suspected he cheated on me, especially near the end, but I could never prove it, and by that time I wanted out so it didn't matter. It seemed like maybe it would be in my favor. If he'd met someone else, he wouldn't care so much about me. I didn't know he'd been seeing Carolina Eddy all that time. I definitely didn't know about Jana." She ran a hand through her hair and paced in a tight little circle.

Cyrus looked like his heart might break, watching her. "I'm sorry, Anya. I truly am."

She gave a dry laugh. "Sorry that my ex-husband was an even worse monster than we initially thought? It just reinforces the validity of my decisions. I just can't believe I never caught him in anything. I thought your office looked at Jana's phone. You really didn't find anything?"

"We really didn't," Cyrus said. "Believe me, if we had, I would have been all over that."

Anya stopped moving and pinned him with a penetrating stare. "How can you be sure? What if there was something on her phone and somehow Vance—or even Dermot, if he knew that Vance had killed her—made it disappear?"

Cyrus said, "The Hadlees have influence, I'll grant you that, but I've never seen it in our office. Dermot goes higher up than us, from what I understand. Not that anyone's ever been able to prove it."

"But if Vance and Jana were seeing one another, how did they communicate?"

"They weren't seeing each other," Josie said. "I think they met at the doctor's office. She was a receptionist. They likely talked there. Maybe more than once. We'll never know, but I think that's where they set up the meeting. Jana wanted to talk to him about something. It couldn't be about her birth family. Anya, do you have any idea what it could be?"

"No. I wish I did."

Josie kept mulling it over as the conversation turned toward arresting Vance, which Cyrus intended to do once they left the hospital. Anya wanted to come.

"Absolutely not," Cyrus and Mettner said in unison.

"I'll stay in one of the cars," she insisted. "You can park it down the road from the farm."

As they argued over it, Josie retreated into her own mind, the unanswered questions surrounding the cluster of cases that all seemed somehow related, however tenuously, to Jana Melburn like a splinter under one of her nails. There was, after all, still the matter of the Sharon Eddy and Kerri Cryer murders. Vance had no real alibis for either murder, and a cadaver dog had alerted to the scent of human remains in one of the Hadlee family vehicles. In spite of that, they still couldn't prove that he'd committed the murders. Again, Josie couldn't see the advantage to Vance in killing either woman. Unless Sharon Eddy's murder had somehow been a warning to Carolina that she should continue to keep all of his secrets. Was the murder of Keri Cryer a stab at Mathias somehow, even though he'd exonerated him? Had he left the bodies in Anya's jurisdiction with the same brand as her to scare her? Antagonize her? Vance was certainly arrogant enough to commit the murders so brazenly and believe he could get away with them.

But then what was the catalyst? Why, after ten years, had he decided to start killing?

Was it Dermot's stroke? That had happened the year before but the murders had only started days ago. Was it Piper's death? That was certainly more recent. For all they knew, Vance could have killed Piper as well. But wouldn't

Vance have told Carolina that? He'd told her everything else. Was that why Vance had gone to bat for Mathias and gotten him out of prison? But why would Vance bother? With Mathias in prison for her murder, Vance would never fall under suspicion.

And who had stabbed Garrick Wolfe? What was his role in all of this?

Josie felt Mettner nudge her. "You okay, boss?"

"Yeah, yeah."

Anya and Cyrus were still arguing about whether or not she could be present when they arrested Vance.

Mettner said, "Walk with me."

She followed him over to the food area, a collection of counters that had a wide selection of dishes to choose from, some pre-made and others made to order. "What's wrong?" she asked as they perused several pre-made sandwiches.

"The pieces aren't fitting. It's gotta be bothering you, too."

"It is. We're no closer to solving our own murders."

"I don't think the evidence is going to get us there," Mettner said. "We've got a lot of circumstantial stuff, but nothing solid. I was hoping if we untangled this mess in Bly, something would bubble to the surface."

"Yeah," Josie said. They walked over to the pizza counter. A woman and a young boy stood hand in hand, studying the menu. Mother and son, judging by the resemblance. "I think the problem is that we're coming at this entire thing from the wrong direction."

"What do you mean?"

"We're focusing too hard on Vance, and maybe even Mathias."

Mettner laughed. "That's all we've got."

The mother and son pointed at the menu simultaneously. They said pepperoni at the same time and then they laughed. They each had a dimple in their left cheek.

"No," Josie said. "We've got Jana. She is what started all of this. Everything."

"We literally just solved her case."

"I'm not talking about her murder," said Josie. "I'm talking about her. Who she was, what she wanted."

Mettner scratched at his chin. "I'm not sure I follow."

As the mother put in an order for two personal pepperoni pizzas, the boy wrapped his arms around her legs. Automatically, she put a hand on his head and began pushing her fingers through his thick black hair. He gazed up at her with adoration.

"Jana was a foster kid. Obsessed with science, sure, but not just any science. Genetics. That's what Hallie said. It makes sense that you'd be interested in genetics if you never knew your biological family."

"She couldn't have been trying to find her biological family through Vance Hadlee."

The mother paid for the pizzas and took her receipt. Looking down at her son, she said something to him. He made a face, and she mimicked it back at him. Again, they looked momentarily identical. When they laughed again, the dimples appeared. "No," said Josie. "But I think she would have been much more observant of families. How they acted. What they looked like. The traits they passed from generation to generation."

What if I told you...

Mettner followed Josie's gaze, watching the mother and son for a moment. "Jana working as a receptionist for one of the main family doctors in their area would have given her access to a lot of biological information about local families. Okay, okay. I think I see where you're going with this. It was something she saw or noticed or realized from working at that office that made her want to pump Vance for information. But what?"

The mother noticed them staring. Josie watched her take note of the bulky spots under their coats where their holsters rested. Then she made eye contact. Like her son's, her irises were a light brown.

Don't you want to know the truth?

Josie flashed to the first time she'd seen Vance Hadlee up close. She clutched Mettner's arm. "His eyes. Mett, it was his eyes."

"I don't—" he began, but Josie was already dragging him back to where Cyrus and Anya were speaking, more calmly now. They both looked up, surprise registering on their faces as they saw Josie pulling Mettner by his arm.

"Anya, the eye condition that Vance has, what's it called again?"

"Heterochromia."

"There are different kinds," Josie said. "The one where you have two different colored eyes."

"Heterochromia iridum," Anya said.

"The kind Vance has which you said was—"

"Central heterochromia."

Cyrus held up his hands. "Wait, wait just a second. What are you—"

Cutting him off, Josie said, "Are there other kinds?"

Anya tapped her lips, thinking. Then she said, "Well, yeah. If I remember correctly, there's also one called sectoral where basically just a section of the iris is a different color than the rest."

Mettner took out his phone and began tapping into his internet browser search bar.

"Mathias Tobin has sectoral heterochromia," Josie said.

Cyrus lowered his hands. "That has a name? I always thought he'd just had some kind of eye injury in childhood or something."

"Are you sure?" asked Anya. "I never saw him that close."

Mettner turned his phone screen toward them, showing an image of an eye with an iris that was half blue, half brown.

Cyrus said, "His isn't as pronounced. In fact, you really have to be close to him to see it. He's got blue eyes and in one of them, there's just a small bit that's brown. But his eyelashes on that side are blond."

"Yes," Josie said. "Anya, you studied this in school, right?"

"I didn't study it for practice, but I definitely took a big interest in it since Vance's eyes were so unusual."

"Is heterochromia genetic?" Josie asked.

She took a few beats to think it over. "I don't remember. I think only in cases of a rare disorder. A syndrome. I can't think of the name of it."

Mettner tapped at his phone again. "Waardenburg Syndrome."

"That's it," Anya said. "But I don't think Vance had it. Although I guess maybe he didn't have severe symptoms? If I recall, with Waardenburg, the most common issue is hearing loss."

"And a white forelock," said Mettner, reading from his phone. "Loss of pigmentation in hair and skin. Other symptoms range from constipation to abnormal facial features, joint problems to deficits in intellectual function."

"But it's possible not to have all of those," Josie said.

"Waardenburg is a group of genetic conditions, so yeah, I'm sure it would present differently across a wide spectrum of patients," Anya said.

Josie said, "Do you remember ever seeing photos of your mother-in-law?"

"No. Not really. I'm sure that Vance showed me, but it was such a taboo topic in the household that no one ever spoke of it. They all felt betrayed and abandoned. You couldn't even say her name."

"When we did the search at the farmhouse, there were photos of her in Vance's room. She had a white forelock and it looked like she was wearing a hearing aid."

Anya's eyes widened. "You think that Susanna Hadlee had Waardenburg Syndrome and passed it down to Vance?"

"And Mathias," Josie said.

"My God," Cyrus mumbled.

Mettner looked up from his phone. "You think Susanna Hadlee is Mathias Tobin's mother?"

"Her and Garrick?" Anya said.

"Think about it," Josie said. "Garrick practiced family medicine before he got into pathology. Cyrus, didn't you say that he delivered the Hadlee children?"

"Yeah, but Mathias Tobin is a year younger than Vance. Three years younger than Lark. That means Susanna would have carried the baby to term while married to Dermot and raising the kids. I mean, I don't remember folks talking about her being pregnant a third time, but if she had kept to the farm during that time, and then Garrick delivered the baby himself, it's possible she could have kept it hidden. Still, she would have to get through the entire pregnancy while living with her husband. How would that work?"

"It was an affair," Mettner pointed out. "I'm sure Susanna Hadlee didn't announce it to Dermot that she thought the baby might not be his. But maybe Dermot suspected or found out and then it became a problem. Maybe he forced her to put Mathias up for adoption."

"Garrick couldn't have taken him," Anya agreed. "Even if he wanted to—even though he wanted to. It would have ended his marriage with Marie, and while he could stay upright to tend to patients and later perform autopsies Monday through Friday, he would not have been fit to raise a child."

Mettner said, "So Mathias comes along, Susanna is coerced into giving him up, she tries to stay in the marriage for a few years, for the sake of the kids she still has, but she can't hack it so she leaves. Or Dermot finally kicks her out. Mathias grows up in foster care."

A tingle started at the base of Josie's neck. "I don't think she left."

"What are you saying?" said Cyrus.

Josie met Anya's eyes. "The box that the state police evidence response team found at Garrick's house, it had—"

Anya's face fell. She finished Josie's sentence. "A hearing aid in it. Oh my God." She wobbled a little and Cyrus took her elbow. "I think I need to sit down," she murmured.

Cyrus guided her over to a nearby table. Josie and Mettner followed. Once they were seated, Mettner said, "What box are we talking about?"

Cyrus tore his eyes from Anya's face. "In Garrick Wolfe's garage, the evidence response team found a metal box with a human bone fragment—likely a skull plate—an old piece of clothing, a necklace and what they believe was a hearing aid. It's been sent for processing."

Mettner said, "Garrick Wolfe killed Susanna Hadlee?"

"He couldn't have," Anya murmured. "I'm telling you. There is no way he could have killed someone."

Cyrus sighed. "It was a long time ago. He might have been different back then."

Mettner stared at Anya for a long moment. Then he turned to Cyrus. "You have photos of this stuff? In your file?"

"Why?"

"How can you be sure that what they found in there was a hearing aid?"

Cyrus said, "We're sure."

Mettner pressed on. "You're leaving out a lot of context. What did the stuff look like? What condition was it in? Where was it found inside the garage?"

Josie felt a spark of excitement. Mettner was on to something.

He added, "And how damn long does it take to process fingerprints? Our guy does it in a matter of hours."

"The state police are backed up," Cyrus pointed out.

"But you could get us photos, couldn't you?" asked Josie. "You could make a call right now. Someone in your office could send them to you in minutes."

Anya put a hand on Cyrus's forearm. He visibly startled. She managed a wan smile. "Please, Cy."

A silent moment passed between them. From where Josie sat, it felt intensely private, like she and Mettner shouldn't be witness to it. She felt relieved when Cyrus broke eye contact with Anya. He patted her hand and said softly, "Give me a few minutes."

FORTY-TWO

While Cyrus was gone, Mettner got them all coffee, which they drank in silence. Josie was beginning to feel the weight of the day and the murder cases her team had been tasked with solving, together with the heft of the secrets they'd started uncovering in Bly. Her head pounded. The sutures on her scalp burned.

"I've got them," Cyrus said, striding back to the table.

He resumed his seat and the three of them crowded in around him, peering at his phone screen. He swiped through a half-dozen photos and then back, showing each one again.

Mettner said, "That's a tackle box."

Cyrus nodded, stopping on a photo of the workbench in Garrick Wolfe's garage. The bright red, rectangular box sat in the middle of the bench.

Anya said, "If this is evidence that Garrick murdered Susanna Hadlee, why would he leave it out like that? I lived with him and Marie for almost a year and I never saw that box."

Cyrus said, "I'm sure he hid it when Marie was alive."

"Keep going," said Mettner.

The next series of photos showed the four items inside the

box. Each of them was crusted with dirt, badly decayed, and barely recognizable. The skull plate was about the size of Josie's hand. The necklace was so dirty that they could not make out the charm. The piece of clothing was dark and frayed, any pattern impossible to identify. At first glance, the hearing aid looked like a dirt-covered rock. It was only in the close-up photo that Josie could make out the small wire that ran from the large piece that went behind the ear to the smaller earbud that sat inside the ear canal.

Cyrus said, "Obviously this is not what most hearing aids look like now, but if this was Susanna's then we're talking the late eighties. The style seems about right for that time."

Mettner said, "I believe you. That's a hearing aid. But look at the items, as opposed to the box."

"What is it?" asked Anya.

Josie said, "The box is new. Clean. In perfect condition. The items inside are obviously extremely old. Like Cyrus said, if these belonged to Susanna Hadlee and we assume that she died at the time that Dermot Hadlee told everyone she had 'left', then that was over thirty years ago."

"It's interesting that you say that," said Cyrus. "Because I also called to see if they'd gotten prints from any of this. Nothing from the items inside the box. Too old, too degraded, and if they tried to get them, they'd run the risk of destroying some of the items. But on the outside of the box, they found two sets of prints."

Mettner said, "Whose prints?"

"Garrick Wolfe's—his are in the system since he had a DUI a few years back—and Vance Hadlee's."

Anya gasped. "Vance?"

Mettner said, "Not Mathias?"

Cyrus shook his head. "Nope. Not Mathias. Only Vance."

Anya said, "But Vance would have been only five years old when Susanna was killed. Maybe six."

Josie felt the puzzle pieces slot into place, a fuller picture of the sequence of events revealing itself. "Vance didn't do anything to his mother," she said. "He found this stuff. Then he put it into this box, and he brought it to Garrick."

"What are you talking about?" said Anya.

"When we talked with Carolina Eddy, she told us that Vance was a mess after his dad's stroke. She said that he kept saying he thought he knew who Dermot was but that he had found things out that changed his mind."

Mettner pointed toward Cyrus's phone screen. "He found out that Dermot killed his mother?"

"I think so," Josie said.

"But how?" asked Anya.

"I don't know," Josie said. "Maybe there was something in the house? Among Dermot's things?"

"This stuff," said Cyrus. "He found these things."

Mettner said, "Even with the hearing aid, I'm not sure he'd make the connection to his mother. Besides, that stuff looks like it was buried for the last few decades."

"It was," Josie said. "When we searched the farm, Lark complained to us that since Dermot's stroke, Vance was consumed with digging along the north end of the property. He'd told her he wanted to put in a pond. She said he'd been using the bobcat to dig."

Cyrus placed his phone on the table and ran a hand through his hair. "He wasn't digging a pond. He was looking for his mother's remains."

Anya touched the screen before it could go black. She swiped until she found a photo of the skull plate. "He found them," she murmured. "Some of them, at least."

Josie said, "He's probably been looking for more. That's why he's digging all the time instead of working on the farm. Dermot's not in any condition to stop him now."

Mettner said, "He put them into his tackle box and went to see Garrick. Why Garrick?"

Anya sighed. "Garrick was like an uncle to him. Vance and Lark were always very isolated on that farm, especially once they were no longer going to school every day, but Garrick was around a lot when they were kids. He was always someone they trusted. Remember, Dermot was the one who talked Garrick into giving me the job in the ME's office. After I left Vance, even though Garrick and Marie had helped me get away from him, he still listened when Garrick asked him to leave me alone."

"He didn't listen," Josie said. "He obeyed. Dermot raised him to obey the father figure. With Dermot's health compromised, the next available father figure was Garrick. Vance went to him for guidance."

"And Garrick told him to exonerate Mathias, first thing."

Anya said, "I wonder if Garrick told Vance that Mathias is his half-brother."

Josie said, "I think Vance already knew—or suspected. Jana Melburn wanted to meet with him not about her own biological family but about Mathias's birth parents. Remember, Mathias told her she was 'wrong' and 'insane' and he said something like he didn't know who was filling her head—probably with this idea that he was related to the Hadlees. It's why he called her meddling."

Cyrus said, "When she said 'could be yours', maybe she meant the farm?"

Anya said, "Dermot would never let him stake any claim on that farm. He would fight him every step of the way, and he'd probably win."

Josie shook her head. "Lark Hadlee told me that she and Vance have a trust fund that was set up by her mother's family so that regardless of the income from the farm, Susanna's children would be provided for. It wasn't contingent on Dermot at all. Only on Susanna. If Mathias is one of Susanna's children, that trust is his, too."

"Jana Melburn wouldn't have known that," said Mettner.

"No," Josie agreed. "Probably not. Unless she overheard it being talked about at the doctor's office. We'll never know. Regardless, she would have thought he had a claim to the farm."

Cyrus's brow furrowed. "But this doesn't make any sense. After Jana was found dead, Mathias never said a word to anyone about any of this. If he had, we would have gone right to the Hadlee farm and talked with Vance. What possible reason could Mathias have had for keeping something like this to himself?"

Josie frowned. She thought of Hallie Kent holding a place in her own home for Mathias year after year because once upon a time they'd been a family. She thought about all the photos of Mathias with Jana. "You're right. If Mathias knew or even suspected that Jana was going to meet Vance, I can't see him covering that up or keeping it a secret. He would definitely mention it to the police. He went out looking for Jana after she left the gas station. If he'd known or suspected that Vance Hadlee was the person she was meeting, he would have gone right to the farm, but he didn't."

Cyrus said, "In the video he does demand to know who she is going to see and it seems like she doesn't tell him. He uses the words 'scam' and 'suspicious.' I don't think he knew anything about the Hadlees. Not then."

Mettner said, "Maybe Jana didn't tell him specifics. I haven't seen the tape of her and Mathias arguing, but I know Noah was only able to read small parts of the conversation. I read the transcript you guys made. Maybe Jana never named Vance or the Hadlees or talked about the farm at all. Maybe she said something like, what if I told you your birth family was wealthy, or something like that?"

"But in his statement, he said that she was meeting someone about her birth parents, not his," Cyrus said.

Mettner said, "Maybe he misunderstood. Maybe he thought she was speaking generally, as in, you grew up a foster kid, too. Wouldn't you want to know the truth? What if you found out your birth family was rich and that all that could be yours? Something like that?"

"I suppose," said Cyrus. "But Mathias has to know the truth now, right? He was staying with Garrick. This damn box was left out for anyone to see. Garrick probably showed it to Mathias, told him everything. So if Mathias knows all this now, why didn't he just come forward? Tell the world? Why bother with all this running and hiding?"

Josie reached across and tapped Cyrus's blank phone screen. "A DNA test can prove that Mathias is the son of Garrick Wolfe and Susanna Hadlee, but it will not prove that Dermot killed Susanna. Not even the box of her things and partial remains proves that. All it proves is that she's dead. Mathias thinks that Dermot Hadlee has been out to get him for his entire life. Whether that's true or not, it seems like a black cloud has been following Mathias since high school. Allegation after allegation until he finally ended up in prison. Dermot was the head football coach when the boys were in high school. How hard would it have been for him to somehow influence these cheerleaders to say it was Mathias who had assaulted them?"

"Especially if it was Vance who had actually done it," Anya choked out.

Cyrus said, "Okay, let's work through this. This is the theory now: Susanna Hadlee had an affair with Garrick Wolfe. The result was Mathias Tobin, who was put into foster care. A few years later, Dermot kills her, buries her on the farm, and tells everyone she left her family. In high school, Vance starts getting into trouble, assaulting cheerleaders. Dermot decides to intervene and somehow convinces these cheerleaders to blame Mathias Tobin instead of his own son. That falls apart. Eight or nine years later, Jana Melburn is working at the Hadlees' family doctor's office and somehow puts it together that Mathias might be related to Vance. She convinces Vance to meet with her so she can talk about it."

"Vance meets with her," Josie put in. "They argue—probably about her theory that Mathias is his half-brother—and Vance kills her."

"Mathias has no idea she was meeting Vance. No reason to suspect Vance at all," Cyrus continued. "By unfortunate circumstance, he falls under suspicion for Jana's murder. Fast-forward a few more years. He's married to my daughter."

He faltered, voice growing scratchy. Anya touched his shoulder. He cleared his throat and plowed ahead. "She is shot in the head while he's out looking for work. When the police come around to Dermot to get Mathias's alibi, Dermot sees an opportunity to get this kid put away for good, and so he refuses to give the alibi."

"Which means Dermot had to know or at least suspect that Mathias was Susanna's son," said Mettner.

"Maybe that's why he killed her," said Anya. "Dermot found out."

"Dermot forbids Vance from giving Mathias an alibi," Josie added.

Cyrus said, "Then Dermot has a stroke. Vance finds something that leads him to believe Dermot killed Susanna and buried her on the north side of the farm. He goes digging. Finds these things." Cyrus tapped against his phone screen. "Takes them to Garrick."

"Who tells him the truth," Mettner said. "He had to have told him the truth about him and Susanna and Mathias."

"Not necessarily," said Josie. "Garrick made deals with people before. Do this, and I'll help you with that. Maybe he just told Vance to give the statement that would exonerate Mathias and in exchange, he'd help him find out what happened to Susanna."

"He held onto the box for safekeeping," said Anya, looking relieved.

Cyrus said, "But if Mathias didn't shoot Piper, who did?"

"Your department should have reopened the case when Mathias was exonerated," Josie said gently. "If we can find Mathias, maybe he could shed some light on it."

"We've still got a lot of pieces that don't fit together," Mettner said, "Even if what we've worked out just now is all true, it doesn't help us figure out who killed Sharon Eddy and Keri Cryer or, if it was Vance, prove that."

Cyrus sighed and shook his head. "It also doesn't tell us who stabbed Garrick. Well, you two take care of your own cases. Right now, I'm going to arrest Vance Hadlee."

FORTY-THREE

Cyrus agreed to allow Anya to be present while he went to arrest Vance if she agreed to stay in Josie and Mettner's vehicle, parked back behind the staging area which was down the road from the farm. It was dark by the time they assembled there, a line of Bly PD cruisers along the side of the road. Cyrus had brought along four of his officers. They made sure their vests were on and all of their equipment was ready, including their radios. Then they huddled around the hood of Cyrus's car. He spread out an aerial map of the farm and used a flashlight to illuminate it. Pointing to the long driveway, he said, "We walk up here to the farmhouse. The front door of the farmhouse is Side A. Moving clockwise, the left side of the property is Side B, the rear is Side C, and the right is Side D. Denton PD will act as perimeter officers and we'll post them on the corners. Detective Quinn, you'll be stationed here on the B/C side, where you will have a view East and North. Detective Mettner, you'll be positioned over here, C/D side, with a view West and South. You two will hold the perimeter while my team begins clearing buildings, starting with the house."

An officer Cyrus had introduced as Margaret Finlay looked around the circle. "Everyone good? Any questions?"

Everyone was ready.

They walked up the road. Josie barely felt the cold February wind whipping around them. Her adrenaline was already pumping. She wasn't sure why. It was an arrest warrant and she and Mettner weren't even on the entry team. While the driveway was not visible in the dark, the farm itself was well lit, probably owing to the fact that the day's work always started before dawn. The lights were ablaze inside the farmhouse as Josie and Mettner passed it to find their positions on the perimeter. She listened to radio chatter as Cyrus, Finlay and the others made entry into the farmhouse. From where Josie stood, toward the rear of the property, she couldn't see the Bly PD entry team or the house. She searched the other side of the property for Mettner but he wasn't visible from where she stood. Her position afforded her a view of the two cowsheds and the milking station.

She heard a noise, carried on the wind, but she couldn't decipher it.

Her radio squawked. Mettner's voice said, "We've got movement on Side B. West side. Might be a person moving near the garage closest to the house."

"Hold perimeter," Finlay answered.

"Copy that," Mettner answered.

Was it Vance? Josie wondered. In his workshop? They'd find out soon enough as the entry team cleared each building.

Josie stomped her feet to get some warmth back into them. Her eyes scanned the perimeter but saw nothing amiss. The radio chirped again but this time, the message was obliterated by the booming sound of a gunshot. Then another.

"Shit," she muttered, heart skittering.

"Side D, Side D," came Mettner's urgent voice over the

radio. "Gunshots from the direction of the first garage. I'm moving in."

Josie answered, "I'm heading that way."

She unholstered her pistol and sprinted around the cowsheds and then the milking station. The back of the house came into view. There was a long stretch of grass between the rear of the house and the other farm structures where no light reached. She fumbled for her flashlight and held it beneath her pistol, panning back and forth. She saw Mettner and hurried toward him.

"What did you see?" she asked when she caught up.

"Muzzle flash," he said. "Then I think the garage bay door opened and closed. I saw light, almost like a fire, and then it was gone. I was too far away to see much more than that."

"Vance has a wood-burning stove in there," Josie said. "That's probably what you saw when the door opened."

"If it was Vance," Mettner said. "The question is, who was he shooting at?"

Her heart galloped in her chest as they kept moving. Her anxiety was in overdrive, every cell in her body painfully alert. Their feet finally hit the gravel path and Vance's workshop came into view.

"Nine o'clock," said Mettner.

Josie looked in the direction he had indicated. Just feet away from the workshop, someone was sprawled face down on the ground, arms and legs thrown wide. Into his radio, Mettner said, "We've got one civilian down. We need a medic and a backup unit."

As Josie and Mettner neared, Josie saw the thin white hair at the back of Dermot Hadlee's head marred by blood.

"Shit," said Mettner.

From their radios came Cyrus's voice. "Finlay and I are headed your way. Medic is en route."

While Mettner knelt to check Dermot for a pulse, Josie

looked around them, searching for threats, ready to respond. Her eyes were drawn to the garage, only steps away. It had no side entry door, only a bay door, which was closed. Unlike the first time they'd been here, there was no padlock on it.

Mettner said, "No pulse."

Muffled screams sounded from behind the door. Josie's chest tightened. Lark.

Josie opened her mouth to speak but before she could, bullets punched through the metal of the bay door, their booms echoing all around. Josie was sure that Mettner yelled something, but she couldn't hear him over the shots.

Bang. Bang. Bang.

She felt the split in the air and the heat, smelled the cordite where a bullet whizzed past her face. Something punched into her vest, low on her left side, spinning her and knocking her onto her back. The air left her lungs. In the back of her mind, she remembered Mettner listing the firearms he'd found on the premises. Dermot Hadlee owned two handguns. A Colt 1911 and a Glock G21. Both took 45 ACP rounds, which was enough firepower to punch through the garage door and still hit them.

Bang. Bang.

Her mind tried to remember how many rounds each one held, but she couldn't think past the pain blooming along the left side of her torso and the panic at the realization that she couldn't move, couldn't breathe.

Josie's ears were ringing. Mettner's hand was on her shoulder. What was he saying? Her addled mind tried to process it. It sounded like "Fall back! Fall back!" She willed her legs to move, relieved when she saw her feet scrabble, trying to back away from the garage door, out of range of the bullets.

Bang, bang.

Mettner pulled, dragging her. They'd only gone a couple of feet when, to Josie's horror, the bay door lifted.

She tried to say Mettner's name.

It was a belated realization that her pistol was still in her hand. Fighting the intense pain in her side, she aimed it at Vance. He stood in the center of the bay, shirtless, jeans unbuttoned, boots unlaced. A sheen of sweat covered his skin. His hair was wet and slick. She had been right. He'd started a fire in the wood stove. Its orange glow pulsed around him. It was as if he were emerging from the bowels of hell. The Glock was in his right hand and the Colt in his left.

He yelled something but over the gunfire still echoing in her ears and the rush of her own blood, Josie couldn't hear it. She felt Mettner let go of her. The impact of her upper body on the gravel sent a hot spike of pain through her rib cage. It was breathtaking in its intensity. The arm holding her pistol flopped at her side.

Vance laughed as he spotted them.

Josie was aware of the boom of another shot, this one much closer. Mettner firing at Vance. Missing.

Everything was happening so quickly and yet the images, the smells, the excruciating pain were burned into her memory for life.

Vance fired back at Mettner almost simultaneously. Vance's body jerked. The Colt dropped. His other hand clutched the Glock, aiming it at them, pulling the trigger. Mettner advanced on him, returning fire, but after two steps, he went down.

Incredibly, Vance was still standing. Blood poured from two graze wounds on his side and arm and from a small hole in his upper chest. Too high up, Josie realized with rising alarm. Not close enough to his heart.

Josie willed her trembling hand upward, pointing her pistol toward Vance. He took a slow walk toward her. She lifted her other hand and wrapped it, too, around the pistol grip, trying to steady her aim. She fired a shot, but she couldn't control her movements. Even as blood leaked from his wounds and the color left his skin, Vance grinned at her. He pointed the Glock at her face. Then his body slammed to the ground.

Josie was aware of Mettner on top of Vance, trying to wrestle the pistol out of his hands. Pushing the pain out of her mind, she got to her knees just as Mettner's body faltered, his movements becoming slow and sloppy. Vance wriggled out from under him. Before he could stand, two figures rushed forward and descended on him.

Cyrus and Finlay.

Josie knew that the entire encounter had only taken seconds, but some part of her wanted to scream at them: what took you so long?

They dragged Vance away from Mettner, kicking his pistol out of reach and turning him onto his stomach. Finlay cuffed him and then began talking into her radio. From inside the garage, Cyrus said, "Clear! Finlay, get another medic for Miss Hadlee in here. Lark, stay where you are. It'll be okay."

Josie lurched toward Mettner. He was face down, not moving. "Mett! Mett!" Even the words hurt.

She labored to turn him over. Fresh adrenaline coursed through her, numbing some of the pain she felt. It was still hard to breathe. He looked up at her, eyes wide and surprised. "Are you hit?" Josie asked. "Where are you hit? Talk to me. Talk to me!"

But he only stared at her. She knew a 45 ACP round wouldn't go through the vest, but it packed enough wallop to break ribs and potentially do other internal damage depending on where it hit. As her hands searched Mettner's torso, probing around the vest, she felt heat leaving his body. Cyrus appeared beside her. "Help me!" Josie cried. "Help. Help."

She didn't recognize her own voice. Hysteria rose from her stomach into her throat, making her feel like she might vomit. Cyrus knelt beside her and started to unhook Mettner's vest. His fingers came away with blood. "He's hit." He leaned down, looking beneath Mettner's arm. "Got him in the armpit. At least once. Maybe twice."

"Pressure," Josie shrieked. "Put pressure on the wound. How long until the ambulance gets here?"

Cyrus didn't answer. Instead, he began stripping. First his vest, then his shirt. He crumpled it and pressed it under Mettner's arm. His free hand searched for more wounds. "I think he must be hit somewhere else. Or this nicked his heart. I don't see—I can't see—"

Mettner's hand gripped Josie's arm. She looked down at his face, so pale now. Lips bloodless. The surprise was gone. Now there was a look that broke her heart into a million pieces. Realization. Resignation. Tears rolled down her cheeks, landing on his. She took his hand in both of hers and squeezed. "Stay with me, Mett."

His body jerked to and fro as Cyrus tore the rest of his vest and shirt off. "I found another one." He took off his undershirt and pressed it against a bullet hole near Mettner's pelvis.

Every time Josie tried to look away, to assess the damage, Mettner pulled her closer, his strength waning.

Cyrus muttered, "We need help."

They looked over at Finlay, who had Vance secured. They couldn't risk her leaving him. Even cuffed and wounded, he was still considered a threat. Just then, a figure limped out of the garage. Lark, her jeans streaked with dirt, her white tank top soaked through with sweat. Her long brown hair was matted to her face, neck and chest, gleaming with perspiration. She lumbered toward them, barefoot, and Josie saw that her wrists were tied with rope.

"I can help," she croaked.

Neither Josie nor Cyrus argued as she approached and dropped to her knees.

Josie moved closer to Mettner's head as Lark took position across from Cyrus. "Use your hands," Cyrus instructed her, pointing to his balled-up shirt. "Hold pressure here." She did as she was told, pressing her bound hands against the shirt, applying pressure to the wound beneath it, while Cyrus attempted to keep pressure on the other bullet hole.

But Josie could tell it was too late. Mettner knew it, too.

"Please, Mett," she begged. "Please, please, please stay with me. Stay with me. A few more minutes. Don't go."

His lips moved even as his grip slackened. Josie put her ear to his mouth, concentrating with everything in her being, trying to hear him over Cyrus and Lark talking to one another and the radios bleating.

"Boss," Mettner whispered. "Tell Amber... tell her I..."

Josie pulled back, saw the life draining from his eyes. "No, no, no, no, no! Don't go, Mett. Don't go. Stay with me. Tell her what? Tell her what? Mett! Talk to me. Talk to me."

She was still blubbering, still shrieking for him to stay, to talk to her, no longer aware of the pain in her own battered body, when Cyrus began CPR. She was still holding his cold hand when Anya came running from the direction of the house. She, too, tried her best to revive him. They kept working on him until the ambulance came, even though he was gone.

It took three people to wrest Josie from his body before they took him away.

FORTY-FOUR

The hospital lights were too bright. Josie knew there was noise all around her, but she heard no sounds. Even her field of vision had narrowed to a single spot in front of her. Still, she saw nothing. Someone pushed her from a vehicle, through the emergency department doors, and into a curtained area. Somehow, her body complied. More hands lifted her vest from her body, then her shirt, pressing the areas where the bullets had been stopped. There was bruising already. Someone said something about broken ribs. If that was all the damage that had been done to her body, she'd be incredibly lucky. When no one was probing her or moving her around, Josie pressed her hands together. If she concentrated hard enough, she could still feel Mettner's palm against hers.

Tell Amber.

The words were a permanent echo inside her head. It felt like that's all there was now. Just her and the inside of her head. Everything else receded. She knew that Anya was with her, knew she was crying. Then Noah came, wrapping her in his arms—carefully, gently. For the first time ever, his touch brought no comfort. Josie's mind recognized when members of the

Denton PD started to show up. Gretchen, the Chief. Sergeant Dan Lamay. Hummel. Chan. Brennan. Dougherty. Countless patrol officers whose names Josie couldn't keep track of. Everyone cried. Josie felt nothing. Heard nothing.

She'd seen everyone. Everyone but Amber. Her body said, "Where's Amber?" to the people gathered around her bed.

It was the first thing she'd said since the last thing she ever said to Mettner.

Tell Amber I…

Someone, maybe Gretchen, said, "She was too upset. They had to sedate her."

Josie nodded. She laid back on the gurney. She wanted to go deeper inside her head, but it wasn't working. She wanted to sleep but her body wouldn't let her. Trinity arrived with Drake. Then hers and Trinity's parents, Shannon and Christian, together with their little brother, Patrick. Then Misty. Harris was with his grandmother. That was a good thing, Josie thought numbly, as she looked around at everyone shedding tears. Except for Trinity. She was the only one not crying, but Josie could tell by the way the corners of her mouth twisted that she was deeply upset. She shooed everyone out of the room, even Noah, and climbed into the bed with Josie, sliding an arm gingerly across Josie's shoulders. Her breath tickled the top of Josie's ear.

She said, "It's not going to be okay. But we will survive this."

Josie closed her eyes. Sleep didn't come but eventually, her breathing mirrored Trinity's, calm and even. It was what passed for rest.

Tell Amber I…

FORTY-FIVE

The days after Mettner died were long. With each one, it felt more and more like the shock and the pain were too heavy to bear. Josie recognized it from when she'd lost her first husband and then her beloved grandmother. This grief, in some strange way, seemed bigger to her. Maybe because it was shared so deeply by so many people. Everyone in her life, everyone around her, traveled at the speed of someone whose life had just been irrevocably shattered. They were all in a fog. The week after his death was a blur. Somehow, things got done. His body was returned to Denton. Funeral arrangements were made. Reports were filed. Statements were given. There were visits and vigils, hugs and condolences that brought no comfort. Every time Josie tried to talk to Amber, she shook her head and walked away.

It was fine. She'd save Mettner's message for when Amber was ready to hear it.

The funeral was a somber, massive, and deeply beautiful thing. Every last detail of it made smithereens of Josie's already shattered heart.

Cyrus lingered as Mettner's body was lowered into the

ground. His parents, brothers, sisters-in-law, nieces, nephews and Amber gathered in a tight knot around the casket, watching its descent. Josie, Noah, Gretchen, Anya, and the Chief hung back. When it was finished, they waited until the family left before walking over to Cyrus.

"I'm sorry," he said, for what Josie knew was almost the hundredth time.

The Chief said, "Thank you for coming."

Cyrus nodded. He glanced at Anya, a note of longing in his eyes. To Josie he said, "Vance is going to pull through. We're set to arrest him for Mettner's murder."

No one spoke.

Josie looked at the Chief. He said, "Give them to him."

From her purse, she pulled the handcuffs that Mettner had owned and used during his tenure as a law enforcement officer. She'd been carrying them around for a week. Cyrus cradled them in his large hands. He nodded as if he were listening to something inside his own head. "I'll be in touch," he said.

When he left, Anya went after him.

FORTY-SIX

Two weeks after Mettner's funeral, Josie sat in Hallie Kent's living room again. Her ribs were still horribly sore but with lots of rest and painkillers, she was getting around fine. If she didn't do too much in a single day. This time, a fire crackled in the fireplace, adding a measure of warmth to the room that might make Josie drowsy under different circumstances. Josie edged the chair away from the hearth and lined it up so that she was facing the couch where Hallie sat next to Mathias Tobin. Hallie laced her arm through his and beamed, just as she'd beamed in the photo that she had sent Trinity a few days earlier, which Trinity had then forwarded to Josie. It was a selfie of Hallie and Mathias, both grinning, cheek to cheek. Her message read, *Thank you for this. Life can finally get back to normal.* The photo had been taken before the sad news that Garrick Wolfe had succumbed to his injuries. Josie knew that Cyrus and his colleagues were devoting every available resource to solving Garrick's murder.

The press had descended on the small town of Bly after the shooting at the Hadlee farm. Trinity had held court like the queen of television journalism. She was planning a four-part series on the events that had transpired in the last month as a result of the Jana Melburn murder. Josie wondered if four episodes would even be enough to explore all the secrets they'd uncovered. She hoped it would be enough to generate leads that might bring answers to the many questions that still remained.

Hallie bobbed up and down in her seat. "So Vance is going to be charged with Keri's murder? And Sharon Eddy's?"

At the mention of Keri, Mathias's face pinched. He extricated himself from Hallie's grip and leaned forward, elbows on his knees, rubbing his eyes. Hallie glanced at him, her expression sobering.

Once the scene at the farm had been processed, the brand they believed was used on Sharon and Keri had been discovered inside Vance's truck. Its sudden appearance didn't sit well with Josie, but the district attorney was thrilled about it. Between the brand found in his truck and the other circumstantial evidence against him, they felt there was enough to charge him with the Denton murders. They also felt the branding and the strength of Anya's testimony about the abuse she'd suffered at his hands would be enough to sway a jury. The fact that Denton's K-9 unit had alerted them to the scent of human remains in the back of the Hadlees' white sedan was dubious, since it was possible that Vance had transported Susanna Hadlee's partial remains in the sedan when he brought them to Garrick. The district attorney felt strongly that they wouldn't even need the car to convince a jury that Vance had killed Sharon Eddy and Keri Cryer.

Josie and what was left of her team had discussed the matter several times. The initial search of Vance's truck, performed by her and Gretchen, had been thorough. Josie was sure that they hadn't missed the brand—it simply hadn't been there. She floated the idea that someone else had put it there after the fact to properly frame him. The rest of the team disagreed. The consensus was that Vance must have been hiding the brand somewhere off the premises when committing the murders. Josie wasn't sold on any of it, but as the district attorney had pointedly told her, it wasn't her job to try cases, only to solve them. When Josie pointed out that the DNA found on Keri Cryer's coat had not matched Vance—or anyone else in law enforcement's databases—he had made excuses. The DNA was on her coat, not under her nails. It could have been unrelated to the crime. The bottom line was the DA was proceeding against Vance no matter what Josie thought.

"We have enough to proceed, so that's what we're going to do," he had said.

But no one could stop her from coming to see Mathias and trying to tie up some loose ends. She'd lost a dear friend and colleague over this case. She wanted the truth—or as much of it as she could dig up with the people who were left alive. Her next stop would be the Hadlee farm, where Lark had agreed to speak with her. With Dermot gone, she was fully cooperating with both the Bly Police Department and Denton. She'd allowed a team from the state police, on loan to Bly, to begin digging up the north side of the farm in hopes of finding the rest of Susanna Hadlee's remains. She wasn't the only person coming forward with information after Dermot's death. The three cheerleaders who'd accused Mathias of rape in high school gave statements to Bly PD that Dermot had paid them to publicly accuse Mathias, just as Josie and Mettner had suspected.

"Detective Quinn?" Hallie's voice pulled Josie from her thoughts.

"I'm sorry," Josie said. "Yes, it looks like Vance will be charged with Sharon and Keri's murders."

Mathias met her eyes for a brief second. Something flitted

across his face. Josie couldn't be certain of the emotion. Fear? Regret?

She said, "Mathias, I wanted to thank you."

"For what?"

Josie smiled at him. "Saving my life."

He returned her smile. "You're welcome."

Hallie looked back and forth between them, grinning widely. She squeezed Mathias's shoulder. "I told you he'd never hurt anyone."

Mathias reached up and covered her hand with his, giving it a squeeze. Then he slyly moved it back to her lap. Hallie didn't seem to notice this veiled rejection, or if she did, gave no indication. Turning his attention back to Josie, Mathias said, "That's not the only reason you're here."

"I had some questions," Josie admitted. "I was hoping to talk to you about a couple of things that still puzzle me."

"Sure," he said.

Hallie patted his knee. "I'll go get us some coffee."

He didn't respond, didn't even look at her. Hallie seemed oblivious, humming a happy tune under her breath as she disappeared into the kitchen. Josie heard the jingle of Flynn's tiny bell. Then a small thump. Hallie said, "Flynn, stop that!"

Josie said, "The night that you talked to Jana at the gas station, what did she say to you?"

"I don't remember it exactly," Mathias said. "It's been a long time, but I'll do my best. Basically, she said that she had found someone who could change our lives. She had arranged a meeting with him. She said everything was going to be different for all of us afterward. She was pretty vague. At first, I thought she was talking about a cult or some kind of pyramid scheme type of thing. I told her it sounds like a scam to me. Them wanting to meet after nine at night? Sounded suspicious."

Josie remembered the video. "She didn't listen to you."

"Not even a little bit," Mathias said. He glanced over at the fireplace where the last log was slowly giving way to ash. "I got scared. The way her eyes looked—it was like when she was little, and Hallie would make her favorite cake. We tried to ration it 'cause she'd eat the whole damn thing till she got sick from it. Then she'd miss school. We were always afraid the state would take her from us if anything even remotely bad happened, so we were careful about everything. Didn't want her getting sick or hurt. We were already on shaky ground with the rape accusations in my past. We were shocked the caseworker even agreed to let us take her, but she said the charges being dropped were good enough for her. The foster care system was already overloaded. Anyway, sometimes, no matter what we told Jana—no TV for a whole day, or no going over to your friend's house if you don't follow the rules—she'd go and sneak the cake anyway. It got to the point where I could tell when she was going to break the rules no matter what the consequences. She'd get that look. Like she'd just found a pass for unlimited cake, and she didn't care what she had to do to reach it. That's the look I saw in her eyes that night at the gas station, and I'm ashamed to say I got physical with her."

That tracked with what Josie and Noah had pulled from the video.

From the kitchen was another sound, something clinking and then rolling. Hallie's voice was faint but audible. "Flynn! Honestly. You're going to get the spray bottle!"

Mathias continued, "Jana said something like, what if I told you that you could finally know where you came from and who you really are—something like that. I said if she wanted to know those things, Hallie and I could help her do it. Not some random stranger asking her to come out at night. She said something like 'Don't you want to know the truth about where you came from?' and we went back and forth. Me trying to tell her that Hallie and I could do that for her and her saying I wasn't listening. Then she said something like, 'What if I told you that you come from a family who was rich?' I told her that sounded insane. She said something like, 'Wouldn't you want to know? What if your birth family had lots of money and it could be yours?' I don't remember her exact words now, but something along those lines."

This was also consistent with the partial transcript they'd developed.

"Jana didn't tell you that she was looking for *your* biological family?"

Mathias sighed. He rubbed his hands over his face again. "I mean, looking back, I guess that's what she was doing. She kept saying, 'Don't you want to know?' but I took that as a general thing. Like she was saying, as a fellow foster kid, didn't I want to know? The same as she wanted to know. The same as probably every kid like us wants to know. I didn't understand how badly I'd misread that situation until a couple of weeks ago."

"I'm sorry," Josie said. She drew in a deep breath, trying to ignore the pain in her ribs. She'd need more ibuprofen soon. "Did you ever talk to Vance Hadlee after he came forward to exonerate you?"

Mathias shook his head. "No. I wanted to but after the way Dermot screwed me—refusing to confirm my alibi and sending me to prison for my own wife's shooting—I wasn't going near that farm. I wasn't going near Bly. Garrick told me about our mom, though. He paid my legal fees, offered me a place when I got out. He showed me the stuff Vance had brought him. Vance had always had suspicions about his mom leaving. When he was younger, eight or nine, I guess, he caught Dermot burning up her things including her clothes, birth certificate, and driver's license. But he was too young to put it together, I guess."

"Garrick told you this," Josie clarified.

He nodded. "Yeah, once I got out of prison. Apparently, after Dermot's stroke, while Lark was handling the medical side of things, Vance went through his personal papers looking for a power of attorney. I guess the two kids wanted to be able to take over the farm if it turned out Dermot was completely incapacitated. Anyway, he found this map of the farm. Dermot had marked an area on the north side, 'Susanna.' Vance said they'd talked about building another barn for years. The north side had lots of room, but Dermot refused to allow anything to be built there. When he saw her name on the map, it clicked, I guess."

"That's when Vance started digging, looking for her remains," Josie said.

From the kitchen came the scent of freshly brewed coffee. Josie's mouth watered, the pain in her ribs momentarily forgotten. She wondered if Hallie had half-and-half. "It'll just be a minute," Hallie called.

Mathias ignored her. Josie wanted to call back and say thanks, but she wasn't sure she could physically do it. "What was Garrick's plan with regards to Susanna's remains? Did he have one? Why not go right to the police?"

"He didn't think there was enough for them to charge Dermot. Even with the stroke, Dermot still had a lot of influence. Garrick wanted to hold onto what Vance had found. Vance was going to try to find the rest of Susanna's remains. Beyond that, I don't think there was a plan. Garrick meant well, but I think the alcohol clouded his judgment. I'm not sure he was thinking straight most of the time. Keri wanted me to get a DNA test, though. To confront the Hadlees. Not for money or anything like that, but just so that people in town would know the truth. I think she thought it would somehow make them treat me better? I don't know. She didn't grow up here, so she really didn't understand how things work in this place."

A loud pop from the last of the wood in the fireplace startled Josie. Her body jerked slightly, sending a white-hot stab of pain through her left side. She tried to stay focused on the conversation. "Did Keri know about Susanna's remains?"

"Are you kidding me?" said Mathias. "No. No way. She would have gone right to the police. I didn't tell her. All I said was that Garrick was my father and that he had told me my mother's identity. He said that when I was born, Susanna was too afraid that Dermot would somehow know I wasn't his and kill me. No one knew it, but apparently Dermot was pretty abusive toward her."

"I'm not surprised," Josie said, thinking of Anya's marriage to Vance.

"Garrick and Susanna agreed that Garrick would tell Dermot I'd been stillborn, and then make sure I got into foster care. The thing was that I really didn't want to get into any of that. I wanted to move forward. Keri didn't understand. Even if no one ever knew that Vance had found Susanna's remains, me going public with the fact that I was related to him and to Lark? No way would Dermot have let that stand."

In spite of the warmth still radiating from the fireplace, Mathias shivered.

"I believe you," Josie said.

"Besides," he added wistfully. "By that time, I at least had Garrick." His eyes drifted toward the kitchen door. Under his breath, he murmured, "Now I've got no one."

Josie wasn't sure if he'd meant for her to hear that last bit or not, so she moved on. "Mathias, what happened the night that Garrick was stabbed?"

"I was out in the garage, staring at that stupid box for the hundredth time, wondering what the hell I was going to do about... my past."

"Your prints weren't on the box," said Josie.

He nodded. "There was no way in hell I was ever going to touch that box. I didn't need my prints anywhere near that."

Josie didn't point out to him that even if his prints had been on the box, he'd been a small boy when Susanna Hadlee was killed. She was going to ask him what possible trouble he could have gotten into by leaving his prints, but then decided that was a stupid question to ask someone who had been put through as much as Mathias Tobin had. Instead, she asked, "Did you hear anything? A car?"

"No. Not until you guys pulled up. I peeked out. Saw the SUV. Waited and waited. I didn't know what to do. I'd gotten so used to running and hiding from everyone and everything that my first instinct was to stay in the garage and wait. Then I realized that I hadn't done anything wrong. Garrick was my father. He was fully prepared to tell people that I was his son. He'd offered me his home, his money, anything I needed. I thought I was being ridiculous. No need to hide anymore. So I walked right up to the front door and that's when I saw—" He broke off as a sob rose in his throat.

"Take your time," Josie whispered. Sweat gathered at the back of her neck, now more from the pain in her side than the dying fire.

After a long moment, Mathias said, "Sorry. I don't know who stabbed Garrick. I never saw or heard anyone. I don't know who would want to besides Dermot, but Cyrus doesn't think that Dermot could have physically done it."

"He might be right," Josie said. Dermot Hadlee had threatened her with a gun and driven her off the road with his truck. She was willing to believe he'd try to stab someone, but at the same time she didn't believe he was physically capable of making it all the way up the north road on foot, stabbing Garrick, and escaping without anyone seeing him. Dermot might have had motive to kill Garrick, but not the means.

Another sob shook Mathias's frame. He wiped at the tears streaming down his face. "Sorry," he said. "Flashbacks to when I found Piper. It's still really hard for me."

"I'm sorry," Josie said. "I'm sure you know that Piper's case has been reopened."

"Yeah. Cyrus told me. That's good. Really good. All this

time, all I wanted was for someone to be looking for her killer. Not just because I wanted out of prison but because my wife's killer is still out there! Once I was freed, I hoped if I could get the whole Hadlee mess behind me, maybe I could help in some way."

"Do you have any ideas as to who might have killed her?" asked Josie.

"I really don't. Believe me, if I had any idea, I would have been hollering it from the rooftops."

Josie thought of everything Cyrus had told them. "Were you and Piper fighting before she died? Cyrus said her wedding ring was missing. Had you agreed to divorce? Separate?"

"No. Not at all. Everything was fine between us. I knew about the ring. It came up during trial prep but I didn't have it. When I found her—" He stopped, his face going ashen. Swallowing, he went on. "When I found her, I was so hysterical, I didn't even notice that she wasn't wearing it. There was so much blood—"

He broke off as more tears rolled down his face. Josie wanted to lean across the space between them and take his hand, but doing so would mean a lot of pain. Instead, she said, "I'm so sorry, Mathias. For everything you've had to go through."

There was a *thwap* from the kitchen and a vigorous jangle of Flynn's bell. Hallie sounded far less amused this time. "Dammit, Flynn."

Mathias called, "Hallie, we don't need coffee. It's fine."

"No, no," she called back. "She's just made a little mess. I've got to get paper towels from the basement."

Mathias rolled his eyes. He stood up and used his shirt-sleeve to dry his face. Letting out a shaky breath, he said, "Let me see what's going on in there. This damn cat."

Josie stood as well, following him. It felt slightly better to stand after having been in the same position for so long. Over his shoulder, Mathias said, "Sorry. Are you a cat person?"

In the kitchen, one of the lower cabinets hung open. On the floor, Flynn lay on her back, her front paws gripping the edge of the cabinet door. On the counter, a sugar bowl and a cup of coffee had spilled. Three paper towels soaked up some of the coffee.

Josie said, "I like cats, but I'm more of a dog person. You don't like Flynn?"

Mathias looked down at the cat. "Flynn doesn't like me."

As if on cue, the cat hissed. Effortlessly, she flipped onto all fours. Her upper body disappeared inside the cabinet. A second later, something shiny pinged against the tile. Flynn turned, coiled her body like a spring, and then pounced on it. She batted it around until Mathias snatched it from the floor. Brow furrowed, he looked inside the cabinet. "She's got all kinds of junk in here." He reached in and pulled out a black ballet flat. "Random shoe," he muttered. "Just one. Bottle cap. And here. A random glove. A singular glove."

Josie's heart stuttered. A distant ringing began in her ears. She stared at the bottle cap as he placed it onto the counter. It was gold-colored, shaped like a miniature king's crown. The cap to a bottle of Crown Royal. Her ribs ached as her breathing sped up. She took the glove Mathias handed her and turned it over. Gray. Knit. The initials S.E. in black thread.

Black ballet flat. Keri Cryer.

Crown Royal cap. Garrick Wolfe.

Gray knit glove with initials on it. Sharon Eddy.

"Mathias," Josie choked. "What's that in your hand? That you took from Flynn?"

He opened his palm and stared at a gold ring. "Random ring?" he said.

"Are you sure it's random?"

He pinched it between his thumb and forefinger and

brought it closer to his face. Josie watched all the color drain from his skin.

Wedding band. Piper Tobin.

Just as Hallie appeared at the top of the basement steps, Mathias looked up at her. Through gritted teeth, he said, "Why do you have my dead wife's wedding band?"

FORTY-SEVEN

Hallie tried to keep the smile pasted on her face, but it faltered.

Mathias held the ring out. "Where did you get this?"

Josie pointed to the bottle cap. "And this. A Crown Royal bottle cap. Garrick was drinking Crown Royal the night he was stabbed." She motioned toward the glove. "And this. This is one of the gloves that Sharon Eddy was wearing when she was killed." She pointed to the ballet flat on the tile. "And that is Keri's shoe, isn't it?"

Mathias turned to Josie, realization dawning. He licked his lips, swiveling his head slowly back toward Hallie. Josie could see his chest shudder when he took in a breath. "Hallie," he said. "You better start talking right now."

She held her hands out toward him, palms up, as if begging. "It's not what you think."

"What did you do?" His voice was quiet at first, calm. When she didn't answer, he yelled. "Hallie! What did you do? Did you kill Piper? Did you kill Keri? Garrick? What the hell is going on here?"

Her face changed from innocent and remorseful to hateful

and angry in seconds. "I had to do something. You kept trying to move on without me."

"What are you talking about?" he said.

She stomped her foot in time with her words, causing Flynn to retreat to the cabinet. "I'm talking about our family!"

"What family?"

A flush colored her cheeks. Rage twisted her features. Josie put a hand to her waist, but her holster wasn't there. She wasn't on duty. She was injured. In that moment, as panic made it more difficult to breathe, the pain in her side reminded her of this fact.

"What family?" Hallie spat. "You, me, and Jana. Even though she was gone, we were still a family. You and me. We raised a child together, Mathias. We were all we had. Just us. Against the world."

"What are you even talking about?" Mathias cried. "We were kids, Hallie. Foster kids. We did what we had to do to get by. It was never meant to be a permanent situation."

Hallie's fists clenched at her sides. "For you! You made it abundantly clear that it wasn't meant to be permanent for you. As soon as Jana died, and you went and threw it all away. You broke up our family, Mathias. The only family any of us had ever known. Did you think I would just let that stand? I had to do something! I lost Jana and then you. I couldn't—I couldn't just pretend that it was all okay. I tried to get you back, but you drifted and pushed me away and then you met Piper. She didn't even know you. Not really. She wasn't right for you. I went over to your house to try to talk some sense into her, to let you go. She was a bitch, Mathias. She said horrible, ugly things to me. She got her gun out and told me to get out. Me! The only person who has always been there for you, no matter what. Your real family. Piper wanted you to be permanent in *her* life, but what about me?" She pounded a fist into her own chest. "What about me?"

Josie was nearest the countertop. Mathias was between her and Hallie. Edging slowly toward the direction of the open cabinet, she positioned herself so that she was almost directly behind him. She could still see Hallie's face, but Hallie couldn't see her hands. Trying not to make any big movements, and moving as fast as her body would allow, she slid her cell phone from her pocket. She only needed a thumb to punch in her passcode and dial Noah's number. As it began to ring, she turned the volume all the way down. She thought she heard him say hello as she slipped the phone back into her pocket. It was the same trick Anya had used.

Josie hoped it would work.

"Oh my God." Mathias staggered backward, bumping against Josie's body. She moved aside so he could lean against the counter. "You let me take the fall for that. You killed the woman I loved—my wife—and let me go to prison for it! Do you know what happened to me in prison?"

Hallie's face morphed into an expression that was appropriately apologetic. "I'm sorry. I never intended for that to happen, but I worked hard every single day you were in there to try to find a firm that would help you get out. Then you did it yourself! It was fine. Everything turned out fine. Except for Keri. You had to start with her. Moving on. Trying to start a family. A *family?*"

Again, she slammed her fist into her own chest. "*I* am your family, Mathias! But even after you got out of prison, you still didn't get it, did you? So I knew I needed to do more. I tried to figure out where everything went wrong and I saw that the problems started when Jana was killed, and everyone thought that you did it. I had to make it right. I knew if I was able to solve her case and clear your name once and for all, you'd come home to me. I got in touch with Trinity Payne. She was going to do an episode. Everything was fine. Then Piper had to go and die. You know even though she died years after the shooting, the police could still say she died from her injuries, which would make it a homicide. I was worried the police would look at you again."

Josie looked around the kitchen for anything she could use as a weapon, if it came to that. There was a full knife block only feet away but even angling her body toward it sent little pinpricks of pain pulsing through her. She cleared her throat. "But Hallie, Mathias was exonerated."

Hallie rolled her eyes. "By Vance Hadlee. I don't think a single person in this place ever believed that he was telling the truth. Besides, it wasn't even the police suspecting you of murder that worried me. It was that this whole town would still believe you were a killer. No matter what. You would never come home to me if these things, these vicious rumors, were still out there. I had to make things the way they were before. When we were happy together."

Mathias said, "So you killed an innocent girl?"

"Sharon Eddy," Josie said, inching closer to the butcher's block at the speed of molasses.

"Maybe she was innocent, Mathias, but her mother wasn't! I knew it! I knew Carolina was lying all these years. I just never knew what she was lying about, or how to prove it. She deserved what she got."

Mathias sagged against the countertop. "You killed Sharon Eddy to get back at her mom because you thought she was lying about what she saw the night Jana was killed?"

Hallie waved both fists in the air in time with her words. "She *was* lying! But that's not the only reason I killed Sharon. She was exactly the same age as Jana was when she died. It's like it was fate."

"Hallie," Mathias croaked. "My God. You sound crazy."

Hallie took a step toward him, and he recoiled. Anger flared in her eyes. "No," she said. "Don't you dare. Don't you dare look at me like that. Every single thing I've done has been for this family. For you!"

"No," Mathias said.

Flynn emerged from the cabinet, sprinting over to Hallie, her little bell jangling. She rubbed her body against Hallie's shins. "Yes!" Hallie said. "Mathias, I had to do something. Every day that went by you were slipping farther away from me. With Sharon Eddy, I could kill two birds with one stone—no pun intended."

At her flip tone, Mathias and Josie flinched simultaneously.

She went on. "I got a job in records at the police department. It was the only way for me to access Jana's file. To see what was there, to try to put together some kind of plan to win you back. You know what other case came in right around the time Jana was killed? The one with that doctor. Vance's wife. He'd *branded* her. Like she was a cow or something. The photos were right there in the file. All I had to do was find a brand just like that, convince the girls to come here with me. That wasn't hard. No one ever sees me as a threat."

Hallie paused and gave a half-shrug. "Not until it's too late, anyway. I had to make up a story to get them into the car. It was harder with Sharon. I used her mother, that druggie Carolina, as my excuse, except that Sharon didn't care that much about Carolina. It took some convincing: Carolina on her deathbed, staying at my place, wanting to say goodbye and apologize for being a shitty mother. Keri was much easier. I told her you were hurt. She got right in. Getting them to turn off their phones was tricky. Sharon was dumb enough to believe her phone was messing with my car's instrumentation."

She laughed and shook her head. "Kids these days. So dumb. Keri turned hers off when I told her that you were at a location you didn't want traced. She knew you were paranoid after everything you'd been through, so eventually she went along with it. Once they were here, I hit them over the head. If that didn't work, I dropped a little Benadryl into their coffee. Then I used the fireplace to make the mark. Sharon was easy. Keri gave me a very hard time." Her face darkened. "She really wasn't right for you."

Mathias looked as though he might collapse. "Hallie, this is —how could you—"

Josie kept her eyes locked on Hallie's face while she reached behind her and slowly pulled a knife from the block. Hallie never even noticed. Her attention was fully focused on Mathias.

She took another step closer to him. Flynn scuttled behind her legs. "It was easy, Mathias. Literally no one ever suspected me. I just had to make sure they were really dead. I lost the most sleep over Garrick. I was really afraid he might make it, or you might be there and catch me, but he was the easiest of them all. I drove up the north side of that mountain. I was going to park near his property and walk, and then the road was closed anyway. It's like it was meant to be! No one would ever see my car there because no one would be using that road. I was sneaking back past his mailbox when I saw headlights coming from the south. He didn't even put up a fight. Just a sad old drunk."

"But why?" Mathias said. "Why Garrick? He didn't do anything."

Josie kept the knife clutched in her hand, behind her back, and started to inch back toward Mathias.

Hallie's nostrils flared. "You stayed with him instead of me! You chose him over me! Even with Keri gone, you went to him. Before she died, Keri told me about him. How he was your father and you'd been staying with him—not just with her. When the police weren't able to find you—and I knew they couldn't find you because they kept asking me if I knew where you might be—I was certain that's where you had gone. Once again, you chose someone else over me. Over us!"

Josie was close enough to Mathias now that their arms were

nearly touching. She wondered if there was a way to quietly slip him the knife. She wasn't sure she could defend him against a physical attack in her current state. She wondered if Noah was hearing all of this, if he'd had someone else call Cyrus, if the Bly police were on their way.

Mathias said, "Hallie, there is no us."

She flew at him. It was so fast that Josie barely had time to register it. Hallie was small, lithe, and lightning quick. One moment she was on the other side of the room, glowering at Mathias, and the next she was on him, knocking him back, clawing at his face, punching his chest.

He flailed, his arm knocking into Josie's side, sending her staggering away from them. The knife slipped from her hands and clattered to the floor. She doubled over, pain replacing her breath. Fighting through it, she tried to stand up straight. Mathias held his forearms over his face, fending off Hallie's punches. Getting nowhere, she started kicking him in the shins. Momentarily, he dropped his arms. Josie saw where Hallie's nails had left three bloody slashes down his cheek.

"Hallie," he grunted. "Stop!"

But she was beyond listening, beyond reason. The sounds coming from her were more animal than human. It wasn't even rage. It was something worse. Josie took a deep breath and shored herself up. She was about to lunge for Hallie when a battery of Bly police officers burst through the door. The strident shouts of her fellow officers had never sounded so good. Hallie was subdued in a matter of seconds. Josie found a chair and stumbled toward it, collapsing into it as she watched Hallie being dragged away.

"It was for us, Mathias!" she screeched. "For our family!"

Cyrus remained in the small kitchen. Mathias had retreated to a corner when the officers pulled Hallie away from him. He cowered, both hands up in a defensive posture. Josie tried to call his name, but couldn't get enough air to speak yet.

Cyrus looked at her. "You okay?"

She gave him a nod and a thumbs-up.

He holstered his weapon and walked over to Mathias. Slowly, he extended a hand. "It's okay now, Mathias."

From behind his hands, Mathias regarded him warily.

Cyrus's face softened. "I'm serious. It's okay. Hallie's in custody. You all did the right thing."

"How—how did you know?"

Josie lifted her cell phone from her pocket and waved it.

Mathias lowered his arms. "Thank God," he breathed. Then he crumpled to the floor, sobbing. Josie felt every single one of his tears like a barb to her heart. He'd lost so much. Everything, really. His whole life had been an uphill battle— from birth to this moment—and now, with Dermot gone and Hallie in custody, he'd won that battle, but been left with nothing.

Cyrus looked over at Josie. She was tired. So tired of loss. Maybe he saw it in her eyes. Or maybe his own losses sent him kneeling in front of Mathias. He gathered him into his arms and put a hand to the back of his head.

"Everything's going to be okay, now," Cyrus told him. "I promise you that, son."

FORTY-EIGHT

The sky was a perfect blue. The temperature flirted with the fifty-degree mark. As Josie made her way through the cemetery toward Mettner's grave, birds swooped and flitted all around, calling to one another in a symphony. Even in the place of the dead, the day was gorgeous. She moved carefully, at an easy pace. Her ribs were healing nicely, and the pain wasn't that bad anymore. She'd be able to return to work soon—although work without Mettner there was impossible to imagine. Noah and Gretchen had told her how strange it was, how unnatural it felt, how the awkwardness hung over the room whenever Amber was there. She'd returned to work a few weeks after Mettner's funeral. She kept to herself, only talking with the rest of them when necessary.

Josie still hadn't given her the message.

Tell Amber I...

If she pressed her palms together, she could still feel his hand in hers, the life bleeding out of it.

Josie saw the dog first. Blue, Luke Creighton's bloodhound and the Denton PD's new K-9 consultant, sat at attention a few feet away from Mettner's grave. Directly in front of it stood

Luke. His broad shoulders were slumped, head bent toward the ground. There was no stone yet, only a profusion of flowers and some rocks that his nieces and nephews had painted and placed there.

We love you, Uncle Finn, read one of them.

It nearly broke her into pieces.

Blue's tail thumped as Josie drew closer. She stopped to greet him, kneeling so she could soak up his wet kisses and nuzzles. When she finished, she walked over and stood beside Luke.

He looked down and smiled at her.

Josie said, "I didn't know you really knew Mett."

"I didn't know him well," Luke said. "But after that Collins case, he approached me. Said that you told the team it was okay to like me."

Josie laughed. "That's not how it went down. I just told them that we should leave the past in the past, was all."

"Whatever you said, I appreciate it. Mett and Amber had me over for dinner after the Collins case. It was nice. I felt... like a part of something again. He didn't have to do that, but he did."

Over the lump in her throat, Josie said, "Mett was a good guy."

Was. The word still made her want to scream.

Luke reached into his pocket and pulled out a large fishing lure with fluorescent green feathers flared at its base. He placed it next to one of the painted rocks. "Everyone always brings flowers," he explained. "Thought I'd do something different."

"Mett loved fishing," Josie acknowledged.

They stood in silence for a moment. Blue let out a small groan and then lowered himself to his stomach. Luke chuckled. "That means he's ready to go. You going to be okay here? Noah's not with you?"

"Flying solo today," Josie said. "I'll be fine."

"And when you leave here?"

She looked up, meeting his eyes. "What do you mean?"

"I know you never wanted to talk about it with me, but Josie, I know you've been through some shit, same as me." He held up his hands. She was so used to them now that she hardly noticed anymore how badly mangled they were. During the case that had ended his career and their relationship, he'd been kidnapped and tortured. Both of his hands had been completely shattered. The surgeons had done their best to repair them and he had excellent function, but they looked monstrous. Scar tissue marred almost every inch. The index and middle fingers of his right hand were almost completely flattened. The tip of his left pinky finger turned outward at an unnatural angle.

Josie thought of the stitches she'd received in the hospital—gone now, with barely a mark left—and how difficult it had been. "Yes," she said. "A lot of trauma, you and me."

"You more than me," Luke said pointedly. "I just hope that Mettner's death doesn't make it worse. Doesn't make you..."

"What?" Josie said. "Make me what?"

"More afraid."

The words went through her, leaving behind a ripple in her psyche. Since their last conversation, she'd thought a lot about all the choices she had made from a place of fear.

Luke jammed his hands back into his pockets and lifted his chin, motioning to someone approaching from the direction Josie had just come. Blue was on his feet, tail wagging furiously. When Amber reached him, she too stopped to pet him, scratching his head and murmuring soft words into his floppy ears.

Luke lightly nudged Josie's arm with his elbow. "Just take care of yourself, okay?"

She tried to say something, but the words got lodged in the back of her throat. She watched Luke greet Amber, hug her, say a few words to her and walk off with Blue bounding after him. Josie felt a strange buzz work its way through her body. Anxiety. She'd been wanting to talk with Amber for weeks, but now that they were here, alone, she wanted to run. She knew, intellectually, that Mettner's death wasn't her fault. They'd followed procedure, breaking perimeter to respond to gunshots; stopping when they found Dermot's body; calling for the medic and backup. They couldn't help it that Vance had started shooting through the door as soon as he heard voices. Mettner had done what he was supposed to do after the initial barrage: try to pull Josie to safety, but Vance had been on them before that could happen. Still, in her nightmares every night, the scene replayed itself in Josie's mind.

Mettner had followed procedure. They both had. But Josie was here and Mettner was not.

His death wasn't her fault, but she still felt guilty.

Amber walked up and stood beside her, studying the piles of flowers, stones, and now a flyfishing lure at their feet. Josie chanced a look at her, tried to talk again. Still nothing came.

Amber let out something between a groan and a shriek. Lifting both hands, she ran them through her auburn locks and turned her head toward the sky. This time, she screamed, long and loud. Josie's instinct was to back away, but her legs wouldn't move. She had to deliver Mettner's message. She could do that one thing for him. Amber should know that his last thoughts were of her.

Finished with her raw display of emotion, Amber turned toward Josie. "I'm angry," she said. "But I don't blame you. You should know that."

Josie wondered if she'd feel better if Amber blamed her.

"I know you've been trying to talk to me since Finn died. I'm sorry. I just wasn't ready."

"No need to apologize," Josie said. "We don't have to talk now if you're still not ready."

"No," Amber said. "I know you were there when he… when he went. I need to know what it… what it was like."

Josie felt like a thousand thorns had taken up residence in her mouth. "It was fast," she managed. "Very fast. He was—he did everything he could to save both of us. He did everything right. It's just the bullets—"

Amber raised a hand. "I already know how he died. The bullets, the vest, his armpit, all of that."

"There's something else," Josie said. She'd thought long and hard about how to deliver Mettner's final message. *Tell Amber I...* She didn't know how he'd intended to finish the sentence. The best she could do was guess. She'd lost many hours of sleep trying to do just that. She'd lost sleep over deciding whether or not she should finish the message. Was it kind or cruel to leave it unfinished? If she told Amber the truth, would she spend the rest of her life trying to guess on her own? Did Josie want to do that to her?

"The last thing that Mett—Finn—said was, 'Tell Amber I...' He, uh, died before he could finish the sentence. But I think maybe he was trying to say, 'Tell Amber I'm sorry.'"

Amber stared at her, unblinking. Then her eyes narrowed. Josie's heart did a double tap. Poking a finger into Josie's chest, she said, "Bullshit."

Josie stumbled backward, feeling the place where Amber had touched her like a bruise. "What?"

"Finn would never say that."

"What are you talking about?" Josie said.

"That's what you would say."

Josie rubbed at her chest, still feeling Amber's finger punching into her sternum. "You're right. That is what I would say."

Amber reached forward and took Josie's hand, holding it in both of hers. "But it's not what Finn would have said, Josie."

Amber's hands were so warm. One of her palms pressed into Josie's, against the very same place that Mettner's hand had been while he died. Did Amber know? Had someone told her that Josie had held his hand?

Josie said, "How do you know that's not what Finn would have said?"

"Because Finn had no regrets. That's how he lived. How we both tried to live. He loved his job. He always knew the risks. We talked many times about the possibility of him dying. The odds seemed slim given that he was no longer on patrol, but we always knew it could happen."

"You were okay with that?"

Amber laughed, squeezing Josie's hand harder. "Of course not, but Josie, Finn loved his job so much, how could I begrudge him that? Especially when his job was what brought the two of us together, not once, but twice. Once when I started and twice when you solved my case. He was grateful to you, you know."

Josie looked away, tears stinging the backs of her eyes.

Amber tugged at her hands. "You saved my life, Josie, and Finn gave me a life. I was alone before I met him. As alone as a person can be. Yes, I lost him just like I've lost everyone who mattered to me before him. You know what the difference is this time?"

Josie couldn't speak, so she shook her head.

Amber's grip tightened. "I have a family now. Finn gave me that. He gave me something I never had before, and it will last me the rest of my life. His parents, brothers, sisters-in-law, all his nieces and nephews. They've taken me in, Josie. Then there's the team, Finn's found family. You, Noah, Gretchen, the Chief. All of you. I just lost the love of my life, but Josie, for the first time in my life, I'm not alone."

"You always have a seat at my table," Josie rasped just before the tears came. She couldn't stop them. They came hot and fast, and pretty soon she was hyperventilating. This was ugly-crying. Amber tried to pull her in for a hug, but Josie resisted, pushing her away. She didn't want Amber to have to comfort her when she was suffering more than Josie.

But Amber was strong, and the more emotion that poured out of Josie, the weaker she felt.

Amber threw her arms around Josie, squeezing her in a bear hug. Her breath was hot against Josie's ear. "I know what Finn was trying to say. 'Tell Amber I love her.'"

FORTY-NINE

Josie moved through her home like she was seeing it for the first time. The well-used furniture. The dog toys strewn throughout. The place on the bottom of the back door where Trout had left marks after scratching to go outside so many times. The framed photos of loved ones in almost every room. Toys that Harris either kept at their house or had left there. The many drawings he'd made them pinned to the refrigerator. His sports schedule. The wall calendar on the side of the fridge filled with events, parties, and visits from family.

She sat in the silence of the kitchen, Trout snoozing at her feet, until Noah came home from work. Trout hopped up as soon as he heard the front door. Josie listened as his little nails clicked against the hardwood floor of the foyer. Noah baby-talked to him, assuring him in saccharine tones that he had missed him all day and that he was the very best boy. Trout made some high-pitched noises of agreement or gratitude—or both.

Noah said, "Where's Mom?"

Trout gave a short bark and came barreling into the kitchen. Noah trailed behind him, his expression half smile and half concern when he saw her. That's how it was now, with everyone, not just Noah. The concern behind the smile. Was she okay? Was she managing? Could she handle this?

Noah walked over and bent to kiss her, one warm palm snaking behind her neck.

She said, "I talked to Amber today."

He froze. "How did that go?"

"Good, I think."

"Want to talk about it?"

Josie stood up and wrapped her arms around his neck. He pulled her in close. She inhaled and felt herself melt against him. "Noah, I don't want to have any regrets."

"Okay," he said into her hair. His hands stroked her back. "What kinds of regrets are we talking about?"

"Big ones."

He brought his hands up and cradled her head, drawing back so he could look into her eyes. Smiling, he said, "Should I be worried?"

Josie laughed. "No. I mean, I don't think so."

He released her. "What's going on, Josie?"

She glanced over at the fridge. They had at least a dozen drawings by Harris at any given time. Looking back at Noah, she said, "What if I change my mind about wanting kids?"

He visibly relaxed, the tension draining from his shoulders. "That's what this is about? Have you changed your mind?"

"I don't know. I'm—I've been thinking about it. When we talked about it before, the reasons I didn't want them all had to do with me being afraid."

He touched the scar on the side of her face, tracing it from her ear to her chin. "I know."

"You said I was enough for you."

"Because you are."

"Do you want children?"

"Not as much as I want to be with you, Josie."

"Noah."

He dropped his hand. "Part of me does, yes. Sometimes I think about what it would be like. It's hard not to think about it with Harris around all the time. God, I love that kid."

Josie smiled. "Me too. Noah, do you ever feel afraid? Of being a parent?"

"Of course," he said. "Even with Harris, I worry about him all the time."

"No," she said. "I mean afraid that you'll screw up. End up like your dad."

Noah's father had left his mother as soon as Noah was eighteen. He'd completely abandoned his family. He'd been waiting for his youngest child to become an adult so that he could leave and start over elsewhere—and he had. He had a new, younger wife, and children. He didn't keep in contact with Noah or his siblings.

"I won't end up like my dad," Noah replied.

"How do you know?"

"Because I'm not an asshole."

"Noah."

"Josie, I know I won't turn out like my dad. I won't do what he did. I see Harris and spend time with him and even though he's not mine—even though we're not related by blood or even marriage—I'd take a bullet for that kid. I could never abandon him. Ever. That's how I know."

She nodded. In a husky voice, she said, "That's how I feel. I've always been afraid that somehow I'd be the kind of mother that Lila was to me: cruel and abusive, neglectful and damaging, but I know now that I'm wrong. I wouldn't be like that at all. It's not—it's not in me."

"I'm glad you realize that. Everyone else sees it. You've spent a lifetime punishing yourself for things that Lila did to you. Josie, if you want kids, we can have kids."

A lump formed in her throat. "I'm not exactly there yet,"

she said. "I just know that it's not the kind of decision I want to make from a place of fear. I'm afraid if I make big decisions based on my fear, I'll... have a lot of regrets."

He closed the distance between them and cupped her cheeks, tilting her chin up toward him. His hazel eyes sparkled. "Take some time," he said. "We can talk about it again after you've had time to think."

She blinked, feeling intoxicated with relief and love and Noah's proximity.

"Josie," he whispered.

"Yes?"

He gave her a mischievous grin. "Just in case we do decide yes to having kids, maybe we should go upstairs and practice how to make them."

Trout whined at their feet.

Josie laughed as Noah scooped her up, carrying her bridal-style all the way up the steps to their bedroom.

In every quiet moment, the last seconds of Mettner's life crowded her mind. Losing herself in Noah was the only way to silence them. As they peeled one another's clothes off, she repeated Amber and Mett's mantra in the back of her mind.

No regrets.

No regrets.

A LETTER FROM LISA

Thank you so much for choosing to read *Close Her Eyes*. If you enjoyed the book and want to keep up to date with all my latest releases, just sign up at the following link. Your email address will never be shared, and you can unsubscribe at any time.

www.bookouture.com/lisa-regan

Please note that this book touches briefly on the issue of domestic violence. If you feel unsafe in your home, I encourage you to reach out and get help. A good place to start is the National Domestic Violence Hotline (United States). The website is www.thehotline.org but remember that your internet history is never truly erased, so to be on the safe side, consider calling 800-799-SAFE (7233). You can also visit my website www.lisaregan.com which has a Resources tab where I have compiled some resources for survivors of sexual assault and domestic violence, including resources in other countries.

With every Detective Josie Quinn book I write, I feel more and more blessed and fortunate to have readers who are so loyal to the series. I am so grateful to all my readers—new and old—who choose to read my books. To say it is a pleasure to bring you these books is an understatement. I am so thankful for all of you!

I absolutely love hearing from you. You can get in touch with me through my website or any of the social media outlets below, as well as my Goodreads page. Also, I'd really appreciate it if you'd leave a review and perhaps recommend *Close Her Eyes* to other readers. Reviews and word-of-mouth recommendations go a long way in helping readers discover my books for the first time. Thank you so much for your enthusiasm and commitment to this series. I know that this was a tough one, especially for my most dedicated readers, in the sense that we've lost Mett, but I hope you'll return for the next several adventures!

Thanks,

Lisa Regan

www.lisaregan.com

facebook.com/LisaReganCrimeAuthor

twitter.com/LisalRegan

ACKNOWLEDGMENTS

Fabulous readers: you are, above all, my purpose and passion in writing this series. Your enthusiasm and love for all things Josie as well as your dedication to the series is an incredible gift that I cherish each day. I see all your messages, comments, posts, emails, and other wonderful ways you have of getting in touch, or just shouting from the rooftops about how much you love Josie, and I am here for it! You really are the very best. Thank you for sticking with me for this wild and wonderful writing journey. You truly make every word worth it!

Thank you, as always, to my husband, Fred, who always selflessly pulls double duty as fantastic husband/father and consultant with each book. Thank you for helping me with weapons and farm research on this one. Thank you for always letting me talk about crazy plot problems over breakfast and then coming up with dozens of ideas that get me unstuck. You are amazing! Thank you to my daughter, Morgan, for always knowing exactly what to say when I'm uber stressed over a deadline and for being the funniest, wittiest, kindest, most fascinating human I know! Thank you to my *first* first readers: Maureen Downey and Katie Mettner. Your speed and incisive critique was absolutely essential. I love you both and can never repay you for all the ways you two always make my writing—and my life—better. Katie: I'm very sorry I had to kill off your namesake. I didn't enjoy it. Thank you to my first readers: Dana Mason, Nancy S. Thompson, and Torese Hummel. Thank you to Matty Dalrymple and Jane Kelly for all the encouragement and for being there for me on a daily basis for anything I need. You two are a lifeline. Thank you to my grandmothers: Helen Conlen and Marilyn House; my parents: Donna House, Joyce Regan, the late Billy Regan, Rusty House, and Julie House; my brothers and sisters-in-law: Sean and Cassie House, Kevin and Christine Brock and Andy Brock; as well as my lovely sisters: Ava McKittrick and Melissia McKittrick. Thank you as well to all of the usual suspects for spreading the word—Debbie Tralies, Jean and Dennis Regan, Tracy Dauphin, Claire Pacell, Jeanne Cassidy, Susan Sole, the Regans, the Conlens, the Houses, the McDowells, the Kays, the Funks, the Bowmans, and the Bottingers! As always, thank you to all the wonderful bloggers and reviewers who faithfully return to Denton to read Josie's latest tale, as well as the ones who've only met Josie in this book. I appreciate your time and your incredible support!

Thank you, as always, to Lt. Jason Jay for answering my endless questions, sometimes multiple times, in such great detail at all hours of the night and day. I am astounded by your generosity. Thank you to Stephanie Kelley, my incomparable law enforcement consultant, who worked so hard with me to get every detail right—or as close to right as fiction will allow. You are such a gift, and I could just listen to you explain things all day! Thank you to Courtney Capone for answering my veterinary hospital questions. Thank you to Leanne Kale Sparks for helping me navigate some legal issues in this book, like getting Mathias Tobin out of prison. You are the absolute best! I'm so grateful for your friendship. Thank you so much to Audrey Brooks and Hope Lawrence for answering all of my cattle farm questions!

Thank you to Jessie Botterill and Jenny Geras for the gift of getting to continue writing this series and to continue working with the best publisher on the planet. I'm so grateful. Thank you for helping me iron out not only the plot of this book, but many more to come. I can't wait for readers to see what we've cooked up in future books. Thank you, Jenny Geras, for your insightful and brilliant edit, and for the care you took to help me make this book shine! Finally, thank you to Noelle Holten, Kim Nash, my copy editor, Jennie, and proofreader, Jenny Page, as well as the entire team at Bookouture.

Made in the USA
Monee, IL
16 June 2023

35965250R00206